ELEMENTARY, MY DEAR

ELEMENTARY, MY DEAR

Autumn Sabol

iUniverse, Inc.
New York Lincoln Shanghai

Elementary, My Dear

iUniverse books may be ordered through booksellers or by contacting:

iUniverse
2021 Pine Lake Road, Suite 100
Lincoln, NE 68512
www.iuniverse.com
1-800-Authors (1-800-288-4677)

ISBN-13: 978-0-595-35686-7 (pbk)
ISBN-13: 978-0-595-80163-3 (ebk)
ISBN-10: 0-595-35686-9 (pbk)
ISBN-10: 0-595-80163-3 (ebk)

Printed in the United States of America

Dedicated with gratitude to all of the stalwart
Sherlockians of FFN, especially Amy, Kathy, Meg, Erin and Ceili.
I couldn't have done it without you.

—MH

CHAPTER 1

In Which I See a Shrink and Get Hit By a Truck

"I had coconut syrup in my hair." Shifting uncomfortably to avoid a spring sticking out of the ratty couch, I tried to resume my train of thought. "You know, and if that isn't bad enough, my crummy pop-can-on-wheels Fiat has busted down again, the history professor from Hell is breathing down my neck and I'm practically running my roommate's errands, with the added bonus of Café Crema Artificially Flavored Coconut Syrup dripping off the shelf and into my eyes."

"And how did that make you *feel*?"

I turned over on the couch, glaring at Douglas Mitchell. He was sitting in his secondhand pleather armchair by the couch, dress shirt buttoned to the neck, slacks creased to razor-sharpness, valiantly trying to pretend that his cluttered dorm was a posh psychiatrist's office. It irked the hell out of me. "How do you think it made me *feel*? I mean, I sure didn't feel like Cinderella goin' to the ball, ya know?"

Doogie sighed mightily and peered at me over the tops of his non-prescription glasses. "Nona, I don't know how many times I'm going to say this. I'm trying to help you, and free of charge I might add. I'm trying to break down your frustrations and get to the bottom of your dissatisfaction, but I can't do it if you fight me every step of the way! Plus, a diagnosis like this is vital to my thesis!"

I groaned and fell back onto the couch. "Okay, *okay*, forget about it. How's this? It made me feel angry, like it was the icing on a really crappy cake. That better, Doogie?"

"That's fine," he said frostily. "And it's Dr. Mitchell."

"But you don't have your degree yet; you're only a third-year."

"No-NA…"

"*Okay*, okay, whatever." I heaved a sigh of my own and continued. "But it wasn't just the syrup that made me angry; it was lots of different things, know what I mean? Like my manager Marie is always hassling me for no reason, and my coworker is constantly bothering me to join his band, stuff like that, you know? And it's always so hard to say no. I mean, I always try to go outta my way and be pleasant and helpful and crap like that, but nothing I do ever seems to be good enough! Every time I try to do my job or help someone out, they spit in my face! Take Trish: there's a perfect example. That little priss chewed me out for forgetting to return her movie to the rental place, even though she was the one who rented it! That was rich!"

"And how did that make you feel? No wise-ass remarks, Nona."

"Which one, the thing with Trish?"

"Yes, let's start there. How do you feel around her?"

"Well, that's easy enough to answer. I feel…I feel inferior, like just because her father is an alderman and she summers in the Hamptons, I'm automatically obligated to take care of her personal business! But my family is just as wealthy and important as hers, so how come *she* gets to walk all over me? I mean, it would be different if she helped me out with things I need; then I'd be happy to help her. But she never offers, and every time I ask her to pick up something for me, like a newspaper from the newsstand, she always says that she's 'too busy.' Of course, I always end up getting the paper myself, but not before she asks me to pick up the latest *Cosmo*, 'since I'll be there anyway'!"

"Hmmm. Have you done anything about it?"

I sighed again. I seemed to be doing that a lot in Doogie's company. "I've put in two apps for a new roommate, but no luck so far. My mom thinks I should transfer outta here. Oh, of course, let's not forget dearest Mother, always pestering me about when I'm going to stop goofing off and get a real job. 'What on *earth* are you going to do with an art degree, Nona? Aren't you ever going to *do* something with your life, Nona? You're so smart, Nona; why don't you become a doctor or a lawyer and do something *useful*?' She drives me crazy!"

"And how does that make you feel?"

I was momentarily stunned with disbelief at the vacuous reply. Where had the boy learned his technique, soap operas? "Are you even listening, Doogie? I just said she drives me crazy!"

"Hmmm." Doogie scratched some more on his legal pad and waved a hand, gesturing me to continue.

After some squirming on the couch and casting about mentally, I regained my train of thought. "I just don't get it, you know? I want to be useful and help people out, but it seems like no matter what I do, I can never do anything right. I'm not efficient enough for Marie and not musical enough for Scotty. I'm not cool enough to hang out with Trish and her circle, but I'm too cool for my mother; she thinks that I'm not serious about my life. My grades are mostly Bs and my professors never have anything out of the ordinary to say to me, you know, not even a 'Good job!' or a 'You can do better than this.' I'm going for a degree in art, and I suppose I'm a good artist, but I don't expect myself to be the next Rembrandt or anything.

"Still, no one seems to appreciate the things that I *can* do; no one values my opinions or asks my advice. It's like nothing I do makes any impact on the world at all! I've always tried to follow my dad's example and be humble, but the result is that I end up a human doormat! Hmm, maybe my mom's right for once in her life. Maybe I do need to be more assertive. I guess…I guess that sometimes I wish that I could…"

Douglas' digital wristwatch beeped shrilly, interrupting my tirade. "And that's the hour," he announced, dumping the legal pad on the coffee table and getting up from his chair. "Thanks for coming, Nona; see you next week."

What? That was it? Shocked, I rolled over on the couch to protest and caught a glimpse of the legal pad on the table. It was covered with what looked like a shopping list. "Doogie, have you even heard a word I've said?" I cried in incredulity.

"Of course I have, Nona." He busied himself with filing the papers, not meeting my questioning gaze.

I heaved myself off of the couch to stand next to the coffee table, peering down at the pad. "Then why does your legal pad read…" I squinted a bit to read his chicken-scratch handwriting. "'Pick up dry cleaning, call Prof. Jarrow, buy snacks for big game this weekend'?"

The blush that flooded his ears was all the answer I needed. I might have known. Dejected, I hefted my backpack and left the dorm, not uttering a word. Doogie could find another guinea pig for his thesis; I wasn't going back there again.

❦   ❦   ❦

I made my way across the campus quad in the drizzling rain, climbing the stairs of the dorm building to my shared rooms. After scanning the hallway, I unlocked the door and pushed my way inside, kicking off my boots and casting my backpack into a corner. Fatigued and foggy, I dug out my secret stash of Gevalia coffee grounds and brewed a pot before flinging myself onto the couch and listening to the October rain abuse the windowpanes. As with most artists, the weather had a profound effect on my mood, and my current mood was as dark as the gathering clouds. Between the constant pressures from my mother and grandmother to conform to preset standards; the callous uncaring of Doogie, who had promised to help me; my spoiled roommate and her obnoxious demands; I could feel all of the stressors crowding my mind, overwhelming me. Times like these called for intense escapism.

Stretching out to the cluttered coffee table, I bypassed my textbooks and seized my tattered copy of *The Return of Sherlock Holmes*, opening it to the first adventure, "The Empty House." Despite the fact that I had nearly memorized the thing, the mystery wrapped itself around my mind, as engaging as the first reading. As the smell of percolating hazelnut vanilla permeated the air, the rain outside suddenly drenched the streets of London rather than New York, and clattering hansom cabs replaced purring taxis, one of the cabs bearing the most brilliant mind in all of literature. Never taking my eyes from the book, I rolled onto my side and stretched my hand over to the coffee table, feeling for the open bag of chocolate chips that rested there.

Bang! The slamming of the door shattered my concentration as I balanced on my side on the edge of the couch, rolling me off of the edge and onto the tile floor. Trish was home. "Oh, God, what a *miserable* day!" came her high, reedy voice, wounded with the unbearable trials of everyday life. As I stared at the floor tiles, trying to find a reason to move, I could hear Trish's rock-my-world pumps click-clacking across the room to the kitchenette, where she invited herself to a large cup of my coffee.

Rubbing my right arm where it had landed between the ground and me, I heaved myself up to the couch again, propping my arms on the back. Trish was a study in sex appeal, from the skintight stretch pants to the barely-there blouse. Her feathery short hair was freshly bleached; it glowed white blond without a hint of brown roots. Jewelry dripped from ears, neck and wrists, even a small stud in her nose. "Isn't it a little early to go clubbing?" I asked. I didn't doubt that Trish would venture out at any hour if there were a drink and/or a man to be had, so I was only half-joking.

She rolled her black eyes as she clutched my favorite blue coffee mug, violent scarlet lipstick rings adorning the rim. "What are you talking about?" she snapped. "I just got back from class. Professor Johnson wanted to give me an extra-credit assignment."

Why was I not surprised? Suppressing a snide remark about 'extra-credit,' I reclined on the couch again, snagged the elusive bag of chocolate and resumed my reading. Before I could lose myself in the story, however, Trish stood over me, mug in hand, glaring icily. "I want to sit down," she announced, looking pointedly at my legs.

I am a short woman and it was a large couch. There was plenty of room for an individual to sit down on the end, even if I didn't move a muscle. "Then sit," I said simply, drawing up my knees and turning the page.

A small crease appeared between her eyes, something I had secretly titled the 'I-want' line. "Your legs are on the seat," she protested, scarlet lips pursing.

Rolling my eyes at the display, I replied, "Then use the kitchen table."

"I want to sit on the couch!" If she hadn't been tottering on three-inch stilettos, she would have stamped her foot.

Despite her protests, I calmly ignored her and turned the page. Finally, with a put-upon huff, Trish marched to the table and almost fell into the chair. Satisfied, I resettled with my novel, but before I finished the next paragraph, Trish's unseen voice broke my concentration.

"You going to the library this weekend?" she asked. I climbed onto my knees to peer over the back of the couch, seeing her sulkily drawing a circle on the varnished surface with a crimson-tipped nail.

"Yeah," I replied warily. "What about it?"

"I need you to pick up a book for me," she announced. "*Advanced Chemistry and Practical Applications*, Chaika and Scollon. You should write that down."

I felt my eyebrows climb nearly as high as my hairline. She wanted me to what? "Huh? Trish, what on earth are you going to do with a textbook on advanced chemistry?"

Trish rolled her mascara-laced eyes in irritation. "Well, I'm not going to *read* it, if that's what you mean," she sneered, as if the answer was obvious. "I'm just going to use a few keywords and carry it around until Brian Parker asks me out. He's a grad up for biochem, you know." A small smile crossed her lips.

"Biochemistry, that's got a cool sound," she purred, already fantasizing about how she would lure the unfortunate Parker into her web.

I was in literal shock. One might imagine that, after the two and a half months of our sharing rooms, I would have become inured to her childish outbursts and ludicrous demands. Instead, as I had ruefully discovered, she continued to surprise me. "And what makes you think that I'm going to get this book for you," I asked, "when you could go and get it yourself?"

"Because," Trish replied, "I've got a big day of shopping planned for this weekend with Katie and Beth; you can't expect me to cancel for a stupid book, can you? Besides, you're going to be there anyway, so just be a dear and get it for me."

I pushed myself off of the couch, surprise mingled with disgust. "Sure, whatever," I acquiesced, swallowing my pride as I went to get a cup of coffee. As I fished for milk in the tiny fridge, I rationalized that grabbing an extra book at the library was preferable to listening to Trish whine for the next month. Finishing with the coffee, I turned back to the couch only to find Trish suddenly stretched across it, toothpick legs sprawled along the entire length, dark eyes smirking at me as she sipped her coffee. Too tired to argue, I dropped like a stone into her vacated seat at the table, propping my head in my hands.

I needed to pick up another application for a new roommate.

The next day it was still raining. I slammed the door to the dorm behind me, threw down my umbrella and kicked my boots across the room in a huff. *Bloody stupid Collins and his bloody stupid lectures…*I stomped to the kitchenette, grabbed the last Corona from the fridge and rooted around for the bottle opener, mentally cursing all the while. *Verdammt, merde, hell, where's the bottle opener, shit, pinche, damn, oh here it is…*Exercising my wrath on the poor defenseless Corona, I swiftly beheaded it and chug-a-lugged, only pausing for breath after a good bit of the contents had vanished. Leaning back against the counter, I couldn't help but reflect on the history class from which I had just come.

Right after my noontide plate of lukewarm *something* at the cafeteria, I had rushed through the downpour to Professor Collins' class on the social impact of modern art. Predictably, the temperamental old fart had turned up the heat to Amazonian temperatures, flooding the lecture hall with a humid dampness, and the rain pattering on the windows proved as monotonous as boring old

Collins droning on and on. It was so hot in the room, and Trish had kept me up half the night with her obnoxious punk rock last night, and suddenly my textbook looked so inviting…

I felt my face heating at the mere memory. I hadn't been the only one to doze off that day, but Ol' Cranky decided to make an example of me. His hand had come down on my desk with a force that you could hardly credit to such a scarecrow, and he had announced to the *whole* class that if I couldn't concentrate on the valuable education he was so *graciously* dispensing, I could leave and not come back. I almost did just that, but dropping out of a class would only provide more fuel for my mother's arguments against me. Gritting my teeth, I apologized and somehow stayed through the class, loathing every second.

I was startled out of my brown study by the phone ringing. Crap, another one of Trish's bosom buddies reporting that Lacy dumped Jimmy and was now dating Tommy, or something equally pointless. Sighing, I crossed to the phone and braced myself as I lifted the receiver. "Hello, Trish isn't here now; can I take a message?"

"Nona!" screeched the voice in reproach. "That is no way to answer the phone, after all I've taught you, is that any way to-" My grandmother's diatribe faded away as I held the phone away from my ear in momentary shock. Oh, no, Grandma. I could already tell that this conversation was an ulcer just waiting to happen.

When the buzzing over the phone lines began to quiet, I swallowed my frustration and replaced the phone to my ear. "Grandma, hi! I'm so sorry, I thought you were someone else."

"Obviously, my dear, but you should never assume things; it's terribly unbecoming."

I caught myself gritting my teeth again; thanks to my relatives, I'd end up with dentures. "How are you, Grandma." The question came out as more of a statement, but as always, Grandma was too caught up to care.

"Oh, miserable, Nona, you know how my arthritis gets in this damp weather. My back isn't faring too well either, and I'm almost positive that the damp is getting into my lungs. I'll be at the hospital with pneumonia before the week is out, you just watch. And then, of course, there's…"

Her voice once again subsided to a murmur as I removed the phone from my ear and shook it violently, strangling my grandmother by proxy. Why, why, *why* did she always do this to me? Couldn't she take a gentle hint?

I stopped shaking the phone, barely hearing her say, "But enough about me, Nona. Nona? Are you there, dear?"

The phone returned to my shoulder. "What did you need, Grandma?" As if I didn't know...

"Oh! I was just calling to tell you that little Crystal Sterling's older brother Harrison is back from Yale, and the Sterlings are throwing a dinner party to welcome him back! You simply must come and meet him, Darling, such a fine young man! His father is a full partner at Sterling & Grey, but of course you know that. The party is next Friday, so this weekend we have to run to Versace on 5th and pick you up something in dark green; oh, you have such pale skin, Darling, we'll buy you something tasteful, diamonds of course, make an appointment at the salon and-"

"Grandma!" I interrupted desperately. "I can't go! I'm studying for my midterms, I have to go to the library this weekend and I'm working next Friday!"

"Oh, nonsense, you can make time! Just play hooky or call in sick, whatever it is you do these days."

A familiar queasiness was building in the pit of my stomach. "I can't, Grandma. I'd love to go, but my midterms are too important!"

Sheer indignation erupted from over the phone. "I beg your pardon? Scribbling essays about globs of paint is more important than spending time with your grandmother, who may not have much longer on this earth?" Now that was bull; my grandmother was the very picture of health. Besides, she'd cling to life with her fingernails until her only granddaughter had married, and married *well*, so frequent hints about her imminent death tended to pass into one ear and out the other. "I simply will not take no for an answer, Nona, so you may stop that awful whining; it is giving me a headache."

"But Grandma, I can't-"

"You can and you will, Nona! Now, not another word! I shall have Daniel bring the car to the university on Sunday, ten sharp. Be waiting by the gate, and please wear something decent this time! Those awful peasant skirts are so beneath you, Darling. See you this weekend! Ta!"

With a sharp click, the line went dead. Dammit. I felt as if I had stepped into the path of a rampaging Mack truck. I briefly contemplated hurling the phone at the wall, screaming obscenities in every language in my repertoire, but in the end I knew it was pointless to fight. If I didn't show up, my grandmother would call me every day for the next week. There was nothing for me to do but be at the gate on Sunday, in something *decent*. Without realizing it, I tweaked the waistband of my brown ankle-length skirt, which was so *beneath* me. I could have argued to her that elastic-waist skirts and slacks were the only things that could conceal my physiological imperfections, but I was too numb to fight, having exhausted all of the questions years ago. Why couldn't she, and everyone else for that matter, just leave me alone? Why couldn't I live my own life, pursue my own dreams, and just exist with my imperfections and flaws intact?

I fled to the relative safety of my room, shutting the door tightly behind me and locking it, the lock serving no practical purpose since I was alone in my apartment. I grinned sadly as I recognized the gesture as unconsciously symbolic. *I'm shutting out this world and all of its demands,* I mused silently. *Chew on that one, Doogie.* Numb with an odd cocktail of frustration and defeat, I stripped for a shower, allowing my critical gaze to linger on the reflection in the bedroom mirror. Cursed with curves in an era that glorified the straight line, thirty pounds heavier than any billboard model, I was far from beautiful in the eyes of modern society. Attractive, sure, if you looked at my face, but otherwise…I skimmed my hands down my figure, sneering at my reflection. Too-wide hips, tiny waist, I was a wasp in more than the White Anglo-Saxon Protestant sense. Once upon a time men would have slavered at my feet, but in the twenty-first century no fashion or trend catered to my figure.

With an unladylike snort, I ceased my arduous self-appraisal and hopped into the shower, trying to scrub away the cultured filth from twenty-three years of good breeding. *Count your blessings, Nona,* I admonished myself. *It could have been Mom.*

Two hours later I stood in the lobby of Brown, Gregg and Eber, looking very out of place among the suited stockbrokers in my brown skirt, sweater and battered backpack. Regardless, I walked to the elevator and punched the appropriate number, traveling upwards. Oddly enough, this high-class place of business was my only refuge in times of adversity; the place where I knew I was always welcome.

The doors pinged open and I made my way effortlessly through the rows of cubicles, none of the suited brokers batting an eye at my less-than-corporate attire. At the end of the hall a short balding man hunched over a wad of papers, deep in consultation with another broker. Hearing the sound of my footsteps, he glanced up and smiled as he saw me.

"Princess!" he exclaimed, using the family nickname. "It's been a while! Come to see the old patriarch?"

I smiled, relaxing for the first time in recent memory. "Hi, Uncle Dave," I returned. "That was the general idea. Is he in?"

David Eber, my father's business partner and my honorary uncle, jerked a thumb over his shoulder. "Walk that way until you see a mountain of paperwork. He should be in there somewhere, unless he's expired from overwork. Maybe you can dig him out for a few hours."

"Overdoing it again?" I asked. "I thought he was talking about retirement."

Uncle Dave snickered good-naturedly. "Child, Jacob has talked about retirement since '93. Go on now, I have to finish up here."

I took that as dismissal and bid him farewell, leaving him to his graphs and columns. Walking further down the hall and to the right brought me to the familiar door, left ajar. I could hear my father even before I stood in the doorway, his boisterous voice uncharacteristically somber. He sat hunched at his desk, sheets of hard copy piled around his desk, the sleeves of his dress shirt rolled up to the elbows and his striped tie pulled down to form a Y on his chest. Head down, he was talking intently on the phone and was clearly displeased with whoever was on the other end.

"Yes, I...yes, I know...no, I haven't heard from her, and I think we should...will you please let me finish? I think that we should-" He broke off abruptly as his dark blue gaze shifted to me, framed by the door jamb. "Princess! No, dear," he said into the telephone, "Nona's here; we need to finish this later, all right? No, *later*. Okay, love you, bye." He hung up the phone and instead of getting up to greet me, he sat back in the leather swivel chair, lacing his hands behind his head with a wry smile on his bearded face. "Of all the gin joints in all the world..." he recited with an air of repetition.

"I had to walk into yours," I replied, paraphrasing the quote from *Casablanca*. "You look good, Daddy," I said simply. "Busy, but good."

"Let's see if I can say the same for you," he retorted, launching himself from his chair and taking my hand, spinning me in a quick pirouette. He took my chin in hand, turning my head this way and that, humming appraisingly all the while.

"Well?" I finally asked.

His grin grew wider and he tugged gently on my long braid. "Gorgeous, as always. Where did you get those eyes, anyway? I don't think there are any angels in the family, are there?"

"Liar." Suddenly self-conscious, I brushed a hand through my bangs and traced a finger down my still-damp braid, wondering how to voice my complaints comfortably.

"You hungry, kiddo?"

That was my dad, always getting to the heart of the matter or, in this case, the stomach. "Starving," I replied.

"Then let's blow this popsicle stand!" Snagging his suit jacket from the back of the office chair and his overcoat from the hook on the door, he swiftly led me out of the office and through the hall. Although he was not a very tall man, his stride was so vigorous that I had to trot to keep up, almost running into him when he skidded to a stop before his secretary's desk.

"Ah!" he cried with an accompanying snap of the fingers. "Rhonda!" The secretary's permed head shot up at the sound of her name. "It's two-fifteen, right? What time is Kowalski bringing his portfolio by?"

Rhonda briefly consulted the schedule. "You have him scheduled for five o'clock, Mr. Brown."

"Call him back and push it off to six, no! Seven, and make reservations at Four Brothers. We'll talk easier over a plate of veal *milanese* anyhow. Got it, Rhonda?"

"Sure thing, sir."

With barely a glance to me, he was off like a rocket through the halls again. Uncle Dave noticed our procession and gave me a congratulatory wink at the success of my rescue mission as I dashed in my father's wake to the elevators and out of the building.

"So, what are you hungry for?" Dad asked as we exited the building, abandoning central heating for the brisk fall air.

I briefly blew into my hands for warmth and contemplated my options. Although my father's bank account could offer me anything I wanted, no matter the price range, I had always preferred to follow in his footsteps and be content with the simpler things in life. "I could go for a hamburger."

"That's my girl. A burger does sound pretty good right now, and I know a great little place in the Village. We gotta deal?"

"*Oui, mon capitan!*" I clicked my heels and saluted with mock-seriousness.

"Aw, get outta here." He raised a hand and waved towards the street, causing a yellow taxi to pull up to the curb. Ever the gentleman, Dad opened the cab door for me as I got in, bunching my skirt in my hands as I scooted over. He slid in next to me and gave the street name to the stocking-capped driver, who nodded and shifted the cab into drive. On the way there Dad didn't ask what was troubling me, and I didn't volunteer anything, steering the conversation into safer channels. We spoke of trivial matters; I described some of my class projects and he told me about a science expo his old college buddy was having at Hudson University.

"You ever hear of Dr. Thomas Ward, Princess?" he asked, continuing before I could shake my head in the negative. "He went to Syracuse with me a couple hundred years ago, was real big on quantum physics before it started to be respectable. He's got this lecture planned this Saturday, some weird theory; he wants all his school buddies along for the ride."

"Oh yeah? What's his theory on?"

He scratched his beard in an effort to remember. "Something about temporal anomalies, random holes in the space-time continuum, pathways and portals to different times and dimensions. All theory, of course, but it reads like Star Trek."

I couldn't help a snort. "He sounds like a crackpot."

"He is a crackpot, but his ideas make sense if you stand on your head and squint real hard," he replied. "Anyway, according to his theory, all that unexplainable stuff like Bigfoot and the Loch Ness Monster are actually prehistoric beasts pulled forward from the past, and UFOs are examples of advanced robotic technology pulled back from thousands of years in the future."

"The truth is out there," I quoted with a grin.

"If you want to believe Tommy, the truth is already here. This expo is his bid for funding, and I do hope he gets it. He's a good guy, hardworking, still thinks he can make a difference, you know? Hey, want to come up to Hudson with me Saturday night and meet him?"

"I'd love to, Dad, but I'm working Saturday night and I have to go to the library."

Unlike my grandmother, my father did not press the issue. He simply shrugged one shoulder in a 'that's life' gesture and asked about my upcoming midterms.

The cab entered Greenwich Village and pulled up to the designated corner. We disembarked and Dad paid the cabbie before turning me down the block and into a nameless hole-in-the-wall diner with a cliché black-and-white tile floor and ancient dessert display. The Formica counter was dented, a light bulb had burnt out and the jukebox had seen better days, but it looked clean and tidy. We had just missed the lunch rush, so we placed our orders almost immediately after sliding into a booth by the front window: two burgers, medium rare, with extra-crispy fries and coleslaw.

"So," Dad began, toying with his silverware after the pudgy waitress deposited two glasses of ice water and steamed into the kitchen, "wanna tell me what's up?"

I sighed and propped my head on one hand, watching the Goths, trendies and students flow past the window. "Grandma called." My father made a noise of revelation, but I ignored it and continued. "She's taking me to a party next weekend, wants me to meet another son of society."

"Uh-oh, she's playing matchmaker with the Mayonnaise Men, huh, Princess?"

"Mayonnaise?"

"Mayonnaise, sure. Rich, thick, oily, and murder on your blood pressure."

I couldn't help but giggle at the analogy. "Nail on the head, Pop. She's taking me on the grand tour on Sunday, formalwear, shoes, jewelry, salon, the works."

"You don't sound wildly enthusiastic, kiddo."

"Are you kidding? I hate it! I tried to be polite and tell her that I was studying for my midterms, but she just bulldozed right over me! Sometimes I wish I could strangle her!"

He cocked his head and grinned wryly. "Be it far from me to plant any ideas in your head, but I hear that the bench is getting real lenient on murder that isn't premeditated. You could go as low as Manslaughter One."

I slapped his forearm in reproach. "Stop it, you're not helping. What it boils down to is that Grandma wants to parade me around before the eligible bachelors, and I'd rather scrub the bathrooms at Grand Central with a toothbrush! What should I do?"

Faced with an echo of his own honest, straightforward bluntness, Dad seemed momentarily disoriented. He toyed with his silverware some more, fiddled with his tie and ran a thick finger around the rim of his water glass, all the while cogitating like mad. In the interim the waitress returned with our meals, and Dad seized the opportunity to tend to his burger condiments as another stalling technique.

I turned my attention to my own lunch and continued to explain. "Well, you know, it's not like this is the first time," I said distractedly, pounding on the ketchup bottle. "I think she's been trying to get me married off since I graduated from high school! I just wish that she could leave me alone, you know? I'm pretty sure that I'll get married someday, but I don't know when or to whom. But I do know that it won't be to one of those stuffed-shirt pretty boys with their brains in their wallets! I just want some time to make up my own mind; is that so awful?"

There was no reply from my lunch companion. I sat quietly for a moment, trying to be patient but getting kind of antsy myself. Jacob Brown was usually a font of good advice, but he was always hesitant to speak against the family. "Well?" I finally prompted before taking an unladylike bite of the burger. Dad was right; the food here was great.

"Well," he finally replied. "I think that you should keep your options open. Don't turn your nose up at any opportunity, Princess, even the ones Beatrice throws at you. I think that you should go to the party and try to have a good time."

This was good advice? "Da-ad!" I protested with a subtle undercurrent of whining. "You don't understand! These men she pushes me at are morons! Their IQs are lower than the city temperature in January!"

He extended his index finger in a patrician gesture. "Now that's exactly what I mean!" he shot back. "You've got all of these preconceived notions swimming around inside your head, and you need to pull the plug and drain them out. Yes, you've been to similar parties before. Yes, a lot of the young men there were not the best and the brightest. Still, that doesn't mean that you should just throw in the towel, sweetheart! I mean, look at me! I'm a self-made man, worked my way up from the bottom of the ladder, but I met your mother at one of *those* parties. I hated those old cocktail things just as much as you do, but if I hadn't let Joe Gregg drag me out that night, you or your brothers wouldn't be here now.

"Now, I know," his voice grew quieter, his words less of a lecture and more of a gentle prod, "I know that you're looking for someone who's right for you, and you should look, high *and* low! You don't want money to decide who you're gonna marry, and that's good, but you shouldn't turn your nose up at some guy just because he does have money."

I sighed, defeated. "So you're saying I should go?"

"I'm saying that you shouldn't turn your nose up at anything life throws at you. Give it a chance, Princess."

Rolling my shoulders, I vowed to attend Grandma's cocktail party with the least amount of ire I could muster, and we polished off the now-cold burgers as Dad changed the subject and filled me in on how Greg and Jack were doing in the wide world.

The hours passed too swiftly for my liking. Of course, Dad was too busy to talk into the evening so six o'clock found us back in another anonymous taxi-cab, wheeling back to my dorm before he returned to the office to finish off the report. When the cab pulled over before the campus, Dad got out to open the door for me. As he gave me his hand to help me out of the cab, something small and hard found its way into my palm. The foreign object turned out to be a pair of crisply folded fifty-dollar bills.

When I opened my mouth to protest, Dad's index finger made a reappearance. "Ah, ah, ah, absolutely not! This is a gift, Princess, and I forbid you to spend it on something practical." He cupped a dramatic hand to his ear. "Waterstone's is calling you, Nona. All those books and movies…"

I grinned as I fingered the money. Leave it to Dad to know exactly where I'd spend the money. "I promise," I retorted, a hand over my heart, "that I shall spend every last penny on something absolutely frivolous."

"That's my girl." Without warning he wrapped me in a tight bear hug and actually lifted me off the ground before releasing me on *terra firma* and reclaiming his cab. As the cab trundled away, he leaned out the open window, waving at me as if a final thought had just occurred to him.

"Proud of you, Princess!" he called as I waved back. "Really, really proud!"

🍁   🍁   🍁

I was nearly skipping as I made my way up the stairs to my dorm, fishing in my backpack for my keys. My father always seemed to pick up my spirits, no matter how bad things seemed. Humming sprightly under my breath, I unlocked my door and entered my dorm, throwing my backpack carelessly against the wall and toeing off my sneakers before I literally jumped in horror, noticing the figure sitting ramrod straight on the frayed couch. I gasped, my stomach swiftly descending to the vicinity of my knees.

"Mother!"

CHAPTER 2

In Which I Go to Dinner with Medusa and the Truck Backs Up

Perched on the sofa was my mother, her skirted suit without wrinkle, her makeup thick yet tasteful and, as always, her stare cold enough to rival the Gorgons of myth. "Nona," she said simply, rising from the couch and gliding over to briefly press her lips to my cheek. "You look…" I could see any number of derogatory comments pass through her mind as she took in my polyester skirt, baggy sweater and decided lack of makeup. Finally she settled on: "…well. Yes, you look well."

"What are you doing here?" It took me a moment to realize that the defensive words were mine.

Mother's mascara-laden eyes widened in mock surprise. "Since when does a mother need an excuse to pay her only daughter a visit?" she asked, edged steel beneath the cracked velvet of her voice.

Sensing the edge, I hurriedly backpedaled. "No, I mean how did you get in?"

"Well, my dear, your lovely roommate was kind enough to let me in before she left. Since I don't have a key to your…(an acidic glance around the living room,) place, I might have been waiting out in the hallway for heaven-knows-how-long."

My tongue was already aching from my efforts to bite it. Elizabeth Brown had elevated spiteful verbal fencing to an art form, knowing exactly which thrust would draw silent blood from her opponent. "Is there anything I can get you, *Mother*?" I bit off, my back going unconsciously rigid. It was best to humor her and play the genteel hostess until I could think of an excuse to leave.

"No, Nona, you cannot 'get me anything,'" she clipped, turning back to the couch and gingerly picking up a large white garment box, being careful not to damage her manicure. "However, you *may* quickly put this on so that we can go."

"Go?" I echoed blankly, the weak feeling in my knees spreading back up to my gut. Had it been only ten minutes before that I had felt so carefree? "Go where?"

"I am taking you out to dinner, and I expect you to look decent." It was not an offer; it was an order. "Now, since I went through all the trouble of buying you something nice to wear, the very least you can do is to put it on and accompany your mother."

I took the box as if it contained a bomb and opened it enough to peek. Instead of an explosive device, it held a lady's silk suit in stark, unrelieved black; as close as I could tell it was a near-replica of the one my mother wore. I shot a desperate glance at my mother, my eyes pleading for mercy. "Please, Mother, I'd love to go, but I…" My voice dwindled into silence at the look on her plastered face. Elizabeth Brown was not like her mother; she needed no guilt trip to make others do her bidding. All she needed was a brief downward twist to her painted lips, a slight wrinkle in the plastic nose and a look in her eyes as cold as the arctic wasteland, reproaching twenty-three years of wasted oxygen with a single glance…

I sighed in submission and hugged the flat box to my chest like a shield. "I'll just be a minute," I mumbled, shuffling into my bedroom to put on the suit.

Of course, once I had wiggled my way into the suit, Mother insisted on doing my hair, undoing the long braid and pinning the mass of brown hair into a bun with ruthless efficiency. She silently bullied me into wearing makeup and supervised the application with all of the aplomb of commissioning a piece of artwork. Finally, as she pronounced me fit for the eyes of the peerage, I was able to glance at myself in the mirror.

A stranger stared back at me with mascara-blackened eyes, the faint red of an artificial blush and the darker red sheen that no natural pair of lips possesses. My hair was pulled tightly against my head in a twist, a few gracefully sculpted tendrils escaping to frame my face in a parody of spontaneity. The unfettered black of the suit was made all the more grim by the white of my equally new blouse, still rigid and unyielding with factory starch. My nylons took up a familiar itching and tinted my legs to a deep tan, obviously contrasting with my pale hands and face. The black pumps elevated me three inches, and it took me a moment before I remembered how to balance. It was miserable. I turned to my observer with a protest on my lips as I took in her own brown twist, black suit, pumps and mascara.

Good God! I looked just like my mother.

After a full half-hour of enforced primping, Mother finally ceased her ministrations. "Are you ready now, Nona?" she stated more than asked, holding out my mink-trimmed dress coat. It was still perfumed with mothballs from the closet in which it had hidden, another of her various "gifts" over my college years, each one with a silent price tag. Suppressing the urge to scream with the ease of practice, I allowed her to maneuver the coat onto me and escort me out of the dorm.

Mother's cab was still waiting at the curb, the meter placidly ticking away, the driver content to wait the hour in exchange for a hefty fare. In a direct counterpoint to my trip with Dad, the ride uptown was frigidly silent. Mother did not feel that conversation was necessary, and I was in no hurry to correct her, silently watching the passing city as the setting October sun coaxed the night-dwellers out of their crevices. The cab pulled up on West 43rd Street before a familiar greenstone bistro with a royal blue awning.

Le Madeleine was my mother's favorite haunt, nestled deep in the heart of the Theater District and catering to the nouveau-riche, non-ignoramus sophisticates who attended Le Miserables out of sheer boredom. Many were the afternoons that Elizabeth M. Brown and her 'friends' gathered in the faux-French garden, sipping superior dessert wine and gossiping about anyone not within earshot, each one secretly convinced of her own preeminence over the other ladies.

We exited the cab and Mother paid the driver, her principles dictating that the driver crawl over his seats to take the bills from her hand rather than have her bend down to reach inside the window toward him. The porter at the bistro door opened the glass front door for us, taking our coats as well, and I did my utmost to imitate Mother's regal promenade. Despite my own desires and inclinations, I had stepped back into a world that I prayed to leave behind me, a life of champagne, silk and strawberries in winter. No sooner had the fragrant, warmed air of the bistro flooded my nose than the 'Commandments' began pouring back into my mind like glorified tap water from an overpriced bottle.

Thou Shalt Not Slouch.

Thou Shalt Not Fidget.

Thou Shalt Not Make a Scene.

Thou Shalt Not Make Conversation with the Hired Help, for these things are simply NOT DONE.

And many, many, many more.

The host didn't bother with confirming our reservation, but instead swiftly guided us to a corner table under a quaint fresco painted on red brick and profusely exclaimed that the waiter would be with us shortly. Ever the gracious lady, my mother bestowed a smile on the man and assured him that his earliest convenience would be fine. It was all an expensive game of pretend; Mother always tipped all of the staff heavily, and in return they treated her like a Rockefeller. She did, however, choose one of the pricier wines from memory to 'refresh the palate.' I was silent as the host fetched and poured the wine with astonishing promptness, not content to hold my tongue but ill-inclined to speak.

Once the man had retired from our service, Mother sipped tentatively at the red liquid and held it in her mouth for a moment, frowning delicately before swallowing. "A fine vintage," she announced with an authority she did not possess. She did not wait for an affirmative response before changing the subject. "So, Nona, how are your studies progressing? I've always believed art is so…fascinating."

Bullshit, I thought. *You've never approved of my studies and never will. But Thou Shalt Not Disagree, for it is NOT DONE.* "Oh, yes, very," I said aloud.

Silence reigned for a few moments as Mother rallied her forces for the next wave of attack. "I had hoped that your father could join us for dinner, but it seems that he is working late tonight. Did you two spend a pleasant afternoon?"

"How did you-?" I stopped short with realization. Mother must have been the voice on the phone that made my father so displeased earlier. This dinner was no accident; it was revenge for interrupting her with Dad. "Yes, it was fine."

Mother smiled, but the expression held no warmth. "It's so kind of him, isn't it? Dropping all of his valuable business clients whenever you beckon and call, no matter how inconvenient it may be. He's such a good man."

I ground my teeth as I smiled, feeling the sting of the hidden accusation. "Absolutely," I managed to scrape out.

A false fingernail circled the rim of her wineglass. "Your father mentioned that you are getting along badly with your roommate. I can't imagine why, she seemed like such a sweet girl."

Trish would be sweet around strangers, I thought bitterly. Aloud I said, "She can be a little difficult from time to time."

Bad move. Mother latched onto the admission like a jackal. "Nona, dear, why do you persist in this charade? I've offered to pay for an apartment off-campus for you. All you have to do is say the word and you can move out next week."

Sure, Mother. Just say the word and kiss your feet. "I'm fine, Mother. I have a job now; I don't need help."

She pursed her painted lips and snapped her napkin irritably before folding it on her lap. "That's your father talking. The man was always too prideful for his own good."

I bit my tongue and let the comment slide, suppressing the urge to say that Dad and his pride were the only things that kept me stable.

Mother smirked a bit at my silence and, savoring the victory, idly shifted her gaze to the door. Suddenly she reached across the table and clutched my wrist in a vise-like grip. "Nona!" she whispered. "Look, by the door!" When I turned to look, she hissed, "Don't be so obvious! What have I taught you?"

I averted my eyes back to my plate and glanced toward the door out of the corner of my eye, the sight sending my stomach southward again. Standing in the doorway and speaking to the host was Harry Garrison, only son of a renowned plastic surgeon and one of the most indulgent partygoers in the city. Almost unconsciously I hunched my shoulders and stared at my plate again, trying to make myself as small a target as possible.

"He wants to marry you, you know," my mother said with uncharacteristic warmth. "Oh, Nona, isn't he dashing? Dr. Garrison moves in the highest medical circles, oh, think of all the opportunities you would have as his daughter-in-law! Let's call him over!"

"Mother!" I whispered desperately. Off the top of my head I could think of several forms of physical pain that were preferable to another evening with Harry, but once she had an idea in her head, Elizabeth Brown could not be swayed. She raised her arm and swirled her hand in artistic circles until she caught Harry's gaze. His face froze momentarily, and I prayed that he wouldn't recognize us and carry on, but someone in heaven wasn't answering for

Harry's face soon cleared with recognition, an ingratiating smile spreading over his face like butter.

"Mrs. Brown!" he exclaimed, slithering more than walking over to our table. Taking my mother's hand, he continued, "It is a pleasure to see your face again. If all women were as lovely as you, my father would go out of business!" Mother visibly melted, every line in her body dissolving into a pile of liquid lassitude.

Without invitation Harry snagged a seat from an unoccupied table and pulled it up to ours, earning a dirty look from the host at the disruption of the table arrangements. He shifted his attentions to me, oozing an oily brand of charm. "And Nona, you look lovelier than ever. Where have you been? I've grown so lonely without you to brighten my day."

I was suddenly glad that my father was working; this incident alone would send his blood pressure through the roof. "I've been busy, Harry," was all I would say.

"Nona has been considering changing her major to pre-med," my mother blurted suddenly.

What? "Mother! I'm not-!"

A swift kick to my ankle silenced me as Mother prattled on. "Oh, dear, there's no need to be embarrassed! There's nothing wrong with changing your mind!" The look in her eyes was a direct contradiction to her light tone, her gaze forbidding me to speak under pain of emotional death.

"Really?" Harry asked, trying to sound interested. Despite his tone, though, I knew that he wouldn't care if I enrolled in clown college as long as he could get me in the sack. "That's great, Nona! Maybe someday you'll be giving my father a run for his money."

Harry and Mother shared a brief plastic laugh before there fell an awkward bout of quiet. Seizing a topic that seemed neutral, I said, "Mother, did Dad mention the seminar he's attending this weekend?" I decided that the following silence was in the negative, so I continued, "Dad told me that his old college buddy is giving a seminar at Hudson U. this weekend. Dr. Ward? Thomas Ward? Anyway, according to Dad, Dr. Ward has this revolutionary new theory on unexplained phenomenon. You see, all of the things in life that we don't know about, like Bigfoot, UFOs or the Loch Ness Monster, might actually be from another time period!"

I began to warm to my topic, picking up speed. "It makes sense, don't you think? I mean, take a look at the possibilities if he's right! If science *could* prove that these holes in time exist, maybe we could harness them for travel! Can you imagine? We could send scientists and explorers back in time to record what actually happened at any point in time! We'd never have to second-guess our history books or-"

"Well!" Harry interrupted loudly, a kind of glazed look on his face as he peered closely at his wristwatch. "That's great, Nona! I'd love to talk about it more, but I'm afraid I have to leave now. 'Phantom' has a seven o'clock curtain! It was so nice to see you again, Mrs. Brown, and you too, Nona. Maybe I'll see you later!" With that, he was up and away from the table before my mother could form a polite response.

As glad as I was to see him go, I couldn't help but feel offended. Harry was always quick with a compliment, but try to start an honest conversation and he was quicker with an excuse.

"Can't you ever be serious?" Mother asked coldly. "Time travel! What nonsense! How do you expect to find a husband if you refuse to act like a lady?"

I turned back to my mother, who was perfecting her icy stare with me as her guinea pig. "What do you mean, Mother? Is *that* the kind of man you want me to marry?" I asked incredulously.

"One can only hope," Mother replied, cold disapproval in her eyes.

I tried to muster a sarcastic smile, but it faltered and died. It was going to be a long night.

❦   ❦   ❦

After a pleasant evening of verbal badgering and belittling, the cab ride back to my dorm was anything but silent.

"What is the matter with you, Nona? Why can't you just spend a civil evening with me? You hardly ate anything!"

"I wasn't hungry, Mother, I already ate with Dad!"

"A bowl of soup and that's all. Did you see the looks everyone was giving us? They probably think you're anorexic! I was so embarrassed!"

"Embarrassed? What the hell did I do? You were the one who *lied* about me, saying I changed my major!"

"Well, I had to say something! How did you expect to attract Harry's attention when you just sit there like a lump?"

I covered my mouth to stifle an exasperated scream, causing the taxi driver to glance worriedly in his rear-view mirror. "Maybe I *didn't* want to attract his attention, Mother!" I shouted, my face heating with anger. "Maybe I think that

Harry Garrison is a philandering jerk! And besides, if I did want his attention, I wouldn't lie in order to get it!"

"That's the trouble with you, girl," Mother announced with eyes forward. "No ambition, no drive. You would be perfectly content to laze about painting pictures for pocket change when there are so many opportunities out there for you!"

"Like what?" I protested. "Law school? Pre-med? Mother, I don't want to be a doctor or a lawyer, I'm no good at those things! I am good at art!"

"This has nothing to do with what you are 'good at,' Nona. You could be a doctor or a lawyer if you would just apply yourself! You have so many more opportunities than I had as a girl; now for God's sake, take advantage of them!"

"This isn't about you!" I shouted, the evening's frustrations building to a head. "Why does everything in my life have to be about you? This is about *my* life and what *I* want to do with it! I'm an artist, Mother! I like to draw and paint and take pictures, and I'm good at it! That's what I'm going to be!"

"So that's it?" Mother demanded, growing icier. "Everything your father and I have given you, all of the concessions we've made, you just throw them in our faces!

"Daddy wants me to do what I love! He's proud of me, Mother, because I'm doing what I want in life!"

Mother was immediately skeptical. "Yes, I admit that is partly your father's fault. It never ceases to amaze me that such an intelligent man can be so ignorant of what his child truly needs." Her foot tapped edgily on the floor of the cab; I could tell she was dying for a cigarette. "But this is what you want, is it?" she snapped. "Tell me then; what are you going to do when you graduate?"

I was temporarily stunned by the left-field question, racking my brain for an answer. "Well, um…maybe I could work for an advertising firm or an animation studio, something like that. I don't know…"

"You see!" she crowed triumphantly. "You don't know! You're abandoning the opportunity for a stable, high-paying career in exchange for what—sitting on the pavement in Central Park, scribbling with schoolyard chalk and praying that someone throws some loose change at you?"

I took a deep breath, knowing it was useless to argue but still meaning to have the last word. "Yes, Mother," I said calmly. "Thank you for finally understanding. That's exactly what I'm planning to do."

Mother finally fell silent, stoically looking out the window and away from me. I thought I heard the cab driver heave a little sigh of relief and smiled to myself as the rest of the drive passed quietly.

When the cab pulled up to the campus dorm and stopped, I opened the door and paused for a moment. "Goodnight, Mother," I said evenly. "Thank you for dinner." I did not expect a response, and she did not disappoint me, refusing to even glance my way. Sighing, I pushed my way out of the taxi and stood on the curb, watching the taillights disappear down the road. Massaging the back of my neck, I tried to pull bobby pins from my hair as I climbed the stairs to my dorm.

Unlocking the door, I yelled for Trish but got no reply; I was blessedly alone. I toed off the pumps, moved to my room and stripped frantically, eager to rid myself of the metaphorical aftertaste of my mother. Only after I was clad in a pair of sweatpants and my rattiest T-shirt, scrubbed clean of every trace of cosmetics and safely ensconced on the couch with a mug of tea did I allow myself to truly relax. Letting my head roll onto the back of the couch, I sighed involuntarily and reflected on the events of the day. After the phone call from Grandma I felt as through a truck had hit me. Now, the truck had just backed up, slowly. *God, why can't Mother just leave me alone? Or even better, why can't she respect my decisions? I'm doing what I want to do! I think.*

Groaning aloud, I let a melodramatic arm fall over my eyes and tried to think positively. Mother would come around, I was sure. After I graduated and was gainfully employed, she would see that I wasn't crouched on the sidewalks in the Park, and then she would start to see that my time wasn't a waste. *After all,* I rationalized, *she's not old and I'm definitely not. We've got time to work this through. She'll come around.* The thought cheered me immensely and I seized the TV remote, idly channel surfing, my outlook looking brighter. *Sure, she'll come around, and Grandma will too, once I meet Mr. Right. And I'm not even close to my prime yet. I've got lots of time!*

All the time in the world.

Freezing October wind snapped at my face as I climbed the subway stairs. I tugged my wool coat closer, trudging through puddles in the light of nocturnal neon tubing. The few pedestrians on the street kept their heads down, the blackness of night weighing heavily on their shoulders. Glowing signs along the promenade proclaimed pizza parlor, laundromat, bookseller, greengrocer. Loud rap music drifted in and out of earshot as a beat-up Ford Fiesta pealed past me, the overblown bass rhythm swarming out of its open windows. The smell of car exhaust and Thai food and endless, bone-weary fatigue pervaded the thick, damp air.

The city so nice they named it twice: New York, New York.

Home, sweet home.

As I walked towards the campus, I hitched my too-heavy knapsack, crammed as it was with schoolbooks, notebooks, my CD player, and most importantly, my dog-eared copy of *The Adventures of Sherlock Holmes*, about which Scotty delighted in teasing me about just because he couldn't pronounce half of the words in it. I was thankful that the rainstorm had passed while I was working, but my soggy boots suffered in the aftermath as I returned to my dorm. Shifting my burdensome backpack, I cursed Trish virulently under my breath. The damn book my roommate had asked for was also weighing down my pack, courtesy of my stop at the library before work. *Advanced Chemistry and Practical Applications* was a two-inch-thick monster. How was toothpick Trish going to carry it around at all, let alone 'pull keywords' from it to impress Brian Parker? Just peeking at the pages and pages of formulae made my head swim.

I plodded along for a few more blocks before coming out of my blue funk, recognizing my surroundings. I was about two streets over from the campus, but a shortcut through a convenient alley would have me home in no time. My head protested the folly of walking through alleyways at night, but my soaking feet whined at the thought of two or more blocks of walking. *Besides,* I thought. *I can see the other side from here! No problem!* With a quickened step, I set off down the dark alley.

As I walked, the noises of the city slowly dimmed until I couldn't even hear the incessant Manhattan traffic anymore. The sudden quiet crawled across my skin in the form of goosebumps as I realized that my heels striking the concrete were the only sounds. Soon, however, a different sound hit my ears, a kind of rhythmic clip-clop with the ring of steel on stone. I had been to Central Park enough times to know the sound of horseshoes on pavement, but what was a horse-cab doing this close to the university?

A puddle of lamplight showed me the end of the street, but when I emerged from the alley, my campus was nowhere in sight. In fact, nothing familiar was in sight! A row of shabby tenement houses lined a cobblestone (*cobblestone?*) street, lit at intervals by weak gaslight lamps. Down the road, I could see a two-wheeled, horse-drawn carriage retreating into the distance.

Okay, now even for New York this was strange. I should have been able to see my dorm building from here, but instead I was on some bizarre movie set!

I must have taken the wrong shortcut. Time to get back to familiar ground. I did a sharp about-face and marched back into the alley, only to smack my nose painfully. The alleyway I had come through was now a solid wall.

CHAPTER 3

❀

In Which I Discover That I am Not in Kansas Anymore

Suffice it to say, now I was extremely scared. It was one thing to be lost, sure, but it was another thing to be so completely lost that you couldn't find from whence you came! In any case, I quickly recovered my composure and decided to set off and find out where I was before my night got any more weird. From the look of the area, I guessed that the movie was set in the eighteenth or nineteenth century, and the sight of that horse cab proved that there were people here. Perhaps a camera crew was shooting a night scene and could give me directions. Either way, I wanted to make sure of my location. So I shouldered my bag, took a deep breath and set off in the direction of the cab.

The streets were so quiet compared to the rest of Manhattan and as I walked the length of the set, I marveled at how everything was so meticulously designed. The model houses were detailed down to the smallest brick, the gas lamps were real metal and there wasn't a trace of mailboxes or fire hydrants anywhere! If I didn't know better, I might actually believe that I had gone back in time! Whoever was making this must have had a huge budget! All I could hear was the whisper of the wind, the sputtering of the lamps and…footsteps, coming closer. Suddenly, from around the corner, a man and a woman appeared, dressed in costume. Their attire looked very similar to the type of clothes worn in that Jack the Ripper movie *From Hell*.

"Thank God!" I whispered aloud. Hitching up my backpack, I dashed up to the pair. "Excuse me," I said a bit breathlessly, the two actors staring at me in shock. "I'm sure I'm not supposed to be here, and I apologize, but I'm really lost. Do you know how I could get to NYU from here?"

The man eyed me up and down, very convincingly astonished. "NYU? Madam, I have never heard of such a place."

"Wow, an actually believable English accent!" I said in admiration. How cute of him to stay in character! "Hey, you're good at this! Do you think I could get in here as an extra?" At their blank looks, I decided that the answer was negative. "Never mind. But really, I'm serious as a heart attack. Which way to the college?"

The man drew the woman close to him in a protective gesture. "Madwoman! Leave us be, or I shall summon a constable!"

I raised my hands in a placating gesture. "Listen, mister, you want me to leave, I'm gone. But I need you to help me get off this crazy set! And why are you talking so funny? You'd think it was the 1800s, not the 2000s."

"What nonsense is this? The year is 1886, fool woman! Be gone!"

"188—what?" For some odd reason, the mention of a date shot like a bullet through the armor of my disbelief. 1886? Shaking my head dazedly, I backed away, continuing down the street. That couldn't be. Was it really the year 1886? No, that was stupid. He was just being a temperamental jerk. Why didn't that idiot just answer my question? *Hmph, actors.*

I continued walking past shops and houses, the length of my journey outpacing any conceivably sized movie set. The wavering light of gas lamps lit my path as I trod the scarred and worn cobblestones. A thin mist swirled around me. In the distance a bell tolled once, some huge clock striking the half-hour. There wasn't a bell tower near the university, was there? Was I even close to the campus? Maybe I really was…No, impossible! Going back in time, what a stupid idea, I should know better. I just needed to keep walking until I saw someone else.

Despite my doubt, the chill air reeked of fog, fish and horse manure, a smell tough to find in the city, or at least in New York City. Could I have somehow fallen back in time? No, absolutely not! That was ridiculous! "This is a dream!" I said aloud, halting on the broad sidewalk. "I've fallen asleep in the library, and I'm dreaming, and I'll be late for work, and Marie will have my head…" I reached my right hand across to pinch my left. The pain was swift and sharp. Yes, I could feel that! Not a dream, then. Good God, then *what*? My mind was caught in a torrent of thoughts and sights and smells, barely registering any one. As a final test, I peered into a darkened shop window, hoping to see an empty storefront, constructed hastily for scenery purposes. Instead, I could see a music store, fully stocked in strings and brass instruments, but somehow lacking electric guitars and keyboards.

Now positive that I was not on a movie set, and equally sure that I was not dreaming, I pushed away from the glass and scrubbed my face with my hands, cursing under my breath. As much as I wanted to deny it, the reality of it all was sinking in fast. All the evidence pointed to something I simply could not accept. I truly was in the year 1886, in the nineteenth century! Oh, God, how did I get here? And more importantly, how was I supposed to get back??

The harsh sound of footsteps ran in my ears again, a single pair this time. Then, shuffling through the fog came a man in disheveled clothes, with a harshly accented voice and the unmistakable reek of cheap alcohol. "Oi, wot's a pretty laidee like you doin' out so late a' noight? You could get 'urt."

Had I still been in New York, I might have been disgusted and oddly flattered. Drunks late at night were simply a nuisance, like mosquitoes, but if this was the Victorian era, then I was in a very precarious position. In such a rigid age, my slim knee-length coat, short work skirt and leather ankle boots probably made me look like a hooker.

Well, I always thought that the best defense is a good offense. Craning my head at the slouching, ill-shaven figure, I sneered in my iciest tones, "Get lost."

He started visibly, apparently still sober enough to register an insult. Judging from his hesitation, I concluded that my response was either entirely unexpected or he had no clue what the hell I had just said. Either way, he snarled something vicious, strode forward and grabbed my arm, most likely expecting me to cower in fear. Instead, I instinctively delivered a swift kick to the 'unmentionables,' causing my would-be attacker to moan loudly and curl up on the ground. Suddenly free, I backed away in a hurry, silently blessing my night courses in practical defense.

I was about to make a clean getaway when a louder noise froze the blood in my veins. Three other ruffians appeared on the scene, taking in both their fallen comrade and me. *Oh, crap.*

"'Ey, there! Wot did you do, you little tart? We'll teach you not ta 'urt our friend, lassie! Get 'er!" they bellowed, charging at me in a drunken frenzy.

Practical Defense flew out the window as I swung my backpack at the closest man, dropped it and fled down the street as fast as I could, 'Hell's Idiots' hot on my heels. Oh, God, not good! I couldn't just run aimlessly down the streets of a foreign city; I would tire out or get lost, and they would catch me eventually. I couldn't fight three of them off with my bare hands. My breath started to wheeze in the cold foggy air, and my ankles ached viciously from the running. My lungs were burning and my vision was starting to blur. I needed help, now! Hell, I needed a weapon!

As I rounded a sharp corner, both needs were miraculously met. I slammed quite accidentally into a well-dressed young man with a mustache and a walking stick. Opportunity! Seizing the stick from the bewildered man, I whirled around and blindly lashed out, luckily making contact with the head of a rampaging ruffian, who stumbled and fell. Thrilled by the adrenaline, I would have enjoyed pummeling him further, but I was robbed of the opportunity by the sudden crack of a gun.

The young man lowered a smoking pistol at the brutes and cried, "Leave the lady be!" Most of his valiant speech was lost on them, however, for they had fled at the sound of the bullet, taking their fallen comrade with them.

Oh, thank God that's over. I suppressed a shudder, trying to shake the horrible feeling of being chased. Tension dropped from my shoulders, replaced by fatigue. If those idiots had caught me…no, absolutely not, not going to go there. I was safe now, at least for the moment.

"Are you all right, Miss?" the gentleman asked in an upper class British accent.

He seemed genuinely concerned, and at least he didn't denounce me as a madwoman, but I had been rubbed too raw to notice at that time. "Well," I snapped, "for someone who's lost, friendless, cold and chased by gutter slime, I'm just peachy! This is a long shot from the movies, that's for sure!" It was inexcusably rude, especially since the man had undoubtedly saved my life, but I was in no mood for idle conversation.

His brown eyes were creased with worry. "Do you need assistance, Miss? Are you injured? If you will accompany me to my flat, I will assist you in any way I can."

Well, this is surely not New York, I thought, *not if men behave like this!* The formality in the man's voice and his good manners, not to mention the fact that he rescued me, made him head and shoulders above about ninety-nine percent of the men in Manhattan. I felt my ill temper slowly begin to drain away. Feeling halfway secure, I took a better look at my benefactor. He was moderately tall, taller than I am anyway, but as I'm only five-four, that isn't saying much. Conventionally handsome, thickset and athletic, he sported sandy brown hair and the aforementioned mustache. He couldn't have been a day over thirty, possibly younger. In one hand he held the pistol; in the other was an odd black bag.

"Well, my mother told me not to take rides from strangers," I said with an effort to smile, sheepishly handing his walking stick back to him. "But I think that, considering the circumstances, I'll take you up on this one."

Curious but satisfied, my gallant champion asked me to wait while he found a cab. I agreed and he left, only to return a minute later in a hansom cab and graciously helped me into it. Suddenly remembering my discarded backpack, I explained to the gentleman and asked if we could backtrack and retrieve it. Thankfully he agreed and we set off down the road as I directed the cab driver along the way I had come.

After a short journey, I spotted my knapsack lying in a gutter by the side of the road. I jumped from the cab once it had stopped and dashed over to it, unzipping it and performing a quick inventory. Everything seemed to be accounted for, thank God, so I shouldered the backpack but hesitated before reentering the cab. My head was whirling with questions: English accents and gas lamps, fog and horse cabs, the huge clock I had heard before? I must be in London! But how did I cross the Atlantic Ocean? And for that matter, how did I get hiccupped one-hundred-plus years back in time? How would I get home again? Was I going to miss midterms? I snuck a glance at my rescuer from the corner of my eye. Who was this guy anyway? He seemed awfully nice, but could I really trust him? If I was in Victorian London, then maybe…I racked my brain, trying to remember exactly when the Jack the Ripper murders had occurred.

After some moments of silent thought, I climbed back into the cab, still unsure of my situation. The gentleman muttered something to the cabbie and we rolled down the streets again before he returned his attention to me. "I am glad to see that you have recovered your satchel, Miss…" He trailed off expectantly, but I was too caught up in myself to notice. "Miss?" he finally prompted. "Might I have the honor of your name?"

Name? I had been so wrapped up in organizing my thoughts that introductions had completely slipped my mind! "Oh! Um, yeah, sure! It's Nona, my name, that is, Nona Brown." God, that sounded dumb. I awkwardly thrust out my hand.

My benefactor caught it and placed it briefly to his lips. Wow. After all of the trauma, it seemed this night was finally starting on an upward curve. "Charmed, Miss Brown," he said. "I am Dr. John Watson."

Looking back, I know I must have looked ridiculous, staring with my mouth open like that. This was Dr. Watson? John H. Watson of literary fame, late of Afghanistan, follower of detectives, carver of cadavers and all-around second banana? But that couldn't be! He wasn't real! Sherlock Holmes and Dr. Watson were just figments of Sir Arthur Conan Doyle's bored imagination! Weren't they?

"Miss Brown?" asked Dr. Watson. "Are you all right?"

All right? I thought, a gritty smile pasted on my face. *Oh, sure I'm all right!* I silently screamed. *I'm sitting in a hansom cab, ten thousand miles from home and one hundred years in the past, having a pleasant conversation with a fictional character, and he asks if I'm all right? No, I'm NOT all right! I've gone completely insane; I'm over the rainbow, Toto, and I'm just sitting here waiting for the men in shiny white coats to give me a new jacket and take me away! How do you like THAT?* Finally, with a supreme effort, I took a deep breath and cleared my head. Hysterics would get me nothing but a one-way ticket to the nuthouse. *Focus, girl,* I thought as I called on my final reservoir of self-control. *Go with the flow.*

"Yes, I'm fine, doctor," I whispered aloud, a little unsteady but otherwise clear. "I'm just *very* confused. And I'll explain everything, I promise, as soon as we get to Baker Street."

It was now my companion's turn to look surprised. "But how did you know we were going to Baker Street?"

I looked out the window so that the good doctor would not see the shocked expression on my own face. I had mentioned Baker Street as a test, to see if this was indeed the same Dr. Watson of murder mysteries. It seemed that my hypothesis proved true. "Well, you'd be surprised at how much I know, Doc," I said lightly, realizing the ironic truth of my statement.

The poor man, oblivious to the weight of my words, asked, "I beg your pardon?"

I smiled genuinely for the first time that night. "Oh, never mind."

CHAPTER 4

In Which I Explain Everything

We disembarked from the cab on a very nice street, lined with well-kept houses and lovely old trees. Dr. Watson paid the cabbie, walked up the steps of one of the houses and unlocked a door marked 221. Once again I pinched the back of my hand viciously, the pain once again removing all doubt as to my state of consciousness. I couldn't believe I was actually here! The most famous address in history, 221B Baker Street, in the era of Queen Victoria! The very thought seemed to defy belief. Watson motioned for quiet and led the way through a dark foyer and up a flight of stairs to the right. I followed him up the stairs, counting as I went. "Fifteen, sixteen, seventeen. He was right," I murmured half to myself. "There really are seventeen."

Watson looked askance at me and pushed the door open into 221B. The sitting room was creased with shadows, lit only by dying firelight, and I squinted to see until Watson lit a gas-lamp.

With the room illuminated, I could not believe my eyes. It was exactly as I had imagined it from the stories. To my right were windows overlooking the street below, a coat-rack and an old-fashioned, cluttered desk. In front of me was the pair of armchairs and the fireplace. To my left was a Victorian sofa, a chemical-stained table with assorted beakers and whatnot, another more orderly desk, a set of bookcases, the dining-room table and a door I assumed led to other rooms. Newspaper clippings and papers were scattered around the room in a jumble, and the smell of tobacco lingered in the air. Beyond this simple description, it was the sitting room that I had pictured so often as I read.

I wandered the room with the reverence of a pilgrim at a shrine, lost in wonder; I shuffled papers on desks, examined the letters stuck to the front of the mantle with a jackknife, ran my fingers over the pipe collection and archaic chemical array, caressed the thick volumes on the bookshelf. Pulling an volume at random, I unlaced my boots, wandered over to an armchair and sank into it, turning pages aimlessly without really reading anything, trying to let the reality of it all sink into my mind. Baker Street. Baker Street!

I jumped at the hand on my shoulder. Watson stood behind me with a glass in hand, wariness and confusion creasing his eyes. Poor guy had been watching the whole time; he probably thought he had a Bedlam patient in his house!

I closed the book and rubbed my eyes. "Oh! I'm sorry, Watson, really, but I just can't believe that I'm here! Here, of all places!"

The confusion deepened. "I fail to understand you, Miss Brown."

I encompassed the room with a sweeping hand. "This, all this, my God, all true!" I paused and thought. "You don't have a clue as to what I mean, do you?"

"I fear not," he replied, handing me the glass. "Perhaps you should elaborate."

I studied the glass briefly, diagnosed the small amount of smooth amber liquid as alcohol and knocked the whole thing back, shivering at the aftertaste. Of course, brandy, Dr. Watson's panacea for all the ills of the world. "Um, elaborate, you said?" I continued, looking up at him and handing back the glass. "God, where do I begin?"

Watson raised his eyebrows at my brusque dispatch of the brandy and accepted the glass, clearing his throat. "The beginning is usually best."

I rolled my eyes as the stale platitude. "Okay," I returned with a smirk, a bit of humor breaking into my mood. "'In the beginning, God created the heavens and the earth, and the earth was…'" I trailed off at his impatient glare. "All right, I get it. The beginning…Well to start, you should probably know that I'm not from London."

He nodded, moving to the sideboard again. "I gathered as much from your accent. You are an American, from New York perhaps?" Returning to the chair, he passed me a slightly larger amount of brandy.

I accepted the brandy and threw it back again, impressed with him despite myself. *Testing the limits, Doc?* I thought silently, feeling much more relaxed. *Judging what kind of woman downs a double-shot of straight alcohol? Let's hear it for amateur psychology.* Aloud I said, "Dead on target, *Herr Doktor*. Your roommate must be rubbing off on you. Where is the Great Detective, anyhow? Sleeping?"

He smiled and blushed with the praise, but it vanished with the latter end of my statement. "Yes, but how did…?"

Uh-oh, here it comes. "Hold on and let me finish," I interrupted, emboldened with at least two shots of liquid courage. I had to get it out now before I lost my nerve. "Okay, in addition, you should probably know that I'm not from this year either. In fact, I—well, I'm a time traveler. I come from the year 2002 A.D." I paused meaningfully, not liking the silence that followed. "Following me so far, Doc?" I prompted.

It was obvious that Watson was not inclined to believe me. "Time travel?" he scoffed, beginning to sound impatient with me. "Such a thing is surely impossible!"

"I know it sounds crazy," I said in a placating voice, "but it's the only explanation I have. I mean, about an hour ago I was in Manhattan in the year 2002, and now I'm…oh, Lord, when am I? What's the date?"

"Today is October 20th, 1886," Watson replied. He glanced at the mantle clock. "Make that the 21st." He was clearly dissatisfied with my story. Glancing at me skeptically, he asked, "Tell me, Miss Brown, how well do you handle alcohol?"

"What?" I glanced down at the empty glass in my hand. Two glasses worth, one finger of brandy each, that was two shots, maybe a little more. Did he think I was drunk? "Hey, wait a minute, Doc. I'm not drunk; I can promise you that." *A little tipsy maybe,* I admitted to myself. As I pondered how to convince him of my truthfulness, I was seized with a sudden, triumphant thought. "I know! I'll prove it to you! I'll prove I'm from the future! Let's see…" I deposited the glass on a side table and leaned forward in my chair, eager to convince him before he sent me packing. "You're Dr. John H. Watson; you room with Sherlock Holmes, the consulting detective."

His brow furrowed in skepticism. "Such things are common knowledge."

I cast about for another scrap of information. "You were in Afghanistan as an army surgeon, attached to the Fourth Northumberland Fusiliers," I said with conviction.

"It was the Fifth Northumberland Fusiliers," he rebutted. He looked no closer to enlightenment.

I hissed under my breath. Damn, it WAS the Fifth! I was losing him! "Ah…you spent your boyhood in Australia!"

His brows lifted. "No, I didn't, I was raised in Hampshire!"

"Really?" I asked. "News to me. I need to speak to whoever wrote that biography…"

"Miss Brown," said Watson in long-suffering tones. "I do not know why you would concoct such an outrageous lie, but I suggest that you abandon this pretense and tell the truth! I cannot help you unless-"

"No!" I cried. "No, I'm telling the truth, I promise! I just need to…aha!" My gaze fell on my backpack, discarded in my rapt wanderings. I leaped from the chair, seized it and hastily pawed through the contents, trying to find something modern that would validate me beyond any further doubt. The book I was reading, *The Adventures of Sherlock Holmes*? No way! Considering to whom I was talking, that might seriously screw up the future or something. My wallet? Nah, I needed something really phenomenal.

"Eureka!" I cried, snatching my portable CD player. "This should prove it!" A swift check of the CD in the machine brought a sigh of relief. It was loaded with my "study music," a selection of classical and instrumental pieces I had burned from other CDs. God forbid, I didn't think that the nineteenth century was ready for Green Day or System of a Down.

"Here, take this," I instructed, handing the headset to Watson. He took it with a mixture of curiosity and discomfort, as if he were handling a poisonous snake. "Put it over your ears, like so," I pantomimed the action. He did as I did, but with a great deal of unease. I checked the volume, pushed play and handed him the player, waiting for his reaction.

It was not long in coming. No sooner did the first track begin than the cynical expression dissolved from the good doctor's face, replaced with a look of pure amazement and delight. He sat in his armchair and listened in fascination as I watched from the floor. With him in such a state, I seized the opportunity to discreetly close my bag before he caught sight of my copy of *The Adventures*. No need for my newfound friend to have any undue knowledge of the future, whatever future that may be.

When the music died away, Watson slipped off the headset and gazed with wonder at my CD player. "Amazing," he breathed, "a concert hall that fits in your hands."

I took the player back, turning it off and stowing it in my bag. "Hey, you're right. That's a nice way to put it."

But no sooner had the bag closed than the skeptical Watson completely disappeared, replaced with a supremely interested one. Seizing a battered notebook and scribbling with great fervor, he fired at me, "How does such a contraption work? What other kinds of machines are there? How is police work done in the twenty-first century? And medicine, what kinds of advances have been made? Tell me everything!"

I couldn't help but smile at his newfound enthusiasm, now that he fully believed my claims. I tried to answer his questions broadly, nothing too specific, telling him about my life in New York. He was amazed to hear that women could vote and hold eminent political positions and equally amazed to hear about the progress of technology, especially when it applied to medicine.

After about half an hour, he raised a hand. "One final question, Miss Brown. Why did my sitting room hold such fascination for you? And how did you know, or thought you knew, details about my life?"

Wow, I thought he had forgotten that. Regardless of his downplayed role in the detective stories and Hollywood movies, the man was no fool. "Well, you see," I began, "we in the future know a lot about you and your friend Mr. Holmes. As a matter of fact, you two are probably the most celebrated investigators in history!" A delighted smile spread over his honest features, and I simply couldn't bear to tell him that most of the world thought the two of them were fictional characters created by an out-of-work optometrist with too much time on his hands. By that time, I was definitely feeling the effects of the brandy and my tiring evening. I attempted to stifle a jaw-cracking yawn, but was unsuccessful.

Watson glanced at the mantle clock again. "Good heavens, but my manners are atrocious this evening! Shame on me for keeping a guest awake until the small hours of the morning! Miss Brown, I fear that we have no guest rooms, but there is a small servant's chamber, which is currently empty. You may stay there for tonight, and tomorrow I shall try to secure you a place with the landlady for the duration of your stay."

"Mmph." I didn't really register the words, but instead allowed myself to be led downstairs. As I paused in the doorway, I could see that the quarters were absolutely spartan: a tiny bed, a washstand and a dresser. However, I wasn't about to complain, at least not right away. Watson was being so nice, after all, and I realized that I hadn't even thanked him. "Thanks, Doc. Really 'preciate all this," I said, a little fuzzy as I swayed in the doorway.

"It is truly nothing, Miss Brown."

"You can call me Nona, if you want. 'M not an old maid yet."

Watson smiled. "Very well then, Nona. Sleep well."

I found I needed no further encouragement and slipped into the room, shutting the door. Deciding not to disrobe in a strange place, I climbed into the bed fully clothed and fell into a deep and dreamless sleep.

※   ※   ※

"Miss Brown?"

Someone was shaking my shoulder and speaking in a light voice. I opened my eyes a crack, but shut them tight against the glare of sunshine. "Ugh. Go 'way, Trish. Class isn't 'til one today."

"Miss Brown?"

Suddenly, the night's events came back in a roaring flood. As I sat up with a gasp, my hand slipped on the side of the bed and I fell down in a heap, hitting the floorboards hard. "Ow! Shit! What the-?"

Looking up, I could see a thirtyish woman, plump and matronly with dark hair pinned to the top of her head, staring down at me in shock. I scrambled to my feet. "Terribly sorry about that…ah…"

She caught my drift. "Mrs. Hudson," she said with what I assumed to be a Scottish lilt in her voice.

"Thank you, Mrs. Hud—Mrs. Hudson?" This was the housekeeper? I had always thought she was old! "Ah, sorry about that, you startled me."

She eyed me askance, looking as if she wanted to wash out my mouth, and I regretted my earlier burst of profanity. "Dr. Watson instructed me to wake you for breakfast," she said. "If you so wish, you may refresh yourself with the facilities upstairs."

Facilities? Oh, she meant the bathroom. This fancy Victorian talk would take some getting used to. "Yes, that would be great, thanks." I smiled in what I hoped was an endearing manner.

She nodded briefly, not endeared. "You go upstairs, through the sittin' room and down the hall, t' the first door on the left." With that, she disappeared through the door.

Absurdly glad that I had gone to bed with my clothes on, I hurriedly made the bed and rushed upstairs. The sitting room was empty, so I bypassed it and walked into the short hall, observing three doors. The first door on the left was the bathroom, so the other two must be bedrooms. I could hear movement in one and assumed it was Watson, so the silent room must belong to Holmes. For a moment I contemplated peeking inside it and catching a glimpse of the Great Detective in repose, but I thought that would be pushing my luck. I was here on the goodwill of total strangers; if they kicked me out, I would be seriously screwed. Therefore, I put temptation out of my mind and entered the first door on the left.

My first thought was "Thank God! Indoor plumbing!" Indeed, I gave thanks that the late nineteenth century was sophisticated enough to have toilets and hot running water. My second thought was "Holy crap! Look at the bathtub!" The Victorian tub came up to my waist; it was that deep. Considering the fact that I had spent a late night fully clothed, I knew my priorities just then. Turning the taps full on and wincing as the water clanged through the primitive pipes, I plugged up the tub and was actually in the process of undressing when reality sank like lead in my stomach.

I was stranded in a foreign era. I was in the 1800s. Barring a miracle, I would never go to class at NYU again. I would never see a movie, never graduate, never listen to the radio as I surfed on the Internet. I would never see my mother or my brothers for the rest of my life. Oh, my God, my family wasn't even *born* yet! As this horrifying knowledge set in, I finally released the roiling emotions I had withheld the previous night. *I'll never see my father again,* I thought bleakly. *I'll never dig him out of the office again, never let him drag me to lunch, never curse the umpire with him at a Mets game, never talk to him after a hard day at work, never again...* I was suddenly grateful for the roar of the tap water as I sank to the floor, pressed my face into a towel and cried myself out.

When my outburst of tears had slowed to a trickle, the tub had filled and was steaming invitingly, so I stepped carefully into the scalding water, scrubbing the tear tracks from my face and taking a bar of soap to my brown hair, trying to regain my composure. The ache of loss was still present in my chest, but it had dimmed to the point where I could think rationally again.

As I cleaned my physical self, I took the opportunity to come to grips with myself and try to assess my situation. Today was October 21st, 1886. If I remembered my Sherlockian history, Sherlock Holmes and Dr. Watson had lived in Baker Street for five years. Next year Watson would meet Mary Morstan during the Jonathan Small case, and they would marry shortly after that. Four years after that event, Holmes would defeat Professor Moriarty and embark on his Great Hiatus. Provided that my memory was not once again faulty, then I at least knew my place in the grand scheme of things.

Suddenly feeling a greater sense of stability, I began thinking about long-term plans, just in case. Chances were high that I might be in this century for a while. Hadn't Watson said that he would arrange quarters with Mrs. Hudson? If I remained here, that would mean he would probably pay for my room himself, but I couldn't allow that. The Dynamic Duo had not yet reached the financially stable epoch of their lives. That raised another important point: how *would* I support myself? I was determined to earn my keep, but if memory served, the world of Victorian London did not present many opportunities for a working single woman. What could I do?

I could draw and paint, of course, but artistry was an unstable position in any era, especially for a woman in this one. I was good with children; perhaps I could be a governess. On second thought, that would require me to live in a household and leave Baker Street. Not wanting to abandon the only person who believed my tale, I decided to save that option for a last resort.

What else? Language tutor? No good. Thanks to the diverse culture of New York City, I could curse fluently in five languages, but that was about it. Wait, I used to play the violin and guitar; perhaps I could give music lessons. The more I thought of that idea, the more I liked it. That position would give me the freedom I desired and would probably pay well. My musical skills wouldn't merit Carnegie Hall, that was for sure, but I could read sheet music and teach others to do the same.

After about half an hour in the tub, I felt cleansed and refreshed in mind and body, confident that I could handle whatever came at me in this brave new world. However, my stomach was grumbling and the water was growing cold, so I pulled the plug and levered myself halfway out of the tub. Just as I had one foot planted on the floor, the door suddenly flew open. There, tall and pale in the doorway, clad in pajamas and bathrobe, austere features frozen in shock, unruly black hair falling into his astonished gray eyes, long white hands slack on the doorknob, was the man, the Master, the Great Detective himself, Sherlock Holmes.

And I wasn't wearing a stitch.

CHAPTER 5

In Which I Abuse a Wall and Almost Burn a Library Book

Before I scandalize anyone, rest assured that my previous observations of Sherlock Holmes took place in a time span of about two and a half seconds. After the two and a half seconds, Holmes gave a little gasp and slammed the door with a bang.

I, on the other hand, leapt out of the draining tub, broke the record for toweling off and shrugged into a worn brown bathrobe hanging on a peg. The belt fell to my hips and the hem trailed on the floor; I assumed that it belonged to Holmes. Well, considering the circumstances, I was pretty sure that he wouldn't mind, and it was considerably less revealing than my modern outfit. God, I was so embarrassed! Caught *au naturel* by Sherlock Holmes, my favorite character in literature! This was a thousand times worse than those dreams where you came to class in your underwear!

I adjusted the belt and ran out into the sitting room, beholding what I had feared: poor Watson getting a semi-intelligible dressing-down from his crimson-faced friend.

"How could you, Watson?" shouted the normally loquacious detective, lit up like a Roman candle. "She was...*I* was...How *could* you!?"

"Holmes, you aren't making sense!" returned the bewildered doctor. "What on earth are you talking about?"

This was probably a good time for me to intervene before things degenerated any further. "Perhaps I can explain, Doctor," I said coolly, straightening to my full five-foot-four and doing my best to glide in, hoping that my own face wasn't burning too badly.

At my entrance, Holmes' expression shifted from shock to embarrassment before finally settling on icy fury. "And who might you be, Miss, to intrude upon my humble home?" he asked with cold emphasis in his voice.

Watson stared in open confusion, but I quailed internally under Holmes' piercing appraisal. Seeing myself reflected in those cold gray eyes, I suddenly wished that I were prettier, or smarter, or taller, or anything more than what I was, for that matter. From the way he stared down at me, Holmes was probably deducing my best friend's middle name and what I ate for breakfast last week! Nonetheless, I rallied my courage and forced my gaze upwards to meet his. Just because he was legendary didn't give him the right to be rude, or to open doors before knocking.

"I am Nona E. Brown, sir," I returned just as icily, choosing my words with care. "And I doubt that I shall need Dr. Watson to introduce you. Judging from your height, your features and the size of your ego, I deduce that you are Sherlock Holmes, the world's most arrogant consulting detective. As to my presence here, I was in an unfortunate situation with a band of ruffians last night, and Dr. Watson was kind enough to rescue me."

His eyes widened as my previous barb struck home, but I gave him no chance to interrupt as I switched tacks to Watson. "Mr. Holmes is upset, Doctor, because he has already made my acquaintance in a most unorthodox way." I smiled sweetly at Holmes. "It would seem that he neglected to knock before he opened the bathroom door."

Ever the Victorian gentleman, Watson gasped with understanding and glared daggers at his friend, who was blushing again. Holmes looked so embarrassed that I decided to back off a little. Perhaps I was overreacting. After all, he didn't have no way of knowing that I was there. I was rather surprised at Holmes' appearance, though. I had been expecting someone much older, at least in his thirties, but I judged him to be around his mid-twenties, and somewhat handsome as well. The illustrations didn't do him justice at all.

Uh-oh, it looked as though Watson was about to do a little overreacting of his own. "However," I amended quickly before Watson could burst in righteous fury. "There's really no harm done and I'm starving, so let's apply ourselves to breakfast, shall we?" Without waiting for a response, I seated myself at the table and proceeded to pour myself a cup of coffee, silently praying that they wouldn't comment further. I was already on thin ice and I was terrified of another misstep. Thankfully, faced with the lady's actions, the gentlemen decided to uncomfortably follow suit.

As the meal progressed in an uneasy silence, I bit my lip and mentally struggled for something to say without embarrassing Holmes again or offending his pride. Before I could say anything, however, Holmes suddenly reached over and patted my hand reassuringly. "Never fear, my dear, we will send a wire to your family and secure you passage on a ship. All will be well."

"Excuse me?" I asked. What was the man talking about?

Holmes smiled in a sure fashion. "It is perfectly elementary, Miss Brown, although that is not your actual surname. You are of the wealthy Von Braun family of New York, and you came to London some months ago without your family's knowledge in search of adventure. However, after your money ran out, you were too proud to beg your family's forgiveness. In desperate straits, you were forced to sell your jewels, your clothes, and finally take to the streets. I hope, however, that you have now realized your folly, and I am sure that your parents will be overjoyed to hear from you."

It took me a second to figure out that he was making deductions about me, but once I did, I wanted to giggle wildly. Poor Holmes! His deductions made a lot of sense in that day and age, given my suddenly cultured voice, un-calloused hands, New York accent and state of *deshabille*, but he couldn't be further from the truth. Well, shameless prankster that I am, I put on an astonished face.

"Why, Mr. Holmes, that is excellent!" I cried, a la Hound of the Baskervilles. "Your deductions are truly remarkable." His smile grew even more self-satisfied and I raised my cup, continuing blithely: "It's too bad they were all wrong."

Sherlock Holmes dropped his fork with a clatter and stared at me in shock. I could see Watson struggling to hide his laughter; he had surely been through similar scenarios before. "All wrong?" echoed Holmes.

"Well, I shouldn't say all," I amended thoughtfully. "I am from New York, but as for the rest…" I trailed off meaningfully.

Holmes seemed a bit dazed. "But I don't understand," he said bleakly.

My devilish little mind had concocted another prank. My, I was evil today! Turning to Watson, I said, "Doctor, perhaps you could shed some light on the matter."

Watson picked up on my ruse immediately and stared me up and down as he stroked his mustache thoughtfully. "Miss Brown is a writer and artist who enjoys playing the violin and guitar. She is twenty-three years of age and is in her final year of attendance at New York University. She lives with a roommate, waitresses part-time, speaks five languages to a very minimal degree and walks a great deal. Her visit to London was entirely spontaneous, and she arrived only last night."

"Wonderful, Doctor!" I praised, clapping my hands lightly. "Right on every point!"

Holmes had a dreadful expression on his face, drawn and pale, and I worried that he might be sick. "I see. Watson?" he said in a tight voice. "Have I been exhibiting signs of an early senility?"

That was it. Watson and I burst into helpless laughter. "It is perfectly elementary, Holmes," Watson echoed with an airy wave. "I met Miss Brown late last night, or early this morning, as I returned from my shift at the charity hospital. Over the course of the evening we had a lengthy chat, during which time I divined all the facts that I have now enumerated."

Now it was Holmes' turn to laugh, partly at the prank and partly at himself. He sighed with relief and wiped tears of mirth from his eyes. "Thank God, Watson!" he chuckled. "For a moment, I feared that the pupil had outstripped the teacher and that I would be reduced to taking notes on *your* cases! But," the detective cleared his throat, suddenly all business, "again, Miss Brown's dilemma still remains to be ascertained."

That was my cue. I gave Holmes the abbreviated version of my trip through time, Watson providing validation of my strange tale. Holmes listened intently, meaning that he slouched in his chair and stared at the ceiling for the entire narration, but when I concluded, he simply shut his eyes and shrugged. "Time travel is a complicated business, I would assume, and quite impossible in this day and age. We lack a greater grasp of technology. Therefore, I fail to see how I may help you."

Well, he was certainly keeping an open mind! "There must be some way to get me home!" I protested.

"I wonder..." Holmes said thoughtfully before returning his attention to me. "Miss Brown, do you think that you could find your way back to your point of entrance into this time?"

I was taken aback and processed the question for a moment. "If I were brought back to the point where I met Dr. Watson," I said cautiously, "I suppose that I could retrace my steps."

"I see!" said Watson in revelation. "You intend to return to that location to see if we cannot return her to her own time!"

"Precisely, Watson," Holmes replied. "We shall wait until nightfall in order to replicate the circumstances, have Miss Brown backtrack to the point of origin and see what may be."

I grinned happily and reapplied myself to breakfast with new vigor. After all, Oz was very interesting, but this Dorothy was ready to go back to Kansas.

The remainder of the day passed uneasily. Holmes made some derogatory comments about my modern clothes and tried to pump me for information about the immediate future, but once he realized that I wasn't going to tell him anything, he seemed to forget about my presence entirely. Watson at least spoke to me, giving me the most in-depth and enjoyable Victorian history lesson of my life! On the other hand, I was eating myself alive with anxiety as we waited for nightfall. If this experiment tonight didn't work…No! I refused to dwell on that thought and instead focused my mind on the present.

After a late supper, the sun having set hours before, Watson called a cab to the door and he and Holmes hastily bundled me into it, one of Watson's heavier greatcoats disguising my 'strange' attire. We rattled through the streets, the light from the gas lamps flashing past the cab window. Not a word was spoken between us as we traveled; we all knew and respected the gravity of the moment. The brougham finally rolled to a stop and as we disembarked, I recognized the ill-fated corner where I had first encountered Watson.

Holmes handed a pair of coins to the cabbie and instructed him to wait. The man agreed and Holmes turned to me. "Now, Miss Brown," he stated, "if you would be so kind as to retrace your steps, perhaps we can put an end to this mystery."

I nodded and led the way up the street. My heels clicked loudly in the silence as the detective and the doctor silently flanked me. This part of the journey was simple enough; when the London Losers had played their sick game of tag with me, I had run in pretty much a straight line. However, all too soon we reached a three-way split in the road. I glanced uneasily between them, sensing Holmes' growing impatience. "Ah," I mused aloud, "to the right, I think." *Stupid! Don't think it; know it!* "Yes, right, this way!" I set off with a lengthened stride, cursing my memory. Damn it, Holmes must take me for some kind of an idiot! His cold gaze always seemed to bore right through me, as if I were a specimen laid out for display. I knew of his attitude towards womankind in general and I admit that I wanted desperately to make some show of brilliance to change his mind, but I only became more nervous as the minutes wore on.

We came to another intersection and I nearly hissed in frustration. I turned left here…didn't I? Nothing in the area looked familiar. Had I taken a wrong turn? I bit my lip in thought for a minute when Holmes spoke up behind me. "Miss Brown, I can think of several better places to be than on a freezing street; might we move it along?"

His acerbic tone was scorching and certainly didn't improve my mood. If he was so *perceptive*, why couldn't he see how hard this was for me? I swung my head around to snap at him when I noticed the building behind his tall form.

"The music store!" I cried in revelation. "I remember now! This way!" I set off down the left road at a near run, the men jogging in my wake. It was all coming back to me. Another left turn brought me to the spot where I had argued with that couple, down the road was where I had seen the hansom cab, and here…I stopped before a blank brick wall, part of a larger store whose sign was obscured in the blackness. "Here!" I proclaimed with all the force of a royal decree. "I came right through this wall!"

Holmes briefly raised an eyebrow and completely ignored the wall, instead directing his attention to the ground. "Ah!" he exclaimed, pulling a magnifying glass from his pocket and pointing to a black mark on the ground. "Observe here! This mark appears to corroborate the lady's claim, Watson! If you would lift your left foot please, Miss Brown?" What? Feeling absolutely idiotic, I complied, my balance shot to hell as I stood on one high heel. As my heel shifted on the uneven cobblestones, my arm flailed for support and came into contact with the detective's arm, which I gripped tightly. He seemed shocked at the contact for a moment, but he neither acknowledged my hand nor removed it from his arm, directing his attention to the sole of my boot.

"Right here," he began, running a long finger across the edge of the sole. "You can see where the peculiar black crepe of the sole has rubbed off in contact with the curbstone, here." I tried to crane my neck over my shoulder to see what he was talking about, but the movement threw me off and I faced front again, feeling like a horse brought in for shoeing. Holmes continued with no thought to my discomfort. "Although I hold some reservations about people walking through walls, the mark is significant. We shall accept it as a working hypothesis. Miss Brown, you may lower your foot." I released him and did so, glad to have both feet on *terra firma*. Holmes looked down at me as if he expected me to thank him for something; the man was rapidly getting on my nerves. How different he was from the storybooks! I really shouldn't believe everything I read.

"Now what do we do?" Watson asked.

That was the sixty-four million dollar question, wasn't it? Taking a deep breath, I strode up to the wall and placed my hand against it, watching for some telltale ripple. Rather than dissolving into a permeable substance, it remained firm. I pushed against it, with a similar lack of results. "Open sesame!" I said aloud, only half in jest. Predictably, there was no change in the stone. I was growing desperate. On the other side of this wall was New York City in the year 2002, and I had to get to it.

I shoved the wall again, this time with both hands. Nothing. I had to get through this wall and get back home; I had classes tomorrow. I had to go to work at the bistro, I had to work on my term paper, people were going to worry about me. I pushed harder, gritting my teeth with the exertion. I had to get through, I needed to go grocery shopping, do my laundry, call my father, go to dinner next week with Grandma—oh God, my father, my mother—my family! My *family*! I was beating against the wall with both fists, its blank face mocking my anger and grief.

"My family! My life! Oh, God! Let me through, you piece of *shit*! Give me my life back! *God*!" With a final shout, I kicked the wall hard and stumbled backwards, landing on the pavement. I buried my head in my hands, sobbing, not caring who saw. "Oh, God, what am I going to do? H-how can this be happening? Oh, God, please, I want to go home…"

I felt a large hand on my shoulder and a tissue pressed into my grasp. Mindlessly grateful, I seized it, scrubbed at my streaming eyes and vigorously blew my nose before I realized that it wasn't a tissue I held. It was a man's white pocket-handkerchief. Oh, no, not that. Humiliated beyond words, I glanced up to see…oh, joy. Sherlock Holmes knelt beside me, the shock on his face dissolving into featureless calm. "Keep it," he muttered, rising smoothly and speaking briefly to Watson before striding away.

Wonderful! I thought, kicking myself inside. *That's the third time I've made an idiot of myself in twenty-four hours!*

Watson looked distinctly uncomfortable, hovering between sympathy and humor as he helped me to my feet. "Holmes has gone for the cab," he said. I didn't know how to reply to that, so I didn't. I was too swamped with emotion to make conversation. After what seemed an eternity of silence, the four-wheeled horse-cab pulled up to us with Holmes already inside. Watson helped me into it before climbing in beside me, and we rolled away. I stared fixedly out the window, trying to ignore Holmes' gaze silently appraising me.

When we returned to Baker Street, Mrs. Hudson was still awake. We didn't explain anything to the poor woman, but with one look at my stricken figure she needed no explanation. She fetched me a pair of aspirin and a glass of water, both of which I thankfully consumed, and pushed me off to bed. Once alone in the maid's room, I could see in the dim moonlight a large white night-gown on the bed, presumably a spare of Mrs. Hudson's. With infinite thankful-ness, I stripped off my clothes and heaped them on the floor, donned the oversized pajama and crawled into bed.

I didn't sleep much that night.

❧   ❧   ❧

The next morning, breakfast was a subdued affair; not a word escaped among the three of us. I picked at my ham and eggs, not really tasting anything I put into my mouth. Holmes seemed unconcerned as he stirred sugar into his coffee, but Watson, bless him, kept glancing at me in apprehension when he thought I wasn't paying attention.

Finally, I couldn't stand the tension any longer. Best defense is a good offense. I put down my fork with resolution and fixed the men with what I hoped was a firm gaze. "Well, gentlemen, what happens now?"

Holmes raised a sable brow. "Miss Brown, if you are intending to be vague, you are succeeding admirably."

I bit my tongue to silence a retort before speaking calmly. "Well, I think it's safe to assume that I may be here for quite a while. I don't have any idea how things work in this time or how I can get by in society. So, what am I supposed to do with myself?"

"I don't see that you need to do anything," Watson commented. "You are already situated downstairs and I see no possible reason as to why we cannot continue in this vein."

Thank God! He was going to let me stay! Before I could thank him, how-ever, Holmes chimed in. "And have her stay here? Absolutely not. I will not have my restful haven poisoned with feminine clutter."

"But, Holmes!" Watson protested. "She would be adrift and friendless in a strange time!"

Holmes raised a long finger. "Nonsense, Watson. I am sure that there is a homeless shelter that will take her in; now the subject is closed."

I sat openmouthed in shock. Jerk! That overbearing, misogynistic jerk! Feminine clutter? I glanced around the thoroughly untidy sitting room. This from Mr. Dysfunctional himself! I was about to tell him *very* explicitly what I thought of his little "haven" when my gaze fell across the chemistry array and an idea sprang to mind, a very sneaky little idea. I knew from *The Adventures* that if I outright argued with him, he would only grow more stubborn, so I pushed myself up from the table and walked slowly over to my bag.

"Gee, it's too bad I can't stay," I said carelessly. "Now I have no place to lay my poor little head." Holmes snorted at the ceiling and Watson glanced at me with unease, but I smiled and winked at the doctor to let him know all was well. "Of course, if I were staying," I continued, rummaging through my backpack, "I'd have a place for all my things, like this book, for instance." I pulled out Trish's library book and sank into an armchair with it.

"*Advanced Chemistry and Practical Applications*," I read aloud slowly. "Whatever shall I do with this?" There was the faint scrape of a dining-table chair as I opened the book at random to a page covered in complex formulae and oblique definitions. "Good heavens!" I proclaimed to the air in front of me, sensing someone trying to read the book over my shoulder without my noticing. "This book isn't even mine! I'm afraid I simply can't do a thing with it! Well," I amended, snapping the book shut, "it ought to make splendid kindling." I stood and made to throw the book in the fireplace.

Hook, line and sinker: the Great Detective hissed sharply and lunged to snatch the volume from my hands, but I twisted and halted him with a hand on his chest, holding the book out behind me. The two of us vaguely resembled the Statue of Liberty play in American football. "Do I stay?" I asked Holmes, shaking the book precariously over the flames.

Holmes glanced slowly from the book to me and back again, turmoil plain on his face, before he grudgingly stepped back. "Very well," he grunted sourly. I held the volume out with a grin and he snatched it, dropping into his armchair and devouring the tome with a scowl on his face. "Salome," he muttered.

I ignored the Biblical insult, stepping back to the breakfast table.

Watson's face was alight with mirth and admiration. "In all my campaigning days," he said grandly, "I have never seen a neater skirmish nor a more clever victory."

"I heard that," came a sulky voice from the armchair.

"You were meant to," replied his roommate.

I shook my head in amusement. Thus was the eventful beginning of my time in London and my life at 221 Baker Street.

CHAPTER 6

❀

In Which I Learn a Great Deal and Solve a Case (Well, Kind of...)

The next month proved to be more instructive than anything I had ever experienced in college. To my chagrin, we had been forced to reveal my mysterious origins to Mrs. Hudson. After we had shown her the CD player and revived her from her fainting spell, the good lady had taken me under her maternal wing. She even took in some of her old dresses for me to wear around the house during my indefinite stay in the 1800s.

It turned that out I was expected to earn my keep by taking on some of the maid's duties. As one can imagine, my twenty-first century self was ill-prepared for such tasks. Mrs. Hudson was a firm taskmistress and put me straight to work stacking wood for the oven, washing windows, scrubbing floors and dusting all and sundry surfaces. When I protested lack of knowledge for a task, such as cooking or sewing, she would simply roll up her sleeves and show me how, muttering all the while at the lack of education for young women in the future.

I was a willing pupil, even with the numerous needle pricks and more squeamish aspects of Victorian food preparation, but despite my compliance, some things were too much for my modern mind to immediately handle. One day during a cooking lesson, she was forced to fetch smelling salts for me after she demonstrated the proper way to gut a chicken. For the next month I was sore and aching, nursing blisters and burns from housework, silently cursing the day I set foot in this wretched era.

The free time that I did have was spent upstairs in the Holmes and Watson quarters. Holmes had eventually reconciled himself to my female presence, at least when he decided to acknowledge me over the bridge of his new book. I spent most of my time listening avidly to the pair discussing their cases or reading books I had pirated from the sitting room bookshelves. I am a hopeless bibliophile and, deprived of any outside influences, I devoured treatises on detection, chronicles of crimes past and the occasional medical journal and yellow-backed novel belonging to Watson.

Watson was my primary companion over the first few weeks. He bought me some clothes that were more suitable for public wear and would often take long walks with me, instructing me on the finer points of Victorian customs. I in return painted a glowing picture of the wonders of the future, giving my companion examples of pop-culture and technological advancements.

Rest assured, however, that my feelings toward Watson remained grounded in strict friendship. Not that there was anything amiss with him; on the contrary, he was well mannered, considerate, intelligent and steady as a rock. It was simply that I was too busy trying to stay afloat to attempt a romance just yet. Besides, I didn't want to rob Mary Morstan of her Prince Charming once the affair with Jonathan Small rolled around.

Holmes, on the other hand, seemed to amuse himself by annoying the hell out of me. Since I began helping Mrs. Hudson with the chores, he treated me like a common servant until I finally yelled at him. He scared me half to death when he unloaded his pistol into the wall in the dead of night, without even a case as an excuse, so I had to yell at him again. He came and went incessantly during his cases, often incognito, and delighted in deceiving me with his disguises. And yet, all in all, his biggest flaw was his stubborn disregard for my problems, a quality that bordered on rudeness.

For example, in the middle of November, I was standing in the foyer, hanging a new picture for Mrs. Hudson. My short stature, however, made it difficult to achieve the desired height, and it is nearly impossible to drive in a nail with your arms stretched straight above your head.

As I stretched up on tiptoe, trying to reach the elusive spot, an all-too-familiar voice sounded from behind me. "What *are* you doing, Nona?"

Startled, I jumped as Holmes emerged from the kitchen, a large index volume in one hand and an apple in the other, wearing the half-amused expression that served only to aggravate me. Dammit, he scared me! That did it; I'd teach him some manners.

"Isn't it obvious?" I asked with an air of astonishment. "I'm doing some experiments on Einstein's Theory of Relativity." His gaze shifted from the hammer and nails in my hands to the small picture resting on the floor and he raised a sable eyebrow in silent, confused questioning. I shrugged in reply. "Hey, ask a stupid question, get a stupid answer." Nothing provoked a reaction from Holmes like the 's' word. He was as proud of his intelligence as a debutante was of her beauty.

Oddly enough, he did not comment at my barb, merely looking up at the spot for which I was reaching. "You are obviously too short to reach that place on the wall."

"No shit, Sherlock," I growled under my breath, noting the ironic propriety of the catchphrase.

If he heard me, he gave no sign but instead took a noisy bite of the apple, handing me both fruit and book. Relieving me in turn of the hammer and nails, he began to drive a nail into the designated spot.

Wow, that was unexpected. I had thought he would just tease me further, but instead he was helping me out! I stood watching him for a while, wondering if I should thank him. "Um," I began, causing him to pause in mid-swing and look at me askance. His gaze told me quite clearly: *No thanks needed or wanted, so spare us both the discomfort, please.*

"How is the Hamilton counterfeit case going?" I said instead, as I had gotten the message.

He nodded at my silent communication. "Very well, actually," he said easily. Pound, pound, pound. "If things keep going in this vein, I shall be forced to burgle his house."

My eyebrows rose to my hairline. "This is 'very well'?" I asked incredulously.

Holmes simply gave me a roguish smile and kept pounding.

I smirked back at him. "You enjoy this sort of thing, don't you? Breaking and entering in the dead of night."

He rolled his eyes in a "Who? Me?" expression and gave one final pound to the nail, handing the hammer back to me. I returned his book and apple and gave him a warm smile, happy that he was finally being a little nicer. He nodded again and headed up the stairs to his rooms.

I picked up the picture and started to hang it on the nail, but stopped in shock. He didn't! "Holmes!" I screeched in fury.

"Yes?" he asked innocently, halfway up the stairs.

I pointed angrily to the nail. "I was hanging a picture! You weren't supposed to drive it in all the way! Now I can't hang the picture or pull the nail out!"

"Oh?" he said mildly. "Well, so much for the Theory of Relativity." With another noisy crunch for the apple, he continued up the stairs, leaving me to curse the detective in English, French, Italian, German and Chinese as I hunted for a stepstool.

Rest assured, of course, that I was not about to let such treatment pass unpunished, harmless though it may be. If Holmes was going to go out of his way to annoy me, well, what kind of friend would I be if I didn't return the favor? The question was how to do it. If I engaged in verbal repartee with Holmes he would surely outwit me, and I didn't want to push the envelope with malicious pranks, although after a few weeks, I did start feeling a powerful urge to add cayenne pepper to his afternoon tea! But in the end I settled for something subtle, inconspicuous and foolproof: physical contact.

Every morning, when I brought up the early coffee, I would greet Holmes with a cheery "Good morning!" accompanied by a kiss on the top of his head or my fingers through his hair, always little things; a hand on his arm, a brush of his wrist, almost accidental but obviously meant. This may not seem like a big deal, perhaps quaint affection or even mild flirting, but I was pretty sure that it rankled the misogynistic, pessimistic detective

So for the next month or so, Holmes and I made war in blatant secret, under the amused eye of Watson The good doctor liked to imagine that Holmes and I were flirting; after a barb from Holmes or an enthusiastic hair-ruffling from myself, he would smile all-knowingly over the top of his newspaper and chuckle to himself.

The remainder of October and all of November passed in a hazy blur as I grew accustomed to my new life. In fact, my days had settled into such routine and monotony that when I finally did participate in the other half of Holmes and Watson's life, I almost didn't realize it.

It was December the tenth, and snow was upon the ground. We were seated in the sitting room in a companionable, post-luncheon silence, Holmes clipping articles for his index volumes, Watson reading and filing the morning's mail, and myself lounging on the window-seat, halfway through Winwood Reade's philosophic *The Martyrdom of Man*. Holmes had declared it too complex for a woman, so of course I had to read it. It was very deep, very layered and a bit depressing, but actually rather intriguing.

However, despite the pleasantly puzzling philosophy, I wasn't really reading it. Instead, I leaned against the window, silently waxing poetic about the falling snow and thinking about Christmas presents. I had decided on a fine writing set for Watson, as a not-so-subtle hint that he should keep careful notes and one day get started on those chronicles. Mrs. Hudson was forever losing her spectacles, so I was looking for a nice chain to hang her glasses around her neck. But what about Holmes? Despite his bad attitude, my sense of manners demanded that I get him a present. What to get for the man that wants nothing? Days of window-shopping had yielded nothing but icy fingers and a growing awareness of my light pocketbook. Mrs. Hudson graciously gave me a fair allowance, but even the amount I had hoarded wouldn't go far towards quality presents.

As I sat and pondered, a large, vague shape clattered down the street, stopping in front of the building and disgorging a smaller, equally vague shape. "Client, Holmes," I chimed, breaking the silence. "I'll get the door." Shifting from my comfortable seat and filing away my Yuletide dilemma, I walked down the stairs as the door was pounded upon. I opened the portal and admitted the sole petitioner, who shook the snow from his coat and handed me his card. From the man's short stature, pinched rat-face and shifty expression, I knew his identity before I had even glanced at the square of cardboard: Inspector Lestrade of Scotland Yard, famed in the Canon for his incompetence and his ability to take all the credit.

I cocked a skeptical eyebrow at the card, ruining my invisible maid persona, but some instinct in me did *not* want this man looking down on me. Brushing past him, I returned up the stairs and into the sitting room, shutting the door behind me before I gave the card to Holmes. "Inspector LeRat to see you, Holmes."

He smiled briefly. "He impressed you that way as well?" I nodded with a rueful smile as Holmes regarded the weather report out the window. "Hmph. Lestrade would often swallow his tongue before coming to me. To do so in weather like this is very promising news, very promising indeed." He returned his attention to me and gestured to the empty breakfast tray on the table. "Send him up, Nona, and bring another pot of that singular coffee you make."

Hmph indeed. 'Singular' was probably the closest thing to a compliment I'd ever get from Holmes. I grabbed the tray and headed to the kitchen, relaying the message to Lestrade on the way. In the kitchen I seized a conveniently perking pot of coffee and proceeded to doctor it, adding a square of baking chocolate, a splash of rum and a few drops of precious coconut extract, my favorite recipe in the winter.

My errand thus completed, I loaded the tray with the silver pot and four cups and headed back up the stairs. I was apparently just in time; all I had missed was the ritual lighting of tobacco and a few astounding deductions by Holmes, Lestrade having made himself comfortable at the table. I filled cups and passed them around before taking one for myself and sitting down unobtrusively on the sofa.

Lestrade drew on his cigar thoughtfully before launching into his tale. "It's an odd business, Mr. Holmes, very odd. Not two nights past, Andrew McGregor of Number 12, Bayberry Lane, was found dead in his study, his throat messily cut. Mr. McGregor was an elderly, reclusive man and something of a miser, according to his son, Jason. His long career as a stock trader had built him into one of the wealthiest men in the City, but he lived in a modest house, kept only two servants, a middle-aged couple, and refused Jason a monthly allowance, insisting that he make his own way in the world." The little inspector paused and tapped his cigar ash into the saucer of his coffee cup.

"How old is this son?" asked Holmes, beating me to the punch.

"Twenty-seven," answered Lestrade.

Twenty-seven! And he wanted an allowance? My estimation of the late McGregor jumped up a few hundred notches. My woman's intuition was painting a picture of a frugal, principled father trying to instill a good work ethic in a lazy son and the lessons not taking. Still, I tried to remain objective.

Lestrade continued his narrative. "Early yesterday morning, Mr. McGregor was found by Mrs. Millet, one of the servants. McGregor's throat was clumsily cut from ear to ear; it would seem that the burglar was surprised by the elderly man and made a hasty job of killing him."

Watson looked up from the notes he was taking. "It was burglary then, not premeditated murder?"

"Definitely, Doctor. A small safe behind a bookshelf was found open and empty. It had contained a sack of loose gems, amounting to roughly half of the man's fortune. They were, however, all properly insured." He paused here to help himself again to the coffeepot, and my opinion of him warmed a bit. If the man could appreciate good coffee, perhaps there was some hope for him. "The bay windows in the study open onto the front yard," Lestrade continued. "They were found slightly ajar when Mrs. Millet came upon the scene."

"I hope that you remembered to look for tracks under the window before you let all of Scotland Yard have their way with the crime scene," said Holmes in a weary voice.

Lestrade bristled righteously. "Mr. Holmes," he said tightly, "the coroner estimated McGregor's time of death at ten-thirty on the night of the eighth, when the snowfall began. Any tracks were buried under three inches of fresh powder. Nevertheless, I can safely assume that the window was the burglar's escape route. In the dead of night with the obscuring snowfall, it would have provided optimal cover."

"If this is all so simple," said Holmes, "why have you brought it to me?"

In answer Lestrade reached into his overcoat and pulled out a small bag, the contents of which he emptied onto the table. Intrigued, I took up my coffee, grabbed Holmes' magnifying glass from his desk and moved to the table to see what Lestrade had brought. Five glittering gems, beautifully cut, winked up at me from the polished table surface. "These five gems were found on the desk of the deceased," Lestrade said with gravity.

Holmes instinctively began to rise from his chair, but I halted him by holding out the magnifying glass with a 'What would you do without me?' smile on my face. Surprisingly, he grinned back and accepted the offering, with Watson looking smug again and Lestrade somewhat annoyed at my interruption.

Holmes systematically inspected the gems with me leaning over his shoulder. With him thus occupied, I took the opportunity to pose a question of my own to the inspector. "What are the alibis for the son and the servants?"

Lestrade bristled even further. "Mr. Holmes, you take too many liberties with your staff! Surely I am not to be interrogated by the hired help!"

What? This weasel was trying to put me down, but before I could put him in his place, Holmes interrupted without taking his eyes from the gems. "Of course not, Lestrade, but Miss Brown is not hired help. Inspector, may I introduce Miss Nona Brown, my fellow lodger. She takes rooms on the ground floor and has most generously been helping our overworked landlady until suitable help can be found. Therefore, I am quite sure she would appreciate a bit more courtesy. Now answer her question."

Wow. Holmes actually helped me out! Will wonders never cease? I stared coolly at the inspector, causing him to shift in his seat. "Ahem, yes, my apologies, Miss Brown. The alibis…Mr. and Mrs. Millet had retired at nine-thirty or so, Jason McGregor half an hour later. None of them heard a thing."

Holmes laid down the magnifying glass and stretched wearily. "Other than their obvious worth, I see nothing remarkable about the gems."

Watson spoke up, punctuating his words with his pencil. "Perhaps the burglar spilled the stones in his haste to escape and neglected to retrieve them."

"That is impossible, Doctor," said Lestrade. "The stones were arranged quite precisely, thus…" He aligned the stones in a straight and orderly row. "Accident is not a possibility. I believe that it is some kind of message, but as to its meaning, for that I come to you."

We all stared at the row of gems for some time when an idea began to grow in my mind. Hadn't I once read a story with five gems like this? No, that had been a calendar with five months. Months…"What are the names of the gems?"

Lestrade briefly consulted his notepad and indicated each stone in turn. "Ruby, peridot, sapphire, opal and topaz."

"And they were found in exactly this order?" I asked eagerly, causing Holmes to peer curiously at me. With an affirmative nod from Lestrade, all the pieces came together. I whistled incredulously. "Whew, that boy has guts to flaunt it like this!"

Watson voiced their unanimous question. "I say, Nona, have you got something?"

"Well, if 'something' means that I've solved it, then I suppose so."

There ensued general uproar as the men surged to their feet. "How is this possible?" roared Lestrade, practically foaming at my impertinence.

"Please, gentlemen, please!" I said over the din. "Let me explain!" They reluctantly resumed their seats as I pointed to the innocent-looking gems on the table. "These gems are birthstones, gentlemen. They are symbolic of the months July, August, September, October and November, respectively." I paused meaningfully. Watson and Lestrade seemed lost, but silent comprehension dawned on Holmes' face. I pointed to each gem and recited, "J, A, S, O, N. Jason. The son murdered his father, opened the window, took the gems from the safe to collect on the insurance and left this message to snub his nose at Scotland Yard."

The inspector's face was alight with revelation and triumph. "By Jove, it makes sense!" he crowed. Lestrade scooped the gems back into his bag and shrugged back into his overcoat. "I'll obtain a warrant straight away; can't have him moving about. Thank you ever so much gentlemen; the cheque will be in the mail!" With a flurry of motion, Scotland Yard's finest was out the door and down the stairs, slamming the front door as he went out.

I stood speechless for a moment. I did it! I had actually solved a case! So now what? "Well," I said to the remaining men who stared at me with incredulity on their features. "Guess I'll get started on the dishes." I gathered up the tray and headed for the door.

"Birthstones?" asked Holmes in disbelief.

I paused and shrugged. "It's a...girl thing."

And I actually made it down the stairs and into the kitchen before I burst out laughing.

CHAPTER 7

In Which I Have a Merry Christmas and Go to My First Opera

Days had passed since the solving of 'my first case,' and I never gave it a second thought. I did my chores, gave my silent opinion on other cases of Holmes', debated with Watson about the necessity of musical progression and made another dent in *The Martyrdom of Man*, just life as usual on Baker Street.

About a week later we were all in much the same positions: Holmes smoking his post-prandial pipe and perusing the agony columns in the afternoon paper, Watson systematically filing the day's mail and I pondering the Christmas present puzzle.

Watson shifted himself from the chair, pigeonholed his letters over his orderly desk, fixed Holmes' correspondence to the mantle-piece for later and, to my great surprise, dropped a white envelope into my lap.

This effectively startled me out of my reverie. "Watson, what's this?" I asked in confusion.

Watson smiled. "I have taken many liberties in my life, but I have yet to stoop to snooping about in a lady's mail." This got a dry chuckle from Holmes.

The envelope was indeed addressed to me, from Scotland Yard, no less! What did I do? No postmark, so a courier must have delivered it, then. I tore it open and peered inside, the breath catching in my throat. What was the meaning of this?

After some seconds, Holmes voice sounded sarcastically. "We are all breath-lessly awaiting some report, Nona. Be so kind as to enlighten us on the con-tents of the mysterious envelope."

In silent response, I picked out a crisp five-pound note, along with a mes-sage reading, "For services rendered with regard to McGregor case." Five pounds! In 1886 that was quite a wad. I glanced up at the men, stricken. "This isn't mine," I protested. God, what would Holmes and Watson think of me? I was stealing their income! And they had given me so much! "This is yours. I didn't do anything with the McGregor case."

"Nonsense, Nona," Watson protested magnanimously. "It's a standard freelance payment. You solved the case; you've earned the fee."

"But I didn't!"

"Nona," Holmes began wearily. "If you are fishing for compliments, then I suggest…"

"I'm not fishing for compliments!" I interrupted. "What I mean is…"

"Then you have nothing to protest," Holmes interrupted back, his eyes flashing with verbal battle.

I broke in almost desperately. "But I *cheated*!"

"What?" chorused the men, snapping to attention.

I addressed the floor in embarrassment. "I once read a detective story that ran along the same lines as the McGregor case, and I applied it to the case. I didn't earn anything!"

Holmes and Watson looked blankly at me for a moment, but then Holmes burst into incredulous laughter. "That's it?" he asked in disbelief. "I thought you might be psychic. Good God, woman, if that's cheating, then I swindle my way into ninety percent of my income! Do you think that the criminal histories on my shelves are for show? 'There is nothing new under the sun.' Ecclesiasti-cus, something-or-other. Most of my cases are solved because I compare them to past cases. That is not cheating, my dear; that is detecting."

"But I-"

"Ah!" He held up a preemptive finger as I opened my mouth. "Not another word. The fee is yours and that's that."

I closed my mouth and looked at Watson pleadingly. "Holmes is right, Nona," the doctor asserted. "Not another word. Buy something nice."

'Buy something nice,' he says, as if I were some fluffy Victorian female. Hmph. I resumed looking out the window and pondering. How on earth was I going to get…Christmas presents! I glanced down at the five pounds clutched in my fist. This was my chance! With the five pounds combined with my savings, I could buy that writing set for Watson with plenty left over for Mrs. Hudson, not to mention Holmes. Goodbye, guilt!

Now for the hard part: getting downstairs to change before they could volunteer to chaperone me. Buying Christmas presents is a little tricky when the recipient of said present is hovering over one's shoulder. Nonchalantly pushing myself off of the window seat, I made my way downstairs without comment from the Dynamic Duo. Sneaking into my room, I hurriedly pinned up my hair and attempted to bend my will against that of the corset. Lacing a corset is not meant to be a one-person task, and the finished result was looser than normal, but I wasn't able to summon up the will to care. So what if my waist was a few inches wider than the social norm? At least I could breathe.

Snaking into the restrictive Victorian dress, buttoning up my shoes, pulling on my long coat and literally pinning a hat to my brown curls, I snatched up my small purse and shoved the fiver deep inside it. So far, so good. Cracking the door open, I could hear Mrs. Hudson busy in the kitchen, and Holmes and Watson were presumably in the sitting room upstairs. The coast was clear. I swiftly crossed to the coat rack, snagged one of Mrs. Hudson's shawls to ward off the winter chill and opened the door.

"Where are you going, Nona?" queried a male voice from behind me.

Caught! I spun around, seeing Watson halfway down the stairs in his carpet slippers. I attempted an ingratiating smile. "Going out for the day!" I chimed with nonchalance.

"Nona, you shouldn't be going out alone, it's-"

"Not proper," I finished. "Well, seeing as how I'm halfway out the door and you're in your shirtsleeves, I won't bother you with escort duty and just carry on. Soonest gone, soonest home, right?" I didn't bother waiting for his likely-negative reply, edging the door closed. "Thanks anyway, I'll be home soon!" Shutting the door firmly, I clutched the shawl around my shoulders and headed down the street in double-time, half expecting Watson to follow. When I reached the corner taxi stand and there was no sign of him, I allowed myself a sigh of relief. Oh, why couldn't Holmes have been coming down the stairs; he didn't give a damn about me anyway. As it stood, either Watson or Mrs. Hudson was going to read me the Riot Act when I got home. However, as I stood on the icy pavement, snow swirling around me, the foreign yet familiar sounds of the city echoing through my frame, with no babysitter to watch my steps, I was too overjoyed to care. "Cabbie!" I called to a passing hansom cab, waving a hand, my internal liberation overflowing onto my face in a brilliant smile. I was free!

❦   ❦   ❦

Hours later I was cruising the Strand in blessed solitude, carrying my bundles. The writing set was perfect for Watson. I had also bought a slender silver chain for Mrs. Hudson to hang her spectacles on and had even found a miniature Christmas tree, in addition to picking up quite a few books that I had long coveted. Now all that remained was Holmes, but I was still at a loss. The only thing I had really considered was a large file cabinet for his papers, but I turned that down; trying to get Holmes organized was like trying to straighten the Leaning Tower of Pisa.

Suddenly, as I passed a jewelers' shop, I found the ideal gift: a beautiful, gold-plated pocket watch and chain. It was practical, lovely and perfectly impersonal. I knew Holmes would appreciate it. The plated pocket watch was a good sight cheaper than its solid gold counterpart, but it still cut deeply into my savings. Didn't matter; I was too caught up in the Christmas spirit to worry about money.

Whistling "Jingle Bell Rock," I noticed the sky growing dark and was about to call a cab when I realized that I didn't have enough money left. All my money had been used for the gifts and my books! I would have to walk back to Baker Street in the dark. Christmas spirit evaporated as I walked over to a cab, trying to calculate exactly how close three pence ha'penny would get me.

However, Fate intervened once more. As I placed my hand on the cab door, a larger hand placed itself upon mine. With a start, I followed the hand up the arm and found the owner, a dapper young man with blond hair and a goatee. He removed the hand quickly, as startled as I. "Forgive me, Miss," he apologized. "I shall seek out another cab."

"No!" I protested. "It's all right, you take this one." He looked incredulously at me and I blushed. Oops. I had committed a Victorian social no-no: being generous to a man. Men were supposed to be chivalrous, not women. To cover my gaffe, I said hastily, "Tell you what, if you're going towards Regent's Park, we can ride together."

The young man seemed willing to overlook my social rift and instead changed the subject. "Why are you headed to Regent's Park? Seems a bitterly cold day for a stroll, don't you agree?"

I most definitely did agree; it was freezing outside. "I live near Regent's Park, but my purse has been emptied by shopping, so I'll have to walk from the park.

"Certainly not!" protested my new companion. "I am staying with friends on Gloucester Road, right next to Regent's. I'm sure I could drop you off wherever you live."

I just loved these Victorian men, so eager to please. I graciously accepted and gave the man my address. He helped me into the four-wheeler and we rattled off down the cobblestone streets.

As we rode, we made general small talk. I gave him my name and learned that his was Darby Edwards. He was the son of a country squire, he told me, and he enjoyed his life immensely. He had been out on the Strand browsing for gifts and was about to head back to his friend's house for a party. I gave my profession as a music teacher and said that I took rooms under the worst tenant in London. All in all, we passed the miles in charming conversation until the cab pulled into Baker Street. As I alighted, Darby peered at the house with curiosity. "Isn't this the street of that detective, Someone Holmes?" he asked.

I nodded ruefully. "Sherlock Holmes, to my everlasting regret. He's the unbearable neighbor I mentioned."

A strange and frightening transformation overtook my new friend. A hard light gleamed from his blue eyes and his lips pulled back into what might have been a smile if it hadn't been so cold. "Really?" he said softly, half to himself. Then as suddenly as the new Darby came, it went, leaving only the charming gentleman who had given me a ride. "Well, Miss Brown, I must be on my way. Best of the season to you and yours." He planted a kiss on my hand and I wondered if I had imagined the earlier harshness. "I hope I shall see you again," he said in a low and flattering voice, but the effect was spoiled by his eyes. The ghost of steel lurked behind those blue eyes, staying with me as the cab rattled away and causing me to compulsively wipe the kiss off of my hand onto my dress. This two-faced stranger may hope to see me again, but the feeling was less than mutual. Even so, I tried to put Darby Edwards out of my mind and concentrated on getting my purchases hidden in my room before anyone saw me.

I had hidden the gifts under my bed, changed back into housedress and mobcap, and was busily making war with a stack of dirty dishes in the sink. It was a bloody and gruesome battle, but I was slowly making headway against the greasy army, blowing holes in its' ranks with cannons of soap and dishrags. So intent was I upon my impending victory that, when a heavy hand was laid upon my shoulder, I gasped and whirled, somehow sure that it was the two-faced Darby Edwards.

"Holmes!" I yelled at the true offender, both relieved and embarrassed. "You scared me! What do you want?"

Holmes looked blank, an odd circumstance. Holmes' face was usually very expressive, especially when he was being sarcastic, but in this case his tone was expressionless. "Who was the man in the carriage?"

How had he known about that? Misguided anger from my scare began to bubble to the surface. "Do you send someone to keep tabs on me, Holmes?" I asked with irritation. "I'm a big girl; I can cross the street by myself."

His brows came down in irritation. "I do not recall addressing your size or age, Nona, and I make it a point to keep track of visitors to my domicile. Now, who was the man?"

I shrugged offhandedly and returned to the dishes. Holmes was just being Holmes, I decided, poking his considerable nose into everyone else's business. "Just a fellow I met on the Strand who offered me a ride home."

"You did not know him?" His voice was a bizarre blend of wariness and (*relief?*) something I couldn't place.

"No, as a matter of fact, I didn't. I've barely been out of this house since I arrived here, Holmes! I can count the people I know on one hand."

"Precisely my point." Holmes moved around to see my face and I was suddenly struck by his purposeful nearness. He had never gotten this close to me before. *And so what?* I thought. *Who cares? Not I! Stupid girl, concentrate! No, not on that!* "You are a stranger in this time," Holmes continued, oblivious to my internal struggle, "and a lovely one at that. You must take every precaution so that men will not take advantage of you."

Was he complimenting me? I would have thought so if he wasn't being so condescending in the same breath. "Gee, I guess I forgot my red riding-hood this time, but I'll be sure to remember next time I go to Grandma's house," I said with saccharine sweetness.

Holmes' voice tightened, a large flaw in his self-restraint. I began to wonder if I was pushing too hard. "Enough of your sarcasm, woman! You go out without a chaperone and do not return until after nightfall, sharing cabs with strange men. You cannot possibly know what kind of dangers await you in a city this size, and since Watson and I have allowed you to stay here, you are our responsibility!"

I simply raised my eyebrows as I retorted, "Mrs. Hudson is the one who allows me to stay here, Holmes, and I pay for my lodging in labor. I am no one's responsibility but my own."

"That is entirely beside the point," Holmes protested. "No matter whose responsibility, you take too many liberties for a single young lady in a city!"

Now that was going a little too far; it was time to rein him in. "Why, Holmes," I began, smiling coyly. "If I didn't know better, I'd say you were a jealous lover!'"

That stopped him. He stepped back quickly and averted his eyes. "Don't be ridiculous, Nona!" he said uncomfortably. "It's nothing like that at all!"

I turned to the sink again, all icy exactitude. "Then you have no business interfering with my social life."

Silence reigned as I progressed in the now-cold dishwater, but I could still sense Holmes still standing behind me. Was I being a witch with a capital B? I didn't think so; Holmes was the offender here, trying to control my movements! On the other hand, perhaps he was just looking out for me. Still, as a native Manhattanite I could take care of myself, thank you very much. But Holmes had no way of knowing about the rigors of New York. Hmph. Just as I was about to negotiate a peace, Holmes spoke.

"Just…be careful." His tone was almost pleading. I turned in surprise, but he had already left the room, leaving me to stare at the empty kitchen doorway.

Never in a million, billion years would I understand Sherlock Holmes.

I lay wakeful in bed, staring at the position of the moon outside my window and guessing at the time. It was Christmas Eve, and I was trying to see if it was late enough to sneak upstairs and plant the presents I had wrapped the night before.

Earlier that day, I had been visiting with Watson to give and receive season's greetings from some of his war compatriots. All involved had a wonderful time, playing music and telling stories over hot cider (or brandy, in the men's case). And as an added Yuletide bonus, a band of the young street Arabs commonly known as 'the Irregulars' dropped by Baker Street just before bed, serenading us with Christmas carols in a child-sweet, slightly off-key choir. Of course, this sent Mrs. Hudson into a flurry of motherly baking, and the two of us dispensed Christmas cheer in the form of fresh sugar cookies. I had often seen the Irregulars pop in and out during a case and had endeared myself to them by always keeping the kitchen door open and turning a blind eye to the cookie jar. They called me "pretty Miss Nona" and often referred to me as "Mr. 'Olmes' laidee-friend," which never ceased to distress Holmes. Holmes, of course, declined all of the festivities, puttering with his chemicals all day. There never was a more proper Scrooge. When I wished him Merry Christmas, I half-expected him to say "Bah, humbug!" and tell me to boil my head in the plum pudding! But I digress.

After the fifth instance of gazing out the window in who-knows-how-long, I threw caution to the wind and got out of bed, reaching under my bed for the green-and-red gifts and the tiny Christmas tree I had hidden there. I crept through the hall and up the stairs in my tartan plaid nightdress, my burden in my arms as I pushed the door open.

The sitting room was empty, lit by the dying fire, with just enough light to keep me from damaging the furniture. I placed the tree and the gifts on the table and stood back to survey my handiwork. The tiny tree winked and sparkled on the linen tablecloth, somehow transforming the sitting room with holiday spirit. Now if only that newfound spirit would rub off on Holmes.

Turning to go back to bed, I stopped in my tracks with a smile. Speak of the devil, and he appears. Holmes was asleep at his desk, lounging in his shirtsleeves with one long arm dangling into space and the other pillowing his head. Well, I had wanted a glimpse of the Great Detective in repose, hadn't I? I crept closer, careful not to wake him. His desk was littered with formulae; he had probably been noting some chemical reaction when the Sandman came in for the K.O. I stood as quietly as the falling snow, taking that obscure pleasure that comes from watching someone unawares. Holmes had lost his superior, faintly sarcastic expression in slumber, seeming tranquil and at peace with himself. The firelight played across his pale face, illuminating the line of his brow, the plane of his jaw, the tilt of his strong nose, the shadow of his lips…

Wait a moment, could I really be thinking like this? Although Sherlock Holmes was a somewhat handsome man, it was definitely not in the classical sense. The nose was too strong, for one; it made him look like a bird. His jaw was firmly lined to the point of Cro-Magnon, especially when he was being stubborn. His entire frame was nothing but planes and angles; if I had so desired, he would be ridiculously easy to caricaturize. I wasn't attracted to him at all, was I? So where exactly *was* I going? Actually, I wasn't entirely sure, but it was probably nowhere good.

With a supreme effort, I cleared my head. How could I be having those kinds of thoughts? After all, it wasn't as if we were even friends! Suddenly, the kitchen conversation from weeks earlier came back to me, when Holmes had seemed so concerned for my welfare. It had been misguided, unnecessary concern, but concern nonetheless. Perhaps Holmes did care, in his own oblique way, and just had odd ways of displaying it.

I wasn't about to wake Holmes and send him to bed; the stubborn man would just pick up the experiments where he left off. Taking the blanket from the sofa instead, I carefully draped it over his sleeping form. Impulsively, I softly combed my fingers through his luminous raven hair, a tender caress infinitely different from my usual contact. "Merry Christmas, Holmes," I whispered. My face was mere inches from his. His breathing sounded in my ears, his heartbeat echoed through my body, the scents of shag tobacco, of sandalwood soap, the warm, clean smell of *him*, filled my nose. My God, was I going to *kiss* Sherlock Holmes?

That ludicrous thought snapped me back to attention. Of course not! The very thought was absurd! He was Sherlock Holmes, The Great Detective; he wouldn't kiss any woman, let alone Nona E. Brown, part-time housemaid!

But he isn't The Great Detective anymore, whispered a treacherous little voice. *You left The Great Detective on the pages of a novel. Now he's just a man. And he cares.*

Enough of such heresy; it was too late at night for such thoughts. That was it; it was late, I was tired and a good night's sleep would put everything into perspective again. Decisively I walked to the door, cast a slightly wistful glance at the sleeping man, and went back to bed.

The next morning I woke with that special tingle that can only be found on Christmas Day. Yawning gustily, I washed up and dressed hurriedly, 'those thoughts' banished from my mind. Mrs. Hudson and I had quite a task ahead preparing a Christmas feast and it would require all of my concentration.

I was bringing jars of preserves for breakfast up from the cellar when Watson came thundering down the stairs in elation, surprising me. "Merry Christmas!" he exulted. "Angels walk the earth this blessed morn, and lo and behold, here is one in my hallway!"

I confess that I giggled at the hyperbole. "Such flattery, Watson! You're certainly in a good mood,"

"As well I should be," he replied. "The writing set is a treasure, Nona. I shall be terrified to use it!"

"Don't you dare!" I protested. "I gave it to you for a reason! You have a real gift for writing, Doc, and I want you to put it to good use someday. Promise you'll use it?"

He did so and formally presented me with a long black box. I deposited the preserves on the hall table and opened it, gasping in delight. My gift was a tiny diamond pendant on a silver chain, beautiful and elegant and utterly beyond his means, which made it all the more precious.

"Oh, Watson," I breathed. "You speak of treasures and then give me this! Help me put it on!" He gladly did so, and I rushed to the hall mirror to see it glitter at my throat. Real diamonds! How did he do it? Any amount of jewelry I had received in my previous life, no matter how extravagant, paled in comparison to this one gift. "I feel so beautiful!" I exclaimed, twirling in my patched housedress.

"I don't imagine you would need a necklace for that," Watson complimented. He was such a dear. I planted a sisterly kiss on his cheek and took immense pleasure in his pleased blush.

And where is Holmes through all of this? I wondered when the door swung open again and Holmes came down the stairs in frock coat and top hat. "I'm going out," he announced, although that was a bit obvious.

I was itching to know what he thought of the watch, but he would see my question as badgering so I merely asked, "Will you be home in time for dinner?"

"More than likely," he replied, pausing at the hall mirror to adjust his hat and brush his coat. Holmes never took much care for his appearance; was he going to see a lady-friend? More importantly, did he even care about my gift?

My doubts were assuaged as Holmes dug long white fingers into his waistcoat pocket, pulled out his new pocket-watch, checked the time and replaced it smoothly before moving out the door. Watson dismissed this as mere eccentric behavior, but my eyes grew moist with gratitude. Holmes had brushed his coat to call my attention and had checked his new watch for the time, disregarding the grandfather clock in the hall. He did care after all. In his own oblique way, he had thanked me. I went to start breakfast.

Days passed and New Year's drew near. Holmes hadn't given me a Christmas gift, but I understood, or at least I thought I did. I just shrugged it off, attributing it to his anti-social nature, and reminded myself that giving was better than receiving. Aw, who am I kidding? I admit that I was a little hurt, but I gave no sign of it.

One evening I returned to Baker Street after a long and exhausting day of running errands. I was too late to start dinner, but I was certain that Mrs. Hudson had taken care of it so I didn't worry. I wasn't that hungry anyway; I just wanted to wash up and sleep.

I unlocked the now-familiar door and stepped through, announcing, "I'm home!" to no one in particular. The fact that Baker Street was my home still felt odd. However, this time someone was there to hear me.

"There you are! I was beginning to worry that you wouldn't make it!"

I craned my head to see Holmes coming down the stairs. He was *gorgeous*. I suppose they called it "full dress", I was never completely sure, but I did know that Sherlock Holmes was six-foot-plus of elegance in a full black Victorian tux, and I was thoroughly enjoying the view.

Grinning foolishly, I called out with a teasing lilt, "Woo-hoo! Feast your eyes on the blue-plate special!"

He rolled his gray eyes at my teasing and began to push me down the hall. "Hurry up, Nona, or we won't have time for dinner before the curtain!"

Despite the appreciable view, I was starting to get annoyed at his manhandling. "Holmes, you're talking gibberish! Make sense!"

In answer he grinned from ear to ear and pulled three slips of cardboard from his jacket pocket. "Behold, a wonder for the ages! I have procured box seats for the encore performance of *Tosca* tonight!"

Of course, the opera; it was one of Holmes' few passions. My heart sank as I surveyed my simple outdoor frock. "Holmes, it's very generous, but I can't go."

"Oh? I hope you know what you are missing, Nona. Have you ever been to *Tosca*?"

"No, I haven't; I've never been to an opera, but…"

"*What?*" he interrupted in true shock. "By God, woman, that is abominable! Have you no entertainment at all in the next millennium? To your room and change; we shall rectify the situation this very night!"

My hopes were ground into the dirt with each passing word. "But I have nothing to wear!" I cried.

Holmes stared at me with an air of weary disgust. "Come now, Nona, don't play such woman's games with me. I have absolutely no patience with them. Now be ready to go in half an hour, or don't come at all!" With that he turned and strode back upstairs.

I felt like screaming. Woman's games? How *dare* he? Had it never occurred to him that I had better things to do than concentrate on new dresses! Did he ever contemplate that perhaps I wasn't as readily outfitted as he? How could I go to the opera? I could just see myself sitting among the other ladies in their opera gowns and glittering jewels, a gray goose among swans. I would go to my room, all right, but I would go to fume and curse and possibly even cry at the loss of opportunity, a Cinderella among the ashes with no mice to keep her company. I stalked into my humble quarters and froze, forgetting to breathe in my astonishment.

On my narrow maidservant's bed was a gown, an exquisite, shimmering, crushed-velvet opera gown the color of crimson Tuscany wine. It burned and glistened with heavy ruby fire in the lamplight. Atop the gown was a pair of long white gloves, dress shoes, a thin circlet of gold, presumably for my hair, and a set of opera glasses. One thing more there was: half a piece of paper with Holmes' cramped, hasty handwriting. It impersonally read, "Merry Christmas, Belated."

I read the note, read it again and crushed it to my breast with tears stinging my eyes. That man, that stubborn, infuriating, thoughtful, wonderful man! Running a shaky hand across my watery eyes, I ran to fetch Mrs. Hudson to help me dress.

Mrs. Hudson was a whirlwind, getting to work immediately. She skillfully twisted my brown hair into an artful bun and fastened it with the circlet. She cleverly painted my face with cosmetics until I was a work of art. She got me into a corset, lacing it properly, but *that* took some difficulty, as you can well imagine. And finally, she draped the gown over my head, pulled my gloves on, fastened Watson's necklace at my throat and turned me toward the dresser mirror.

I hardly recognized myself. Instead of the tattered, mousy housemaid I had become accustomed to seeing in that piece of glass, there stood an elegant Victorian brunette with creamy skin, red lips and a tiny waist. Flashing back involuntarily to my dissatisfaction with my shape in the twenty-first century, I couldn't believe how *right* this looked.

Mrs. Hudson regarded me with satisfaction, considering me at a job well done. "A prettier lady Covent Garden will never see, Nona-bird," she said with motherly pride. "And no one deserves it more than you." She held out a hooded opera cloak the same shade as my gown. "Here's my Christmas present, Nona-bird. Heaven knows you'll need it with the snow."

"You knew about this?" I asked in disbelief.

"Of course, my dear! You don't think that Mr. Holmes would go out shopping for gowns, do you?"

Since she mentioned it, it did seem rather silly. I hugged her briefly so as not to muss the gown. "Thanks for *everything*, Mrs. H," I said, meaning every word.

She smiled fondly. "Enjoy your night, my dear."

Steeling myself with a deep breath, I glided out into the hall. Holmes and Watson stood waiting by the door, both looking more handsome than they had rights to look. At the sight of me, the good doctor placed a hand over his heart. "If the Lord strikes me down this night," said he, "I shall die a happy man, having glimpsed Heaven with my final breath."

I blushed at the poetry and thanked him, turning to Holmes to seek his appraisal. He was staring at me and continued to stare until Watson nudged him. "Hmm?" he finally said. "Oh yes, very nice, cab's waiting outside." He turned to the door.

Watson seemed offended at his lack of loquaciousness, but I was actually surprised. I had expected a caustic remark on how women took forever, or some such, so I was both surprised and flattered at his reaction. With Holmes you learned to take compliments as they came, which was hardly ever. Ah, well, *c'est la vie*. I took Watson's arm and went to my first opera.

The evening was a blur; I can only remember bits and pieces of it now. I remember the opera house vaguely, all wood, velvet and crystal. I can hardly recall the opera itself. *Tosca* was a tragic, Romeo-and-Juliet type of story: boy meets girl, boy loves girl, girl loves boy, boy gets executed for treason, girl throws herself off tower, very depressing stuff. The music was lovely, though. I blame my faulty memory on a long day of errands and the several glasses of champagne I drank during the show rather than on any lack of interest.

My clearest memory, ironically, was of the return home to Baker Street. I had momentarily dozed off in the cab, and when I foggily came to, I was floating up the walk to the house. It took me a moment to realize that I was being carried by a pair of strong arms. I breathed the fragrance of tobacco, sandalwood and musky aftershave. It was Holmes. A deep and soothing lassitude stole over me as I burrowed deeper into his embrace, for to an emancipated woman of the twenty-first century, being carried by a man was a very new and very pleasant experience and served to bring 'those thoughts' forcefully to mind.

In any case, Holmes bore me into my room and laid me on the bed, but Mrs. Hudson averted any hint of scandal as the morally towering Scotswoman shooed him away. The good lady saw me out of the gown and into my night-dress, which was fortunate, because I never could have managed in my inebriated state without ripping something. Finally in tartan nightgown and loosened hair, I crawled under the blankets and fell exhaustedly to sleep.

However, that was not the end of my eventful day. Much later that night, when everyone was abed, I awoke to the creak of my door as it opened. My back was to the door, preventing me from seeing the intruder, but I could see his long shadow on the wall I faced, revealing the nighttime prowler to be Holmes. What was he doing, sneaking into my room? Was he going to sift through my drawers, thinking I was too drunk to wake? How rude! I lay very still, listening for the telltale scrape of drawers, but it did not come. Rather, light footsteps moved deeper into the room to stand over my moon-shrouded form. Dammit, what was he doing? Looking at my window? My bed? Me? I dared not turn and peek at him but lay almost quivering in curiosity.

Then suddenly, slowly, gentle fingertips brushed my hair and jawline in the lightest of touches, stopping the breath in my throat. With that the footsteps hurriedly retreated, the door swung shut and I was left alone and wakeful, going over the turmoil of thoughts in my muddled head. Holmes had visited me in the night. He watched me while I slept. He touched my face in what could only be termed a caress. I lay awake, watching the moon for quite some time.

It was about then that I began to use 'Sherlock Holmes' and 'love' in the same train of thought.

CHAPTER 8

In Which I Take Up Cross-Dressing and Holmes Doesn't Take My Advice

Despite my own inclinations, the night of the opera did not send Holmes and me leaping into each other's arms. On the contrary, we continued to go about our lives teasing and aggravating each other as if nothing had happened, but there remained an edge to our play. To be perfectly honest, I think Holmes' new feelings terrified him. With his nocturnal admission of regard, it was as if he had unleashed a dangerous animal and was powerless to imprison it again.

Also, as long as we're being perfectly honest, I was scared too. I had never envisioned myself entering into a lasting relationship with any man, at least not in my college days and certainly not with a Victorian-minded man that I once assumed was fictional! Yet I knew that in nineteenth-century culture, a relationship with Holmes could only end in one of two ways: marriage or heartbreak. Both were far too final for my twenty-first century mind.

In the days and weeks that followed, Holmes and I were actually driven apart, each seeking solitude to reorganize his or her thoughts. However, since cases for Holmes were not abundant in January of 1887, we were forced into contact, each grating on the other's nerves with our heightened awareness of each other, striving desperately for normalcy. Watson sensed our dilemma, perhaps even diagnosed it, but was powerless to provide a cure. Holmes and I needed time apart to discard our shattered viewpoints and forge new ones, and we got it in spades.

❦   ❦   ❦

Towards the end of January, London was the focus of an unseasonable rise in temperature. The snow half-melted into a dirty brown slush, destroying any inclination of leaving the house. Holmes was particularly grouchy, chafing at the weather, the lack of activity and the previously mentioned emotional quandary. What was worse, Watson was slowly healing from a case of his own, nursing a two-week-old bullet hole in his shoulder.

Watson had frequently come across Mrs. Feeny, a very young mother, during his shifts at the charity hospital and deduced that her visits were too frequent for coincidence. Doing some "independent investigations"—his phrase, not mine—outside the Feeny house, he discovered that Mr. Feeny was an abusive alcoholic roughly three times his wife's age! A gentleman of action, Watson immediately intervened and took a bullet through the shoulder for his pains. Holmes, of course, was furious at Watson for not consulting him and for acting so rashly, but it didn't take a great detective to see that he had been simply overwrought with concern for his friend.

Thus was the unhappy beginning for the new year; Holmes pacing the sitting room in a huff, poor Watson suffering silently in his armchair with his arm in a sling, guiltily indulging in morphine to cut the pain, and myself at the window seat…well, bored stiff. Conversation was useless; I had read everything on the bookshelves at *least* once, and there was no mail to sort that day. After some minutes of grinding inactivity, I decided to track down Mrs. Hudson for another lesson in the womanly arts. Learning how to embroider had to be more interesting than doing nothing at all. My plan was sound but soon thwarted; Mrs. Hudson was laid up with cramps from what she called 'woman's sickness' and asked to be left alone. I granted her request with utmost sympathy, ruefully regarding Midol and tampons to be two of the things I missed the most about the modern era.

Out of ideas, I went to the kitchen and ate an apple out of sheer boredom. God, what a dreary day. My mind felt wrapped in wet blankets that fogged my thoughts to such an extreme that I hardly heard the pounding at the door. "Hmm, what? Door? Oh, door!" Forcibly pulling myself from the doldrums, I hurried for the pounding portal. Whatever idiot was out and about on a day like this was probably a client, and therefore deserved Heaven's blessings for rescuing us all from the jaws of boredom.

I pulled the door open to admit a portly, finely dressed man of later age, his expensive trousers dripping slush onto the polished floorboards. I took the card from his gloved hand. It read, "Wouter von Twiller, Vice-Chairman, Sumatra Shipping Company, Amsterdam, Netherlands." Holland? Wow, what a trip! I applied a formula to the situation, more practical than the ones used by Holmes with his smelly chemical reactions. Long trip plus wealthy client equals important case, just what Holmes needed.

I dashed upstairs and remembered to shut the door before saying, "Eureka! I've got it!"

Holmes and Watson turned to me, startled. "*It* is an indefinite pronoun in this sentence, Nona," Holmes stated sarcastically. "Be so kind as to elaborate."

"*It* is the answer to all our problems, Holmes," I returned, a bit sarcastic myself. As I said, there was now an edge to the game. "Of course, if you'd like, I'll tell the client to go and…"

The word "client" got Holmes moving. He swiftly crossed the room, took the card in his hand and for half a second, held my eyes with his. For that brief moment I could read in his eyes confusion, fear, wariness and…desire? It couldn't be, could it? That second of indecision was bliss and claustrophobia at the same time; the sheer possibility of Sherlock Holmes holding me, kissing me, *loving* me, was enough to both excite and terrify me. The moment was fleeting, over when Holmes detached his gaze from mine and regarded the card, and yet the feelings it stirred remained. Also, on some unexplainable level, I knew that the contact had also affected Holmes. Almost unconsciously I retreated to the door, a deeper instinct telling me to back off *now*, before I did something stupid.

Holmes turned to me again, hard and blank as slate, whatever emotions I had guessed at buried under an avalanche of self-control. "Bring the man up, Nona," was all he said, his glacial voice enough to make me doubt my earlier instincts. We most definitely needed some space. I turned and went downstairs, relaying the summons to von Twiller, but I did not follow him up. Instead I went to my room, shutting the door tightly and half-heartedly working by hand on a new outfit I was making for myself. The rhythmic rise and fall of the needle helped to calm my frayed nerves but also left me itching to know what kind of case Holmes had received. I stitched for half an hour, heard the front door slam, and continued work. If there was one thing I learned in Baker Street, it was that patience was a virtue. I gave my project another ten minutes before heading back up the stairs to inquire about the new case. As I cracked the door open and peeked in, I did not expect the scene upon which I came.

Holmes was crouched on the floor in his Inverness traveling cloak, inspecting the contents of a suitcase. A quick glance affirmed that it was Holmes' own. Watson had risen from his chair and spoke with the tight voice of a man in argument. "Holmes, you must know that every cell of my being cries out against this endeavor of yours. You are not a foolhardy man, but this seems to push the limits of reason!"

Holmes wearily sat back and combed a hand through his hair. "Watson, you are simply overreacting. I will go to Amsterdam, clear up this mess, collect my fee and return before Valentine's Day."

"Baron Maupertuis is the most wanted man in Europe!" protested the doctor stridently, clutching his wounded arm close. "His smuggling rings have eluded the police in three countries on the Continent! His wealth and power rival the higher echelons of nobility! And you are going to topple him, alone, before Valentine's?

"Precisely."

Baron Maupertuis? I thought. *Why does that name ring a bell?* I racked my brain for some obscure reference, finally concluding that I must have read about him somewhere.

Watson's face grew darker still. "Holmes, you will be isolated in a foreign country against a foe of mammoth proportions. Do you even speak Dutch?"

"No, but I suppose I'll muddle through somehow," came the blithe reply.

"You'll muddle yourself into an early grave if you persist in this foolishness!" Watson argued stridently.

Holmes snapped the suitcase shut with more force than necessary and rose from the floor. "Perhaps it would be less risky if I had a friend to accompany me, someone who does not embark on imbecilic ventures, only to receive nothing but pain for his carelessness!" It was all too obvious that this biting rebuke was meant for Watson, who turned away with a hurt expression as Holmes paused suddenly. "Forgive me, my dear Watson," the detective said softly. "That was unworthy of me."

"Yes, it was," agreed the doctor gruffly, his back to the detective in a silent rebuke of his own.

It was now Holmes' turn to look pained. "If your intuition proves true, Watson, and this endeavor is as dangerous as you make it, then I do not wish to have what may be our last words to be hurtful ones. So I will offer my apologies and end it here."

The detective took up his deerstalker hat from the coat rack and clamped it over his tousled hair before turning to go, but before Holmes could reach the door, Watson spoke quietly from his place by the fire: "Good luck, Holmes."

Holmes paused by the door, relief inscribed on his face at his friend's absolution. "I pray that I shall not need it, Watson, but my thanks all the same."

With a start I remembered my position by the nearly closed door. Feeling like an eavesdropper, I scurried down the stairs and took up a convenient mop lying by the wall, beginning to clean up the slush tracked in by von Twiller. When Holmes came down the stairs, dressed for the journey with suitcase in hand, I feigned astonishment at his intended purpose. Actually, my surprise needed very little forcing. Finally garbed in the peculiar costume so treasured by illustrators, Holmes seemed to at last look the part of the Great Detective, man of myth and legend, at whose name the most hardened of criminals could not help but shudder. I broke the self-inflicted spell by speaking: "Off to Holland, Holmes?"

He appeared equally surprised to see me. "Nona? I thought you were working."

I gestured with the mop. "I am working, and it would seem that you are as well."

His face grew suspicious. "How did you know I was going to Holland?"

Oops. To cover my mistake, I waved an airy hand. "I'm from the future, Holmes. I know practically everything."

Holmes cocked a skeptical eyebrow. "Is that so? Do you know the outcome of this case, then?"

I was about to open my mouth and emphasize the "practically" part when the floodgates of memory opened wide and I realized that I *did* know! I had read about the Baron before! In the opening of the story "The Regiate Squire," Watson had made a tantalizing reference to Holmes' victory against Baron Maupertuis in the spring of 1887, one of the foremost criminals in Europe. Unfortunately, the case had stretched on for months and finally left Holmes bedridden in a state of extreme nervous exhaustion. My past was Holmes' future. This moment in the foyer would be the last I would see of him for months as he abandoned himself to dangerous, unyielding, laborious work, finally collapsing under the strain.

With my previous reactions to Holmes, I thought that I would be exulting at his departure, but every instinct cried out in anguish at the thought of his leaving for months on end. "I'm sure everything will turn out fine," I managed to say.

We stood there for another minute, each one not looking at the other as we sought a safe way to say goodbye. Holmes surprised me by speaking first. "Will you write to me?" What an odd request for Holmes! My confusion must have been obvious because he clarified, "To keep me updated on the criminal news, the agony columns, things like that." Well, that at least made sense. I agreed to keep him informed on the doings of England and he gave me the address where I should send the letters. Another uneasy silence descended upon us. "Nona, I don't know what to say," Holmes admitted quietly.

Say you love me, screamed an internal voice. *Say you love me and you can't live without me and you don't want to leave me and you'll write me as often as you can, say anything, just say SOMETHING!* But all that came out was, "How about goodbye?"

Holmes nodded like a man in a daze. "Goodbye," he murmured, taking my hand and placing it to his lips, letting the pressure linger for a second longer than politeness prescribed. With that, he turned and walked out the door.

Some unexplainable force propelled me out the door after him, causing me to cry his name. "Holmes!" He turned on the street, looking up at me with (hope?) an unreadable emotion in his gray eyes. *I love you!* cried the inner voice. *I love you and I won't see you for months and I know you'll be busy so don't forget me; don't forget what we started; don't let this die because I love you, Sherlock Holmes! I love you!* "Don't work too hard."

The light in his eyes died, and he nodded again before setting off down the icy street in search of a cab. I watched him go until he disappeared around the corner. I wondered if he knew he had packed away my heart in his suitcase. I wondered if I would ever get it back again. And I wondered if I really wanted it back at all.

Valentine's Day came and went, and spring came to London town, bringing sunshine and birds and flowers, but no Holmes. True to my word, I faithfully clipped crime articles and agony columns, enclosed them in envelopes with handwritten notes of my own, usually admonishing him not to work too hard, and sent them to the Netherlands several times a week. In reply Holmes sporadically sent messages back to London, sometimes postcards and sometimes telegrams, assuring me that he was still alive and updating me on the progress of the case, not exactly the average brand of love notes.

With the advent of spring, there was no lack of activity. Mrs. Hudson enlisted my help for a spring-cleaning of mammoth proportions; with Holmes' extended absence, the valiant lady finally vanquished the clutter that had so densely occupied the sitting room.

Once Watson's wound had healed, the two of us took advantage of the lovely spring weather and spent a great deal of time outdoors, for no express purpose other than to leave the house. He even took me to a garden party at the house of some of his acquaintances, but my social debut met with disaster. I do have to say that it wasn't entirely my fault. After all, how was I supposed to know that Priscilla had a childhood fear of snakes? It was only a half-grown garden snake, and it was really her own fault that her dress was cut so low.

After I had written Holmes about the unfortunate consequences of my presence at the function, I received a terse postcard in reply. "Damn you, woman!" Holmes had written. "You will be the undoing of my reputation! I am still laughing even as I pen these words, and the Dutch must think me stark, raving mad! Never send me such stories again!" There were no more garden parties after that.

With Holmes' extended truancy, I quickly realized that I was utterly lovesick. However, allow me to reassert that love did not turn me into a simpering, sighing ball of fluff as it usually did the typical Victorian woman. Perish the thought; I did my chores with the same level of competence, I could still hold conversations and run errands with ease, and my public life was much the same as always. Yet my thoughts were bent on my heart, and my heart was with him.

Holmes' presence, or rather his absence, was continually felt in Baker Street: his vacant place at table, his empty armchair in the morning, his silent violin at night. It was as if he had swiftly died, but in some ways it was worse. The days and nights of waiting made it worse.

For all of January I had longed for time to think. Now that I had too much time on my hands, I started thinking. I turned my musings toward marriage, mapping out possibilities and worst-case scenarios with utter practicality, determined not to fall prey to "blind love." Somewhere in the beginning of March, I realized that if I were to be Holmes' wife and lover (Mrs. Nona Holmes; the thought still stopped me cold), I would require a deeper participation in his life. I needed to become a detective, or at least know my way around the profession. The question was how to acquire such knowledge. I had book learning by the bushel, gleaned from the treatises, monographs and histories of my first few months, but how would I gain practical knowledge and experience in an era that frowns on women taking up such professions?

It was this question I pondered during the Great Spring Cleaning of '87. I was in Holmes' bedroom, dusting and straightening and changing the sheets and curtains. Mrs. Hudson specifically wanted the entire house scrubbed and aired out, so if I lingered in this room longer than the others, that was surely no one's business but mine own. As I dusted and polished, I noticed an oddity; Holmes had two wardrobes while Watson had one. Why? This at least was a mystery easily solved.

Inspection of one wardrobe revealed ordinary clothes, but the contents of the second were more extraordinary. Costumes for Holmes' disguises were hung on these racks with stage makeup and accessories on a series of shelves. *So, this is how he does it!* I mentally crowed.

Unable to resist the pull of curiosity, I shamelessly pawed through the various articles. A boatman's sweater and red kerchief, a butcher's bloodstained apron, a priest's cassock, even a lady's dress! But what was this? I pulled out a jacket that was surely too small for Holmes. Perhaps it was a leftover from the Irregulars' scavenging; just like that man to not throw anything away. It was then, quite accidentally, that I discovered the answer to all my problems.

Snatching up the jacket along with an overlarge linen shirt, a pair of worn trousers, scuffed boots, a cloth cap and a pair of battered glasses, I quietly dashed downstairs and into my room with my treasures. Quivering with mirth, I pinned up my hair, undressed, changed into the borrowed clothes and placed the non-prescription spectacles on my face before turning to the mirror. The effect of the baggy clothes was most satisfactory: instead of the feminine curves of Nona E. Brown, there stood a poor, stout, nearsighted and perfectly androgynous London youth of about seventeen.

"You're perfect," I told my reflection.

"Thankee koindly, mum," my reflection replied. No, that wouldn't do, Cockney was too hard to keep up for any length of time. I switched to a milder Irish brogue that sounded somewhat convincing. "Many thanks for ya compliment, lassie."

That was much better. Feeling something like Dr. Frankenstein, I struck up a conversation with my 'monster.' "Now you just need a name," I told my creation, "something Irish."

"Casey O'Reilly," suggested the youth.

"Too generic," I replied.

"Patrick MacDougall," proposed the youth.

"Too hard to say," I rebutted.

"Bertie Flynn," submitted the youth.

"Close," I allowed. "How about Bernie Flynn?"

"Bernie Flynn," brogued the young Irishman, "'s' got a lovely ring to it, lassie."

I formally lifted a hand and the boy in the mirror did likewise. "Then I christen thee, um, Bernard Liam Flynn, but Bernie for short." With this mock-pompous pronouncement, I was struck with the schizoid goofiness of the whole situation and burst into giggles, as did Bernie. At least this problem was solved. As Bernie Flynn, I could regain my former freedom, walk unchecked in the lesser parts of London, and acquire all of the practical knowledge I needed. With that end in mind, I changed back into my housedress and stuffed Bernie under my bed, leaving him secure in the knowledge that he wouldn't be waiting too long.

        ❧   ❧   ❧

The day of Bernie's debut actually did not commence until nightfall. It was the middle of March, and it had been a fairly ordinary day. I had received a telegram from Holmes, which read:

N-

STILL ALIVE STOP NOT WORKING TOO HARD STOP FOX IS CLEVER BUT HOUNDS CLOSING IN STOP

H.

And that was it. Telegrams charge by the word and therefore are brief by nature. It was probably prudent of Holmes not to send any details, but such rationale did not soothe my irrational worry. My poor, pining heart longed for a written affirmation of affection, but knowing Holmes, it would not be soon in coming. So, he wasn't working too hard, was he? Oh, come now, I knew him better than that. What happened to the fifteen-hour days that I had read about? At the risk of sounding smothering, I dashed off a reply telegram.

H-

CORNERED FOXES ARE DANGEROUS STOP USE UTMOST CAUTION
STOP FUNERALS EXPENSIVE THESE DAYS STOP YOU ARE TERRIBLE
LIAR STOP DONT WORK TOO HARD STOP

N.

As sunset drew nearer, I complained of a headache and announced my decision to retire early. I declined both Watson's modern medicine and Mrs. Hudson's folk remedies, protesting that I only needed sleep. Eventually the pair
released me and I fled to my chamber, shutting and locking the door. Giddy
with anticipation, my headache miraculously gone, I rescued my alter-ego
from his dust-bunny prison under my bed and made a hurried transformation. I made some last minute adjustments, untucking my shirt, tearing a hole
in my jacket and fraying my pants cuffs with a nail scissors before I pronounced myself fit to be seen in public. With a deep breath I crept out my window that, unlucky me, faced the open street, and strode out onto the sidewalk,
relishing in my freedom from heavy, confining skirts.

Caught up in my liberation, I almost froze in despair and shock as I saw
Watson coming out the front door! I had completely forgotten about Watson's
volunteer work at the charity hospital! He would see me and lock me in my
room! I frantically racked my brain; should I dash into an alleyway and hope
he hadn't spotted me? No, I decided, this was as good a time to test my disguise
as any. Nevertheless, I pulled the brim of my cap down and hugged my coat
closer as I walked slowly past Watson, who was coming down the front steps.

My fears were completely unfounded. Either he was occupied with other
thoughts or my disguise was better than I thought, for Watson walked right
past me without even glancing my way. Thank God; Holmes would have surely
recognized me, and I would have never heard the end of it. That thought
reminded me of why I had set out in the first place. Squaring my shoulders in
what I hoped was a manly fashion, I headed to the stop for the horse bus and
then the heart of London.

❋   ❋   ❋

My first excursion as Bernie Flynn was unsatisfying. London's market dis-
tricts were a lot like New York City, only dirtier and smellier. Furthermore, I

had gotten a little used to the respect due to a lady, but Bernie Flynn got all the respect due to his class, that is to say, none. I returned to Baker Street late that night, footsore and disillusioned, ready to throw in the proverbial towel. However, some obscure force (the thought of Holmes) reminded me of my purpose and I continued in my endeavors.

On my second excursion a few days later, I headed out in the daytime, trying to get a different feel for the city. Portobello Road bore no improvements; it was still dirty and smelly, but now it was also *noisy*! Men and women of about every class crowded the street, hawking their wares from street stalls, advertising the latest theater, or just milling about to exchange gossip. I bought a bruised apple from a fruit vendor with only three teeth, obviously not a sampler of his own wares, and I munched it as I wandered up and down the streets, wondering what I should do next. Gone were the tidy streets and pleasant shoppers of the Strand; these coarse people pushed, yelled, sang and spit with no sense of decorum. It was thoroughly enlightening but really did not teach me anything about detecting, which was what I had set out to do. *Oh, let's face it,* I moaned internally. *I'm hopeless. I don't know the first thing about directions or local slang, not to mention basic sleuthing skills. I would need some kind of guide or mentor if I wanted to…what the?* I felt a tickle at the pocket where I kept my money. Almost without thinking, I whirled and reached out, snaring the would-be thief by the arm. Pickpockets in New York were notorious, and it had taken me three missing purses before I learned the warning signs of the pickpocket. "Now, see here, you…" I trailed off in shock as I recognized the struggling tow-headed boy in my grasp. "Tarkers?" I gasped. It was one of the Irregulars!

His struggling ceased as he peered at me intently. "'Ere naow, do Oi know you? 'Ow do you know moi name?"

Uh oh, you're Bernie Flynn now; remember, Nona? Think of something! "Um…ah…"

Tarkers looked at my hand and drew a sharp breath. "Miss Nona?" he hedged tentatively.

Damn! I was caught! Releasing the lad, I turned on heel and attempted to vanish into the crowd. *Stupid, stupid, stupid! Shows how much YOU know! How did the little Arab figure it out? Oh, I hope he knows enough to keep his mouth shut!* I ducked into an alley and slid against the wall, trying to catch my breath and recover from my shock. Okay, enough was enough. If I couldn't fool a ten-year-old boy, it was time to pack it up and head home. I might even make it back to Baker Street in time for tea…

"Cor, you were roight, Tark! It is Miss Nona!"

"Oi told you it were her, Wiggins."

My head snapped up. At the mouth of the alley was Wiggins, lanky leader of the Irregulars, with Tarkers in tow. Wiggins half-raised a hand to his dirty hat, probably wondering whether or not he should take it off in my presence. Lady or no lady, I was not a very prepossessing figure at the moment.

Finally, he gave up. "Erm, beggin' your pardon, Miss Nona," he said uncomfortably. "What you be doin' on Portobello Road dressed up loike a lad? Is Mister 'Olmes back from the Neth…the Nether…back from 'Olland yet?"

I couldn't help grinning at his earnest nature. "No, Wiggins," I returned in my usual voice. "Holmes has not returned, and I would appreciate it very much if you didn't mention this to him. I was trying to learn how to disguise myself so that I could help with cases and whatnot, but I'm afraid that I'm not very good at it."

"Naow, Miss Nona, you're awfully good at disgoises!" Wiggins protested. "I never were have guessed if not for your 'ands."

"Moi 'ands? I mean, my hands?" Damn, this was catchy. I peered at my hands, trying to use the eyes of a stranger. They were shapely and long-fingered, with elegant almond nails, lady's hands. "Oops. I see your point."

"If you would boit your nails, it would be perfect," said Wiggins, nodding his head sagely. "As a matter 'o fact, if you want to act loike one 'o the lads, we could learn you 'ow."

Well, I hadn't expected my mentor to come in the form of a fourteen-year-old boy, but beggars couldn't be choosers. I gratefully accepted and followed Wiggins to begin my 'edification,' chewing on my nails the whole way.

Over the remainder of March, I lived a double life, dividing my time between Watson in Baker Street and my life on the streets as an honorary Irregular. Wiggins, Tarkers, Simpson, Chumley, Gardner and Smith schooled me incessantly in the finer points of the hard-knock life.

"Come on, Bernie, you can't let me notice you," instructed Simpson during Pickpocketing 101.

"No, Bernie, Piccadilly is *that* way," illustrated Gardner in London Geography.

"Well, Bernie, if you want proper distance, you have to 'awk it back real good," taught Smith. I don't believe I should describe that particular class.

By the beginning of April, I had graduated from the School of Hard Knocks 'magna cum laude' and renewed my solitary jaunts with bolstered courage and enjoyment. The results were much better. Through Bernie I made several new friends, including a jovial bibliophile who broadened my vocabulary of unprintable words to include Russian. I could trace a man from one end of the city to the other, even if he took a cab (although that involved a lot of guesswork and luck). I could tell any manner of man, from a carpenter to a tailor, by the cut of his clothing. And, wonder of wonders, I even got a steady job as resident Irish fiddler at a respectable pub on the weekends.

I felt secure and self-reliant, no longer dependent upon Holmes and Watson. I had grown from a Manhattan college art major into something entirely more bizarre, but infinitely more satisfying. I felt ready to take on Holmes.

❧   ❧   ❧

I found myself counting down the days to the fourteenth of April and the conclusion of Holmes' case. When it finally arrived, I greeted it with a bittersweet enthusiasm. My insides were awash in a turmoil of eager anticipation and dread of the unknown. The telegram that arrived at lunch only confirmed what I already knew, but the feelings intensified with a dash of concern for Holmes' well being. I was stitching in my room, trying to contain my excitement, when Watson burst in quite agitated with the telegram in hand.

"We must go to Lyons," said he. "Holmes is gravely ill."

"Thank God!" I burst out. Watson was understandably dumbfounded and I hastened to explain. "No, Watson, I don't mean that! I've just been waiting for you to say that all day! The case is over now and Holmes can come back, so let's get going!" I hauled my suitcase, packed and ready, out from under the bed.

Here we go with the dumbfounded again. "You knew?" spluttered Watson. "But how did…" I cocked an eyebrow skeptically and he trailed off. "Of course, the future; I had forgotten. Call us a cab while I pack, would you?"

I did so, and within the hour we were on a train heading towards the Channel and France. During the long and tedious trip, conversation was barely existent between us. In its place, books were our companions: a medical journal for Watson, a beginner's French dictionary for me. Watson was obviously perturbed. He seemed to play the Doubting Thomas, refusing to accept my reassurances concerning Holmes' health until he could see it for himself.

I was nervous as well, not over Holmes' physical state, but over his emotional one instead. Had he reconciled himself to his affection for me? Was he willing to accept affection from me? Or would he brusquely shove me away as he had previously done? I knew then that I loved him, but did he love me? These questions tormented me as the train rattled down the tracks towards Lyons, Holmes, and the answer to all of our questions.

The Hotel Dulong was a first-class establishment, with marble, heartwood and silver filigree everywhere. I was almost afraid to walk in for fear of scuffing the immaculate floor. Watson, however, had no such compunctions; his military background was obvious as he marched up to the front desk and asked for Mr. Holmes' room.

"Ah, *oui!*" cooed the oily concierge with an accent like treacle. "*Monsieur* Holmes! He iz ze hero *internationale*, non? He is in ze room...how you say...three and twelve. Zooch a peety, zat...Wait! *Monsieur et Mademoiselle!*" His cries went unheeded as Watson and I headed for the wrought-iron elevator. A trip up three floors and a walk down to the end of the corridor brought us to Holmes' door, under guard by a uniformed member of the *Surete*, the French police force. He was probably there to keep any villains or paparazzi away, but I was tempted to believe that he also served to keep Holmes *in* his room. We assured him of our affidavits and he allowed us inside.

The interior was an almost-palatial suite, elegantly and expensively furnished; only the best for international heroes, I supposed. However, I did not give much thought to the trappings, for lying asleep on the bed with a French doctor at his side was the object of our journey.

The usual phrase for a man in his state is 'pale and wasted,' but this was certainly not the case. Pale he was, ill and weak perhaps, but not wasted. 'Wasted' implies an illness brought on without a greater purpose. Holmes had suffered long days of few meals and less sleep, days of backbreaking, mind-racking, footsore work that had driven him to this state of collapse. But because of Holmes' trials, one of the most dangerous criminals in Europe was now behind bars, and three countries were safe from his influence. Holmes was not wasted; he was beautiful.

Watson and the French *medico* were engaged in a lengthy, highly technical discussion in the sitting room of the suite, leaving me with the slumbering detective. I sat gently on the bed and examined him more closely. He was much thinner, his cheekbones more pronounced and the bones in his wrist more prominent. The black of his uncombed hair made his face all the whiter by comparison, but his breathing was strong and steady, and his face was at peace. There was nothing that a week or two of rest and good meals would not cure.

Although his form did not move, my alert ears noticed a subtle change in his breathing. He was awake, the little sneak, and didn't want me to know. In response, I crossed my arms and sighed in exasperation.

"You worked too hard, didn't you?" One gray eye flew open to regard me in irritation. "I told you; I told you not to work too hard, but would you listen? Nope, don't listen to Nona, mm-mm. And now look at you."

The eye closed and his lips crept into a smile. "Very well, Nona," he said quietly. "Next time I shall pace myself and allow the villain to escape."

Such relief! If Holmes could be sarcastic, it wasn't too serious. I told myself that the little thrill in the pit of my stomach was due to that knowledge and not due to the sound of his voice. "Well, good, as long as we're in agreement." This got a dry chuckle from my patient.

He opened his eyes to regard me fully. "Did you miss me?" he asked softly.

What to say to that? The truth, I supposed. "Yes," I admitted, all teasing gone. Let him make what he wanted of that; I decided that I had nothing to hide.

Holmes reached out and took my hand in his thin one, sending my heart to my throat as he raised it to his face. His touch was pure electricity. Was this the penultimate moment I had been hoping for since January? Holmes paused, peering at my hand. "You've been biting your nails," he said. "Were you worried about me?"

My bubble of hope unceremoniously burst. Dammit, dammit, *dammit*! Why did the man have to be so dense? I rolled my eyes in exasperation. "Come off it, Holmes. Three months straight is quite long enough to play detective." He just grinned impishly at me.

Watson finally broke away from the doctor. "Dr. Beaupre has assured me that…oh, you're awake." He took a seat at Holmes' bedside.

Holmes nodded cordially, the formality marred by a delighted grin. "Watson, old boy, you're looking well."

"I wish I could say the same for you, Holmes."

"Nonsense, I'm right as rain. We can catch the next train to London," argued Holmes, trying to push himself up from the bed.

I pressed him back, marveling at how easy it was now. "Oh, no you don't! You don't start pulling that on us for at least a few days! Then we'll talk about going back to London." Surprisingly, Holmes gave in with only a minimum of protest.

We spent the rest of the evening listening raptly as Holmes told us of his struggles against Baron Maupertuis, the evil Flaubert and the Giant Rat of

Sumatra. I can only agree with Watson; the world is not yet ready for that tale. Only one more point of our reunion deserves mentioning: since he took it earlier, and throughout the entire course of the evening, Holmes had not released my hand.

CHAPTER 9

In Which I Shake the Holmes Family Tree and Discover a Rotten Apple

Walking into the familiar sitting room late at night, I found that the lamps were cold, but the fire was lit. I could see Holmes staring pensively into the flickering hearth. He was probably in a reflective mood and wanted to be left alone, so I turned to go back downstairs. "Wait," called Holmes softly from his armchair. "I need to talk to you."

What could he want? It was too late at night for sarcastic repartee, and Holmes had no case at present. What was there to talk about? Moving closer to the armchair, I could read mental distress in every line of his long body. I laid a tentative hand on his shoulder, unsure of his reaction. His shoulder was tense and he subtly flinched at my touch. "Holmes," I said quietly, lest my voice betray my roiling emotions. "What can be troubling you so?"

He drew a deep breath before replying. "I have been thinking a great deal about…a great many things. About my life, and the future, and you." He turned and tried to smile at me. "Mostly you."

I was overwhelmed. Such an admission from Holmes! Fish would sooner walk on land! However, I could only stand in shocked silence as he haltingly continued. "My time in Holland was long and arduous, but not entirely constant. When I had a moment to myself, I would read the notes you sent me. I would comb them with my eyes, searching for some hidden meaning, some obscure hint, only to return them to my pocket in despair. And yet, I would fold and unfold them, keeping them close, often smoothing them out for another reading."

He shakily rose to his feet, his eyes dark gray pools in the firelight. "I have known loneliness for years, Nona, and I do not wish to know it again. Your letters have tethered me to the real world when I wished to bury my heart in my work. Your wit and laughter remained with me no matter where I went." His long fingers traced a path down my jawline. "You kept me sane," he whispered.

Unable to help myself, I seized his trembling hand and pressed it to my cheek. "You will never be alone again," I whispered fiercely, holding his eyes with my own. "Not while I'm here."

"Nona." He breathed my name with unmistakable hope, stepping closer to me. His eyes were jagged shards adrift in a sea of pain. "I'm so confused. I-I never imagined that…"

I silenced him with my fingers on his lips as my hand snaked around his neck. "I love you, Sherlock," I said, finally freeing the words I had yearned to speak for so long.

His breath seemed to catch in his throat, and his free arm pulled my waist closer. "I," he struggled, his face inching closer to mine. "I—God help me, Nona, I love…" I could smell his tobacco and sandalwood soap. Our eyes closed, our noses brushed, and then…

Knock, knock, knock! "Nona-bird, are you going to lie abed all morning? Get up, girl, there's work to be done!"

My eyes flew open in the harsh, dust-speckled sunlight, taking in the sparse furniture of my humble room at Baker Street. I lay in shock for a moment, then rolled over and screamed something especially foul into my pillow, with a few desultory kicks for good measure. Why, why, *why* did I have to wake up just then? And everything was going so well! With an ill-mannered groan, I heaved myself out of bed on July the 27th, 1887, to begin the day's chores.

Holmes had quickly recovered from his ordeal in Holland, solved another case along the way and returned to Baker Street soon afterward. That brief hiatus was the last rest he had for a while. All of May and June brought no lack of cases to our door. Holmes was oblivious to the cause of his good fortune, placing the reason on fame from the Netherlands-Sumatra case, but had he read anything but the agony columns, he would have discovered the true cause.

Unbeknownst to Holmes, Watson had been slipping past case details to enthusiastic reporters, giving the detective credit for his cases rather than letting Scotland Yard steal the glory. Eager for a hero, the papers easily seized on the stories and mentioned Holmes' name at every opportunity, so the months following were busy ones for all of us.

Those months were also times of great changes for Holmes and me. Despite my frequent dreams, Holmes had yet to nerve himself for the lover's leap of faith. It grated on my patience but I strove for understanding, not wishing to push too hard, and my efforts were not entirely fruitless. Holmes must have overcome his emotional obstacle in Holland, for he no longer tried to drive me away. On the contrary, he began to try and include me in his world. At his suggestion I learned the basics of chemistry and I actually did fairly well, although I did have to replace the wallpaper after I accidentally mixed silver nitrate with Holmes' carbonucleic solution. After that instance, Watson was usually elsewhere during chemistry lessons.

Holmes also began to accept my invitation to get outside more often, and we would stroll up and down the Strand like the proper Victorian couple, Holmes reading the life history of our fellow pedestrians to my unending amusement. When clients arrived with their peculiar problems, I became less of a housemaid and more of a contributing associate. The teasing and physical contact continued, but at some point, it had transitioned from blatant rivalry to blatant flirting. Our relationship blossomed in the spring sunshine, but in the dead heat of summer, there came a case that would shake our fledgling love to its very core.

It was too hot for chores. It was too hot for anything. After a half-hearted dusting, Mrs. Hudson reluctantly bowed to the thermometer and released me from further duties as she went to the market, so the late morning sun found me draped over the divan in the sitting room with my eyes closed, trying to will the limp breeze to pick up a bit through the open windows. *Stupid era,* I thought sourly. *No air-conditioning, no swimming pools, no nothing.* Looking at Watson just made me resentful; after war service in India and Afghanistan, heat didn't bother him in the slightest. I was seething with envy as he sat unconcernedly reading the paper. Holmes was little better, doing a wonderful job of ignoring the sweltering heat, but every now and again he would fidget irritably and glance out the window. Whether this was due to the weather or the lack of cases I wasn't sure, but if he even got close to the desk drawer where the morocco case was kept, I was going to say something controversial and start a heated discussion to distract him. It was too hot to argue, but anything was better than *that*.

Through the open windows came the distant clatter of a horse-cab as it rattled down our street. *Don't stop*, I willed it silently. *Don't stop here; it's too hot for casework. Besides, I'M the one who has to get up and get the door...* The cab rattled to a stop right below our window. *Dammit.*

"Aha, we have a visitor, it seems. Get the door for our client, won't you, Nona?" Holmes sounded almost smug. If it had been any more than "almost," I would have punched him.

"He's your client, Holmes," I retorted from my prone position. "You get the door." Okay, maybe it wasn't too hot to argue, but it was *definitely* too hot to move.

An urgent-sounding knock sounded downstairs. I glared at Holmes, who cocked an eyebrow back at me. With my second ill-natured groan of the day, I pushed myself up. "And I thought men were chivalrous," I announced snootily, both of them just snickering in reply.

I grumbled my way down the stairs as the pounding began again. "This had better be important," I muttered as I opened the door. It was. The man on our doorstep towered over me as tall as Holmes, but he was so overweight as to seem even more imposing. With slightly greasy black hair, watery gray eyes and a doughy face, he was an almost repulsive figure, but there remained a sharpness and intensity I had seen in only one other person.

I was floored. "Mycroft! You're a full year ahead of schedule! What are you doing here? My God, has Parliament collapsed?"

There are no words to describe the elder Holmes' utter shock as he stared down at the short, mousy housemaid who knew of his governmental importance, a secret kept from ninety-nine percent of the population! "How on earth...?" he spluttered in a baritone voice worlds apart from the tenor of his sibling.

Oops. Me and my big mouth. "Um..." I hastily amended, speaking a whole sentence in the space of a word: "I'mgonnagogetHolmes." With that, I practically flew up the stairs and burst into the sitting room, temperature forgotten. "Holmes, Mycroft is here!" I exclaimed, hearing heavy footfalls on the stairs behind me.

Holmes and Watson had risen to their feet in surprise when I felt a vise painfully grip my wrist. Twisting around, I found it held in Mycroft's enormous hand, which was squeezing it with a force that you could hardly credit to the man.

"Who sent you?" he roared at me, crushing my wrist. "Talk, spy!"

My wrist bones screamed in protest. Tears sprang to my eyes and it became increasingly harder to think straight. "Holmes!" I wailed. It sounded pathetic, I know, but I felt that I was justified.

"Mycroft, unhand her! What is the meaning of this?" Holmes demanded angrily, stepping forward.

The elder Holmes released me, and I swiftly crossed the room to the safety of the dining table and Watson, glaring daggers at Mycroft. Watson, slightly overwhelmed with the situation, quickly regained himself and examined my wrist for permanent damage.

"That woman is a spy!" exclaimed Mycroft. "She knows of my position, my line of work! She has likely been sent here to collect information!"

"I am no such thing!" I retorted, racking my brain for a suitable excuse. "Holmes, Sherlock I mean, just told me that his older brother was a very important person in the government! I just guessed!"

"And you expect me to believe that?"

I was getting angry. "I expect you to go to hell, butterball!" I spat, turning Mycroft so red I thought he would drop of a heart attack. Lord, it was hot.

"Both of you, shut up!" cried Holmes in exasperation. "And please explain what's going on!"

"How do I do that if I have to shut up?" I sassed at him, arming sweat from my forehead.

"My thoughts exactly," grumbled Mycroft, displeased at his brother's impertinence.

The three of us began to talk at once, our voices escalating in volume as each tried to speak over the other. The temperature in the room seemed to rise with our voices until it was almost unbearable. Finally, when I thought that things would surely come to blows, the crack of a gunshot silenced us, and we all stared at the forgotten occupant of the room.

Watson replaced his revolver in the drawer, closed it and spoke quietly, his voice carrying across the noiseless room. "Now, I think that everyone should sit down." We three looked about the room shamefacedly and did so, Watson at the table, Holmes and Mycroft in the armchairs, and myself on the divan. No one mentioned the new pockmark in the wall as Watson continued, "I know that this heat wave has us all a bit edgy, but we must strive to rise above our discomforts and behave like human beings. Now, let's begin with introductions like civilized people."

Mycroft cleared his throat. "Of course, Doctor, and I already know your identity. I am Mycroft Holmes, Sherlock's elder brother." Watson's eyebrows climbed at this, but Mycroft continued. "What I would like to know is who is she?"

Holmes interrupted, which was fortunate, because I otherwise would have been rude. "That is Miss Nona Brown, my…fellow associate." Hmph, how diplomatic. At least he didn't say 'housekeeper.' "And she speaks the truth, Mycroft. You know how careful I am about such things."

Mycroft stared me down in apparent disbelief, but I just stared back. Finally, he simply shrugged. "I suppose that is believable. After all, it is in a woman's nature to make uneducated guesses."

Rudeness must be a family trait, I thought, biting my tongue.

The portly man reverted his attention to his brother. "Sherlock, I must urgently speak with you, privately."

I wasn't about to budge, but Watson hastily rose from his seat. Holmes waved him down again. "You may trust them both implicitly, Mycroft. I have handled many of the most delicate cases with their assistance."

"Very well," acquiesced Mycroft, "as long as I may have the doctor's word that he will be silent upon this instance. This cannot become fodder for the lurid stories of Fleet Street."

"I beg your pardon?" asked Holmes, turning to stare at Watson.

Watson fidgeted uncomfortably in his seat. "I—I'm sure I don't know what you're talking about." Poor Watson, he never could prevaricate.

"Come now, Doctor," Mycroft continued. "The information you have been giving to the newspapers does make for entertaining newsprint, I admit, but this case cannot be mentioned."

Holmes opened his mouth to speak but closed it again, understanding spreading across his sharp face as he glared at his friend.

Watson, clearly uncomfortable under the scrutiny, replied, "Well, certainly, I agree, but aren't we straying a bit off topic?"

"Indeed!" I added. "The subject at hand, if you please? I wish to end this before the heat drives us all mad."

Holmes turned around again, but not without a final glance at Watson to assure him that the discussion was far from closed.

"It is an exceedingly simple matter, Sherlock," said Mycroft. You must come home with me to North Riding."

Holmes' face grew pale with shock, but quickly hardened in a sneer. "And what made you think that I could ever be persuaded to set foot there again?"

"Sherrinford has been arrested for murder."

"*What!?*" Holmes cried, leaping from his seat with fists clenched. It was the largest display of emotion I had yet seen from the man.

Mycroft remained in his seat, speaking coolly. "Father has been able to push for house arrest, but he mentioned that the evidence is against Sherrinford. If we do not solve this case before trial date, the family name will be permanently besmirched no matter the outcome. And if we do not solve it at all..." He let the phrase trail off meaningfully.

Holmes was pacing back and forth before the mantle, his face tight and troubled. He seemed to be struggling with a difficult choice, with none of the options appealing. Sherrinford I had vaguely heard of before; he was a rumor in my era, the unmentioned eldest of the Holmes brothers and follower in the father's footsteps, but what could be stopping Holmes from returning to help him?

"Sherlock," said Mycroft quietly. "You must try and put the past behind you. Sherrinford needs you. I will help you if you are afraid, but..."

At the word 'afraid,' Holmes went stiff and glared at his brother. "I am *not* afraid," he grated, "and the only help I will need is assistance in packing." With that, he turned on heel and disappeared into his room, Mycroft following behind.

Once they were gone, I pushed Watson to his feet. "Hurry, Watson, get packed, or they'll leave without us!"

"Wait" he protested, totally lost. "What makes you think we are going? This is a family matter."

"So? That's all the more reason! Four minds work better than two, and besides, if this Sherrinford is up the creek as far as I think, he'll need all of the help he can get! Now hurry up!"

"But..." he began again.

I stared gravely at Watson. "If you were being accused of murder, wouldn't you want all of the help you could get?"

He finally agreed and went to his room. I flew down the hall and into my own room, hauling out my large suitcase from under the bed. The first thing I packed was Bernie Flynn and his secondhand fiddle, just in case there was dirty work involved. Next went two of my nicer dresses for dinner, and I hoped that I would have access to an ironing board at the Holmes estate or I would be a wreck. My toiletries, my underthings, my saved money, all were crammed into the suitcase. Finally, in went my prototypes after I changed into one for traveling.

All summer long I had been working on practical outfits, something to allow mobility during a case without the need to disguise my identity or my femininity. The prototypes were a unique blend of masculine and feminine apparel; they consisted of a man's undershirt, waistcoat and trousers, all taken in and altered to fit. To avert scandal, I added a pleated knee-length skirt over the trousers with a sash and bow at the small of my back. Combined with a man's straw hat, feminized with a silk rose in the hatband, of course, a lady's summer coat and my button-up boots, the effect was rather snazzy and I was very proud of it. Now, if only it would pass the board of censors.

Kneeling on the suitcase and finally buckling it shut, I dragged the stubborn luggage out into the hall just in time to see Holmes come downstairs dressed for travel with a similar valise in hand, followed by his brother. "About time!" I cried, feigning impatience.

The Holmes brothers gawked at me openly, speechless. I judged the outfit a success. "What are you doing, Nona?" asked Holmes, his voice an octave higher in surprise.

"And here I thought you were a genius," I sighed.

"Surely you can't be considering going with us," Mycroft rumbled with warning in his voice.

"Of course not," I agreed. The pair glanced skeptically at my lack of argument as Watson banged out the door and down the stairs with his own suitcase. "*We* are going with you," I finished.

"Absolutely not!" roared Mycroft. "This is a personal affair!"

"Which is why we are going to help you," I countered.

"This is none of your business," warned Holmes, his gaze including both Watson and me.

"This is a partnership, Holmes," said Watson firmly. "Your business is our business."

"This is outrageous!" Mycroft grunted angrily.

"I don't see what we will gain by standing here arguing," I said. "Watson and I are going, even if we have to purchase our own train tickets and stay at a hotel at our own expense." I could make good on that threat too; between Bernie's fiddling on the weekends and Mrs. Hudson's allowance, I had hoarded a goodly sum. "Now, are we leaving, or are we going to stand here until we miss our train?"

Holmes regarded the both of us with astonishment, and a brief flash of understanding passed over his face before he turned to go. "Let's be off, then," he said hoarsely, unwillingly touched by our friendship.

❦   ❦   ❦

During the long train ride Mycroft somewhat grudgingly repeated the particulars of the case for Watson and me. Sherrinford, their eldest brother, was the epitome of the country gentleman and a true philanthropist at heart. Hardly a person in the tiny village of Kingston-on-the-Hill did not have a tale of some kindness done by Sherrinford Holmes. He was known affectionately as "The Squire," although the title still technically belonged to their father, Sir Siger Holmes. Now, however, Sherrinford and his family were imprisoned in the family manor with constables constantly prowling the grounds.

Two days earlier one Sylvia Pittston, a very young widow, was found dead of a gunshot wound near a secluded area of the town creek. Mrs Pittston had been one of the many receiving aid from the Holmes estate. In the pocket of her dress was a note from Sherrinford, asking her to be at that specific place the previous night. On that evidence and the fact that the gun recovered at the scene matched one in Sherrinford's collection, he was charged with willful murder. I had a great many questions, but that was the extent of Mycroft's knowledge.

Throughout the train ride north, Holmes was totally silent. His arms crossed tightly, he stared blankly out the window as the countryside rolled by. It was not unlike him to brood wordlessly during a case, but this time something in his manner betrayed a deep sense of anguish. Holmes *was* afraid of something, afraid and deeply hurt as well, but I could not guess at the cause. Did he not get along with his brother? Did he have some kind of quarrel with his parents? Was there some awful memory at North Riding that he did not wish to confront, some secret shame? There was no way for me to know, and I berated myself for thinking like a Gothic romance, but his subtle pain tore at me. I ached to comfort him, but Holmes abhorred weakness, especially in himself, and he would not accept even if I offered.

There was not an abundance of talk for the remainder of the trip.

❦   ❦   ❦

The sun was a melting ball of gold on the horizon, dipping steadily towards the blossoming earth, when we disembarked at the small "stop only on request" station at Kingston-on-the-Hill. What a difference! The beautiful North Riding countryside overflowed with rolling green hills, dotted with flowers and towering trees. A fragrant breeze blew gently across my face, removing any memory of the oppressive city heat. Watson was similarly affected, breathing deeply and enjoying the lack of soot and dust. Holmes typically ignored the pastoral perfection, standing with arms folded moodily.

A shout from the end of the platform arrested our attention as the train continued on its steam-driven course. "Halloa! Master Mycroft! Master Sherlock!" At the end of the wooden platform was a white-haired elderly man, waving enthusiastically atop an open carriage with a pair of patient horses. "Welcome home, my lads!"

Mycroft returned the wave and seized his bags, leading us to our rendezvous. The man leapt from his perch and clasped Mycroft's hand with affection. "So many years, my lads! It would be truly wonderful if not for the tragic circumstances. Nonetheless, Adelaide and Theresa will be overjoyed. Master Sherlock, I heard about your wonders on the Continent, simply tremendous. And of course, Theresa never misses a copy of the *Times*. But who are your companions?"

The likeable man ceased his excited monologue, peering at Watson and me intently, with a longer glance at my strange attire. Holmes gestured to us briefly. "These are my associates, Dr. Watson and Miss Brown."

He shook the doctor's hand and bowed slightly over mine. "A pleasure. Trevor St. Clair, the family accountant, at your service. We were not expecting additional guests, but we have plenty of room, and I'm sure that the Squire will welcome all the help he can get. But what are we doing, standing about and jawing while daylight slips by? Come along now; we must get to the Manor!" Mr. St. Clair took my bag and tied it on a platform on the back of the carriage, as did the men with their own luggage. We guests got into the open coach and the spry St. Clair clambered into the driver's seat, flicking the horses' reins and sending us down the dusty dirt road.

The breeze was delightful and the coach was quite comfortable; I was thoroughly enjoying myself. My high spirits were not very infectious, however. Holmes seemed to grow more dismal with every revolution of the carriage wheels, and Mycroft stared intently at the passing countryside. Well, who could blame them, considering what had brought them here? That thought quickly sobered me and my good spirits dried up.

"Lots of changes in North Riding since you were here last, young masters," said St. Clair from his perch. He gestured to an expanse of land to the west. "The Richardson estate has dried up after that affair with the Milverton scoundrel, whole family turned out. If not for Master Sherrinford, they'd be living on the streets of London by now. As 'tis, they're working on a little farm now; it's not the life of luxury, but at least they aren't starving."

After a few more moments of silence St. Clair gestured again, this time to a sprawling house in the distance. "At least the Edwards' are still around. Sir Roger's getting along badly with your father these days, but young Darby used to stop by at least once a week, of couse, before the arrest."

Wait a minute. Edwards? A shudder tap-danced down my spine as I recalled the bipolar man from last Christmas. Darby Edwards? Could it be the same man? I thought that he didn't know Holmes…I pondered this tidbit in silence as we clattered down a long, shady lane, canopied by lofty oak trees. The dying sunlight filtered through the spreading branches, dappling the ground in ever-changing patterns. The beauty took my breath away.

Soon the carriage emerged from the oak alley onto a large expanse of common ground. At the end of the lawn stood an enormous manor house, sweeping and elegant, probably centuries old. Ivy crept up the stone front of the mansion, branching out to cover the newer wings of the house as well. Extending from the manor house out in back, I could catch glimpses of wide fields, servants' quarters and stables.

Wow, this was where Holmes had grown up? What on earth could have made him reluctant to return? Wild horses couldn't drag me away from this! As I was about to voice my opinion to Holmes, I was halted at the sight of his face. He stared at the lovely manor with a pale, drawn face, eyes and mouth tight with tension, the face of a man being twisted by a deep, internal pain. He caught my concerned gaze and gave a sickly smile, increasing my worry tenfold.

"Home, sweet home," he croaked uneasily.

The coach pulled up to the steps and a suited man I assumed to be the butler came down to take our bags. "Welcome to Oakstaff Manor, gentlemen, oh, and lady. Welcome indeed. The Squire is waiting to receive you in the library."

Between himself and St. Clair, the pair of them began to untie the baggage to be taken to our rooms. But wait! What if a maid unpacked my bag and saw my alter-ego? That would be disastrous! I whispered a request to St. Clair, asking that my bags be left unopened and giving as my excuse the fact that I treasure my privacy, before following the others up the broad stone steps.

The foyer of Oakstaff Manor was most impressive in carved wood paneling and tapestries, an enormous staircase leading up to the second floor and several doors on either side. Watson and I would have goggled in awe, but Holmes and Mycroft set a brisk pace, moving swiftly through a door on the far right-hand side. I could only assume that this new room, with high ceilings, Turkish carpets, stuffed couches and books to the vaulted dome, was the library. Likewise, I assumed that the pushing-forty man that rose to greet us, one of three figures assembled on the couches, was "Squire" Sherrinford Holmes.

The squire was tall, of course, a trait that seemed to run in the Holmes bloodline, with brown eyes, dark brown hair and a closely trimmed beard and mustache. The eldest Holmes was a happy medium of the extremes found in his brothers; he was as broad as Mycroft, but the broadness spoke of vigorous activity rather than too many rich meals. He did not seem to retain the sharpness of genius that was an integral part of Mycroft and Sherlock, instead portraying an honest, but rather commonplace, intelligence. Sherrinford crossed the room and embraced his brothers who, wonder of wonders, returned the affection.   •

"By Jove," he rumbled deeply. "Has it been so long? Mycroft, you look a bit extended around the waistline; didn't I warn you about that all those years ago? And Sherlock, the last I saw of you was at the wedding, what, seven years past? How the time flies!"

Introductions were duly made, and it seemed that Sherrinford was also an avid reader of the London papers, so he was very glad to make Watson's acquaintance after so many mentions in the *Times*. The squire's gaze lingered a bit over my outfit with a dubious glance cast at Sherlock, as if unsure of his brother's involvement with such an unorthodox creature, but he was polite enough to me. The other two occupants of the room then joined our circle; a thirty-something woman, graceful and demure with brown hair and black eyes, was Mrs. Holly Holmes, Sherrinford's wife. However, the other man, Sir Siger Holmes, took me by surprise.

For some reason I had expected an older, grayer version of Holmes, but apparently Mother Nature had hiccupped in this hereditary legacy, for Holmes resembled his father not in the least. Sir Siger was a shorter man, his brown hair losing the battle with gray, with sour creases about the dark brown eyes and terse, silent mouth. His eyes were pools of glass, utterly reflective, never betraying a hint of emotion. The perpetual frown deepened as he shook Watson's hand, and he openly scowled at my waistcoat and skirted trousers. This was a hard man.

Okay, I thought. *So the guy's a Scrooge. Big deal. Now I can kind of see where Holmes gets his wonderful attitude.* I moved away from the circle and went to study the bookshelves, so when I turned back, I saw what no one else did. Sir Siger caught the gaze of his youngest son and burned into Sherlock a look of hatred and loathing so strong that I flinched internally. Holmes looked away quickly, seemingly unconcerned, but I could see his hand clench and his mouth tighten. I began to get an inkling of what was troubling Holmes.

🍁   🍁   🍁

After a brief round of polite conversation, we were excused to our rooms to freshen up for dinner. Holly led me up to my room, apologizing for their lack of readiness.

"I had no idea that we would be entertaining a young lady," she said, "not with Mycroft and Sherlock being so…well, adverse to the feminine population. I do hope you'll be comfortable." I found that to make perfect sense and assured her that whatever she had would be fine. My chamber was actually beyond my expectations, done up in dark blue and white décor. There was a large canopy bed, a wardrobe, a washstand, a large dresser, thick carpeting and a bookshelf. There was even an ensuite bathroom. Compared to my room in Baker Street, this was a palace!

I thanked Holly profusely and she departed, saying that she would "send Theresa up" in case I needed assistance in preparing for dinner.

The first thing I did was unpack my thankfully untouched suitcase. Poor Bernie and his violin case vanished behind the bookshelf as the other two prototypes and my wrinkled dresses went into the wardrobe; the least damaged frock I laid out for dinner. Everything else I hastily stuffed into a handy dresser. That task done, I left my hair pinned up and went to take a quick bath.

I didn't soak in the tub, but instead merely scrubbed off the dust of the trip, not knowing how long it would be before dinner was announced. Not more than fifteen minutes later, I drained the tub and climbed out without mishap. Toweling dry, I shrugged on an emerald silk bathrobe that seemed made for me. Ah, luxury! As I tied the robe around me, I was about to fix my hair at the dresser when the door banged open. A small boy of about six leaped into my room in a panic and shut the door, spinning and regarding me with astonishment. He obviously had thought that the room was empty.

Well, at least I was decent this time. Before I could inquire as to what on earth he was doing, a shrill voice sounded from down the corridor. "Master Virgil! Master Virrrrr-giiiiiiiiiillll! How dare you hide from me! Once I lay hands on you, I'll see you spanked within an inch of your young life!"

That explained a lot. Placing a finger to my lips, I pointed under my bed. With speed borne of desperation, the lad wriggled into the enclosed space. Not more than a second later, the door banged open a second time, revealing a towering stick of an old woman about as old as the Flood with iron-gray hair in a severe bun that only emphasized the web of wrinkles on her face.

"I'm sorry, miss," she clipped, her facial expression and tone of voice suggesting the very opposite. "I am looking for my young charge who had once more eluded me, a boy of six years. Have you seen him?"

Yeesh, this was a governess? She looked more like a Gorgon. I drew myself up regally, the image of an affronted lady. "I assure you, Mrs...." I trailed off.

"Miss," the harpy stressed. "Miss Gertrude Hill, if you please."

"Well, Miss Gertrude Hill, I think that I would know if a little boy ran into my room, don't you agree?" Please note that I did not lie; that was essentially true.

She seemed to accept it. "Very well," she said, inclining her head without changing her expression. "Sorry to have disturbed you." With that, she swept down the hall, leaving me to shut the door. *Nice people they got here,* I mused sourly. *Maybe Holmes had the right idea after all.*

Cautiously the young criminal crept out from under my bed. "Thank you, miss," the lad said with a cultured voice, brushing dust from his trousers. "Sorry to barge in, miss. This room is always empty." He was a bright, charming boy with a tangle of black hair, dark gray eyes and a smattering of summer freckles. Protruding from his trouser pocket, I could see the handle of a small magnifying glass. Remind you of anyone?

"Well," I laughed. "It's not every day that I get to aid and abet a felon, so I suppose you're excused."

The boy extended his hand, probably as he'd been carefully coached to do. "My name is Virgil Cyril Mycroft Sherlock Holmes, Esquire. Who are you?" he asked solemnly.

I took the tiny hand just as gravely, noting the length and dexterity of the fingers. Heredity was a funny thing, wasn't it? "Pleasure to meet you...um, Master Virgil. I am Miss Nona Ermingarde Brown."

"I'm a detective!" announced the lad, removing the magnifying glass for my approval. With formalities out of the way, he was an excited six-year-old again. "I'm the second greatest detective in the whole wide world!"

"Second greatest?" I asked. "Who's the first?" *I bet I know the answer to that.*

"My uncle Sherlock!" *Ah, so this is Sherrinford's boy.* "He's even better than Monsieur Dupin! My uncle Sherlock saved the whole wide world from Baron Mapertis, you know. Father read about it in the paper. And when Uncle Darby read it, he said that Uncle Sherlock is a glory-hogging git, and Grandpapa said he is too, but Father said that Uncle Sherlock is a noble man." He paused uncertainly. "What does 'noble' mean, Miss Brown?"

"'Noble' means someone who is good and who always does the right thing," I replied. Here was Edwards again, who obviously disliked Holmes. And what of Sir Siger, denouncing his grandson's hero in the lad's presence? That's a real nice guy.

Virgil nodded, satisfied. "I thought so. Anyway, did you know that there's a mystery at the Manor? My father can't go outside and play with me until it's solved, so..." here he brandished the magnifying glass like a sword, "I'm going to solve the mystery so Father can play outside again! I just wish that Uncle Sherlock could come and help. I know he could solve it."

Oh, Lord, such a face he made! I'm such a softie for kids; I just had to say something. "Actually, Virgil, that's why I'm here. I'm a friend of your uncle and I came here with him and Dr. Watson and your uncle Mycroft to solve the mystery."

"Hooray! Hooray!" cried the boy, leaping about in glee. "Uncle Sherlock is going to solve the mystery!"

A knock came on the door and I went to open it. This new intruder at least had the decency to knock. The open door revealed a young woman slightly older and taller than myself, with a wealth of reddish-brown hair and eyes a few shades lighter than the Holmes' gray. "Miss Brown?" the woman asked politely. "I'm Theresa St. Clair. Mrs. Holmes sent me to inquire if you needed anything."

Virgil ran forward and clasped Theresa around the legs. "Oh, Miss Theresa, did you hear? My uncle is here!"

Her polite demeanor melted away into genuine warmth as she pried herself loose. "Oof! Yes, young sir, I had heard! Have you been bothering Miss Brown, you little scamp?"

"Oh no!" I protested. "Actually, Master Virgil and I were having a very entertaining discussion."

"Very well," said Theresa in mock severity. "I'll let you go this time, but next time..." She began to tickle him and he squirmed loose, fleeing with childish glee down the hall.

We watched him go. "Charming little devil, isn't he?" I smiled.

"He'll be beating ladies off with sticks by the time he's twelve," she agreed. I welcomed Theresa inside and apologized for my state of undress, readjusting the robe. She waved it away. "We're all ladies here. If you don't mind me saying, miss, my grandparents and I are thrilled that Sherlock has brought help along.

We all dearly hope this gets cleared up, for the Squire's sake. But enough of that, is there anything I can do for you?"

"Why, yes, as a matter of fact, there is something. Let's start with what the hell is going on here!"

"I beg your pardon?" Theresa seemed oddly flustered. Sometimes these Victorians and their delicacy drove me nuts.

"You know, with Holmes, I mean Sherlock, and his father. What is going on between them?"

"Oh, that. Well…I suppose that Sir Siger has never gotten over Sherlock's defiance. The other sons bowed to their father's wishes in their choices of careers. Sherrinford returned to Oakstaff after university to become a country gentleman, since he is the heir and all, and Mycroft went into government work as his father had prescribed."

Don't I know it, I thought silently.

"Sir Siger had wanted Sherlock to be an engineer," Theresa continued, "but Sherlock wanted to become a detective."

An engineer? Sir Siger expected Holmes to be content with a desk and a slide rule? Where was this man when his son grew up?

"Eventually, after he returned from university, Sherlock left home and went to London. The rest you know."

That was it? It couldn't be. A little squabble over career choices couldn't possibly lead to the depth of hate that I saw burning in Sir Siger's heart, could it? There was something she wasn't telling me, but I wasn't going to pry…not yet anyway. Instead, I gestured to my frock on the bed. "Is there enough time before dinner for me to commandeer an ironing board and take care of this dress?"

The change of subject seemed to relieve her. "Dinner won't be for another hour. I'll take care of it, Miss Brown." Well, to think that I had rushed my bath for nothing. She draped the gray frock over her arm and turned to the door.

I halted her before she could leave. "Hey, um, Theresa? I don't believe that the Squire killed Mrs. Pittston any more than you do. So, just out of curiosity, do you have any ideas who could have framed Sherrinford?"

"Darby Edwards." The name grated out of her mouth like sandpaper.

I was startled at her vehemence. "What? Why him, Theresa?"

She shook her head briefly, regaining herself. "I…can't explain it. Not now. But I *know* it was him." With that, she was gone, leaving me totally lost. I lay down on the bed, mind whirling. Someone had framed Sherrinford; my instinct told me that. But who, and to what end? I had a feeling in my gut that

that the 'who' was answered, but the 'why' still lingered. And what of Holmes and Sir Siger? Perhaps the career dispute was part of it, but so many things were still unanswered. It seemed that I had two mysteries to solve: The Adventure of the Country Squire and The Adventure of the Detective's Past.

❦   ❦   ❦

Theresa promptly returned with my freshly pressed frock, leaving me plenty of time to prepare myself before the dinner gong sounded. Dinner was delicious, I suppose, but I never tasted whatever I put in my mouth, too concerned with watching Holmes from the corner of my eye. What I saw was not encouraging. Holmes positively shone at table, chatting and reminiscing with the others with uncharacteristic exuberance, but he only pushed the food around on his plate while the level of wine in his glass rose and fell with regularity. It was with great relief that the meal ended and we rose from our seats.

Holly retired to the library with a pot of chamomile tea, and I knew that I was expected to join her, but instead I followed the men into the billiards room as they settled around the large green felt table, lighting cigars and pouring glasses of cognac.

"All right, gentlemen, I can see that you are doing a marvelous job at ignoring the matter at hand," I announced, purposefully loud.

The men craned their necks to regard me. "Shouldn't you be in the library, young *lady*?" rasped Sir Siger in a hoarse smoker's voice.

"I probably would be, if I weren't in the middle of investigating a case of murder and fraud," I returned icily. "But seeing as how I should be present when the case is discussed, I shall join you." Having made the first offense, I crossed the threshold into the kingdom of men. I could hardly sit quietly in a corner; they would walk all over me without even noticing. So, calling on Bernie Flynn, I strode into the room, took the cognac glass from Holmes' hand and perched myself on the billiards table, sipping the fiery-sweet liquor.

Holmes cocked an eyebrow at me and I cocked one back before addressing the room entire. "Why don't we begin by drawing up a working list of suspects?" I asked.

"A capital idea," said Holmes, coming to my rescue before anyone (i.e: Sir Siger) could object. "Watson, since you have so much experience with pen and paper of late, perhaps you could take this down." Apparently he hadn't gotten past the whole newspaper thing. Watson looked slightly abashed as he drew out his ever-present notepad from his jacket pocket.

"Well," Sherrinford spoke up. "I am not sure of the rest of you, but I personally think better when my hands are occupied. Would anyone take me up on a game of billiards?"

"Me!" I cried, but I was right in the middle of a sip, so it came out "Mmph!" I swallowed and set the glass down, taking a cue from the rack on the wall and chalking it. "I'll play you, Squire."

Mycroft began to chuckle and I shot him a withering glance. Sherrinford looked down in amusement. "I hardly think it would be fair," he protested.

"Don't worry," I blithely replied. "I'll go easy on you." It was only half-bluff. I had watched my father play billiards countless times and, although I had rarely played in his circle, I was nothing to laugh at with a cue stick, the veteran of thousands of pool hall games in New York. Mycroft's chuckling grew louder.

"Don't underestimate her, Sherrinford," called Holmes. "She'll surprise you every time. In fact, I'd bet five pounds that she beats you simply for the shock value."

"I'll take that bet." Sir Siger's hoarse voice echoed through the room and the tension increased tenfold. Holmes steadfastly looked away, not meeting his father's corrosive gaze.

"Well," said Sherrinford with forced joviality. "It seems that there is money riding on this one, Nona. What shall we play, straight for one hundred points?"

I nodded mechanically, no longer sure of my abilities. Straight billiards is devastatingly simple: hit two of the three balls on the table with your cue ball to score one point. Since a scored point led to another turn, it was possible for an expert to score upwards of five hundred points without relinquishing control of the table. If we were only playing to one hundred points, it promised to be a quick game. Suddenly I desperately wanted to win for Holmes, even if it was just to spite his hateful father.

Sherrinford graciously allowed me the first shot and I bent to line it up, carefully testing the feel of the cue. As I judged the distance and angle, I caught Sir Siger's eye across the table. With a bitter grin I looked him in the eye. *En garde!* My cue lashed out and struck home on my cue ball, sending it across the felt table and into the first ball, ricocheting into the second. One point for me. *Like riding a bicycle,* I thought with satisfaction, feeling better about my chances.

As I lined up my next shot, Watson spoke for the first time. "Any thoughts on suspects, gentlemen and lady?"

Oh yeah, that was why we were here, wasn't it? "Well, Sherrinford," I posed as my cue lined up. "You're the pivotal player here. Any ideas?" My cue ball struck the object ball, but missed the third by a hair. Great.

"No, not really. I don't believe I've made any enemies." The lord of the manor struck out and easily caromed into both balls. Just great.

"'The only man without enemies is a dead man,'" quoted Sherlock, a little dismally. "Men do not murder for no good reason."

"Actually, you'd be surprised, Holmes," I said. "Some people who are mentally unbalanced don't need a reason." Sherrinford scored yet another point. "Dammit," I muttered softly, feeling Sir Siger's razorblade grin.

"Oh come now, Miss Brown," protested Mycroft. "A man simply wakes up and decides to kill a perfect stranger? Such a thing has never happened."

"Not yet, anyway," I said, thinking of Jack the Ripper. Sherrinford missed his shot; my turn again.

"Well, let's just keep that option open," said Watson, ever the peacemaker.

I lined up my shot. The lineup was a piece of cake, that point was as good as mine…Suddenly a harsh, dry, utterly false cough rang out, skewing my shot and causing me to only clip the cue ball. "Excuse me?" I stared down the unrepentant Sir Siger. "Do you mind?"

"That was bad form, Father," said Sherrinford quietly. "Nona, take the shot again." In a huff, I did so and easily took the point.

The game and the discussion drew on as the Holmes family dug up past grudges, unpaid debts and outstanding offenses. Watson's list grew in length as Sherrinford and I traded turns, and I marveled at how many of the names actually applied to Sir Siger rather than Sherrinford himself.

Finally I was setting up for my hundredth point with Sherrinford trailing by only two. "I believe that's it," said Watson, reviewing his pad. "Anyone else?"

"Darby Edwards." I was so busy lining up my shot for my final point that I didn't realize that I was the one who had spoken!

Sherrinford looked shocked. "What? Come now, Nona, Darby is one of our closest family friends. As a matter of fact, he is my son's godfather! What causes you to suspect him?"

I quickly regretted that I had spoken. What to say to that? The truth? *Oh, I suspect him because he gave me a ride at Christmas and your accountant's granddaughter doesn't like him? Oh yeah, that's convincing.* "A hunch, I suppose," I said lamely.

Sir Siger barked a laugh, a cold, cruel sound that made me cringe inside. "Woman's intuition, my dear girl? How *very* typical." I am not a coward, believe me, but that sneer made me want to curl up and die. My view of my cue ball faltered.

"'A woman's guess is surer than a man's certainty,'" came Holmes' voice. "Who wrote that? Kipling?"

"Longfellow, I believe," rumbled Mycroft. "Kipling said that the female of the species is deadlier than the male."

"Ah, well, that applies as well," Holmes said easily, leaning back in his chair and catching my eye with a smile, albeit a shaky one. That was it, I was winning this game for him come hell or high water, and Daddy Dearest could just eat my dust! I lined up my cue, barely breathing in my concentration. It was a trick shot; I would have to hit the object ball slightly off center to get it to hit the remaining ball. With a wish and a prayer I let fly with the cue, accidentally using more force than necessary. The object ball careened across the table, missing Sherrinford's cue ball and hitting the bank like a battering ram. *No!* I cried inside, but the ball didn't stop. It bounced off the bank and back across the table as if the game was pinball instead of billiards, hitting the opposite bank and drifting slowly back again, towards the remaining ball! The men had ceased talking, all attention on the billiards table. I think I crossed about everything that could be crossed as the object ball rolled closer…closer…and lightly tapped Sherrinford's cue ball.

"Yes!" I cried, pumping my arm. It was an absurdly lucky shot, but I had won!

"By Jove!" breathed Sherrinford in shock and admiration. He turned to me as if seeing me in a whole new light.

"Luck," snorted Mycroft, but the gleam in his eye made the effrontery more ruse than not.

"Skill," protested Watson, always the gentleman.

"Hey," I spoke up. "I'm with Mycroft on this one. That was stupid luck."

"Nevertheless, my dear," said Sherrinford, "I believe you carry away the laurels this time." He clasped my hand warmly, and I felt that I had won more than a game of billiards. "Sherlock has a point, I see. I shall never underestimate you again."

"Hear, hear," called Watson amiably.

Well, that had been fun and a close game, but now Sir Misanthropic could put his money where his mouth was, thank you very much. But even as I thought of the bet, Sir Siger was moving toward the door.

Holmes rose to his feet. "Father, wait, what about…?"

The bitter man coolly regarded his taller son. "You would stoop to taking money from your *father*?" he accused, stressing the last word. At that Holmes paled and turned his head away, leaving Sir Siger free to leave the room.

Hateful, spiteful man. I had a suspicion that if Sherrinford had won, Sir Siger would have had no qualms about collecting from his son. I snorted quietly as I returned the cue to its rack. "Bastard," I muttered, but the word carried in the quiet room. The declaration seemed to be a dagger for Holmes; he stiffened visibly, his eyes going wide with pain, and he hurriedly left the room, leaving me in a state of confusion. What was going on?

"What?" I asked rhetorically, lost and hurt. "Was it something I said?"

CHAPTER 10

In Which I See My First Corpse and Flirt with a Suspect

That was *it*. I was going to get some answers, come hell or high water. Leaving the men in the billiards room, I dashed out into the foyer, but Holmes was nowhere in sight. Damn! Oakstaff was so huge; he could be anywhere! *Okay,* I mentally lectured. *Calm down and think for a minute. Where would Holmes go in a state of distress?* Well, at Baker Street when a case was going badly, he would hole up in his room and scrape on his violin until we all thought we'd go nuts! That was as good a place to start as any. Of course, I had no idea where his room was, but I thought it wouldn't be too hard to find.

It turned out to be harder than I thought. I tried asking the butler, but he refused to tell me, probably trying to avert scandal. After some minutes of verbal wrestling, he finally acquiesced and gave me directions to Holmes' quarters. Of course, me being me, I got hopelessly turned around and asked a maid for directions. She too was scandalized by my request, and I had to start all over again, mentally cursing the prudish Victorians.

About fifteen minutes later I finally reached what I thought was Holmes' room. Steeling myself with a deep breath, I knocked on the door. "Holmes?" I called softly. "It's Nona. Can I come in?" I waited with hands clasped to hide their shaking. The door remained shut. I knocked again, louder. "Holmes? You can't be asleep already, so let me in!" No reply. Perhaps I had guessed wrong and Holmes was elsewhere. I tried the brass doorknob; it was locked tight.

Well, so much for that theory. I recommended banging, not caring if I woke any early retirees.

"Holmes, let me in!" I pleaded. On impulse I placed my eye to the keyhole to see if the key remained in it. If it was, I could pull a nifty little trick with a kitchen skewer and a page of newspaper. No such luck; Holmes had taken the key from the lock, but this also gave me a limited view of the room. The room's only lamp was turned on low, cloaking the room in shadows. I could dimly see the bed; the dark form on it was Holmes. How could he be sleeping through all of my banging? Was he just lying there and ignoring me? "Holmes, *wake up!*"

The shadow on the bed moaned and shifted, throwing its arm over the side and dropping a small object, which rolled into the lamplight. A syringe. No amount of pounding would wake Holmes now.

Stifling a cry, my heart aching, I launched myself from my crouch by the door and barreled down the hall in the general direction of my room. I was so incredibly pissed. Not with Holmes, well, maybe a little for not telling me what was going on and for seeking comfort from a needle and not me, but more so with the loathsome Sir Siger, who had somehow driven his youngest son to this pit of despair. What kind of a father was he? I really had no experience with broken families; despite the pressures from my mother, my own home life had been fairly stable. I couldn't imagine the pain of growing up with an emotionally abusive father and a...wait. What about Holmes' mother? Was she dead now? Had she abandoned the family? I had a hunch that she played a large part in this particular Greek tragedy.

I marched double-time to my room, seeing red, ready to lash out at any fool who crossed my path. Luckily (or unluckily, however you want to look at it) I reached my room without encountering anyone and entered alone, slamming the door. I paced my chamber in a huff, teeth grinding and fists clenched, trying to surmount my muddled emotions with rational thought as heart warred with mind.

Okay, time to calm down and think. What could Holmes—

Poor Holmes! How could that heartless monster be so cruel? If only I could...

Matter at hand, if you please! Now what could Holmes and Sir Siger—

Damn that wretched devil! If he were here, I would rip off his...

No! Concentrate! What could be the problem between those two? There was so little data that—

I've got enough data to justify blowing a hole in Sir Shithead! Teach him to mess with my man!

"Gah!" I cried in frustration. "This is too much!" I threw myself onto the bed, exasperated with my feelings and the entire situation. There was no use in racking my brain for reasons. I needed more information before I could even theorize. Best thing would be to get some sleep. Holmes would want to see the crime scene first thing in the morning and then talk to the coroner, the constabulary, any witnesses, a few suspects, plus I would have to find time to collar Holmes and force the truth out of him. It promised to be a busy day and I needed my beauty sleep, so I washed up and changed into a light nightdress I found in the wardrobe. I turned off the lamp and climbed into the large, soft bed, fully expecting the cognac and the stress to send me off to Dreamland. But every time I closed my eyes, I could see Holmes alone in the darkness, trembling in the clutches of morphine-induced nightmares.

Sleep was long in coming that night.

❦   ❦   ❦

After had seemed an eternity of tossing and turning, I had slipped into the limbo between deep sleep and wakefulness sometime in the small hours of the morning. A few hours later, the morning sunshine forced itself into my room as I woke bereft of alarm clock. Still fogged with sleep, I staggered out of bed and threw open the bay doors to check the forecast on the balcony. The sun seemed only inches above the horizon, illuminating the cotton-like clouds. The oak trees swung in the gentle breeze, the fragrance of distant wildflowers pervaded the air, and the trill of birdsong filled my ears. It promised to be a glorious day.

Nevertheless, the lovely weather did very little to raise my spirits. In direct contrast to the sunshine, I was instead filled with melancholy, bemoaning my predicament. Between Holmes' internal problems, the mystery of his past and Sherrinford's current dilemma, I felt completely overwhelmed. I was suddenly filled with a fierce homesickness. Even though I had given up all hope of returning to the twenty-first century, I longed to be back in my dorm room with my terrible roommate, with nothing to worry about but getting to work on time and turning in my assignments, knowing that my father was right across town, always willing to lend a wise and sympathetic ear...

A flash of blue along the road caught my eye as I moped. A uniformed constable armed with a long-range rifle slowly prowled the brush, scanning for any signs of movement. That sight brought me back to myself and reminded me of why we were here in the first place. I couldn't linger in the past now, not when there were more pressing tasks to handle. Suppressing a nervous chill and forcing myself to get a grip, I moved back inside to wash and change into one of the prototypes.

As I went downstairs to the dining room for breakfast, a heavy feeling grew in the pit of my stomach. After last night I had no idea how Holmes had fared, and I dreaded facing him, fearing what I would see. Pausing outside the dining room door, I steeled myself internally, put on a game face and walked through.

"There you are! I was about to send someone to wake you!"

The acerbic voice was strong and steady, the clothes were fastidiously neat, the hair was properly combed and the collar was pressed. Holmes was sitting at breakfast with Watson, Sherrinford and Holly. Mycroft and, thankfully, Sir Siger were nowhere in sight. More importantly, though, Holmes looked absolutely fine, not a hair out of place.

It took me a moment to recover from this contradiction to my expectations, but I rallied gamely. "Good morning to you too, Holmes," I returned, taking a seat next to him. "I trust you slept well."

He didn't answer, changing the subject. "Be sure and eat, Nona; we may be working through luncheon." He certainly wasn't taking his own advice, picking at his plate again. Conversation drifted away from the case as we tried to keep to lighter diversions. I did not contribute, watching Holmes out of the corner of my eye. I had worried that he would be a wreck after last night, but here he sat, perfectly groomed and chatting away. Maybe I was reading too much into this after all…

Suddenly my hopeful rationale melted away. Under the corner of Holmes' jaw, below the ear, I saw he had missed a spot while shaving. In all the months I had known him, that was a first. Of course, there was any number of explanations: poor lighting, dull blade, or even simple forgetfulness, so why did it make my stomach tie in knots? I made no further attempt to eat, all concentration instead on the first-class actor beside me.

There was no road to the crime scene and we would be traveling on horseback, so we pushed ourselves from the table and moved to the back of the house. As we passed the music room, however, a childish sneeze arrested our attention. I caught a bare glimpse of a thatch of black hair and a tiny hand before the culprit vanished into the room.

The movement caught Sherrinford's notice and he smiled. "Ah, that's right, Sherlock, you haven't met your nephew yet. Virgil, come out and meet your uncle!"

There was a pause; then Virgil's tiny form crept out, eyes cast down and feet shuffling. Poor kid was probably terrified to finally meet his hero.

I nudged Holmes discreetly. "This kid idolizes you," I murmured. "Be nice."

Introductions were duly made, but Holmes did not take his nephew's hand or even smile. Instead, he sank down to Virgil's level and peered intently at the boy. Virgil was obviously nervous, but he returned his elder's gaze with the same intentness. Again I was struck by their similarities.

Holmes' arm snaked out and removed the magnifying glass from the boy's pocket. "You wish to become a detective?" he asked softly.

"Yessir," replied Virgil, making it one word.

"Do you know what it takes to be one?" Holmes asked, voice cold.

"Ah, observation and de...deduction, sir?" was Virgil's hesitant reply.

Holmes eyebrows climbed and I knew his interest was piqued. "Is that a question, Master Virgil?"

"No, sir."

"Very good." Surprisingly, Holmes dug into his waistcoat pocket and removed the gold pocket watch I had given him for Christmas. Taking the lad's hand, so like his own, he placed the watch into it and carefully wrapped the tiny fingers around it. "Then using observation and deduction, perhaps you can tell me about this watch."

Despite his youth, Virgil sensed a challenge and rose to meet it. He inspected the watch carefully, opening and closing it, running his fingers over the serial number stamped on the inside, even raising it to his ear to listen to it tick. Finally he handed it back to his uncle. "I'm sorry, sir, but all I can tell is that it's very special to you and it was a present."

Holmes' eyebrows climbed higher. He obviously hadn't expected Virgil to come up with something, much less be correct! "And how did you know that?" asked Holmes with delight.

Virgil pointed at the watch as he spoke. "When you put it in my hand, you wrapped my fingers around it, as Mother does when she lets me hold Great-Grandmother's French china, so it must be special. But it's just an ordinary watch and isn't worth a lot of money, so I de...de..."

"Deduce," prompted Holmes.

The lad nodded. "Yes, I deduce that it was a present, and that's why it's special." Impressed, Holmes pocketed the watch again and rose to his feet. With a burst of emotion, Virgil cracked his polite exterior and cried, "Uncle! Will I ever be a detective, Uncle Sherlock?"

Holmes looked down on the small boy and replied seriously, "You *are* a detective, Virgil, and I shall require your assistance in the case, if you would."

Well, this was a dream come true for Virgil! "Anything you need, Uncle Sherlock!" he said proudly, squaring his tiny shoulders.

"While we are here, Virgil, you must be absolutely observant. Stay watchful for anything out of the ordinary. If you see anything amiss, anything at all, come and report to me right away. Understood?"

"Yes, sir!" he beamed. I thought the boy would explode with pride and excitement, and I also noted the smile Holmes was wearing, departing from his usual cold exterior. Someday I knew, or at least hoped, that Holmes would make an excellent father, worlds above his own.

"Well, it would seem we have another detective in the family," came a sneering, smoker's voice. Speak of the devil. Sir Siger emerged from the study down the hall, coming to face our group. "And where would the Great Detective be off to this fine day?"

Almost unconsciously, Virgil moved closer to his uncle as his grandfather drew nearer. "Uncle Sherlock is going to solve the mystery so Father and Mother can go outside again."

"Ah, yes," came the scornful reply. "I have been wondering when you would get around to it." The reproach in his voice was the lash of a whip. Careful not to let anyone see, I slid my hand into Holmes' own, almost wincing as he squeezed it painfully. "Isn't it ironic," Sir Siger continued, "that the fate of the family name should rest on your shoulders, *son*?" My hand was getting crushed; I regretted my comforting actions.

Watson, wonderful man, came to our rescue, taking Holmes' arm and addressing the elder Holmes. "I'm sure you will excuse us, sir, but we have a great deal of work to complete and we have no time to tarry." With that, the good doctor moved swiftly down the hall with Holmes and me in tow, leaving Sherrinford and the others behind. Sherrinford's voice rose unintelligibly, but with a definite tone of argument as we exited through the back door of the manor and out into the stable yard.

The wide-open sky, fresh air and warm sunshine lifted ten stone from my back, and I heard Holmes and Watson expel pent-up sighs. Our horses were waiting for us, three thoroughbred beauties. A stableman led me to my horse, a silver-gray mare, very ladylike, but I noticed a problem straight away. "Stable boy, this saddle is faulty," I said.

"Impossible, miss," he replied. "That's Mrs. Holmes' own sidesaddle. Couldn't be finer."

Sidesaddle! Absolutely not! I had never ridden a horse in my life, unless you counted the carousel ponies at Coney Island, and they expected me to ride sidesaddle? "That's the problem. Change this to a man's saddle, please, and be quick about it!"

"But..." The man trailed off as he examined my clothing again. "Yes, miss." He led the horse off into the stable.

Holmes looked up from inspecting the saddle girth of his own chestnut steed. He looked that dreadful shade of pale again, but his eyes were still bright. "What's the delay, Nona?"

I jerked my thumb back to the stable. "Little problem with the saddle. He tried to give me a sidesaddle and I made him take it back."

"Do you mean that you'll be riding like a man?" asked Watson, more curious than scandalized. These two at least were somewhat used to my modern ways.

I gestured to my prototype. "You think I wear this for the shock value?" I threw back.

"The thought had crossed my mind," deadpanned Holmes. If it weren't for my gnawing worry for him, I would have called him something derogatory.

My horse was led out again and I stood by it, trying to hook my right foot in the stirrup and heave myself up like in the Westerns. It wasn't working. After a few tries, I finally noticed Holmes standing a few feet away, looking greatly amused. "Couldn't you do something useful?" I shot at him. *Like telling me what's going on with you...*

"You've never ridden a horse before, have you?"

"Brilliant, Holmes! What was your first clue?"

"First of all, you're mounting from the wrong side." Oh. I knew that. He removed my foot from the stirrup and led me to the other side. "Always mount from the left side. Now, place your left foot here," I placed it in the stirrup, "grasp the pommel with your left hand," I did so, "and in one swift movement, stand up in the stirrup and swing your leg over the saddle." That was the hard part. I stood and swung, but my left foot shifted and I slipped backward, falling ungracefully into Holmes' waiting arms. His knees buckled as he caught me and he grunted with effort, almost dropping me, but he regained himself and set me down right-side-up.

I hadn't gained weight since Christmas, so why was this so hard for him? At that moment of weakness, all my fears seemed to be confirmed. The sight of his pale skin and the shadows forming beneath his eyes only spurred me on.

"Holmes, please, what's wrong?" I pleaded, trying to capture his gaze with my own. "You can tell me."

For the briefest moment I thought he would acquiesce, but then he retreated into his icy shell again. "I am perfectly fine, Nona."

"Morphine and excessive alcohol can hardly be considered *fine*, Holmes," I retorted. "What is going on?"

"None of your business!" he hissed angrily, surprising me. "Now cease your badgering and get on the horse, or we shall leave you behind!" Not even when I first made his acquaintance was he this harsh. I complied, clambering ungracefully onto the animal as Holmes mounted his own steed. A little nervous, I gave my horse a nudge with my heels and it began to walk, thankfully slowly, following the others. On our way out of the stable, I caught sight of Watson. The shadow in the doctor's eyes showed that he had seen Holmes sway uneasily as he mounted as well as I.

The ride was fairly short so I didn't have much time to talk to Holmes further; I was too busy trying to control the rather stubborn Duchess. The Dynamic Duo was no help, calling out advice that made little or no sense at all.

"Sit up straight and throw your shoulders back!" called Holmes.

"Then the bouncing up and down gives me a headache!" I returned.

"Grip the horse with your knees, Nona!" instructed Watson.

"My legs aren't long enough!" I protested.

"Then try leaning forward!" insisted Holmes.

"I thought I was supposed to sit up straight!"

And so on and so forth.

None too soon we reached the crime scene, a small curve in the creek's path, hidden by dense shrubbery and guarded by a pair of constables.

"Oi!" called one of North Riding's finest as we drew up our horses. "Clear off, you! This is a restricted area!"

"Pardon me, gentlemen," said Holmes with an easy smile. "I am Mr. Sherlock Holmes, and this is…"

From the constables' reactions, it might have been a royal proclamation. They backed up and stammered with wide eyes like confused children. "Sherlock Holmes and Dr. Watson! Forgive us, sirs, we didn't know it was you, we thought you might be coming, didn't touch anything 'cept the body, read all about you in the papers, sirs, anything you need, just say so." We dismounted and moved past the constables, who ceased their stammering and now watched us in awe from the edge of the glade.

Holmes looked back at the officers and then shook his head at Watson. "Perhaps those articles are good for something after all." With that, he took a magnifying glass from his pocket and set to work. There wasn't a whole lot that Watson and I could do at this point, so we settled against a pair of trees and watched the Master work. Holmes almost scurried around the scene, muttering and humming, peering at the ground, the water's edge, pacing and measuring and talking to himself the whole time.

Looking up to the constables, he pointed to a spot on the ground and asked, "This is where the body was found?" receiving an enthusiastic pair of nods in reply. "Watson, come here." Watson shifted himself from his seat and walked over, but I didn't move, content to watch. Holmes pointed to the ground and they both hunkered down. "What can you tell me about this soil?"

Watson touched the dirt, pinching it between his fingers before shaking his head. Watson had played similar, more active roles in many other investigations, but usually he edited his own involvement out of his reports. "Mrs. Pittston supposedly died from a single gunshot to the heart. Even if she died instantaneously, the corpse would have bled copiously, but there is no trace of blood in this soil. Has it rained since the murder?"

"Not a drop." Holmes gestured to the creek trickling behind him. "People are beginning to complain that North Riding will see a drought."

"Then I see no possible explanation for the lack of blood. Do you, Holmes?"

"I do," he sighed, "but lack sufficient data. I will not cloud my mind with theories before all of the facts are in hand." With a final sweep of the scene, we turned back to our horses. "There is no further need to preserve the scene," Holmes directed to the constables. "You may be excused." We rode back across the fields double-time, Holmes explaining on the way: "The rest of our errands may be completed from the comfort of a carriage. We will head back to the manor, wash up and change, and head to the morgue."

"S-Sounds like f-fun," I stammered as Duchess did her utmost to throw me off. I clung on gamely, but was entirely sore by the time we returned to the manor and I had to be helped off the dumb animal. Despite Watson's protests that I 'did rather well for a first time,' I limped upstairs to change. After our trip to the coroner's office we would be interviewing suspects, so I swapped my prototype for a more respectable dress, thankfully free of the smell of horses.

Feeling slightly better, I went downstairs to rejoin Holmes and Watson at the front stairs. They helped me into the familiar trap, piloted once more by the genial St. Clair, and we set off.

Holmes checked his watch. "It is nearly eleven now," said he. "Inspector Langford should be waiting for us when we arrive."

The watch brought something to my memory. "Holmes," I asked innocently, "was Virgil correct in his deductions?"

Holmes broke into a smile. "He was, actually. He has the makings of a fine sleuth."

"So my Christmas gift *is* special to you?"

That statement jerked his head up and he colored uncertainly. "Umm, well..." he stuttered.

I shook my head, content with my victory. "Never mind, Holmes," I said indulgently, hearing St. Clair chuckle from the driver's seat. For the rest of the drive we applied ourselves to the scenery.

The coroner's office was at the far end of the main street of Kingston-on-the-Hill, and we passed a flower shop, a post office, a pub (which I filed away for Bernie Flynn) and several other shops until we came to the police station and criminal morgue. Inspector Langford was waiting for us by the door as we pulled up, a short, stout, balding man with more hair in his mustache than on his head. Regardless of his rather comical appearance, he somehow managed to retain an air of efficiency and professionalism that some in my old college used to call the Executive Vibe. He cordially shook our hands and welcomed us inside without fanfare. The constabulary was a neat and tidy empire, clerks typing away at official reports and uniformed constables filling out forms. Langford apologized for the paper trail, saying that since the murder he'd kept a tighter rein on his force, making the men fill out official reports after their shifts. We commended his efforts and he led us into his office.

"I'm not afraid to come out and say it," he began without preamble. "I don't think the Squire did it, but I can't tell you who did. That's your job, I suppose, Mr. Holmes. My job is to make your job as easy as I can."

"Then perhaps you can answer some questions for me, Inspector," said Holmes sharply. "Who had access to the crime scene before we did?"

If the man was offended by Holmes' brevity, he gave no sign. "Mr. Smythe, an elderly chap who found the body; Dr. Jameson, the coroner; and myself. Dr. Jameson and I were very careful of our footprints."

"You examined the existing prints yourself?"

Langford nodded. "That very day. I saw the perpetrator's prints going to stand by the creek, and I saw where he had left the scene."

"Where did you find the lady's footprints?" Holmes asked.

Langford did a double-take, then looked at Holmes levelly. "I just realized this, and you may take me for a blind fool, Mr. Holmes, but I saw no woman's prints."

"Neither did I. That is simply because there were none to be found."

"Then how did Mrs. Pittston reach her ill-fated rendezvous?" I queried. "Surely she did not float!"

"Perhaps the killer obliterated her tracks," postulated Watson.

"And left his own behind?" Holmes shook his head. "No, the evidence does not add up. We need more data."

Various questions flew back and forth for the better part of an hour before Langford suggested that we examine the body itself. We agreed and the inspector led us down a hall and a flight of stairs into a network of basement rooms. The autopsy bay was old and cold, with walls and floor of ancient stone and various shelves of wicked-looking surgeon's paraphernalia. Through a miracle of modern architecture, a large glass skylight had been installed in the roof leading up to the outdoors, allowing for both proper lighting and ventilation when necessary. Thus, the autopsy bay was neither cloying nor eerie. I was mildly disappointed.

On a steel gurney in the center of the room was a white sheet, covering a rather obvious series of lumps. "Here she is, gents," said Langford brusquely. "See if you can get anything out of her cause she ain't talking to me." Morgue humor. No one laughed.

We all crowded around the gurney and stared silently, leaving the gruesome task of uncovering the body to our resident MD. Watson's face was a blank as he drew back the sheet and we got our first good look at Sylvia Pittston. I had expected to be horrified at the sight of my first real corpse. I had expected to be fighting nausea and making disgusted noises as people do in the movies, but instead I felt a strange detachment. The figure on the table looked no different than one of the corpses on *C.S.I.*, maybe even a bit less sensational.

Watson drew the sheet back to mid-torso and let it drop. That was all we needed at the moment. The body's skin was pale, but was no longer rigid with rigor mortis. The features were quite lovely in a frozen kind of way. The only blemish in the skin was the perfect bullet hole exactly above the left breast, the *only* blemish. There was no Y-incision, no stitching, nothing. Watson voiced our unanimous thoughts. "There has been no autopsy performed here."

Langford gaped for a moment, then let loose with a string of very creative obscenities before he remembered that I was in the room. "Damn that Jameson!" he concluded. "Bloody drunkard's been cutting corners again!" He turned to us apologetically. "Terribly sorry, gents, miss, but Jameson has done this sort of thing before. If a corpse comes in with an obvious cause of death, he'll skip the autopsy altogether so he can get to The Goose and Crown by opening time. Not after today, though; he's through on my force."

Holmes was livid. Of course, for Holmes this meant only a narrowing of the eyes, a clenching of the fists and a tight voice, but Langford understood the general motivation. "Do you mean to tell me that my brother has been threatened with the gallows on the mere weight of a note and a gun?" Holmes grated softly.

"Yes, it does seem rather flimsy, I know," stumbled the inspector, "but it's the only evidence we have. If you can find contradicting evidence, something that negates what we have, then I'll shake your hand and exonerate the Squire with a smile! Until then, my hands are tied!"

"Well then," sighed Watson, shrugging out of his jacket and rolling up his sleeves. These were the moments that never found their way into print, the times when Watson took the reins of the case himself, usually proving himself invaluable. "It would seem that I have my work cut out for me, if you'll pardon the rather grisly pun. Do you have any objections, Inspector?"

"Nary a one. I was just about to ask if you would, Dr. Watson. I believe that I trust you more than I would Jameson. Have you any experience with autopsies?"

Watson shrugged ruefully. "I must admit that I prefer my patients breathing, but since my association with Mr. Holmes, my experience with cadavers has significantly increased." He turned to address Holmes with an amused expression. "You know better than anyone else that you can't rush a criminal autopsy, so you and Nona best get started on the suspects without me. I shall meet you back at the Manor around tea time, hopefully with better news."

Ever the dramatist, Holmes bowed low and walked backwards out of the room. "Watson, I leave this matter in your highly superior hands," he said grandly, gratitude lacing his complimentary words. Holmes and I returned to the floor level and the summer sunshine, leaving Watson and Langford to their stomach-turning art.

❦   ❦   ❦

After the tension of the autopsy room, a rather amusing surprise awaited us back at the carriage. Apparently we had taken longer than expected, for old St. Clair was stretched out and snoring in the back, hat shading his eyes. I stifled a giggle with my hand. "Guess the poor old boy got tired of waiting. Should we wake him?"

Holmes shook his head, helping me up to the wide driver's seat before climbing up himself. Taking the reins in hand, he clucked to the horse and we creaked down the path again, Mr. St. Clair never stirring. Well, this was a handy little reversal of roles, the young baronet driving the cart while the servant slumbers. With the old accountant asleep and Watson otherwise engaged, the two of us were quite alone, sitting very close together on the hard wooden seat as the breeze pushed back our hats. "Well, Holmes, looks like it's just you and me now."

"Indeed," came the indifferent reply from my traveling companion.

No sense in beating around the bush with Sherlock Holmes. "So, are you finally going to explain it?"

Slowly he turned toward me and cocked a very deliberate eyebrow. "*It* is an indefinite pronoun in this sentence, Nona," he said icily, recalling shades of those bitter winter months. "Kindly elaborate."

Fine. If he wanted to be stubborn, that was peachy, but I wasn't about to let him off because of it. "'It' is the sorry situation between you and your father."

"I dislike repeating myself, woman," he said haughtily, flicking the reins with irritation. "I have told you that it is none of your business."

"And I am telling *you* that's a load of…hogwash," I shot back, mentally censoring myself. This was neither the time nor the place for getting angry. "You are obviously distraught, Holmes, and that makes it my business."

"Distraught?" His voice climbed an octave. "I am no such thing!"

"Oh no?" I asked in mock amazement. "Then your diminished appetite, increased alcohol intake and hurry to leave the billiard room and seek hypodermic sanctuary are all a part of some master plan?" He said nothing, very uncharacteristic, and I did not fail to press my advantage. "This is disturbing, Holmes. It scares me. I hate to think of anything causing you pain, and I want you to tell me why you are hurting. I want to help you. Trust me, Sherlock." On impulse, I slipped a hand into his long white one, hoping to provoke the same reaction as before.

Wrong move. At my touch, Holmes stiffened as if jabbed with a live wire and burned me with a look. His gray eyes were cold and dead as coffin nails, sending a shiver through me despite the sunshine on my shoulders. "This is none of *your* business," he spat slowly. "I do not need your feeble ministrations, nor do I desire them. We will not speak of this again." He lifted his jaw and stared resolutely ahead, leaving me to contemplate the passing foliage. I felt horrible. All I wanted to do was help, and here I was, making it worse. We weren't even a couple yet and we were already having our first fight!

The first few interviews were unproductive: first with an old colonel, next with a spurned girlfriend, and finally with a retired foreign magnate, none of whom were very serious candidates. We had been forced to wake St. Clair, who had been embarrassed beyond words, before we reached the first house for the sake of a good impression. Holmes conducted the interviews with icy exactitude and I played the silent observer, never giving much thought to the interviews themselves. The carriage rides were silent as death as Holmes and I nursed our wounded prides, neither one of us looking at the other.

The fourth house we visited, last for the day, was a sprawling one with fading paint and ill-maintained gardens. "The Edwards," Holmes announced, a frown twisting his features. The sick feeling in my stomach increased exponentially. What if Darby Edwards recognized me? How would Holmes react? *Oh, I know exactly how he'd react,* I thought, *he'll get all jealous and protective...* Right about then I got an idea, a nasty little idea on how to pay back Holmes for all of the worrying he was putting me through.

St. Clair pulled up to the front steps of the house and the butler greeted us, leading us into the parlor. Darby was expecting us, blond hair combed and goatee properly trimmed as he greeted us with a plastered smile. It was very odd; there was nothing about him that screamed "murderer," but for some reason my stomach twisted and I looked down when he spoke.

"Sherlock Holmes!" he exclaimed, reaching for Holmes' hand. "As I live and breathe! Who would have thought that I would see you darken my doorstep again?"

"Edwards," was all Holmes would say, half-heartedly shaking his host's hand.

The grin widened, taking on a mocking quality. "Oh, come now, old boy; you're not still sore after I beat you in the fencing tourney all those years ago!"

Time to put my idea into action. I turned my head up and widened my eyes to almost bovine proportions. "You beat Mr. Holmes at fencing, Mr. Edwards?" I gushed absurdly. "You must be very skillful!"

"Why, if it isn't Miss Nona Brown!" he cried, taking my hand and kissing it extravagantly. "I would say that you have grown even lovelier in the months since I saw you last, but that would be an impossibility."

Oh yeah, like I was going to fall for that. "I am flattered that you remember me, Mr. Edwards," I demurred, looking away lest he see the lie in my eyes and I see the steel in his.

"You know each other?" Holmes asked incredulously.

"Oh yes," I nodded. "Mr. Edwards very graciously gave me a ride home after my Christmas shopping last year." I redirected my syrupy words to my prime suspect. "I was so hoping that you would stop by for New Year's, Mr. Edwards."

"Just Darby, my dear. Regretfully, I had been called home for some financial transactions, but perhaps I could make up for it over luncheon sometime?"

"Oh, that would be splendid, Darby!" I prattled, inwardly vowing never to set foot anywhere with Darby Edwards alone.

Holmes cleared his throat. *Loudly.* "Perhaps we could return to the subject at hand, Edwards."

We were all seated in the parlor and Holmes progressed with the usual questionnaire, but this time I kept interrupting with inanities, usually directed towards Darby. This served a double purpose: it annoyed Holmes to distraction and made Darby think that I had an empty head, a trump card that could prove useful in the future.

The interview was blissfully short. Holmes bid Darby a curt farewell and I smiled prettily at him, silently noting the predatory gleam in his eyes as he glanced at Holmes. My certainty of his guilt rose a few hundred notches, but what could possibly be his motive? Simple dislike? That would be difficult to prove; the man was Virgil's godfather, for crying out loud! At any rate, Holmes and I climbed into the trap and sped away.

We were barely out of sight of the house when Holmes turned to me, not bothering to conceal his anger. "What was that?" he rasped, eyes aflame.

"*That* is an indefinite noun in this sentence, Holmes," I mocked with an indifferent air. "Kindly elaborate."

His voice quivered with rage. "*That* was that little performance you put on back there."

"That was me ingratiating myself with the primary suspect, Holmes," I shot at him, "something I noticed that *you* neglected to do. As long as he thinks I have a head full of fluff, Edwards won't bother to guard his words around me. He might let something slip."

Holmes could find no fault with my reasoning, although I could see him trying. "Why didn't you warn me at least?" he asked.

I stared him down levelly, trying to emulate his earlier cold expression. "None of *your* business."

With a start, Holmes realized his own echo in my words. Face burning with anger and perhaps shame, he crossed his arms in a huff and refused to look at me, but I had made my point. Now he knew how I had felt at his hands, but was I driving him away? I needed something to bridge this widening gap.

"Did Edwards really beat you at fencing?" I asked.

"He cheated," Holmes grunted sourly. "His father paid off the judge. We were both fifteen years old."

I shook my head, trying to picture Holmes as a fifteen-year-old. "I can believe that," I said softly, turning my head to the scenery.

I didn't look around, but I could feel him looking at me as we rode back to the Manor. We had reached an impasse, a truce of sorts, before battle could be rejoined or peace negotiated. The trouble was that I didn't know which it would be.

❧   ❧   ❧

My stomach was complaining by the time we arrived back at Oakstaff Manor. Holmes had been right; we had worked right through lunch. I hoped the tea tray was substantial. We were met by Sherrinford and Holly, who were eager for news, but regretfully we had very little to assuage their fears. Mycroft was absent, barricaded in the study writing letters and telegrams to his agents for background information on the suspects.

Tea was a somber affair as we sat on the veranda, the afternoon sun slowly descending towards the horizon. We strove to keep up the illusion of normalcy until the butler entered the veranda. "Inspector Langford and Dr. Watson have arrived, sirs and madams." No more than two seconds later, we were up from the table and headed to the foyer as fast as propriety would allow. I was awash with nervous anticipation. Had Watson's autopsy yielded any new evidence to exonerate the Squire, or had he found a confirmation more damning than before? A small part of me refused to believe that the gentlemanly Sherrinford could do such a thing, especially with no obvious motive, but my certainty did little to alleviate my anxiety.

Watson and Langford were waiting in the front hall, the subdued expressions on their faces sending my stomach to my feet. Langford stepped forward with his hat in hand, looking up at the stricken Sherrinford. "Well, sir, we performed the autopsy," he began haltingly, twisting his hat nervously. Oh no, oh God, no. "And what we found…I'm sorry, Squire, but there's no help for it. I am forced to acquit you."

Sherrinford's eyes widened as if he was struck. Holmes snaked forward and grabbed the constable by the lapels. "Now listen here," he grated in fury, "you can't possibly…I beg your pardon?"

Langford was grinning openly now as Holmes released him. "You heard me. The Squire is acquitted, exonerated, henceforth freed from suspicion and released from house arrest."

"But *how*?" The question unanimously sounded from all of us.

In response Langford jerked his thumb in the direction of Watson, who smugly took up the explanation. "Deflation of the lungs, an inordinate amount of blood in the cadaver, the point-blank precision of the bullet hole and traces of down pillow under the fingernails. Mrs. Pittston was smothered with a red velvet pillow roughly six hours before nightfall, shot post-mortem, kept in hiding until sundown and then artistically placed at the crime scene."

"Which accounts for the lack of blood and footprints at the scene!" exclaimed Holmes. He wrung his friend's hand, eyes shining. "Wonderful, Watson! Your brilliance is blinding this evening!"

"Agreed," rumbled a grateful Sherrinford. "My family and I owe you a great debt, Dr. Watson."

Flustered with the praise, Watson colored and cleared his throat. "Ahem, it was really nothing, of course. And it still remains to discover Mrs. Pittston's true murderer."

"Correct, Watson," murmured Holmes, falling into deep thought. He turned to Langford again. "Have you told anyone else of my brother's new-found freedom?"

"We didn't have the chance, Mr. Holmes," Langford replied. "We came straight here from the station."

"Just as well," said Holmes. "It is imperative that you not tell anyone of Sherrinford's exoneration. If the news found its way into local gossip, the killer would cease to be complacent and become more cautious. In the meantime, we must continue the investigation as if nothing has happened."

"That's all well and good in public, Sherlock," said Sherrinford. "But I propose that we use the safety of these four walls to celebrate!"

Holmes couldn't contest that and Sherrinford led the party to the drawing room for liquid celebration. I, however, branched off from the main party and sought solace in the library. Seizing a book at random from the bookshelves, I wrapped myself up in an armchair and didn't even open the book, content to let my mind wander. Sherrinford was free of suspicion; I knew it couldn't have been him. Now all that remained was to find the real murderer. Actually all that remained was how to prove that Darby Edwards was the murderer.

My mind was pleasantly drifting when the door opened and closed behind me. I pivoted in my seat and saw Sir Siger coming up behind my chair. Stiffening with disgust, I opened the borrowed volume to a random page and pretended to read. I wasn't about to let him chase me out of the room.

Sir Siger stood facing the bookshelves, his back to me. "It would seem that our man Friday has come up with some compelling evidence," he rasped.

For the record, Sir Siger had just insulted Watson. The baronet had compared Watson to "Friday" of Robinson Crusoe, a savage and slave of Crusoe; a polished and educated nineteenth-century insult, but an insult nonetheless. I kept my tone nonchalant and retorted, "Dr. Watson has proved invaluable on many cases."

He chuckled with a sneer. "It does not surprise me that my son's freedom is due to the mediocre general practitioner rather than that…publicity-seeking charlatan."

Now he was insulting Watson and Holmes in the same breath! Disregarding civility, I grated, "Where do you get off with accusing your eldest son's saviors with such atrocities? Where do you get the gall?"

He turned to fix me with a steely stare, his dark brown eyes seeming black for their harshness. "You speak of things you do not know, young lady."

"Then enlighten me!" I cried in challenge. "What is there for me to know?"

"He hasn't told you?" Sir Siger fairly crowed. "He hasn't told you! Oh, I wonder what you would think of Sherlock if you knew. Stay far away from him! He wishes to marry you, no doubt, bind you to him with vows that can never be torn asunder. Perhaps after he marries you, the truth will come out, and then you will scarcely retain your shining opinion of the great Sherlock Holmes! Then you will regret your vows!"

That was *it*! I wasn't going to stand for this any longer! Marching up to the hateful man, I stood on tiptoe, looked him hard in the eyes and proclaimed, "Sherlock Holmes is the finest man I have ever known or shall ever know, and if he *should* marry me, then my one regret would be gaining *you* as a father-in-law!" With that flung at him, I glided out of the room, the effect somewhat spoiled when I slammed the door hard.

I stormed through the halls aimlessly, blind with rage. My thoughts knew no coherency, always returning to the question, "What is going on?" Holmes wouldn't tell me, Sherrinford and Mycroft probably wouldn't, and there was no way in hell I was asking Sir Siger. How could I...

Sir Siger had wanted Sherlock to be an engineer, but Sherlock wanted to become a detective. Eventually, after he returned from university, Sherlock left home and went to London. The rest you know.

No, I didn't know, but I had a hunch about who did. Theresa St. Clair.

❦   ❦   ❦

After a brief discussion with a maid, I was barreling across the field behind the Manor, headed for a small, homey cottage on the fringe of the wood. That was the St. Clair residence, and the smoke trailing from the chimney proclaimed them to be home.

I marched past the orderly garden and up the whitewashed steps, banging loudly on the door. "Theresa, open up! It's Nona Brown!"

A few moments later, the door opened and Theresa stood there in a faded housedress, reddish-brown hair tied back in a braid. "Miss Brown, how can I help you?"

"Please," I wheezed, a little out of breath. "Please tell me...I'm going out of my mind...Please tell me what's going on with Sherlock, please!" I was growing desperate.

Theresa's eyes went wide and she tried to shut the door, but I wedged my foot in salesman-style and forced it back open. "Miss Brown, I'm sorry, but I can't!"

"*Please!*"

"What is going on here, Theresa?" said a strong yet elderly voice. I pushed back the door to see a little, white-haired lady in a blue shawl, peering at me with astonishment. This was probably Mrs. Adelaide St. Clair.

I pushed past Theresa and stood before the lady in desperation. "Please, ma'am," I pleaded, too worried and exhausted for pride. She looked at me so kindly that for some reason all of the words and emotions I had pent up inside me just came roaring out. "I'm so anxious about Sherlock, and no one will tell me anything, and he's just, I don't know, Mrs. St. Clair, he's...spiraling downwards and I don't know why and I want to help him but I can't because I don't know what's going on!" I paused and took a deep breath, waiting for her reply. If she gave me another excuse, I would scream.

Thankfully, she did not give me another excuse. Instead she smiled very kindly at me, as if she knew my frustration. "Are you lovers, girl?"

The words snapped me to attention. "What? No. No. No. What? Not at all. No. Uh-uh. No. What? No."

Her smile grew wider. "Do you love him?"

There it was. There in spoken words was the big question, and I definitely knew the answer. "Yes," I half-sobbed, admitting it aloud.

It was if a spell had been broken. Mrs. St. Clair sighed then, resigned but content. "Theresa, put the kettle on," she said, her wise eyes never leaving my face. "We have a long story to tell and it's best done over tea."

CHAPTER 11

In Which I Hear a Greek Tragedy and Meet a Vampire Slayer

I struggled to keep my composure as I was led into the St. Clair's tiny kitchen. The setting sun provided the bare minimum of necessary light through the open windows; if the story was to be as long as I expected, we would have to light the gas lamp on the kitchen table. Adelaide pressed me into one of the hard-backed chairs and sat across the table from me as Theresa busied herself with the teakettle.

As I looked at Mrs. Adelaide St. Clair, I realized why I was so comfortable in her presence. She was a tiny woman with glowing blue eyes that matched her shawl and a long braid of snowy hair. The wrinkles on her face and hands seemed to enhance her appearance rather than detract from it. However, her true worth lay in the wealth of expression in her eyes. She seemed compassionate and trustworthy, and I had only known her for two minutes. It was this compassion that seemed to remind be of my father, soothing my wearied nerves and keeping me from fidgeting until Theresa joined us at table.

"You should know, Miss Brown," Adelaide began in a clear voice, "that I would not be telling you this if my husband had not told me of your devotion to Sherlock. I am afraid that curiosity has always been his besetting flaw. In fact, he volunteered to be your driver in order to satisfy his curiosity. Either way, I believe that Violet would have wanted you to know."

Mr. St. Clair had been listening to Holmes and me the entire time? Oh, I had totally overlooked him! Still, it wasn't like I was trying to hide anything, and if his snooping got me the information I needed, then I minded even less. A fragment floated back up to me. "Violet?"

Adelaide nodded. "Lady Violet Holmes, Sir Siger's poor wife, God rest her soul. I was her chambermaid and confidant, even before she was married."

Now here was something concrete. Lady Violet was Holmes' mother and, from the sound of it, most sincerely dead. "What happened to her?" I asked, wavering between eagerness and respect for the dead.

"I am getting to that, impatient young woman," she replied sternly, but without rancor. I subsided into silence and she continued. "Sir Siger Holmes was an officer in the army, but was honorably discharged when he inherited the manor and title after his elder brother died in a fall from a horse. He knew he needed a wife, so he found one in Violet. Theirs was originally a marriage of convenience, but Sir Siger grew to love his delicate wife and she was devoted to him in turn. They had three children, as you know, Peter, Robert and William. After..."

"What?" I interrupted. "What did you call them?"

Theresa picked up the explanation. "Oh, those are their first names. The names they use now are their middle names."

"So Holmes' full name is William Sherlock?"

"William Sherlock Scott, actually."

I grinned with the sheer revelation of it. William Sherlock Scott Holmes? What was it with this family and long-winded names? I wasn't even about to guess with Mycroft and Sherrinford. I found that I preferred Holmes' middle name; William sounded so...ordinary.

"We run far afield of our story," said Adelaide, directing us back on course. I listened raptly. "After Sherlock was born, Sir Siger's restless spirit propelled the family on travels across the Continent. The boys received very little formal schooling, learning from experiences in the back of a carriage. Those were wonderful times for the Holmes', travel and adventure, never lingering in once place for more than two years. Trevor and I managed the estate in their absence and I often received long letters from Lady Violet, telling me of Paris or Munich or Venice, wherever they happened to be at the time.

"The Holmes' returned to Oakstaff in the spring, seven years after their departure. Trevor and I were astonished at how the boys had grown. Sherrinford was nineteen then, a fine young man, so much like his father. Mycroft was fourteen, forever with a book under his arm, just beginning to round out, and little Sherlock, his mother's favorite, who had been a babe in arms when they left, was a lovely boy of seven. Sir Siger was his usual gregarious self and Lady Violet was as sweet-tempered as ever. The first year at Oakstaff was simple and carefree, but the next fall, however, brought a great tragedy to the Holmes household.

Sherrinford was at Oxford that year, Mycroft absorbed in study of his own and Sherlock left with only his parents. The only child in the area close to his age was Jamie Richardson, but he lived on the old estate some distance from the manor. Thus, whenever an invitation came from the Richardsons to tea or luncheon, Sherlock would always accompany the elders.

"That fall was a time of fear for North Riding. A notorious thief, known only as the Black Fox, had been pilfering the houses of the wealthy, sometimes in broad daylight! The thief's daring made Sir Siger uneasy, and he ordered his family and all of the retainers to stay close to the Manor, but the Richardsons had no such misgivings and once more extended the usual invitation to tea. Sir Siger forbade the outing because he had business to tend to and would be unable to escort them. Young Sherlock was bitterly disappointed by the refusal and confided in his mother, who sought to placate her husband to please her son. Sir Siger was still wary as he would not be able to escort them but wanted to please his wife, so he agreed to let the pair go so long as they returned before nightfall.

"From here I can only tell you what I learned from hearsay. As Lady Violet and the Richardsons took tea, Sherlock and Jamie were running amok on the grounds, playing boyish games. Lady Violet accidentally spilled some tea on her dress and excused herself to the kitchen to try and repair the stain. After some minutes, a gunshot was heard and Mr. Richardson ran to the kitchen. The kitchen door leading outside was open, and Violet…was already dead. The only conclusion was the Black Fox." Oh, God. My stomach twisted at the thought of Holmes' poor mother and in anticipation of the rest of the tale, for I had a funny feeling that I knew where this story was going.

"The entire village was shocked. Condolences were sent from as far as Town. Sherrinford returned from university for the funeral but left again soon after. Sir Siger was bereft and would spend days at a time in seclusion, leaving his sons to practically fend for themselves. Mycroft, though only fifteen, was already studying for the entrance exam at Oxford to follow his brother, but he interspersed his own studies with the education of Sherlock." Adelaide's face creased into a smile at the memory. "The two of them would sit on a bench in the village street and tell the entire lives of anyone who passed by. I won't pretend to know how they did it, but they were always right.

"However, a few months after Violet's death, it became obvious that there was a change in Sir Siger. He became withdrawn and sullen to his neighbors and openly hostile towards his youngest son. I believe that Sir Siger blamed himself for not being firm with Lady Violet and refusing to let her leave the Manor but, unwilling to shoulder the guilt himself, he cast the burden on Sherlock, blaming the boy's desire to attend the tea for causing Violet's death."

What??

"The next year Mycroft passed the entrance exams and went off to Oxford. The lad was nowhere near adulthood, but none of us were surprised at his acceptance. In his absence I pleaded with Sir Siger not to neglect Sherlock's education. Finally, he acquiesced and hired a rather promising professor with a turn for mathematics. However, Sherlock loathed him and the fellow only stayed for a year and a half." Her expression grew thoughtful. "What was the chap's name? Professor Arty-something?"

Theresa interjected. "That was his last name. James Moriarty."

What?? "Moriarty!" I cried with astonishment, startling the two St. Clairs.

"Yes, I believe that was the name. Why?" asked a curious Theresa.

I gripped my chair beneath the table and forced myself to speak clearly. "I...knew a Moriarty once. The name just surprised me." They were distracted from further questions by the whistling of the teakettle. I was absurdly grateful. Holmes' arch-nemesis, the Napoleon of Crime, had been his childhood tutor? Oh, the irony.

Theresa went to prepare the tea and Adelaide continued with her history. "After the tutor's failure, Sherlock was sent off to a boarding school in a nearby town, and Sir Siger became all the more abrasive. Although he did not drink, seeing himself as too strong for the crutch of alcohol, he forsook no opportunity to lash out at those close to him. As the years passed, Sir Siger's grief began to slowly...well, unhinge him, and he sought to exile the memory of his wife. In his anger he sold or destroyed all of her belongings and never spoke her name again, trying with all his might to banish her face from his mind.

"However, his efforts were daunted when the children returned home from school for holiday and he saw Sherlock. It would be no exaggeration to say that Sherlock greatly resembles his mother. In fact, there is very little of Sir Siger in him at all. Sherlock was a living testament to Violet Holmes, and it haunted Sir Siger. At first unconsciously, then consciously, he shifted the blame from himself to his youngest son.

"Things were easier for everyone when Sherlock was at boarding school, but when he returned for Christmas and summer holiday, Sir Siger would avoid him, degrade him, do all in his power to remove himself from the situation. He even started a rumor suggesting that Sherlock was not his son!" Oh, no. All of a sudden, the 'bastard' comment in the billiard room made perfect sense. I mentally kicked myself. How could I have been so dense? "Sherrinford and Mycroft were outraged and tried to help Sherlock all they could," Adelaide continued, "pleading with their father, but their efforts seemed to have little effect on Sir Siger or the boy.

"Trevor and I watched this vein continue for years, each year Sir Siger a bit more vindictive, each year Sherlock a bit more withdrawn. Oh, the squire never left a visible scar on his son, but the scars on his soul went twice as deep for it. The squire's final stroke came after Sherlock's own return from university, when Sir Siger insisted that he become an engineer. By that time, Mycroft was already in London and Sherrinford was at Oakstaff.

"Sir Siger knew of the lad's decision to become a detective, but that simply provided more fuel for his insistence. I do not believe he seriously cared about the boy's career; he simply wanted an excuse to cast him off. He got his excuse. Sherlock refused to bend to his father's wishes and the man practically disowned him, granting Sherlock a monthly pittance and sending him to Town. He has never returned until now.

She sighed, signaling the end of her tale. "So, young lady, now you know." She paused suddenly and her face softened. Dipping into the pocket of her housedress, she withdrew a handkerchief and handed it to me. I took it, not understanding until I placed my hand against my face. My fingers came away wet. Berating myself, I wiped saltwater from my face. *Stupid girl! Crying in front of strangers! Shame on you!* Actually, I had been so caught up in the story that I had not known I was crying. Everything was finally explained. Here was the reasoning behind Holmes' introspective nature, his zeal for justice, his distance from mankind and his reluctance to return to Oakstaff.

Rising from the table, my cup of tea untouched, I haltingly excused myself, thanked the St. Clairs and stumbled out into the deepening twilight. I walked slowly across the field back towards the Manor, trying to surmount my emotions once more.

The man blamed his eight-year-old son wanting to play with his friend for causing his wife's death? I thought bitterly. *What a twisted son of a bitch!* The lengths to which people will reach to vindicate their consciences staggered me. My heart was breaking for Holmes, but if he detected even an ounce of pity from me, his pride would be severely damaged. As I walked, I trampled my emotions into the soil of my soul, to be retrieved when the time was right.

❦   ❦   ❦

When I entered the back door of the Manor and headed for the library, I came upon a most welcome distraction. *Miss* Gertrude Hill was walking stolidly across the foyer, dragging her struggling, tear-streaked charge behind her. You could hardly credit the woman with such strength, but despite the lad's best efforts, all four feet of him were being pulled across the floor.

"Let me go!" shrieked Virgil, twisting in vain. "I have to see Father and Uncle Sherlock!"

Miss Hill merely tightened her grip. "I will not have you bothering your elders with such outlandish stories! Since you already ate supper, you shall go without breakfast tomorrow as your punishment."

This set Virgil wailing afresh. Something about the situation rubbed me the wrong way, so I intercepted the pair. "What's all the trouble, Miss Hill?" I asked, perfectly sweet.

"Miss Brown!" cried Virgil with relief.

Miss Hill did not acknowledge the boy. "Master Virgil has been inventing stories and wishes to disturb his parents. I will not tolerate nonsense in my charges."

Inventing stories? What was so bad about an overactive imagination in a six-year-old? However, one glance at Virgil's wide, teary eyes suggested that this was more than a case of tall tales, for the boy seemed honestly upset. Could this pertain to the case? Following my instinct, I decided to take the matter into my own hands. As gracefully as I could, I detached the boy from his governess, who was highly offended at my intrusion as Virgil gratefully clung to my skirt.

"See here, Miss Brown, the Squire trusts my judgment in the rearing of his son!" she cried, balking like a bantam rooster. "You have no right!"

"I am sure that is true, Miss Hill," I replied with formality. "Your judgment is certainly not in question here, but I believe that this may be more than meets the eye. I assure you I shall take full responsibility for Virgil." I excused myself over the protests of the governess and headed for the library, sniffling six-year-old in tow. My instincts told me that Virgil knew something of import to the case, and therefore had the right to an audience.

Our entry into the library was greeted by surprise. Holmes, Watson, Sherrinford, Holly, Mycroft and Sir Siger were arranged around the couches and chairs, sitting up at our approach.

"Nona, where have you been?" asked Watson. "We tried to locate you for supper, but-"

He was cut off as Virgil detached himself from my skirt, dashed forward and reattached himself to Holmes' leg, wailing, "Amiss, Uncle Sherlock! I saw something amiss!"

The room dissolved into general uproar, only adding volume to the boy's wails.

Sherrinford and Holly moved to comfort their son, but Holmes had other ideas. "Virgil!" he snapped at his nephew, seizing him by the arms. "Take a deep breath and hold it!"

The command in his voice broke though to the child and the room quieted as he complied, standing with held breath and dripping tears. "Now let out half," Holmes ordered. Virgil did so, exhaling a measured breath. "Half again." The lad obeyed. "Now all of it." Virgil sagged as he exhaled. "Now," said Holmes in the quiet that followed. "Tell me what you saw."

"Uncle Darby is a vampire!"

"*What?*" came the general consensus as all adult eyes seemed to focus on me. Sir Siger glowered at me and I felt like kicking myself for the second time that night. *Well, so much for pertinence to the case.*

Holmes, however, did not bat an eye at the outrageous claim. "Go back to the beginning, Virgil, and tell me everything you saw." He sat back in his chair and steepled his fingers, fixing his nephew with his unfathomable gaze.

Suddenly aware of this scrutiny, Virgil made a valiant effort for maturity, straightening and scrubbing at his face as he began his narrative in a shaky voice. "I-I was up in the nursery after supper. I was watching the grounds with my telescope." He paused and turned to his father, "The one you gave me last Christmas." Sherrinford nodded and gestured for his son to continue. "When I looked near the stables, I saw Uncle Darby."

"Darby Edwards!" exclaimed Mycroft. "You are quite sure of this, Virgil?"

The boy nodded in the affirmative, warming to his tale. "Yes, it was Uncle Darby, but he was dressed funny. He was dressed up all raggedy, like the black-smith when he's working hard." Darby Edwards in rags, not five hours after we left him? That smacked of disguise. "But he was talking to someone else! It was one of the maids! It was...Jenna or Emma; I couldn't tell."

Virgil frowned with thought before continuing. "They were talking very close together, and...I watched and...he *bit* her on the *neck*!" His tiny eyes were wide with remembered horror. "I dropped the telescope and ran away as fast as I could! I told Miss Hill what happened, but she didn't believe me. Miss

Brown did though," he added, casting a beatific smile at me. "And that's exactly what I saw, Uncle Sherlock, all of it."

Now we adults were in a moral quandary. What Virgil had described sounded suspiciously like a romantic assignation, but how to explain that to a six-year-old? And if we didn't explain, the boy's nights would be haunted by vampires. Faced with the problem, I did what my father had done when I complained of monsters outside all those years ago.

"Virgil," I began, putting a hand on the boy's shoulder and sinking to his eye level. "This is very serious, what you've told us. So here's what I want you to do. Go to the kitchen and get some dried garlic and rosemary. Sprinkle a tiny bit of both by both the front and back doors, and don't go outside or let anyone in, no matter what. Keep paying attention to anything out of the ordinary. We're all counting on you to keep the vampires out."

Virgil was dumbfounded by the thought of an adult taking him seriously, but as he glanced about the room, he saw nary a glimmer of amusement among his elders. "I won't let any vampires in this house!" he exclaimed bravely, running off to the kitchen.

That should keep the scamp occupied, I thought, *and banish any nightmares he might have* There were smiles and a few good-natured chuckles around the room before we discussed the more serious matter at hand. I seated myself on a sofa next to Watson, trying not to look at Holmes.

"Edwards and an unknown housemaid," mused Mycroft around a cigar. "If this is true, it forces a rather obvious explanation to spring to mind: perhaps he is pumping her for information. Can anyone suggest an alternate reason?"

There was a chorus of grumbles and groans in the negative. "Playing on the affections of a maid to gain knowledge of the household," said Holmes thoughtfully, lighting a cigarette. "Efficient, if rather cold-blooded. What are you grinning at, Nona?" Oh, sure, like he had any call in criticism. Milverton's housemaid sprang forcefully to mind, until I remembered that that particular case hadn't occurred yet. I waved away his comment and he let it go.

"Now hold a moment, brothers mine," rumbled Sherrinford. "I still find the idea of Darby Edwards as traitor a bit far-fetched. For years he has been a devoted neighbor and an excellent friend. What possible motive could he have?"

"It is motive that eludes us and motive that we need." Holmes drew deeply on his cigarette. "We cannot prosecute Edwards until we have evidence, we cannot obtain evidence without searching his home, and we cannot search his home without adequate reason. Hence, a motive." He stood and discarded the cigarette in the crackling fireplace. "Perhaps a discreet conversation with

'Jenna' or 'Emma' will yield some results." Typical Holmes, he strode from the room without another word. I saw no further reason to linger, so I politely excused myself and followed my grumbling stomach to the kitchen.

❧   ❧   ❧

Having missed supper in favor of Greek theater, I headed to the kitchen in hopes of wheedling a sandwich out of the cook. On my way I passed a diminutive vampire slayer with an intent expression on his freckled face, headed for the front door with two jars in his fists. I somehow managed to keep back my smile until I passed him.

The cook, one Mrs. Clark, was appropriately sympathetic and whipped up a cold ham-and-mustard sandwich and an apple. She hesitated a bit over my request for strong coffee, but acquiesced after a warning. I didn't need the warning; I had no intention of sleeping much that night.

When my sandwich was crumbs, my apple a core, and the whole meal drowned in two cups of coffee, I felt somewhat myself again and set out to pass the time until bedtime. The library had emptied, but I spotted Sherrinford gleefully helping his son scatter garlic and rosemary in the front hall. I smiled again at the sight and moved on. Holmes was nowhere to be seen; he was probably in the servant's quarters questioning Jenna and Emma. Mycroft was in the study, pouring over something official-looking, so I did not disturb him. As I prowled the hallways, I was halted by the sound of piano music coming from the music room. Following the sound, I peeked into the spacious room and gaped at the musician. It was Watson!

Watson sat at the piano, coaxing a simple tune from the ivory keys with his surgeon's hands. The tune he played was much like the man himself: uncomplicated, unpresumptuous, definitely British, but soothing and a joy to hear. I had no idea that he was musically inclined! Suddenly, it struck me that I actually knew very little about Watson. The good doctor was usually content in Holmes' shadow and often steered conversation away from himself completely.

The song ended and I burst into spontaneous applause from my place in the doorway. Watson pivoted on the piano bench, scarlet from collar to hairline, but relaxed at the sight of me. "Bravo, Watson!" I exclaimed. "That was wonderful! I had no idea you could play!"

He sheepishly returned his gaze to the keys. "It's nothing, really. I took a few lessons as a boy, and I just thought-"

"Watson," I interrupted his self-depreciation. "Just say 'thank you,' okay?"

He grinned like a boy. "Thank you," he echoed dutifully.

I came over and sat next to him on the spacious piano bench, poking a key experimentally. The lone note sounded harsh to my ears, a fitting parallel to my state in life. I wanted to talk to Watson about Holmes and the situation I was in, but I was at a loss as to how to phrase it without sounding foolish. I chewed the inside of my lip and burned holes in the ivory as I pondered.

Once again Watson solved my problem for me. "Thinking about Holmes, Nona?"

I snapped my head up. "How did you know?" Oops. There went my big secret.

He smiled. "You look very pensive. You've been wearing that look a great deal lately, especially when in connection with Holmes." He paused. "Am I in error?"

I sighed. Of course Watson knew about my feelings for Holmes; I think he knew before I did! Well, I had wanted to talk, so I suppose I got my wish. "You're right, Watson, and you know that. I-I know that I…love Holmes, but he just…well, I just…I want to…I don't know. I want to tell him…you know, how I feel, but…oh, hell. What are you snickering at, Watson?"

His shoulders shook in silent laughter. "Oh, Nona, I was just thinking on how perfect Holmes and you are for each other. I find I am tempted to believe in fate."

"What brought *that* up all of a sudden?"

"The two of you are both too proud for your own good." He raised an eyebrow, sliding into lecture-mode. "If either one of you had just broken down and confessed your feelings at any time before this point, you and I would not be having this conversation right now! Sometimes I have wanted to simply-"

"Whoa, Watson, back up! You said 'either one of you.' Am I to assume that you think Holmes might love me too?"

He gave me a look that said, quite plainly and unmistakably, *Duh.*

Holmes loved me? Holmes loved me! I wanted to scream and shout and jump for joy with the certainty of it, but I forced myself to play the role of devil's advocate. "You are basing this conjecture on what?"

"Observation and deduction," he said loftily, earning a snort from myself. "Naturally, Nona, you lack eyes in the back of your head, so you cannot see when someone looks at you from across a room, nor can you notice the person's expression. Simply put, I can. I have watched Holmes watch you with a rather heartfelt expression for roughly four months now. I have watched you do the same to him. I have been patiently waiting for the day when you both surmount your damnable pride and finally accept your feelings, and thus far my waiting has been in vain."

I felt my face light up with happy revelation. Holmes loved me. Oh, happy, wonderful, glorious day. "Hopefully, Watson, you won't have to wait much longer. So, oh guru of the softer emotions, what do I do now?"

He appeared thoughtful, the doctor considering possible treatment. "When we return to London, perhaps a swift kick in the trousers." I laughed aloud at that, but he continued. "As for now, nothing."

"Nothing?"

"Holmes has the case to attend to, and I do not believe that a confession of love would be helpful to his concentration." His expression grew grave. "Bide your time, Nona. The opportunity will present itself, I am sure. But when it does, be sure to seize it."

Good old Watson. I gave him a sisterly kiss on the cheek. "Thanks for the advice, Doc, and not a word of this to Holmes."

He returned his gaze and hands to the piano keys. "As always, Nona, I am the very soul of discretion. Best of luck to you, my dear. I fear you will need it." He resumed playing as I left the room and returned to my chamber.

After a long, luxurious bath, I whiled away the hours lying on my bed and staring at the ceiling, inventing any number of scenarios in which I confessed my love to Sherlock Holmes. Invariably, each scenario ended with him kissing me until we were both threatened with suffocation. The moon rose outside my bay windows and the stars appeared and finally I deemed it sufficiently late enough to emerge. It was time to put my plan into action. I rescued Bernie Flynn from behind the bookcase, destination: The Goose and Crown Pub. Chances were good that the genial Irish fiddler could probably glean more information than the unconventional lady detective could. I quickly slipped into my alter-ego, put on my glasses, took a moment to compose my thoughts, seized my fiddle and headed out the door on my mission.

The manor was deathly still. Creeping through the darkened hallways and down the grand staircase, I strained my eyes for signs of life. There was none to be seen, so I breathed a sigh of relief despite the deepening shadows. Relaxing a bit, I walked across the foyer, boots crunching on dried rosemary, and reached for the brass doorknob. Suddenly, before I could react or even think, a pair of strong arms gripped me from behind, pinning me tight! A male hand smothered my startled cry, rendering me speechless. I could only stare wildly as a rough, coarse voice rasped in my ear.

"And just where do you think *you're* going?"

CHAPTER 12

In Which I Battle with Demons and Start a Bar Fight

I was utterly terrified. I couldn't struggle, paralyzed as I was with shock. My violin case fell to the floor with a noisy crack in the dark silence. My breath was rasping through my nose; I could smell my assailant's musty clothes…and shag tobacco…and sandalwood soap…I experimentally craned my head back and in the weak moonlight beheld a brilliant smile and a pair of dancing gray eyes.

"Holmes!" I cried, but he was still covering my mouth with his hand, so it came out "Hmmphs!" He laughed quietly and released me as I turned on him in a hushed rage. "Holmes! You…you b-big dumbass!" Stupid me, I stopped myself just in time before I could say "bastard." "You jerk! You scared the living crap out of me!"

He grinned impishly, never batting an eye at my modern diatribe; add a few freckles and he would have been a much taller Virgil. "Childish, Nona, I completely agree, absolutely juvenile. It really was unworthy of me." Despite his self-denouncement, the grin grew impossibly wider. "But I just could not resist!"

It was then that I noticed his attire. Gone was the gentleman's evening suit; Holmes was clad in a common laborer's outfit, complete with cloth cap and red bandana handkerchief. He eyed me up and down as I did the same to him. After days of peeking at him out of the corner of my eyes and steadfastly avoiding his gaze, I used the opportunity to feast my eyes upon him. At the same time, though, I was internally cringing, knowing that after months of freedom

I had finally been found out. Now Holmes would breach any number of arguments, forbid me from using Bernie again, and probably try to confine me to
my room for the remainder of the case. Whether or not he would succeed,
however, was another matter entirely.

Instead, he simply cocked a sardonic eyebrow. "Great minds think alike, I
believe the adage runs. Headed out on the town, Nona?"

I was stunned by his nonchalance. "Well I, well, yes, but I-"

"Perhaps you would allow me to escort you?" he asked, taking my hand and
bowing over it, as courtly as if we were in a shimmering ballroom rather than a
dark foyer. "The walk will be so much more pleasant with a companion,
wouldn't you say, Miss Brown?"

"You aren't mad at me for this?" I asked. My mind refused to surmount his
easy acceptance of my cross-dressing.

He straightened, not releasing my hand. "Nonsense, you're a big girl; you
can cross the street by yourself." I blushed a bit at that echo of my own words,
glad for the night to hide it. "This is no surprise to me, Nona."

The weight of his words staggered me. "You knew about this? How? When?"

He smiled again, raising a slender finger. "If I may be permitted to answer
the last question first, since early June. As to how, it was quite accidental, I
assure you. One night as I was walking back to Baker Street from the conclusion of a case, I noticed Wiggins conversing with an older urchin. I would not
have thought twice about it if not for the ears."

"The ears?" I echoed foggily.

His hand left mine and traveled to the side of my face, tugging softly on the
offending organ. "They are the only part of the body unable to be disguised.
Your costume is quite good, Nona, and your attention to minutiae is admirable. If you had pulled your cap down over your ears, you would have escaped
my sight completely."

"Only to be spotted because I was wearing my cap low in the summer," I
retorted. Actually, I was glowing inside from his praise, my honest pride
destroying any hint of embarrassment.

Holmes laughed, quietly but heartily, at my rejoinder. "Touché, Nona!" he
exclaimed, placing a hand over his heart to cover an imaginary wound. Was it
my own imagination, or was he getting closer? "I am pleased to hear of your
faith in my deductive abilities."

"Stop teasing me," I protested, trying not to sound breathless.

"I am quite in earnest," he replied softly.

"Then stop fishing for compliments." God, how I loved him. More than anything else, I just wanted tangle my fingers in his tousled hair and press my lips to his. Why had Watson told me to wait? It was becoming increasingly harder to remember.

For a long second, we were suspended in the age-old dance of courtship, simply gazing at the other. If he had moved even half an inch closer, I wouldn't have been able to restrain myself, and gladly so. But alas, I was undone; he moved a step backwards.

"The constables outside are still on twenty-four hour guard," said he, "and they are ignorant of Sherrinford's exoneration. I doubt that our presence would be welcome. However-" he said quickly, forestalling my question, "I know of an alternate route." He extended an arm to me as if we were about to stroll down the Strand. "Shall we, Miss Brown?" he asked with a smirk.

I rolled my eyes, hiding my romantic frustration in mock exasperation. "You're in one of your moods again, aren't you?" He did not reply and I sensed that perhaps this was an apology for his behavior in the carriage. Personally, I do not believe in grudges. I slipped my arm into his and he led me back into the manor, our first fight reconciled as strangely as it had begun.

♦   ♦   ♦

Holmes led me into the now-familiar library, lighting with a match a pair of candles on a side table and handing one to me. Shutting the library door, he also shut out the moonlight, leaving the flickering candles as our only illumination.

Holmes gestured and led me over to the far left corner, pointing to a thick volume in the middle of a shelf. "If you were casually browsing this library, would you reach for this volume?"

I lifted my candle and peered at the book's inscription. "Record of Financial Accounts, 1600-1700AD," I read aloud. "Certainly not."

Holmes smiled once more. I believe that he had smiled more in the past three minutes than in the past three days. "I was counting on that." He reached out and pulled back on the volume, causing an audible click. Handing his candle to me, I watched in awe as he pulled back on the bookcase and it swung back like a door, revealing a descending stone staircase!

"A secret passage!" I exclaimed. "Oh, this place is awesome!"

"I take it that it meets with your approval." Holmes took his candle back and led the way down the dusty stairs.

At the bottom of the stairs, I could not believe my eyes. The staircase opened into an enormous underground chamber, wrought with gray stone and arched ceilings. Silent stone angels with sightless eyes guarded several marble sarcophagi, lined orderly throughout the chamber. At the far end an arched doorway led deeper into the bowels of the earth. The gravity and dignity of this place was overwhelming.

"The family crypt," said Holmes softly. There was no one to hear us, but the atmosphere demanded respectful silence or at least hushed voices. "Four generations of my family have been buried here."

"Wow," was all I could say. Holmes had a faraway look in his eyes, and he drifted among the marble tombs, lost in the ties of blood. I didn't begrudge him the time; we were in no rush. Candle in hand, I perched myself nearby and looked around the room. The air was stale and dry, permeated with the dust of hundreds of years and hundreds of bones. Most graveyards gave me either a sense of peace or eeriness, but the Holmes vault seemed...dissatisfying to me, and I couldn't imagine why. Swinging my legs, I rocked back and forth on my seat, letting my mind drift...

"GET OFF OF THERE!"

I vaulted off of my seat and halfway across the room, beholding a white-faced detective. Looking back, I realized what I had been sitting on: one of the sarcophagi. *So?* I thought. *It's not like whoever it is will mind, thank you very...*My mouth went dry as I approached the tomb and read the engraved inscription.

Violet Holmes, nee Sherrinford
1829-1870
Beloved Daughter, Wife and Mother

I was too shocked to think straight. I-I had been sitting on...I shuffled backwards as fast as I could, bumping into a marble coffin on the opposite side, watching Holmes in mortified silence. He completely ignored me, his outburst forgotten as he slowly approached the tomb. His expression a studied blank, he laid a trembling hand on the surface, his face almost as white as the stone itself. Eyes closed with strain, he drew deep, regular breaths, seemingly trying not to sob. His pain was tangible.

I refused to stand for it any longer. The emotions I had previously buried erupted to the surface in a volcano. Striding purposefully forward, I seized his free hand in a vice grip, drawing his eyes to mine in surprise. "It was not your fault," I enunciated, tightening my grip on his hand as he tried to pull away. "If it was anyone's fault at all, it was the Black Fox's, *not* yours."

At that moment I joined the infinitesimally small ranks of those who had completely stunned Sherlock Holmes. He stared at me without comprehension for several seconds until finally, terrible realization dawned in his eyes.

"You-you know?" he gasped. "You *know*? How??"

"Yes, Sherlock, I know. I know everything, and the how is not important. What is important is that *you* know that your mother's death was not your fault."

Holmes shook his head dazedly, his normally keen mind buried under an avalanche of emotion and confusion. "No, he said...he always said..." He slid down to sit on the floor, eyes vacant.

I fell to my knees and took his beautiful hands in mine. The time for subtlety was past; this was all-out war I waged against the inner demons that had long tormented this suffering man. "He was wrong, Sherlock. Your father felt guilty when your mother died, so he tried to blame you for it. And you've been letting him! Siger has been killing you for years, and you've been letting him! You have to realize that, Sherlock! Everything that man has said about you is a lie, including your being a bastard-"

At that word, Holmes' face suffused with shame and he turned from me. "How can you know that," he whispered in harsh reproach, "and still see any worth in me? How can you know that my blood is tainted and not revile me? Do not pity me, Nona. I could bear your scorn, your disgust, but not your pity."

My hands left his and flew to his head, turning it and forcing him to meet my gaze. "It's not pity; I just don't believe it's true! And even if it is true, Sherlock, I don't care! Do you hear me? I don't care! Neither does Mycroft or Sherrinford, and if Watson knew, he wouldn't care either! You and your father are the only ones who care, and your father he is, even if he doesn't deserve a son like you." His face weakened and I let my tone soften, my hand straying to brush his hair out of his eyes. "I don't care about your birthright or your past. I care about you, Sherlock Holmes, the world's greatest and most infuriating detective. Please, Sherlock. Your blood does not dictate who you are. Don't let him torture you any longer." I took a deep breath and went in for the final plunge. "Your heart is far too precious to bear false shame."

Even if I live forever, I shall not forget the face of my beloved that night. Holmes' expression was a cacophony of pain and hope in the flickering candlelight as the walls around his soul crumbled to dust. A single tear slipped from his shining eyes and traced a path down his pale, sculpted face. Gently, I raised a hand to brush it away, only to have it enfolded in his larger one. "You…care about me?" he asked softly, the utter need in his normally acerbic voice bringing me to the point of tears. I nodded slowly and with absolute seriousness. Holmes' breath hitched slightly and he hesitated half a second before slowly moving his face closer to mine. I closed my eyes in anticipation, preparing to relish the moment that had haunted my dreams for, oh, so long…

"*Who dares to disturb the tombs of the dead??*" A sepulchral, disembodied voice boomed out, echoing across the stone chamber. With a shared gasp, Holmes and I flew apart, Holmes hurriedly snuffing his candle as I fumblingly did likewise. The room was plunged into utter darkness, leaving me flailing around in search of Holmes, visions of ghosts and goblins and things that go bump in the night flashing through my head. My waving hand found the side of Holmes' head, and he swiftly caught it and held it tight as the voice continued in the pitch-blackness. "*Who comes among the tombs of the dead at this fateful witching hour?? Quake, ye mortals, and despair, for this night you shall join our ranks!*"

My stomach clenched in fear as deep laughter rang out. Suddenly, light flared out near the base of the stairs, revealing…Mycroft! The elder Holmes was nonchalantly lighting a candle of his own, a large, thick envelope pinned under his corpulent arm.

Mycroft! I wanted to kill the dirty rat. To think that Holmes and I had almost—oh, I wanted to *kill* him!

"Are you children enjoying yourself?" Mycroft said with more than a hint of a smirk on his doughy face.

"My *dear* Mycroft," replied Holmes tightly as he re-lit our own candles, no emotion on his face save irritation. The walls of his soul had been hastily rebuilt with no evident weakness in their foundation. Was he as disappointed as I, or just annoyed at the trick? There was no way I could tell. "Have you some ulterior motive for delaying us, or do you simply delight in frightening Nona?"

Excuse me? Frightening Nona? Who is he kidding? Thankfully, I was spared from interjection as Mycroft continued. "I believe I have something of interest for you, my dear Sherlock. It arrived for you by courier a few hours ago." He passed Holmes the envelope and Holmes handed me the candle. He made to open the envelope, but stopped as he saw it had already been unsealed.

I barely had time to notice that it was from the Land Office in London when Holmes gestured sharply to the writing on the front. "My dear Mycroft," said he, "have you neglected to observe that these particular documents are addressed to Sherlock Holmes?"

Mycroft glowered at his younger brother, annoyed at being caught snooping. "Read the documents, Sherlock."

Holmes pulled out what seemed to be copies of deeds and transactions, all of which made zero sense to me. However, Holmes seemed to glean a great deal from them and embarked on one of those non-conversations that only he and his brother could pull off.

"It would be worth thousands."

"He paid but a fraction."

"The scandal?"

"Of course."

"Does he still own it?"

"Sold not three months past."

"Then Sherrinford-"

"Likely."

"*More* than likely."

"Could someone *please* tell me what's going on?" Yes, that was me.

Holmes returned the papers to Mycroft, answering my demand offhandedly. "In the proverbial nutshell, Nona, a few years prior, Darby Edwards circumspectly purchased the Richardson estate from its ruined master for less than a quarter of its true worth. Then quite recently he sold it."

"And?" I prompted impatiently.

"*And* we need more data before we can theorize further, which we will not obtain by standing here all night."

"I do not envy you your task, Sherlock," Mycroft rumbled, "but I wish you good luck, both of you." He paused thoughtfully. "Do try to stay out of trouble." With a terse nod for his brother, Holmes turned and strode towards the doorway at the opposite chamber.

Hesitating for a moment, I caught Mycroft's gaze, drew a swift finger across my throat and mouthed, "I'm going to kill you." Was it a trick of the light, or did the man wink at me? I never found out, for I was soon speeding after Holmes.

🍁   🍁   🍁

I ran after Holmes down a subterranean tunnel, my candle flame wavering and violin case rattling. I slowed and walked next to him, once more resorting to watching him from the corner of my eye. He seemed in no hurry to resume our former scenario, his own gaze steadfastly forward. A part of me (a rather large part) wanted to seize him and pick up where we had left off, but with a great deal of reluctance I turned that down I wanted Holmes to make the decision about a relationship on his own without being forced into it. I was back to the waiting game. *Gonna kill Mycroft, gonna kill that freaking butterball...*

My brooding was broken by Holmes' voice, but he did not breach the subject for which I had hoped. Instead he gestured to the expanse of tunnel we were currently occupying. "You know, Nona, compared to the rest of Oakstaff, this tunnel is actually quite recent. The manor's foundation was laid in the late 1500s, but this tunnel was constructed only about a century or two ago, in the days of the Tudors."

In anyone else I would have thought it an odd topic for conversation, especially considering our recent actions, but Sherlock Holmes in full steam could weave a conversation from antique violins to Tibetan meditations to the mysteries of heredity with nary a seam. I suspected him of intentionally changing the conversation, but I did not object, allowing myself to go with the flow of discussion. "I'm assuming that it was built for a reason."

Holmes nodded. "The tunnel was dug in secret by my great-grandfather during the Anglican Reformation. He sympathized with the Catholic clergy and built the tunnel to hide them from Henry VIII and Elizabeth."

"Wow, that's incredible! A piece of history is sitting right under your house. I never knew that much about Tudor England, you know; we just skimmed over it in history class. Actually, we skimmed over Victorian England too." Holmes gave me a funny look and I pointed at myself. "I'm from two centuries in the future, remember?" He made an enlightened noise and returned his gaze to the tunnel. "Holmes, that reminds me; ever since I got here, you've been remarkably blasé about my time traveling. You've never questioned my story and you've hardly ever asked me about the future or what things will be like someday. Why is that?"

"As you well know, Nona, a favorite maxim of mine is that when you eliminate the impossible, whatever remains-"

"However improbable, must be the truth," I finished. "Yes, yes, but that doesn't answer my question."

"When I first made your acquaintance," Holmes continued, smiling a bit in remembrance, "I validated your claim through simple process of elimination. There were three explanations to your outlandish allegation: you were lying, you were insane, or you were telling the truth. A liar would never invent such an outrageous story as time travel and the clarity of your words and expression removed the doubt of insanity. Ergo, you were telling the truth. Watson's corroboration only strengthened my own deductions."

"And that's it?" I asked incredulously.

He nodded in reply. "And as to my lack of interest in the future, Nona, that is merely because I will not be alive long enough for anything you tell me to be of any usefulness. It is my belief that the mind should be properly organized with only the essentials, as a room in a house, lest it become cluttered with unnecessary information."

"Actually, Holmes," I argued, "studies in the future have suggested that people only use about two percent of their brains. Can you imagine all of the things we accomplish with only two percent? Imagine if we went up to fifty percent!"

"Really?" Holmes' interest was piqued. "That is an interesting tidbit." He paused and looked at me askance. "Perhaps the future holds more than one benefit for me after all."

❦   ❦   ❦

For the remainder of the walk to the village, Holmes and I were engaged in furious debate with myself expounding pop-psychology and him dissecting it. Holmes' intellect was breathtaking and the flow of conversation continued unabated between us as we reached the end of the tunnel, deposited our candles, ascended a ladder, exited via a concealed trapdoor and traversed some two miles to the pub.

The Goose and Crown Pub was only one step above seedy, a semi-reputable gathering place for the lower members of the village. Lurking in the shadows, Holmes and I crept to a grimy window and peered inside. Lights were burning brightly, revealing several men scattered at tables across the ill-swept floor, drinking, talking, drinking, arm-wrestling, and drinking. Did I mention they were drinking?

I whistled incredulously. "It lacks a woman's touch," I mock-appraised. "But it possesses a certain rustic charm, don't you agree, Holmes?" I glanced at him with a smile, but he had a look on his face that reminded me of my father the night of my senior prom. My grin vanished. "Holmes, whatever you're thinking, you can stop thinking it right now!"

His somber expression deepened. "I have made an error in judgment. This is not an appropriate venture for you."

I rolled my eyes. "Holmes, please. If I can stand a corpse in the morgue, I can put up with a bunch of drunks."

He wasn't about to surrender easily. "You are a young lady, Nona, and since you have no living relatives, you fall under my jurisdiction. Your are my responsibility and I must insist that you stay behind."

Okay, it was that kind of chauvinistic crap that really irked me about that century. "Holmes," I began, trying to curb my tongue, "there is a time and a place for chivalry. This is neither. Ah!" I said as he opened his mouth. "Like you said yourself, I'm a big girl. I am no one's responsibility but my own. Besides, you'll be in the same room as me at all times. Now, I'm going in there, so don't follow me in for about five minutes."

Holmes opened his mouth, closed it and opened it again. "Very well, Nona," he finally said. "I doubt that I would acquiesce if not for your previous performances in this alter-ego. You have a certain flair for the stage, Nona."

Just one more shock to that already shocking day. "You had me followed back in London?!"

"I followed you myself."

"But I never saw anything when I went out!"

Mischief lit his gray eyes. "That is exactly what you were supposed to see. Off with you now, lest the spell you cast over me wears off."

Did he mean what I hoped he meant? Damn his ambiguity! I tugged my cap lower, snatched my fiddle case and launched myself from my crouch by the window, walking through the weather-beaten door.

The usual murmur of voices in such an establishment had been boosted by alcohol to an unintelligible drone. None of the windows were open, amplifying the night's summer heat. I tried not to show disgust as I pushed my way past half and fully-inebriated farmhands, stockboys and general loafers, lamenting their lowly stations in life.

I sat at the bar and plopped my fiddle ostentatiously on the scarred and polished surface, lest anyone wonder about my trade. Lowering my voice an octave and adding an Irish lilt, I called, "Pint o' ale, barman, and gimme yer good stuff."

The burly barman glanced up at me from his futile task of cleaning the spotted mugs with a blackened washcloth and grunted in acknowledgement, ambling off to fulfill my order. A moment later he returned, depositing a glass of dark, foamy ale. I took a wary sip, expecting watery, home-brewed swill. Instead, it was of a rather decent quality and the glass was cleaner than expected. Mentally, I moved the barkeep up a notch or two. Still, I didn't do more than sip at the drink; the idea was to obtain information, not to get drunk.

Not more than a couple of minutes later, the bartender spoke. "You a fiddler?" he asked tersely.

"Aye," I replied, keeping to the Irish accent.

"From where?"

"Limerick." I meant the town in Ireland, not the bawdy poems.

"Care to give us a tune?"

This was my break. People are more open to entertainers and bartenders than often their own families. However, I didn't want to jump the gun. "Nothing's for free," I brogued in response.

"The drinks are, if you play for us."

That was good enough for Bernie Flynn. I removed my fiddle from its case, played a few experimental chords, tuned a loose string and launched into my opening song. No matter where I played, I always began with "Down the Old Plank Road." It was a Chieftains reel I remembered from the twenty-first century, an Irish jig with just enough American bluegrass to pique people's interest. Apparently it worked, for soon conversations ceased and toes were set to tapping at the sprightly tune.

After the song ended, enthusiastic applause echoed through the pub. An ill-kept fellow with a red kerchief came up to the bar, placed an empty glass next to me and dropped in a handful of change. I barely had time to catch a gray-eyed wink before several other men shoved coins into the mug, calling out for requests and favorite songs. I complied with the voice of the people, interspersing the requests with my own personal favorites.

I played for about an hour, running through Irish jigs, English ballads, the occasional American bluegrass and once a Cajun zydeco reel. The Goose and Crown crowd had doubled during my concert; I had two mugs filled with change, and the barman was so pleased with the increase in business that he looked ready to adopt me! Replacing my fiddle, I pleaded sore fingers to my expectant admirers and they grudgingly subsided, returning to conversation and ale. I flexed my tired digits (I wasn't lying when I said my fingers were sore!) and entered into discourse with the other fellows at the bar, hoping to steer the conversation to Darby Edwards.

Finally, as I commented on my earnings for the night, one of the farmhands said, "You could play a good night or two o' whist on those coins, fiddler."

I shrugged nonchalantly. "It'd depend on who yer playin' with, I'm sup-posin'. Wid one a' you fellers I'd last a good while, but against one o' these fancy-mansion harse breeders, I'd not last a single hand."

Drunken guffaws from around the bar. "Don't you know it, fiddler! If you staked that against the Edwards whelp, he'd outbid you even if he had ace-high nothing!"

Edwards! Finally! "Edwards? Sounds like too rich a bloke fer me."

"Bah! Edwards wishes he were rich, makes a good show of it too, but for all of his fancy house and carriage he ain't better off than any of us."

"Really?" It took no effort to imbue my voice with interest.

The storyteller nodded sagely, the veritable voice of wisdom. "Yessir, fiddler. Edwards came into money a couple a years ago, lots o' money, but he invested wrong and gambled the rest away. Now he's almost penniless, an' too proud to work for a living like any 'onest man. Sir Roger oughta be ashamed to raise such a layabout son. He'll be beggin' to the Squire soon, and no mistake."

A penniless Darby? That could explain the current state of disrepair of his manor. How very interesting, if it was true, that is. I filed the information away as the conversation drifted away into, what else? Sherrinford Holmes and the murder case.

Nothing they could say would enlighten me on THAT particular topic, so I scanned the room, looking for Holmes. I spotted him at a common table with several others and I silently wished him more luck than I was having. I raised my glass to my lips, only to suppress a gag reflex as a familiar figure appeared in the doorway. Speak of the devil! It was Darby Edwards!

The country lord's son was obviously slumming, dressed in the dirty com-moner's outfit that Virgil had described. I cast a furious glance at Holmes, but his back was to the door and he remained oblivious to our suspect's entrance. My mind was awash in turmoil as I turned back to the bar, praying that noth-ing would happen. I must have somehow angered the fates, for Darby Edwards walked up to the bar and took a seat next to me!

My first thought was that he had seen through my disguise and had come to reveal me, but as the supposed murderer ordered a drink and settled onto his stool, I realized that I was safe. I gripped my mug like a vise and tried not to hyperventilate. I should have known that Darby's corrupt-but-still-Victorian mind could not surmount the idea of a woman, let alone air-headed Nona Brown, cross-dressing. However, I deduced that Holmes was in greater peril than myself; Darby would probably be expecting him to show up and therefore would be looking for the detective.

My fears were confirmed as I noticed Darby slowly scanning the room. After a half-interested scan, he returned to his drink, but if he scrutinized the patrons, he would notice Holmes! Who knew what he would do; the man was a ruthless murderer!

Seemingly from fate itself, a ridiculous solution formed in my head. It was foolish, utterly impractical and almost guaranteed not to work, but I confess that for lack of a better idea, I acted upon it. Tightening my grip on my glass and shifting in my chair, I waited until Darby took a sip of his drink next to me. As he tilted back, I lashed out with my foot and threw his stool back, knocking him to the ground! In the momentum, I flung the remaining contents of my mug onto a burly man sitting directly behind Darby, drenching the man's head! Cracking my voice and switching to Cockney, I roared, "Ey, lads! Drinks are on 'IM!"

Drunken laughter pealed out as the burly man rose from his seat in fury, glaring down on the bearded man who had supposedly soaked him. Darby sat up on the floor, shaking his head dazedly, utterly unprepared for the large boot that connected with his midriff and collapsing again with a whoosh of exhaled air.

A drunken toff sprang to Darby's aid, probably more for the thrill of a brawl than any affection for Edwards. He was joined by another and another until it blossomed into a full-fledged bar fight. I ducked past the brawl, retrieved my violin, and tried to make it clear, but a stray fist caught me painfully in the shoulder and I stumbled against the bar. Before I could react, a set of thin arms hauled me to my feet and unceremoniously shoved me out the door.

Shutting the door, Holmes hauled me up and upbraided me with a mixture of anger and concern. He certainly seemed none the worse for wear. "Are you injured, Nona? What kind of fool stunt was that? I did not know you had a malicious streak."

I brushed his hands away and removed my glasses, wincing at the ache in my shoulder. "It wasn't malice, Holmes! It was providing us with an escape route! Surely you noticed that the guy I knocked down was Darby Edwards."

"Edwards?" echoed Holmes incredulously. "This certainly complicates matters. What did—?" He was interrupted as half a chair came crashing through the pub window, followed by the roar of the angry barman. "Perhaps we could continue this discussion on the return to Oakstaff?" Holmes suggested.

I wholeheartedly agreed as we slipped into the shadows and back toward the Manor.

♦   ♦   ♦

When we were some distance from the village with only the moon for illumination, we slowed from our breakneck pace and caught our breath, slowing our pace to a walk. "Now," Holmes grunted. "Tell me exactly what happened." I recounted all that I had heard and did at the bar, trying to leave out nothing. "Firstly, Nona," Holmes began when I had finished. "That was a foolhardy, reckless, imprudent stunt to perform. True, it was problematic that Edwards appeared, but you and I were committing no crime by frequenting the pub, and if Edwards had seen us, he could not have complained to anyone without exposing himself. Your actions were entirely unnecessary."

Great. I contemplated my dimly-seen feet as we walked, fully conscious of my error. "However," he amended with a smile heard rather than seen. "I will not deny that I rather enjoyed the sight of that cad getting trounced. Execution was a bit shaky, Nona, but full marks for a satisfactory result."

That took some of the bite from his rebuke and I grinned in spite of myself. "So, Holmes, did you glean anything from your efforts?"

"In actuality, Nona, you seem to have gotten the better of me in that respect. I unearthed nothing that I had not previously deduced. The rumor of Darby Edwards in dire financial straits adds another layer to an already-layered case."

"It does seem rather complicated, Holmes."

"On the contrary, it is exceedingly simple. We have data in hand; it merely remains to set it in order." I knew what that meant. From his dingy coat pocket emerged the black briar pipe that Holmes favored and a tin of tobacco. Holmes charged the pipe with dancing fingers and lit a match to set it to smoking. In the brief flare, I caught a glimpse of his profile: chiseled features set, brow furrowed, eyes alight with the scent of his quarry. It reminded me once again that this was Sherlock Holmes, at whose name the black-hearted and unmerciful could not help but shudder.

"Quite the three-pipe problem, eh Holmes?" I asked with jocularity.

"Quite." The brevity of his voice brooked no further conversation. Our walk home was silent, save for the gears winding and grinding in the Great Detective's unfathomable mind.

✤   ✤   ✤

Holmes and I descended through the trapdoor, relit our candles and traversed the length of tunnel without comment. I admit that my throat constricted as we passed through the crypt again, but there were no interruptions this time. We ascended together to the second floor of Oakstaff, pausing before the double doors that led to the ballroom. Here our rooms branched off in separate wings. Our adventure was at an end.

"Well, goodnight, Holmes," I said awkwardly.

"I am afraid not," he replied. "This is assuredly a three-pipe problem and so far I have only consumed one. I do not believe that I shall be retiring tonight."

"Do you want me to sit up with you?" I asked, trying not to yawn. The two cups of Mrs. Clark's coffee were rapidly wearing off.

"No, my dear Nona." *My dear?* "I would not dream of robbing you of your beauty sleep, which you do not need, of course," he hastily amended. "Come, I shall see you to your room."

"Oh, Holmes, there's no need-"

He silenced me by guiding me down the hallway to my room. "As I have recently learned, my dear, there is a time and a place for chivalry. Indulge me."

Okay, he wanted to be overly polite, fine by me. I allowed him to escort me to my door, which I opened and paused in, pulling off my hat and glasses. "Goodnight, Holmes," I said more firmly. With each passing moment, a warm bed was sounding better and better.

Holmes hesitated, as if searching for something to say. "Goodnight, Nona," he said finally. I turned to shut the door, but was halted by an almost-timid, "Nona?"

"Yes?"

The hesitation was longer this time. "Thank you," Holmes said quietly, not meeting my eyes.

I had a funny feeling that I knew what he was thanking me for. "It's true, Holmes," I replied. "*All* of it." Emboldened by my adventurous evening, I actually drew a gentle hand down his astonished face before murmuring "Goodnight," and firmly shutting the door. Safe in my sanctuary, I mechanically stripped, washed and changed, my thoughts decidedly elsewhere. Finally, I slipped into my featherbed and closed my weary eyes with his beloved name on my smiling lips.

I had very pleasant dreams that night.

❦   ❦   ❦

I stretched luxuriously on my poster bed as I drifted up from a wonderfully satisfying dream concerning a detective, two gold rings and a great deal of thrown rice. Early morning shafts of summer gold poured like molasses through the glass of the balcony doors. Dust motes danced like fireflies through the beams of light. I was well-rested, utterly content with my place in the world and very much in love, so all things considered, I felt pretty good that morning.

I washed and leisurely dressed, finally meandering into the breakfast room, confident that Holmes had solved the case as I slept. It may *sound* a bit presumptuous; I mean after all, he was just a man, but he *was* Sherlock Holmes. My anticipation built as I made my way to the well-lit dining room. The breakfast table held the usual suspects: Holmes, Watson, Sherrinford and Holly. Sir Siger, I had learned, did not usually come down for breakfast and Mycroft (*oh yeah, I have to kill him, don't I?*) was once again absent. I encompassed the room with a smile and slid into a vacant chair next to Holmes.

Apparently he had learned his lesson, for the first phrase out of his mouth was a very pleasant, "Good morning, Nona." Was this surprising meekness accompanied by a subtly wry twist?

I settled the napkin in my lap as a maid appeared with a tray of breakfast, setting it before me. I glanced up at Holmes with a conspirator's smile. "Good morning, Holmes. Any luck last night?"

"Regrettably, no." Well, so much for my insight. His expression shifted to mild annoyance as he toyed with his fork. "My vigil was surprisingly unrewarding. Something is eluding me, something…" He shook his head a trifle wearily.

Watson cocked an ear at our conversation. "Trouble with the motive, Holmes? Already exhausted love, money and/or revenge?" Holmes did not answer, lost in abstracted thought.

At that point, Jupiter condescended to join us at table, dropping ungracefully into the place on Holmes' other side. "Have a productive night, Sherlock, Nona?" Mycroft rumbled, sounding altogether too pleased with himself. Holmes, still silent, mechanically pushed the sugar bowl towards Mycroft as he accepted a cup of coffee from the maid.

"Productive?" echoed Watson confusedly. "I say, did I miss something last night?"

I waved it away with my coffee spoon, imbuing my voice with forced nonchalance. "Just a little reconnaissance in town, Watson, nothing very interesting."

"Oh, nothing but the fact that you were in disguise as a man," mused Mycroft, heaping sugar into his coffee and obviously deriving great pleasure at the incredulous stares suddenly fixed on me. I gritted my teeth as I smiled sweetly at him. The man was just evil lately! A bit of pawky humor I didn't mind, of course, but really!

"You were dressed as a man?" asked Holly, astonishment tingeing her voice.

Sherrinford was having just as hard a time swallowing it. "Nona, I recognize that you are more independent than most young women, but surely that is a bit much!"

Regaining control of myself, I simply raised an eyebrow over my coffee cup. "Sherrinford, I thought you said you would never underestimate me again." When redirecting a conversation, my mother had taught me, it is far easier to use their words than your own. Outmaneuvered, the Squire lapsed into silence and Holly uncomprehendingly followed suit. Watson, having overcome his initial shock, regarded me with a bemused eye, as if he had expected something like that from me.

Mycroft chuckled to himself at the stir he had caused and sipped his coffee, only to swallow reflexively and clutch his napkin to his lips in disgust. "Salt!" he cried. "Someone replaced the sugar with salt!"

Holmes stirred from his abstract state. "Really?" he asked, innocent as a lamb. "Oh dear, brother mine, that is a shame. I wonder who could have done that? Quite the little mystery." A subtle pressure on my hand under the table solved that particular mystery for me and I chewed on my lip to halt a grin. It would seem that I was not the only disappointed party in last night's rendezvous. Vengeance was sweet, but Mycroft's coffee was assuredly not.

The overweight Holmes brother fixed his junior with a sour glare as the tainted beverage and faulty sugar bowl were whisked away and the conversation shifted to other channels. Sherrinford seemed sedate and serious as he broached a new topic. "Sherlock, how much longer before this case is concluded? I have been going over the accounts and since my, ahem, arrest, I have suffered a substantial decrease in thoroughbred sales. And since we are calculating loss, I must mention that my reputation has not emerged immaculate as well. If this continues, I shall never find a customer again!"

Holmes smiled comfortingly. "Lay your fears to rest, Sherrinford. Once I have all of the facts in hand, your name will be cleared beyond reproach. As to when that will occur, I believe that your bet is as good as mine. I may solve the case in the next five days or five seconds."

"Count your blessings, Squire," I chimed. "At least we can already prove that you are the innocent party here. Who knows? If the case had gone to trial, you might have been ruined! With your reputation in tatters, you'd most likely have to sell the entire estate!"

Holmes' head snapped in my direction. "*What* did you say?"

Hadn't he been listening? He seemed awfully inattentive this morning. "I said he might have had to sell the whole estate."

Disregarding the incident, I reapplied myself to my bacon and eggs, my fork halfway to my mouth when a voice breathed, "Eureka," and a masculine mouth pressed itself to my cheek!

Dropping my fork with a clatter, my hand flew to my face as I turned to Holmes in astonishment, but his chair was empty. I pivoted just in time to see his back retreating through the door to the foyer. Had Holmes just kissed me? I found the thought delightfully appealing, but rather hard to justify.

I shook my head in confusion. "What the hell was-?" I stopped short at the myriad of reactions that careened around the breakfast table. Sherrinford was in shock, plain and simple, his solid jaw literally hanging open. Holly winked at me conspiratorially, one woman of the world to another. Mycroft looked about to explode with repressed laughter, shaking like the proverbial bowl of jelly. And Watson…oh, he was the worst. The good doctor was insufferably smug, smiling down at me with an I-told-you-so written all over his face. "What?" I queried haughtily, earning a snicker from Mycroft. I icily returned to my meal, not succeeding in keeping the embarrassed blush or the triumphant smile from my face.

CHAPTER 13

In Which the Mystery is Solved and I Attend a Ball

Holmes was absent until that evening, when he returned in disarray and exhaustion. What could he have been doing? After drifting about in boredom all day, I finally spotted him in the foyer and pressed him eagerly for explanations and details. Stubborn man, he refused to breathe a word until properly groomed and refreshed, asking me to gather everyone into the library. A bit put out, I scattered maids and valets in every direction, summoning all pertinent adults into the library. Some minutes later we were gathered anxiously in the familiar room like opera-goers awaiting the rise of the curtain. The only exception was everyone's favorite sadist, Sir Siger, hunched in an armchair with a put-upon attitude.

Holmes glided into the room, his clothes and appearance perfection, standing in the center of the room like the dramatist he was and waiting for our undivided attention, which we quite willingly gave. "Everyone," said he, "I am pleased to announce the conclusion of this case. Evidence has been brought to light that points an unerring finger at one Darby Edwards, who is in gaol awaiting trial as we speak." He paused dramatically, monitoring our reactions.

He must have been disappointed. The lot of us, myself included, sat in utter awe, shocked into silence by this rapid conclusion. The case was over? As in solved? As in everything figured out?

"How?" asked Sherrinford finally, voicing our unanimous question. Watson caught my eye and silently mouthed a familiar word.

Holmes' smile grew more self-satisfied. "Elementary, of course." Watson rolled his eyes, his silent prediction validated, and I had to stifle a grin. "Although," Holmes continued, "I must confess that in this instance, I did not reach the conclusion alone. I admit that I suspected Edwards from the beginning, but I only concentrated my efforts on him after Virgil's fortunate observation. Mycroft's official inquiries and Nona's observations helped me to piece together a plausible motive." Caught up in the moment, Holmes began to stride across the floor as if he were on a stage, with us as his spellbound audience. "The course of events ran thusly: Some time prior, Edwards had purchased the Richardson estate following the blackmail scandal, paying only a fraction of the cost. However, being the man he is, he squandered the fortune through gambling and poor investments, forcing himself to sell his newly acquired land to offset his debts. His financial ruin left him on the edge of poverty, and in his desperation he sought to recreate the cause of his earlier good fortune with his wealthy friend and neighbor, Sherrinford Holmes.

"With his open access to Oakstaff Manor, Edwards easily appropriated one of Sherrinford's firearms and a sample of his handwriting. He kidnapped Sylvia Pittston, whom Sherrinford was aiding financially, and suffocated her at his manse. He kept the body in cold storage in the cellar until nightfall, forged a meeting note in Sherrinford's handwriting, shot the cadaver and placed the body at the 'scene of the crime.' When Sherrinford was arrested, Edwards only had to bide his time. Eventually, the name of Holmes would be anathema in polite society and all trade with a murderer's kith and kin would cease. When the family was forced into poverty, Edwards would make an offer for the manor and estate, thereby restoring his wealth.

"Of course, I had not pieced this together until this morning," (He shot a swift glance at me,) "when I went straightaway to Langford with the motive. By noon we had amassed a small force of constables and stormed the Edwards estate. Edwards the younger was taken into custody and we scoured the house from top to bottom, but due to Watson's comprehensive autopsy, I knew exactly what I was looking for. We discovered a recently and clumsily mended red velvet pillow with the remnants of long scores down the back, as well as several long blond hairs in the cellar's cold store, which match the unfortunate Mrs. Pittston. Therefore, I can safely deduce that Darby Edwards will find himself at the end of his rope very soon. Curtain, end play."

There was a laden pause, and then we burst from our seats, raving with relief, applauding and congratulating Holmes, pounding backs and shaking hands, cheerfully drowning the detective in heartfelt admiration and releasing the past tension amongst ourselves. I thought my heart would burst with pride. If not for the multitude of onlookers, I would have gladly launched myself into Holmes' arms. Instead, I contented myself with a friendly hand on his wrist, jesting, "I knew there must be *some* reason you were called the world's greatest detective!"

"World's greatest detective!" barked a harsh smoker's voice, laden with inestimable scorn. Our festivity drained away as Sir Siger lurched into our midst, the fury on his hard face making him a likely candidate for another North Riding murder case. The Holmes patriarch stared down his taller son, hate dripping from every syllable. "I am afraid that I fail to see your involvement in the solving of Sherrinford's case, *my son* From your own mouth you admitted the key roles of others, leaving you to stitch the pieces together and walk away with the credit. Charlatan! I suddenly find myself believing that the case was solved, not by a thieving false detective, but by a mediocre constable, a little girl and a quack! Fools, the lot of you!"

False detective? Quack? Little girl! How dare he insult me in front of everyone! And Watson! How dare he tear down his son, who had saved his estate and reputation! Red mist rose before my eyes and I noticed Watson clenching his fists in restraint, but we were halted from action by Holmes. He stared levelly at his father, a first since we had arrived, and said quietly, "I may tolerate your words to me, *Father*," he nearly spat the word, "but you will never slander my friends so. I forbid it."

The patriarch snapped. "How dare you?" howled Sir Siger. I was actually becoming afraid for Sherlock; I cringed inside at the man's livid, raging face. "How dare you forbid me? After what you have done, how dare you speak to me that way! You selfish, ungrateful-!"

Just then, a miracle happened. Out of the blue, Sherrinford interposed himself between his livid father and his icy brother, a solid and effective brick wall. "Shut up, Father," he intoned in weary disgust. "We have grown tired of this."

Sir Siger was plainly shocked at his heir's insubordination, stepping backwards. He struggled for words, but the invectives the bitter man had heaped upon his youngest son must not have applied to his eldest. Mutely, Sir Siger appealed to Mycroft, meeting with the same cold disapproval. I let my full loathing for him show plainly as we faced him down.

Checkmated by our seamless unity against him, the dethroned lord of the manor snarled wordlessly and stalked to the door. As he cast a glance over his shoulder, I was finally able to see what he really was: a man twisted and haunted by self-justification, cowardice and shame. I *almost* pitied him. Then, as swiftly as he had exploded, the volatile man vanished from the room.

Sherrinford hastily apologized to both Watson and I and he fled to reason with his father, Holly and Mycroft following in his wake. Only the Baker Street residents were left in the library, with the sound of the fire and the smell of books for company. Breathing deeply and calmly to regain himself, Holmes settled slowly into the center of a wide sofa. After a shared glance, Watson and I bookended him on either side. Simultaneously, we three heaved sighs of relief and leaned against the sofa back, staring at the vaulted ceiling, regaining our equilibrium after the conclusion of the case. We must have made quite the picture as we sat, regarding the ceiling, recovering our friendship in silence.

After some comfortable serenity, I addressed my compatriots, carefully avoiding Sir Siger's previous outburst. "Well you know, as far as cases go, that was rather anti-climactic. I was expecting a big confrontation with the murderer, a shoot-out, the whole nine yards." I shifted idly. "Kinda disappointing."

"Well, Nona," replied Watson. "Seeing as that none of us were blackmailed, poisoned, stabbed or shot to death, I'd call it a rather satisfying ending."

The three of us enjoyed a chuckle out of that, but when we had quieted, Holmes spoke in a rather serious voice. "I wanted to thank the both of you for assisting me."

I heard Watson shift in embarrassment. "Come now, old boy, it isn't as if you couldn't have completed the case on your own."

"I most likely would have," Holmes acquiesced. No candidate for false modesty here, folks. "But could I have done it before trial date, and without damaging the family name? That much remains uncertain. And that is why I value your help."

I turned my head to regard his stark profile. "Knock off the melodrama, Holmes; you stink at it. Your thanks are dutifully noted and gratefully accepted. After all, that's what friends are for." Holmes turned toward me at my stale platitude, his gray eyes strangely alight. For a second I was sure he would kiss me, in front of Watson no less! However, he suddenly rose from the sofa and strode for the door. "I'm going to bed," he announced abruptly, walking through the open door and leaving us staring after him.

Not again! Frustrated beyond belief, I placed my hands over my face to suppress a groan. Good God, how much longer would I have to wait? I uncovered my eyes to see a disgruntled doctor glaring at me with his arms crossed. "What?" I snapped irritably.

He shook his head. "Stubborn fools, the both of you." Rising to his feet, he said, "We may as well turn in early, Nona. We return to London in the morning."

"We do?" I asked. "So soon?"

"The case is over, Nona. We are no longer needed here."

"Well, I know, but...oh, never mind." Watson spared me a puzzled glance and left the room as I reluctantly went to my own. Actually, I found myself enjoying a brief love affair with the stately manor and grounds, relishing in its spacious wings and fine country weather. Of course, my huge room and feather bed might have something to do with it as well. Still, perhaps in the familiar rooms at Baker Street, Holmes may prove to be a bit more pliable to his emotions. With mingled dread and anticipation, I turned out the lamp and fell asleep, leaving my packing for the morning.

   ✿   ✿   ✿

Breakfast the next morning was a rather subdued affair, at least for me. Sherrinford and Holly were positively effervescent, bubbling over with plans for the immediate future now that their freedom was assured. The only thing that made me feel remotely better was the announcement that Sir Siger had barricaded himself in his rooms, refusing to set foot outside until Holmes was off of the premises. Good riddance, as far as I was concerned. I picked at my food, seeking to delay the inevitable declaration of departure, when a phrase from Holly broke through my blue funk.

"...and of course, we are inviting all of our neighbors for the party. It will be a smallish affair, but everyone has been so supportive of us, so I'm sure that everything will be ready in the ballroom by the end of the week."

A ball? This weekend? Hot dog! A delirious grin broke out on my face at the thought. A ball, with me in a lovely gown, and musicians playing, and heaps of admirers, and Holmes...

Sherrinford addressed his brothers with long-suffering tones. "Of course, we will convey your condolences for not being able to attend."

My bubble burst. Of course, Holmes, Mr. Misanthropic himself. No way was he staying for a fancy-dress party, and I couldn't very well stay without him. There went my lovely daydream. My spirits took another dive and I regarded my plate with sudden interest.

"Come now, Sherrinford! For ages you have badgered me to spend more time with the family, and now that I am here, you shove me out the door! Kindly make up your mind!"

My head snapped up, as did everyone else's. The voice certainly sounded like Holmes', but Sherlock Holmes would never willingly stay for a ball...would he?

Sherrinford was nonplussed. "Do I take it that you wish to stay, Sherlock?"

Holmes leaned back comfortably. "If you are willing to tolerate the three of us for the week, then I would be honored. Watson, Nona, what about you? Any yearnings for London?"

Watson glanced at Holmes oddly, then shrugged. "I am perfectly willing to stay."

"Count me in!" I exclaimed eagerly before Holmes could regain his sanity and change his mind. I wasn't sure why he had made such an uncharacteristic move, but I wasn't about to argue.

"And you, Mycroft? Will Jupiter stray from its orbit any longer?"

Mycroft fixed Holmes with a piercing glare, as if to unravel his sibling's insanity with the pure force of his mind. Apparently not finding an answer, he grunted, "I suppose that the office will survive until Monday."

Sherrinford clapped his hands briskly, his honest face aglow. "This is marvelous, brothers mine! Marvelous! Of course, since this is quite spur of the moment, we shall commission wardrobes for you all, save you the trouble and expense."

"Capital," agreed Holmes, but at the mention of formal clothes, a hint of uneasiness tinged his eyes. I hastily changed the subject before Holmes could renege on his commitment and eagerly made mental plans for a new gown. The weekend couldn't come fast enough.

❦   ❦   ❦

That monumental breakfast was a Monday, and the days until Saturday's ball were a flurry of activity. Invitations were sent, decorations commissioned, kitchens working overtime in the joyous rush as all of Oakstaff rejoiced at the liberation of its lord. During this period, thankfully, there was seen neither hide nor hair of Sir Siger.

I dutifully attended a fitting for my ball gown, after which Holly made it clear that I would help the most by staying out from underfoot. So in the days that followed, I made myself scarce, chatting with the St. Clairs over a more leisurely tea, playing hide-and-seek with Virgil, even allowing Holmes and Watson to coax me into another round of horseback riding, which was actually enjoyable

Friday, the day before the ball, found Oakstaff in a slump. All of the eager RSVPs had arrived, the preparations were made, and the entire manor rested in preparation for the next night. I was strolling through the garden when I came upon Theresa St. Clair reading a large leather-bound book on a stone bench. I greeted her and she marked her place, waving me to a seat next to her. When I inquired after her reading, she grinned shyly and showed me a myriad of articles and newspaper clippings concerning Holmes' cases in London and abroad.

"My grandfather likes to keep scraps as a hobby. He couldn't be any prouder of Sherlock if he were his own grandson," she said. "I know it's foolish, but as for myself, it's difficult to put the gangly youth of my memories and the hero of these stories into the same man."

"It's not foolish," I commented. "I understand completely. Try living with him day after day! If you ask me, the articles and stories definitely gloss over his faults!" We shared a laugh at that, but then it was my turn to grow somber. "You know, Theresa, I wanted to thank you and your grandmother for letting me know the truth."

Her gray eyes peered into my brown ones. "Did it help?" she asked simply.

I smiled, thinking back to the conversation among the crypts and Holmes standing up to his father. "You know, I think it did."

"Then you are welcome."

We sat together and admired Nature's bounty, until I remembered something that had nagged at my memory. "Um, Theresa, I've been meaning to ask you this. Earlier in the case, why were you so sure that it was Darby Edwards? I mean you turned out correct, of course, but what made you suspect him?"

Theresa suddenly averted her head, disappearing behind a curtain of reddish hair. "Edwards is going to the gallows?" she asked abruptly.

"Well, yes, we think so," I replied hesitantly. Where was she going?

"Will I be called upon to testify?"

"Testify?" I queried. "Theresa, no one is asking you to do anything! Why would you have to testify?"

She hesitated, but then she sighed. "Edwards," she said hollowly, pushing her hair back. "I thought he loved me, at least at first, but then he started asking questions about how much money the Squire had, what his income was, things like that. When I refused to tell, he started threatening me. Finally, he stopped chasing me down, but he said that if I told anyone that he was making inquiries, a teacher he knew would kill my grandparents."

Edwards, that wretched, wretched man. All of my instincts against him were suddenly justified. "So why are you telling me now?" I asked Theresa, puzzled.

She smiled honestly. "Because you are a good person. Call it feminine intuition if you like, but I can tell. I saw it in your concern for Sherlock and I see it now. I can trust you with a secret. Besides, a jackal in a cage is no threat, even to mice." Her face darkened. "Will you tell anyone?"

I thought about it for a moment, surprisingly touched by her trust but torn by my duty to justice. But what about the reference to a teacher killing her grandparents? Could this teacher be a certain professor of infamous regard? Perhaps not, but better to not take the chance. Finally, I said, "I won't tell a soul."

She nodded in relief, smiling.

A sudden commotion from down the path attracted our attention. Thoughts of Darby Edwards vanished from my mind as Holly dashed up hurriedly. "There you are, Nona!" she gasped. "Come quickly, both of you; you have to see this!"

Both confused, Theresa and I followed Holly into the manor and down the halls to the music room, where odd-sounding piano music floated down the hallway. It was a simple waltz, but every third note was strangely emphasized. Holly motioned us to silence and we listened by the cracked music room door. Voices were heard above the music.

"One-two-three, one-two-three, one—oh, good heavens! Come on, Sherlock, it's a bit like riding a bicycle! You never forget, really!"

"Oh, it's very nice for you to say 'come on,' but what am I supposed to do with my left foot while I'm turning with my right? And you've made me lose count!"

"You aren't supposed to count, Sherlock; let the music count for you!" The third notes grew even harder as the pianist pounded away.

The three of us ladies peered totem-like through the crack in the door, beholding a sight I shall never forget. Sherlock Holmes promenaded about the music room with an ungainly Sherrinford as his dancing partner, a lace tablecloth pinned around the Squire's waist to simulate a dress. Watson stoutly wielded the piano, mutilating a waltz as Mycroft studied the prancing pair, critically commenting on his younger brother's performance.

I stuffed a sleeve into my mouth to keep from giggling. My afternoon had just gone from tragedy to comedy! Or was this farce? "One-two-three, one-two-three!" barked Mycroft. "One-two—oh, look out!"

With twin shouts and a sound of ripping fabric, the eldest and youngest Holmes brothers tripped over the tablecloth and went down in an ungraceful heap. The music stopped as Watson snickered at the cursing brothers, allowing the women's laughter and applause to echo throughout the room as we pushed open the door. "Bravo!" I cried between giggles, clapping loudly. "Bravo! Encore!"

Sherrinford and Holmes clambered to their feet, blushing outrageously. "Nona, whatever you were going to say, don't say it!" growled Holmes.

"Actually, Holmes," I began, overcoming my laughter, "you've saved me an embarrassing request. I never learned how to dance and wanted to beg lessons, but I wasn't sure if I should. Now I know we can learn together!"

Holmes straightened his jacket in a huff. "I already know how to dance, Nona; I was merely refreshing my memory."

I rolled my eyes. "Fine, in that case I can learn and you can refresh your memory at the same time. I might be a better dancing partner than your brother anyway." I grinned at Sherrinford. "By the way, Squire, you simply *must* give me the name of your seamstress."

Sherrinford grumbled something about "trade secrets" and fumbled with the tablecloth as Holly and Theresa snickered, his wife finally removing the torn article.

"Well," rumbled Mycroft, "it seems that we have a change of partners. Doctor, if you please." Watson nodded and returned his hands to the ivory, awaiting the signal. "Nona, I believe that you receive the better end of the proverbial stick in this lesson," Mycroft continued. "Since the woman allows the man to lead in the dance, your task is to anticipate Sherlock's movements and try not to step on his feet."

I grinned outwardly, but my insides were quaking as I stepped closer to Holmes. I slipped my hand into his larger one, suddenly aware of every movement of his long fingers, and almost flinched as his other hand snaked around my waist, pulling me closer to him. I picked up my skirt with my free hand (I wasn't wearing a prototype that day) and gazed up at my dancing partner. He looked almost as nervous as I felt. "Begin," intoned Mycroft, and the waltz started again.

I tried not to look at my feet as I stepped in time with Holmes, counting in my head while he spun me across the floor. *One-two-three, one-two-three, hey, this is easy! One-two-three, one-two-!* "Ouch!" I released my partner and clutched my injured appendage. "Ow, Holmes! That was my foot!"

Holmes was about to apologize, but Mycroft forestalled him. "Now, now, the blame is partly yours, Nona. As I said earlier, you need to anticipate Sherlock's movements."

"How am I supposed to do that?" I retorted. "It's not like I'm psychic."

"I believe it is comparable to your actions in Baker Street," said Holmes, "when you often foresee what I need before I ask for it."

"But that's not prediction; that's just using my head."

"Precisely." He held out his arms with a touch of his old impatience. "Use your head, Nona, and try to anticipate where and when I move."

Rising to the challenge, I resolutely stepped into his embrace as the song began again. We whirled about the room, as I closely watched Holmes' movements and he concentrated on his footwork. After several revolutions, however, we fell into step with each other and began to relax. Watson's playing became less emphatic and more melodic, Mycroft's corrections grew far and few between, and Holmes and I lost ourselves in the flow, oblivious to all but each other.

Some time later, Watson abruptly ceased playing, but Holmes and I were so caught up in each other that we continued for a few steps before the silence caught up to us. "I'm sorry, Holmes, Nona," apologized Watson, flexing his sore fingers. "I just can't play any longer."

"That's quite all right, doctor," rumbled Mycroft, an odd tone to his voice. "I believe that they have grasped the rudimentary basics, at any cost." The man was staring at me, as if seeing me for the first time.

I grew a bit uncomfortable under Mycroft's scrutiny. "Well, good, I'm glad. Um...then I'll be in the library, I suppose." With a smile for the whole room, I retreated to the library. Once there, I shut the door and reflected on what I had just seen. As I left the music room, I glanced at Holmes and almost froze. I had finally glimpsed what Watson had termed Holmes' "heartfelt expression," although I believed it to be more than heartfelt. I called the look in Sherlock Holmes' gray eyes, love.

I couldn't wait for Saturday night.

❦   ❦   ❦

I paced the floor in my room, strains of music floating up from the ballroom downstairs. It was nine-thirty in the evening and the ball was in full swing, dozens of affluent guests laughing, drinking and dancing as they toasted to Sherrinford's innocence. I was itching to join them, but instead I was confined to my room in my bathrobe. Holly had forbidden me to prepare early, arguing that as the heroine of the hour, I should be fashionably late and make a proper entrance. So I paced and I fidgeted, willing Holly closer with each step.

The taller lady finally glided into the room, resplendent in a dark crimson gown and accompanied by a maid. The servant bore in her arms a gown of the same shade as my bathrobe, a vision in emerald silk, which she laid on the bed before departing and leaving me in Holly's capable hands. First seating me at the vanity, the lady of the manor seized a silver-chased hair pick and ran it through my brown hair, twisting the mass onto the top of my head. "You'll be drawing eyes tonight, Nona," she mused softly as she pinned my hair in place.

"You really think so?" I asked abstractedly as she slid the pick into my elegant bun, leaving it to gleam artfully.

"I do," she replied, looking at me thoughtfully, "although I think that there is only one pair of eyes that will concern you here." I colored slightly, which of course was all the confirmation she needed. Holly turned me to face her and applied foundation to my upturned face, smiling. "I never thought that I would see the day when Sherlock returned to Oakstaff Manor. I expected your presence even less."

"In what context?" I asked, turning my head for the powder brush.

The older woman laughed quietly at that. "You are as cautious with your emotions as he! I meant in the context that Sherlock arrives at Oakstaff with a young woman that he obviously favors, else she would not have accompanied him. When you arrived here, Nona, I did some observation and deduction of my own. I knew that this lovely young lady must be intelligent, for she assisted in the investigation in a murder case. She must be independent, an obvious assumption from the fact that she disdained fashion precepts. Finally, she must care deeply for my brother-in-law, evidenced by the obvious concern in her eyes. Am I correct so far?"

"Absolutely brilliant, Holly. Holmes would be seething with envy."

"No more talking." She dipped a tiny brush into a jar of rouge, carefully applying the substance to my silenced lips. "Now for my deductions. Briefly put, based on what I observed, I deduced that Miss Nona Brown both earned and deserved the love of my lawful brother, and also that I would be honored to have her as a sister-in-law." She paused and looked down at me kindly, then suddenly seized a handkerchief from the vanity top and dabbed it to my eyes. "Now, now, don't cry; you'll spoil all of my hard work." I did feel about to cry, from gratitude and thankfulness. It would seem that although Time had torn my family from me, my mother and father and brothers, the temporal entity had graciously replaced them with these wonderful people.

Holly pressed the handkerchief to my lips to blot the rouge and turned my head to the mirror. She had plied her craft well, for I hardly recognized myself. "Holly, you are a wonderworker," I breathed.

"Yes, I know," she replied simply. "Now let's see you into that dress." I dutifully discarded the bathrobe, but since I was wearing corset and petticoats underneath it, I was practically fully dressed. Holly gasped slightly. "Heavens, Nona, your shoulder! What happened?"

I turned to regard my shoulder, a fading yellow bruise serving to remind me of the brawl at the Goose and Crown. I tried to downplay it. "Oh, that, just a little accident in the village."

"When you were dressed as a man?"

"Holly…" I said warningly.

She threw her hands up in exasperation. "Very well, Nona, but we cannot have that bruise showing. Your dress is off the shoulder and I doubt that a yellow patch would improve your skin." She fetched the foundation and powder, gently coloring the bruise into a fleshier shade.

My stomach gave a little thrill at her words. Off the shoulder? I tried to picture Holmes' reaction to me in such a daring Victorian frock. It wasn't working. I supposed that I would simply have to wait. The bruise now miraculously gone, Holly slid the dress over my head and did up the tiny buttons in the back, completing my transformation. The emerald dress clung to my every curve, emphasizing what had previously been neglected. The gown was indeed off the shoulder, the straps falling to the sides of my arms and the neckline perilously low. In the twenty-first century, I had worn spaghetti-strapped shirts and jean cutoffs with no discomfort and a great deal more exposure than this garment, but that was in an era with less regard for indecency. The rules had completely changed with this dress. I had never worn anything so…alluring. "I don't think I can do this," I murmured uneasily.

"Of course you can," whispered Holly in my ear. "I felt the same way before balls or functions at your age. The anxiety will pass, but you must overcome it first." She stepped back and regarded me with a satisfaction that reminded me of Mrs. Hudson. "Are you ready, my dear?"

I thought about straightening my shoulders, but considering my present apparel, I decided against it. "As ready as I'll ever be," I replied and followed her out of the room, doing my damndest to glide.

❦   ❦   ❦

"Announcing Miss Nona Brown!"

The butler's stentorian tones broke through the murmur of the guests and the orchestra's symphony as I descended the large staircase as carefully as I possibly could. In the tradition of manor houses, the ballroom entrance overlooked the grand room, with a large staircase sweeping down and chandeliers swinging from the high ceiling. The chamber glittered in white décor as flowers adorned tables straining with refreshments. A small orchestra played in a corner to the delight of the dancing couples, and the bright electric glow spilled out of the towering windows onto the patio outside. The ballroom had been wired for electricity, so Edison bulbs had replaced candles, the pervasive bright glow recalling memories of my own era.

The seventy-odd guests turned to peer at me, their attention arrested by the unconventional young woman who supposedly wore trousers under her skirts and did not faint at the sight of a corpse. Their whispers echoed around the room as I descended the staircase, feeling more like Cinderella than ever. By the time I reached the bottom of the stairs, I was flooded with well-wishers and curious onlookers, men bowing over my hands and women eagerly exclaiming over my triumph. I had imagined it to be a thrilling experience, but the crush of humanity simply made me feel claustrophobic.

Fobbing off the masses with a few desultory words of thanks, I broke from the main group, snatched a champagne glass from a liveried servant and went in search of Holmes. My eyes circled the ballroom twice, but there was no sign of him. Had he chickened out after all? My spirits fell at the thought of not dancing with him, but I perked up at the sound of a familiar voice calling my name. It was only Sherrinford, though, in the company of a dashing young officer whom he introduced as Major Edwin Wentworth. I graciously took his hand and was about to excuse myself when Major Wentworth spoke. "Might I have the honor of a dance, Miss Brown?"

Well, to be perfectly honest, I hadn't expected to dance with anyone but Holmes. However, the man was nowhere in sight, and I was not about to sit and pine until he finally, if ever, decided to make an entrance. "Certainly, Major," I replied, handing my glass to Sherrinford and allowing the major to escort me onto the dance floor. Thanks to my impromptu lesson the day before, I knew the basics of the dance and was able to follow Major Wentworth without incident.

After the dance was over, Wentworth was replaced with Mr. Sterling, a London stockbroker; Sir Garret Fitzwarren, a local horse breeder; even Lord Sebastian DeBracy, son of the Baron DeBracy. Each of my dance partners was eager to hear of the case, and when not speaking of the murder, they lauded their own achievements, emphasizing their available marital status. It was rather amusing and I listened to each one very politely, but I always found some reason to abandon them at the end of every dance.

Finally, given a brief respite from the dance floor, I tackled the appetizers and indulged in a spot of gossip with some of the local ladies before resuming my scan of the ballroom. The clock chimed eleven and the ball was going stronger than ever, but still with no sign of Holmes. I decided that he wasn't going to show and resolved to enjoy myself in any case.

"Nona!" I pivoted at the voice to see Watson approaching, quite a gallant figure in a new evening suit. "There you are! I see that you were finally able to shake your pursuers."

I laughed at that. "Yes, some of them were very tenacious, but I believe that I've lost them." I lightened my voice, keeping it casual. "By the by, you haven't seen Holmes around, have you?"

He fixed me with a knowing look. "As a matter of fact, Nona, I have just come from him. He desired my presence in my medical capacity."

"What for? Is he sick?"

"Well, my dear, he claims to have come down with the most sudden case of stomach flu in medical history."

I raised an eyebrow. "Claims?"

He regarded his fingernails smugly. "I gave him my medical opinion, placing the cause of his distress on nerves. He, of course, ignored my comments."

"Do you think he'll be coming down?"

"Oh, I believe so." He glanced at the ballroom door. "Eventually." He shrugged, casting the matter away. "As long as we are waiting, Nona, perhaps you could favor me with a dance?"

"Why, Doc, I thought you'd never ask!"

The next few dances were much more enjoyable. Even with the slight handicap in his leg, Watson was an admirable dancer and we chattered away as we twirled to the music. At the end of our third dance, however, he begged off due to the Jezail bullet. We corralled a pair of chairs and continued to talk companionably.

I was trying to explain to him how people danced in the twenty-first century when the butler sounded again. "Announcing Mr. Sherlock Holmes!"

I looked up towards the staircase, as did everyone else, and there was Holmes, coming down the stairs as cool as a cucumber, nary a hint of nervousness. If the assembled guests had been eager at my arrival, they were almost frenzied at Holmes' His feet had barely touched the floor before a circle of eager females surrounded him, begging him for every little detail of the case.

Finally! I was about to dash over to him when a small, smirking part of me recommended that I stay put. *He wants to be fashionably late?* I thought. *He can reap the consequences.* Turning back to Watson instead, I said coolly, "It seems that your patient has made a miraculous recovery."

Watson turned in his seat, seeing Holmes trying to extricate himself from the nearly indistinguishable mass of silk and chiffon. "And when the patient recovers," he said with a wry smile at me, "the doctor is no longer required." Standing from his seat, he bowed dramatically over my hand, wishing me luck with his eyes more than his words before discreetly making his exit.

I smiled my thanks as I watched him leave, although he did not see it. Watching from the corner of my eye, I could see Holmes steadily weaving through the crowd, stopping only for polite nods and brief greetings before moving on. Although I was seemingly engrossed in the waltzing couples, I was unsurprised when a large hand lifted my gloved one off my lap.

"Here you are!" Holmes exclaimed softly as I glanced up at him. For a moment, the detective held my gaze as tightly as my hand, trying to communicate something vitally important. A new light smoldered in his gray eyes and my breath caught in my throat before he gently pulled me to my feet, continuing in a teasing tone, the light still present. "As I slowly drown in a sea of vapid compliments, you sit idle and do nothing. Surely you did not fail to observe my predicament?"

I looked past him briefly, noting the predatory gleam still present in many sets of pretty eyes, before turning back to Holmes. "I observed, of course, but I didn't think you needed a rescue party."

"Are you mad?" he asked in mock disbelief. "Give me bloodthirsty murderers by the bushel; they at least make better conversation than that lot!"

I burst out laughing at that. Gone was the withdrawn, terse stranger that had haunted Oakstaff a week prior. This was the Holmes of old, the sarcastic, sardonic, brilliant Holmes that I knew and loved so well. "Well, Holmes, I'll be sure to throw you a rope next time. What on earth kept you so long? It's nearly midnight!"

"I was feeling a bit under the weather, Nona." The tone of his voice brooked no more conversation on the subject; he was incredibly touchy when it came to his weaknesses. Instead, he changed the subject. "I see that your bruise is healing nicely."

"What?" My hand flew to my shoulder. "You can tell?"

He shook his head. "No, I cannot." At my puzzled expression, he continued. "Over the past few days, you have held your shoulder a bit stiffly, suggesting a bruise you most likely acquired at the Goose and Crown. However, since it is now so slight as to be concealed with cosmetics, I deduce that it must be healing nicely." I did not reply, simply drinking in the sight of Holmes in evening dress. What wass more, he seemed to be doing the same to me. Finally he spoke again, "You are very beautiful this night, Nona."

I blushed a bit. "Thank you, Holmes. You are, too. I mean," I amended hastily as his eyebrows climbed. "You know what I mean."

We stood together in an awkward silence for a moment longer until Holmes cleared his throat haltingly. "Well, Nona, if you are not averse to the situation, then perhaps…we could exercise our newly-acquired skills."

"Holmes," I said firmly. "Are you asking me to dance?"

"Well, yes."

I placed my hands on my hips, fully aware that I was giving him a better view of my bare skin. "Then ask me properly."

A hint of a sardonic smile surfaced on his lips and he bowed over my hand. "Miss Brown, would you grant me the supreme honor of a dance?"

I smiled graciously. "Mr. Holmes, I would be delighted."

And so we danced.

❧   ❧   ❧

The hours flew by as I floated across the floor, Holmes' presence the only thing that anchored me to the ground. Never had I felt so graceful or light or…well, beautiful. We effortlessly matched each other's movements, allowing ourselves to talk freely as we danced. We spoke of the case. We spoke of Holmes' past and my future, and sometimes we did not speak at all, content in each other's arms as the music carried us away to night's Plutonian shore.

Midnight came and went. Fatigue, summer's heat and sore feet broke the spell upon us and we sought refuge on the spacious patio. Seated on the low, wide railing, I arranged my skirts and took in the perfect night. The moon and stars were jewels, scattered by Mother Nature to adorn our special night. The fragrance of garden flowers pervaded the air, a scent that the finest *parfumiers* of Paris could never hope to duplicate. Golden light poured through the windows and muted strains of music were heard. But most importantly, Sherlock Holmes sat across from me, the light in his eyes not inspired by electricity or the bejeweled moon.

"Why did you suspect Darby Edwards, Nona?" he asked suddenly.

Oh, *Lord*. The most romantic night in the history of history, and he wanted to talk about the case? "Well, Holmes, I guess you could say woman's intuition." He snorted at that, prompting me to continue. "Off your high horse, Holmes, it's a respectable claim. It has been scientifically proven that the clusters of nerves in a woman's brain are closer together than in a man's. A woman has the ability to process data much faster than men, hence 'woman's intuition.'" I smirked a bit. "In fact, you could say that every woman is a born detective."

That got a reaction. For a moment Holmes looked as if he were about to drop dead of shock, but then he threw back his head and laughed heartily. "Every woman—oh!" he gasped, brushing tears of mirth from his eyes. "Oh, Lord, my livelihood! My occupation! Never tell another living soul, or I shall be ruined!" I knew he spoke in jest, but I agreed anyway. Holmes heaved a sigh, shaking his head. "How do you do it, Nona? You can turn my world upon its head and make me enjoy it! If I solve ten thousand mysteries in my lifetime, I fear that I shall never solve you."

"I'm glad to hear it," I replied. "If you figured me out, I would cease to be interesting and you would soon discard me for the next problem."

His jocularity subsided and he gently took my hand in his. "I would never cast you away, my dear Nona."

"I know, Holmes. I was only teasing."

He did not release my hand. "Your worth to me runs far deeper than mere intellectual stimulation." He lifted my hand and placed it reverently to his lips.

A sudden and delicious shiver ran down my spine. Watson had said that Holmes gazed at me with a 'heartfelt expression.' I wondered if he knew how much of that was an understatement.

~*Excerpt from the private journal of Dr. Watson*~

It did not take a great detective to see the emotion that my friend, Mr. Sherlock Holmes, harbored for the delightful young lady that had so abruptly entered our lives nearly a full year prior. At the slight risk of degrading my journal's opinion of myself, I must confess that a small part of me was secretly saddened at this. Early in my acquaintance with this singular young woman, I had entertained fantasies of courtship and marriage with the enchanting Nona Brown, but they had come to naught. I had quickly observed her decided preference for my eccentric friend and indeed noticed his decided preference for her. That being the case, I surrendered myself to the course of events and was determined to wish them all happiness, taking great precaution to conceal any erstwhile emotions. It is occasions such as those that give me reason to doubt Holmes' ready condemnation of my acting abilities, but this is neither here nor there.

At the conclusion of Holmes' case, which I had mentally titled 'The Adventure of the Country Squire,' I found myself attending a ball in celebration of a satisfactory ending. We, or rather Holmes had saved Sherrinford Holmes and his kin from death and scandal, thanks to the aid of Miss Brown. Now that the case was behind us, I greatly hoped that Holmes could turn his attention to a more emotional problem, the solution of which required more than brainwork and tobacco poisoning.

My hopes were brought to fruition when, as I drifted about the hall in search of conversation, I came upon a curious sight. The two elder Holmes brothers, Sherrinford and Mycroft, peered circumspectly around a curtain through the open portal leading to the patio. Intrigued, I crept up behind them to discover what was so interesting. To my surprise, I saw Holmes and Nona seated upon the balustrade, hands clasped, gazing steadfastly into each other's eyes.

"Good heavens!" I whispered to the other men. "This is simple spying! I really must protest!" Despite my fine words, however, I admit that I made no effort to leave.

Mycroft turned his massive head to regard me slyly. "Come now, Doctor," he replied *sotto voce*, "you may as well stay, for medical purposes if for nothing else."

"Medical purposes?" I echoed just as softly. "Whatever do you mean?"

He turned to observe the oblivious couple on the terrace. "For if Sherlock kisses her, Doctor, I fear that I shall have a heart attack in front of God and everyone."

"Then I will not be of much use to you," I replied.

"Why ever not?"

"Because I shall join you."

Sherrinford Holmes waved us into silence and I made no further attempt to renege, fully absorbed the powerful human drama before me.

~**~

"Do you ever regret your coming here, Nona?" asked Holmes quietly. "Here, to this time?"

"Regret is a rather strong word, Holmes," I replied. "I miss my family, of course, and sometimes I wish that I could replace my modern conveniences, but regret?" I shook my head emphatically. "No. Never regret. This is the greatest thing that has ever happened to me."

"The greatest?" His long fingers tilted my chin up to face him. "Why?" It was little more than a whisper.

My heart pounded faster. "Because..." His free hand pulled me closer. "...I found..." My hand crept to his neck, pulling him downwards. "...you..." My eyes closed in anticipation. "...Sherlock Holmes."

Our lips had barely brushed when a frantic scream pealed through the ballroom, halting conversation, music and dance. Possessed of one mind, Holmes and I ran into the room, passing a dazed Watson, Mycroft and Sherrinford. Holmes swiftly located the source of the disturbance. One of the upstairs maids trembled with shock in the arms of a liveried man, gasping for breath. "Sir Siger," she heaved. "His chambers—oh, so much *blood*!"

Holmes went rigid and dashed up the stairs, his brothers and Watson in tow. I attempted to follow, but ball gowns were not made for running. By the top of the stairs, I was forced to disregard propriety, shedding my heeled shoes and holding my skirts around my knees to run after the men. I followed their noises through the halls before rounding a corner, coming upon a strange sight. The usually pompous Mycroft was on his knees, being violently sick. Watson leaned against the wall, breathing heavily, looking as though he were trying to prevent imitating Mycroft. The door next to him stood ajar and I walked past him to enter it. Watson gasped suddenly and reached out for my arm. "Nona, don't! It's too horrible!" But it was too late. I pushed Watson away, walked into the room and saw.

Blood, so much blood. It was all over the desktop, dripping on the rug, small spatters on the wall. Still, the most horrific sight was the source of this crimson spectacle. Sir Siger lay slumped over his desk, his hate-filled face almost obscured by the bullet hole in his head, a revolver on the floor where it had fallen from his limp hand.

Sherrinford was crouched against the wall, sobbing, but it was Holmes, Sherlock, that made my stomach clench in fear. Holmes was on his knees, staring at his father, a piece of bloodstained paper in his nerveless hand. His eyes were empty, blank slate gray, devoid of any spark of consciousness. Kneeling beside him, I gently took the paper from his hand just long enough to read its message: three words in Sir Siger's harsh, angular script.

Not my son.

Suddenly filled with a vehement rage, I tore the paper in half and took Holmes into my arms, helpless tears coursing down my face. Holmes fell into my embrace, as limp and senseless as a rag doll, his empty eyes staring as I rocked and cried. Damn Siger, damn him, damn that wretched devil. He could not be satisfied with torturing his son in life; he had to continue after death. I imagined that I could sense the man's spirit, twisted and ugly, laughing over us all. He laughed because he knew. He had crushed his son, had broken him, and I knew that Holmes and I would never be the same.

Our love would never be the same.

CHAPTER 14

In Which I Run Away from Holmes

We did not stay for the funeral. Somewhere amidst the chaos of the following day, Holmes received a forwarded telegram from an august personage in the Foreign Office, urgently requesting his services. I was stunned at the thought of Holmes working during this traumatic time, but apparently he had other ideas. So it was that barely twenty-four hours after the ball, Holmes, Watson and I were silently steaming back to the great cesspool. Holmes was silent and withdrawn on the train, barely speaking a word to Watson or myself, but I thought that I understood. Work is the antidote to sorrow, or so I believe the adage runs. I tried to shrug it off and hoped that this case would help Holmes to put his life in perspective again.

No sooner had we settled back in Baker Street than Holmes set off to meet with the august personage, whose name I withhold. The case was one of blackmail, which made Holmes' course of action clear. Holmes had often put forth that the best way to defuse blackmail was by counter-blackmail. For the next week Holmes worked feverishly to dig up any dirt against the blackmailer himself, sometimes disappearing from Baker Street for days at a time. When he was present in our rooms, he refused our offers of assistance with a biting phrase or an angry snarl. The frenzied nature of his exertions began to seriously frighten me and Watson as well. By burying himself in his work, Holmes was cutting himself off from us, left only with the poison his hateful father had planted in his mind.

Within a week's time, however, Holmes succeeded in coercing the black-guard into silence and the august personage was greatly relieved, expressing his thanks monetarily. However, the period of mental resolution that I thought would follow did not come. No sooner was the case finished than Holmes returned to Baker Street, seized the morocco case and disappeared into his room, locking the door. No entreaties or threats from Watson or myself could induce the door to open. The worry in the pit of my stomach deepened, tempered with a new emotion: anger. The more I dwelled on Holmes' situation, the less pity I was able to muster. As much as I knew he was hurting, he simply *had* to recognize the folly of his self-destructive actions. To continue as he was, falling deeper into depression, was nothing but long-term suicide. Of course, the thought that that might be exactly what he wanted never crossed my mind.

On the third night after Holmes' self-imposed imprisonment, I marched with purpose up to 221B, intent on drawing Holmes out of his shell, come hell or high water. I could no longer stand by and watch the man I loved kill himself. Throwing open the door to the sitting room, I halted to find Holmes sitting boneless in his armchair, clothes rumpled, his pale, drawn face weakly illuminated by the sputtering oil lamp. At first, I feared him prey to the needle again, but a hasty glance to the side table revealed otherwise. A bottle of whiskey that had adorned the liquor stand, full that morning, was now practically empty. I turned to Holmes in astonishment. "You've been drinking," I breathed, unwilling to raise my voice yet.

Holmes rolled his head towards me, his eyes glazed and bloodshot pools. "How astute of you, my *dear* Nona," he slurred, the sarcastic emphasis in his normally precise voice making my breath catch. "I am, as you so brilliantly deduced, drinking." Raising his glass in a scornful toast, he downed the remnants of his glass and shook his head at the reaction.

I crossed my arms to stop their shivering, hiding my concern under a veil of effrontery. "I believe I should now ask *why* you are drinking. Morphine suddenly lose its potency?"

"On the contrary," quipped Holmes in a terrible parody of goodwill. "It would be the preferred alternative. However, my supply is depleted and, (he glanced at the mantle clock,) since it is Sunday, the chemists' shops will be closed. In the meantime-" He broke off and waved a trembling hand at the sideboard.

I finished the sentiment for him. "Any port in a storm, Holmes?" He did not deign to reply, eyes closed in exhaustion, and my heart wrenched anew at the depths to which he had fallen. However, I was not about to let him get off that easily. Rounding his chair, I stood before him with a frown. The time for subtlety was long past, and in his inebriated state bluntness was demanded. "Holmes, I know that this has been a difficult time for you, but it has to stop. You need to get a grip."

"Grip on what?" he muttered listlessly.

"On your life!" I retorted. "Holmes, you are throwing your life away, drowning in a sea of self-pity! You need to stop running away and face this head-on. Your father was a sick, twisted man, and that-"

"Enough!" He suddenly cut me off with a snap, shakily rising to his feet. "I grow weary of your badgering! You will not speak of this again!"

"Like hell I won't!" I shot back. All of my worry for the past week and a half began bubbling to the surface in misguided anger. "You expect me to just stand by and watch you kill yourself? That's what you're doing, Holmes, killing yourself! I refuse to allow it! Now knock it off and come to your senses!"

"Oh, isn't it simple for *you* to preach," Holmes replied angrily, disrespectfully jabbing me with a long finger as he towered over me. The smell of his pipe tobacco and aftershave, which I so treasured, was drowned under the reek of alcohol. "The flawless Miss Brown, who knows everything in history! You know nothing of that which I am dealing! What do you know of loss?"

The anger erupted. "How dare you?" I shrieked in fury, knocking his hand aside. "How dare you speak to me of loss? Little less than a year ago, O Great Detective, I lost a mother, a father, two brothers, three grandparents, five uncles, six aunts and twelve cousins! How *dare* you speak to me of not knowing loss!" Holmes stiffened and retreated to the sideboard as I continued my verbal barrage, my emotions flying out of control. "Selfish, that's what you are, Sherlock Holmes! You're so wrapped up in self-pity that you have no regard for how anyone else feels! Do you have any idea what you're doing to me and to Watson? You pride yourself on observation, but you can't see the very people under your ridiculous nose!"

"Shut up!"

"*No!*"

"Merciful *heaven!*" exploded Holmes, throwing his gaze to the ceiling. "How much longer must I endure torment at this she-devil's hands?" His attention snapped to me. "Always and forever meddling in my ways, ever since you arrived! You're never content to leave well enough alone, are you? Constantly badgering me on this and that, day in and day out, you traitorous little harridan! By God, had I known last October what I know now, I'd have thrown you out into the cold and let you freeze, like the heartless creature you are!"

His words cut me to my very soul. *What I know now...thrown you out...*These awful words spewed forth from the man I loved, who I had thought loved me. I tried to tell myself it was the alcohol talking, that he did not really think this, but as I stared at the man before me, standing with disgust in his bloodshot eyes, I could not convince myself. "Get *out!*" I screamed, a last-ditch effort.

"This is *my house!!*" he roared back.

There was nothing else for it. I turned and fled in defeat down the stairs as Holmes stumbled back to the safety of his own chambers. Blinded by my tears, I was only partly aware of Watson walking through the front door, returning from the charity hospital.

"Nona, my dear, what are-"

"Out of my way, Watson!" I did not pause to see his reaction as I dashed to my room and slammed the door, locking it securely. I threw myself on the bed, buried my head in my pillow and, fairly certain that no one could hear me, cried myself out.

I must have dozed off for when I returned to myself, my window was edged with light as dawn crept into London town. The fog that tiptoed through the streets was yet out of danger, but it would flee as the sun grew higher. A light mist covered the glass pane; it had rained last night. My pillow was damp with a different kind of rain as I scrubbed my eyes and tried without success to repair the wrinkles in my housedress.

After last night's purging, I felt very empty and quiet, but there remained a twinge in the region of my chest. My worst fears had been confirmed. The poison that infected his mind had spread to his heart. Holmes hated me, perhaps as strongly as I loved him, and love him I did, even after such an episode, which accounted for the tension in my heart. As jumbled as my thoughts were, only one thing was clear; I could not bear to stay and suffer more taunts, watching my other half slowly slip into oblivion. At twenty-three years of age, I would run away from home, or as the case were, run away from Holmes.

With none of my usual resolve, I washed up and drew out my suitcase, meaning to be gone before anyone awoke. Pausing often to wipe my eyes, I cleaned out my sparse drawers and emptied my closet, eyes blurring with fresh tears as I ran shaking hands over the beloved crimson opera gown. The red velvet beneath my hands called up bittersweet memories of that long-ago night when I had dared to hope for Holmes' love. More with regret than with bitterness, I left the gown to gather dust in the closet and instead turned to throw out the flowers I had placed on my washstand.

My bed was soon remade with military precision and my few books were placed in a separate valise. I changed into my most respectable town dress, not wanting to wear a prototype and draw attention to myself. That done, I snapped the latches on my bags and glanced about the room. There was no trace of me left in it, no hint that anyone had ever resided there, and that was exactly how I wanted it.

Nodding with as much satisfaction as I could muster, I crept past the staircase with a forlorn glance cast at the familiar door above and quietly snuck out the front door. Leaving my bags on the steps, I walked to the corner cabstand and soon was rewarded with a four-wheeler. I instructed the cabbie to stop by 221 to pick up my luggage, and he complied. As I watched the cabman pile my luggage in the black brougham, I let myself relax a bit, relieved that I would be able to vanish quietly. Best for all...

The slamming of the front door made me jump, my precautions brought to naught. Watson stumbled down the stairs in waistcoat and carpet slippers, stricken to the core. "Nona, what on earth are you doing?" he cried, confusion in his brown eyes as he took in the cab and my baggage.

I turned my gaze to my hemline, my outburst last night returning full force. "Watson," I began haltingly. "I-I'm sorry for shouting at you last night. I was just..."

He gently reached out and took my hands in his. "What happened, Nona?"

That was it, but the tenderness in his voice was enough to raise a lump in my throat. My words came out in short bursts as I tried to hold back the floodwaters. "Holmes—and me—I was going to talk to him—he screamed at me—I screamed at him—and he said—he said...oh, Watson!" Harsh sobs escaped from the prison of my heart.

With only a moment's hesitation, Watson stepped forward and drew me into his arms, letting me rest on his shoulder. "Don't go," he breathed into my ear. "Please don't go."

As I stood there in the morning fog, stifling my tears, momentarily secure in the embrace of my dearest friend, it suddenly occurred to me that I was leaving more than Holmes behind. But at the thought of Holmes came a summoned image of his pale face and burning eyes and my resolve returned. "No, Watson," I said resolutely, scrubbing my eyes. "I can't stay. I still love him; I'll always love him, but after what happened, I-I just can't." I snorted bitterly. "I can't say that Holmes will miss me, though."

"Damn Holmes!" cried Watson vehemently. "I will miss you! Nona, I do not know what happened between you and Holmes last night, but I beg you to reconsider! Is there no alternative at all?" Touched by his devotion, I could still only shake my head in mute sorrow. His shoulders slumped in defeat and he sighed. "Where are you going, then? At least give me that crumb of comfort!"

"I wish I knew, Watson, but when I do find out where I'm going, I'll send word." I attempted a sickly smile. "Don't worry about me, doc. I can take care of myself." I turned to get into the cab, the cabbie already mounted on his perch and looking slightly embarrassed at the display before him. Watson, gentleman to the bitter end, helped me into the cab and shut the door after me. I squeezed his hand reassuringly and cast one final, hopeful glance at the second-story windows, willing Holmes to come to the window and stop me. The curtains remained motionless; there was no austere silhouette. The die was cast.

I turned to the doctor one final time, trying to ignore his silent pleading. "Goodbye, Watson," was all I said before rapping on the roof of the cab to send it rattling down the cobblestone street. As I watched from the rear window, 221B Baker Street and the figure before it grew smaller and smaller, until we turned a corner and it was gone entirely. I was adrift in the great cesspool that was London.

The small trapdoor in the roof of the cab snapped open. "Where to, miss?" grunted the cabbie through the opening.

That was a good question. Where was I going? Could I bunk with the Irregulars as Bernie Flynn? No, Holmes would surely find out. Throw myself upon the mercy of Mycroft? He might be willing to help, but Pall Mall was too close to Baker Street for my comfort. I needed to go somewhere far from Holmes, outside the reach of his web of informants, but where? The obvious choice suddenly slapped me in the face and I addressed the cabbie with a decisive air. "To Charing Cross, my good man. I have to catch a train to North Riding."

~*Excerpt from the private journal of Dr. Watson*~

It was with a heavy heart that I watched the cab roll away down the street. A depression thicker than the fog settled into my bones as I slowly made my way back into the sitting room, mindful of my game leg. It was my leg and the pains that accompany it that had awakened me so early, leaving me awake and alert as the cab clattered up to our door to carry Nona away. Devoid of coherency, I collapsed into my armchair and stared vacantly for an interminable amount of time, trying to surmount the fog of sadness.

Some time later Mrs. Hudson bustled into the sitting room with breakfast and coffee. The thought of food was repugnant at the moment, but I remained silent in my seat. "Nona isn't up yet, I suppose," said Mrs. Hudson, oblivious. "Poor thing looks so worn out these days; think I'll just let her sleep."

Too cowardly to correct her, I grunted noncommittally and she soon left. Her departure left me unabashedly glad, while Nona's was slowing evolving into horrible reality. I feared that my heart was on my shirtsleeve as reality settled more heavily with each passing moment.

The final blow came some half an hour later when Holmes appeared in the doorway in his dressing gown and two days' worth of stubble, blearily shielding his eyes from the sun's glare. "Close the curtains, Watson," he croaked in a stiff voice, shuffling to the table and pouring a prodigious cup of black coffee. I, however, made no move toward the windows, watching him intently. By the time he lowered himself into his own armchair, I had deduced what had happened the night before. I should be a poor physician if I failed to diagnose the symptoms of the common hangover. If Holmes' condition was connected to Nona's tearful departure…

My sorrow quite suddenly plunged into cold-blooded rage. Despite Holmes' arrogance, his idiosyncrasies, the thousand annoyances that never ceased to irritate me, never had I been pushed to this level of wrath with an intensity that bordered on hatred. All I had given up, all I had sacrificed…Keeping my voice low and level, I turned to Holmes and said the two words I had never thought myself to utter.

"You idiot."

His reaction was sharp and sudden. "*What* was that?" he asked, incredulity tingeing his voice.

Bloodshot though they were, Holmes' eyes were of such a piercing intensity that I nearly faltered in my resolve, but summoning up an image of Nona's tear-streaked face, I plowed on. "You, Holmes, are a dense, foolish, obtuse and thick-headed *idiot*."

Holmes' brows drew together in a glower. "I readily admit that drinking excessively is an unwise choice of recreation, but I fail to see how it merits this degree of abuse."

Finesse was not my strong point, and even with a pounding headache, Holmes would run circles around my meager wit. Abandoning tact, I stated bluntly, "Where is Nona, Holmes?"

"A test of my questionable mental acumen, Watson?" Holmes asked facetiously. "Very well, Nona is most likely in the kitchen helping Mrs. Hudson repair the debris from breakfast."

"Wrong," I replied gruffly.

Holmes sat back wearily. "Watson, if you insist on playing games, at least give me something for this beastly headache first."

"Nona is gone, Holmes."

That simple sentence arrested his attention. "Gone where?" he asked more cautiously.

"I do not know."

"And when will she return?" said he.

"In all likelihood, never."

Holmes was stunned. "Never? Why on earth not?"

Did he think me so dense as to believe him innocent? "I believe that you can answer that question better than I, Holmes," I snapped angrily. He still seemed lost, so I decided none-too-gently to jog his memory. "Nona left Baker Street in *tears*, Holmes. She wept as she got into the cab. I don't believe that she left of her own volition. The question remains: What could *possibly* have happened between last night and this morning to make her leave weeping?"

"But she was here last night," murmured Holmes in thought. "We were talking, and then...I don't remember."

"You don't remember?" I exclaimed, rising from my seat. Never had the need to speak burned so urgently in my blood. "The most exceptional woman in London has been driven away in tears, and you don't *remember*? In that case, Holmes, allow me to make some deductions. Last night, you were in the sitting room, proceeding to get dead drunk. Nona comes in, wanting to dissuade you from your path of self-destruction. You hurl the most foul and hurtful imprecations upon her, breaking her heart and sending her out of the room in tears. This morning, unable to bear your idiocy any longer, she packs her few belongings and disappears into the fog, and Heaven only knows where she is or if she is still alive at this moment!"

Memory flooded back into the detective, washing his face of any hint of color. His lips formed the words, "My God," but no sound issued forth.

I, however, was not finished. "By God, Holmes, I have no idea what you said to her, but judging from her reaction, it must have been monstrous! How could you? That dear woman…oh, Holmes, you blind fool! You held her heart and soul in your unworthy hands, and you discarded them both like rubbish! How could you? It is unthinkable that you would be so cruel to a stranger, but even more folly for her, Nona loved you!"

My harsh words were plainly a dagger to his heart, but I was too infuriated to be concerned with niceties. "Loved me?" he echoed weakly.

"Yes, for what it's worth, she loved you with all of her precious heart. And here is something you never thought to deduce; I loved her too!" I was aghast that I had actually said the words aloud, but now the die was cast, and what was done could not be undone. "I watched her grow towards you, Holmes, and I discarded my own inclinations, never thinking to impose upon you. I had hoped that you would someday return her love, that my efforts would not be in vain, but due to your pride and foolishness, you have thrown it all away! Now she is gone!"

Holmes' expression was one of sorrow I had never seen paralleled in my entire career of dealing with death and disease, and I momentarily fancied that the ironclad Sherlock Holmes would finally break down and weep. But instead, he rose from his chair, fixed me with a steely gaze and roared, "And *good riddance!*"

My righteous anger floundered in a sea of confusion. "What?" was all I could gasp.

Holmes folded his arms protectively about his lean frame. "Good riddance! The woman was nothing but a nuisance, always poking about my work! I knew this would come from taking in a woman, Watson; I just knew it!" He cast a devil-may-care expression at me. "Now, old boy, I believe the playing field is clear for you. Marry her, murder her, whatever you wish; it's all the same to me."

"You mean you do not love her? You do not care for her at all?"

He laughed, harshly and coldly, laughed! "My dear Watson, whatever gave you that idea?"

I simply stared at him, horrified. "You-you are inhuman!"

Holmes crossed his arms tighter, as if donning armor. "If only, Watson," he said bleakly. "If only." With that, he disappeared into his room.

Angered beyond words, I thrust myself into my coat and hat and headed out the door, scorning cabs in my fury. I burnt off my furious energy in continuous motion, hardly slowing my stride until the sun rose higher and scorched the fog from the earth. Only then did I stop and allow myself to think. Holmes apparently did not care for Nona. Could this possibly be the tragic fulfillment of my long-abandoned desires? No, I reasoned, Nona still loves Holmes; she admitted it herself. Still, given enough time and the proper motivation…I cursed myself for exploiting such a volatile time, but the thought was tenacious and refused to release me. Another feeling prodded me as well: hunger. I had not eaten breakfast and it was nearing luncheon, so I caught a cab back to my rooms, despite fears of a confrontation with Holmes.

I let myself in and was greeted with the sight of Mrs. Hudson furiously dusting, the red in her eyes not entirely due to the dust. Upon seeing me, she dropped her dust rag. "Oh, Dr. Watson!" she cried. "Is it true? Is Nona-bird truly gone?" I consoled the good lady the best I could and uneasily inquired if Holmes was upstairs. "No, Doctor," she moaned. "He went out this morning just after you left, and I haven't seen him since." Placating her with vague assurances that all would be well, I hinted about luncheon and was rewarded when she steamed off to the kitchen. Holmes did not return for lunch, or supper, and by the time I unhappily retired for the night, he was still absent.

I saw Holmes the following morning, but only as he headed out the door. That first day set the precedent for Holmes' ensuing behavior. For the next week or so I caught only glimpses of him as he left in the morning and returned at nightfall. Every evening upon his return, he would almost hopefully ask if there was news from Nona. Still angered with his ruthless behavior, I always replied with a curt "No," upon which he responded, "Well, thank God for good news." Each instance only served to further irritate me. However, I did not know nor endeavor to care what errand sent him out every day. In hindsight I can only ruefully claim that I saw, but did not observe.

Early in September, when the days were beginning to cool, I was reading the afternoon paper in the sitting room, once more alone. I was mulling over a telegram I had received earlier, a terse note from Nona informing me that she was well and staying with Sherrinford Holmes at Oakstaff Manor. A burden lifted from my heart upon learning that she was safe and sound, but now I was faced with a different problem.

How was I to act upon my newfound knowledge? Should I tell Holmes? Certainly not, I decided, he would not care one way or the other. The question was, should I act upon it? Would Nona be receptive to me, not as a friend, but as a man? The thoughts weighed on my mind so heavily that I did not hear the footsteps on the stairs until a light knock sounded on the door, startling me into alertness.

I bade the visitor enter, and in strolled Wiggins, captain of the unofficial Baker Street Detective Force. The begrimed lad grinned and snapped me a cheeky salute, which made my inner military veteran cringe in horror. "Mr. 'Olmes in, doc?" he queried.

"I fear not, Wiggins," I replied evenly. "I do not know when he will return, but you are welcome to wait."

"Naow, guv, s'orful noice of ye, but Oi carn't stay. Jus' tell Mr. 'Olmes 'at we ain't found 'er yet."

"Found whom?" I queried.

"Miss No-na," he enunciated, as if I were hard of hearing. "Mr. 'Olmes 'ad us on th' scent since Mond'y last. Sure 'opin' Oi finds 'er first an' wins th' fiver."

"Holmes offered five pounds to the lad who finds Nona?" I asked incredulously.

The boy nodded vigorously. "As' roight, guv, n' as' why Oi gotta be goin' back t' work. Give 'im the message, woan't ya?" I agreed, and the young businessman was gone out the door as promptly as he entered.

Instead of clarifying matters, this new tidbit only muddied the waters further. Holmes was searching for Nona, quite frantically if he was going out every day and offering two weeks' standard pay to the first street urchin who spotted her. Could this mean that his previous words were nothing but prideful bravado and that Holmes did care for Nona? Knowing Holmes as I did, I found that explanation not only probable, but likely. My own dilemma was how to equate myself into this convoluted triangle. Could I be misjudging Holmes' actions? Should I be patient and, above all, silent in hopes that Nona could forget Holmes in favor of a more stable alternative? Drawing a medical analogy, I resolved to perform one last test before I prescribed a cure.

Once again, Holmes did not return until late. Although he was usually adept at concealing his inner expressions, in this instance even the casual observer could see fatigue in every line and limb. Holmes trudged into the sitting room, rather damp from the fog and drizzling rain, removing his shoes and coat with a lethargy that bespoke his exhaustion. Before he could rally his forces, I made a preemptive strike, speaking with familiar casualness from behind the evening newspaper. "Any sign of her, Holmes?"

"Neither hide nor hair," he almost moaned, dropping his sodden overcoat on the floor, not wishing to expend the energy to hang it up. "It is as if the earth itself has swallowed her up. Mycroft's agents are useless, should be ashamed to-" His monologue ceased abruptly in realization, but I had all the data I required. Holmes glanced at me with mingled wariness and amusement at my sudden guile. "That was devious, Watson," said he, the same blend of emotions emerging in his voice. "There are hidden depths to my Boswell." He threw himself into his armchair and studiously ignored me, gazing pensively into the hearth flame. Presently he spoke, "Might I inquire as to how you deduced the situation?"

I rattled the paper as I nonchalantly turned the page, reveling in my minute triumph. "As much as it would please me to give you my twenty-step process of deduction and elimination, the truth is actually more simple. While you were out, Wiggins came by with a status report."

"And?" Holmes said eagerly, forgetting his pretense.

I shook my head and his face fell as he relapsed into abstraction. I did not broach conversation, content to wait Holmes out.

My patience was soon rewarded. Holmes cleared his throat uneasily. "Well, Watson," he said lightly, "what do you make of it?"

I smiled inwardly at the wordplay. That selfsame phrase had been used at the beginning of many of our most challenging cases, but this case was proving to be more challenging than either Holmes or I had faced before. "What will you do when you find her?" I queried.

He tossed his head irritably, annoyed to be the questioned instead of the questioner. "I shall tell her to return."

"Tell?" I echoed.

His face relented a bit. "I shall ask her to return."

"Ask?"

He realized that I would not be daunted. Shrinking into himself, Holmes said more to the flames than to me, "I shall apologize in the humblest terms in my vocabulary and beg her to return."

I am certain that anyone else would see Holmes as staring blankly into the fire, but as one who had learned to hear the words he did not say, I could read anguish in his tight eyes, in his rigid back. When I coupled this with an image

of Nona's brimming eyes, there was no other option left to me. Over the pro-
testations of my heart, I discarded my paper and withdrew a creased telegram
from my jacket pocket. Wordlessly I handed it across to Holmes, who took it
with a puzzled air. He scanned it briefly and his eyes went wide with amazement. "North Riding!" he cried. "Of course! Fool that I am, I could not see the
wood for the trees!" He leapt from his armchair and dashed to the door, stoop-
ing for his coat and boots.

I rose from my own chair. "Holmes, you can't possibly leave now!"

"Why ever not, Watson?" said he, halfway into his coat.

"By the time you reach Kingston-on-the-Moor, Nona and the rest of the
household will be in bed. Somehow I doubt that being rousted from a sound
sleep will put her in a forgiving state of mind, not to mention that an apology
will not have a productive effect if the speaker collapses from exhaustion halfway through."

Holmes cocked a sardonic brow and grudgingly returned the coat to its
stand. "Very well, Watson," he replied. "I shall obey my doctor's orders."

"For once," I could not help but mutter as I returned to my chair.

Holmes began to make his way to the bedrooms, presumably to sleep, when
suddenly he paused in the doorway. "Watson," he began with his back to me, "I
owe you an apology as well. Will you forgive my cavalier treatment of you this
past week?"

An apology from Holmes was rarer than snowfall in June, and I was
momentarily stunned into silence. When I recovered, I simply replied, "Pride
makes a poor suitor, Holmes. Remember that tomorrow." He did not turn, but
simply progressed onto his rooms. I remained in my chair until the fire died
out, making no move to relight it. The damp chill made my leg ache, but such
discomfort was easily forgotten, shadowed by the blade in my heart.

~**~

I trudged through the field at the rear of Oakstaff Manor, Virgil at my side
with his child-sized violin securely in its case. I had been Virgil's "music
teacher" for roughly a week, giving the lad violin lessons to offset my room and
board. Sherrinford and his family had welcomed me with open arms, not even
caring to hear the cause of my troubles, for which I was unabashedly grateful.
They agreed that I could stay indefinitely, but balked at the notion of my earning my keep with household chores. I in turn balked at the suggestion of my
being a freeloader. It was Virgil's new governess, Theresa, who suggested a

compromise with the position of music teacher. The duties were light with only one charge and lessons five days a week, and the benefits included free room and board along with a weekly stipend of two pounds six.

However, I *earned* my wages. Virgil was a promising student, but he was woefully inexperienced. Unlike the piano player, who simply memorizes a series of keys in a song, the violin player must create his own notes After the first two lessons we were forced to move the practice area to a copse of trees some distance from the Manor, out of respect for others' auditory senses. By the third lesson my regard for my own instructor and violin teachers everywhere skyrocketed.

As pleasant as it was to be back in Oakstaff, I found little joy in my situation. When I was not tutoring Virgil or spending time in his and Theresa's company, I was alone, drawing. Art had been my major in college, but since I arrived in London I had woefully neglected the practice; I simply had not the time to spend on sketching and painting. If my sketches over the week were placed in a chronological row, even the basest of art lovers could see the stages of emotion through which I was going: light, feather-touch landscapes when I waxed melancholy; boldly-lined still life when I vented my rage; realistic portraits when I finally found peace with myself.

The two of us reached the patch of oak trees and settled into the shade. The temperature was dropping in the advent of the English fall, but the sun's glare was enough to make the shade welcome. Virgil opened the case, ran rosin along the bow and asked, "Do you think you'll be able to tell me today, Miss Nona?"

"That depends on how much you've been practicing," I replied, settling on a large rock. I had promised Virgil a story about his uncle if he could run through his scales without a single faulty note. I had been hesitant about the offer at first, fearing that I could no longer speak of Holmes, but after a week of intense introspection and artistic therapy, I found myself no longer angry with Holmes; heartbroken, yes, but not angry.

Virgil nodded vigorously. "Oh, yes, I've been practicing in the cellar. I tried in the kitchen, but Mrs. Clark told me I was curdling the milk, so I went to the cellar."

I smiled at the image. "All right then, let's begin with the C scale. Fingers ready…and begin." I smiled encouragingly throughout the next half-hour; it was the only way to keep the grimace from my face. After the half-hour, I interrupted with: "Let's give your fingers a rest, okay, Virg?"

Virgil's tiny shoulders slumped. "I'll never learn how to play."

"Now, now, it's okay," I soothed. "Everyone has to start somewhere. When I was six, I couldn't even-" A twig snapped, stopping me. Someone was approaching. I turned to Virgil. "You didn't forget to clean your room again, did you?" He shook his head and another twig snapped, nearer. And who should appear from behind a tree but the object of my thoughts, Sherlock Holmes!

Virgil crowed with delight and ran to clasp his uncle's knees, but Holmes only patted his head abstractedly, his level gaze on me. I returned the gaze as I said, "I think practice can end early today, Virgil. Take your violin back to the house, please." The boy threw me a questioning glance and I tried a smile. "We'll be along in a minute. I'd like to have a word with your uncle." Holmes flinched almost imperceptibly as Virgil obediently packed up his instrument and crunched off in the direction of the house. Once his footsteps died away, I addressed my erstwhile love, not rising from my seat. "How did you find me?"

Holmes shrugged uncomfortably. "It was not difficult. One had only to follow the incessant screeching."

I shook my head, irritated. "No, I mean how did you follow me from London?"

A ghost of his old ironic smile flashed across his face. "As I said, Nona, one only had to follow the screeching. Virgil should expect a stern letter from the Prime Minister soon." I ignored his hyperbole, turning my eyes to the forest floor. Holmes cleared his throat. "So, are you ready to come home yet?"

"Yes, I think I am," I replied blithely. "It is almost teatime and Mrs. Clark produces an excellent tray."

"That is not what I meant!" Holmes growled.

"I know perfectly well what you meant," I retorted, turning my head in effrontery. The nerve of him, just showing up and asking if I was ready to come home! Of course, the fact that he showed up at all was suggestive, as was his use of the word "home."

"Nona," he began again, "I have never been adept at expressing myself-"

"You did an admirable job of it last week!" I snapped.

"Damn it, woman! I am trying to apologize!"

"Then stop bandying words and just apologize!"

Holmes drew a deep breath, stepped forward and did something utterly shocking; he clumsily descended to one knee at my side and took my hand in his. "Nona, I-I am heartily sorry for the cruel things I said to you that night. I offer no excuses, for the blame is surely mine. I have been selfish and foolish, and I regret it. Please accept my apologies, Nona, for it is all I have to offer. Please forgive me."

Stunned would be too kind a word for my reaction; I was utterly, totally flabbergasted. An apology from Holmes, on bended knee no less! His mono-tone words had a note of frequent rehearsal to them, but the sincerity in his eyes drove any thoughts of duplicity from my mind. Touched beyond words, I could only murmur, "I forgive you, Holmes, and I'm sorry for shouting at you."

Holmes burst into a beatific smile and leapt to his feet. "Thank you, Nona, thank you! Quickly, you must hurry and pack, there is a train to London in an hour!"

I wasn't letting him off that easily. "Pack?" I asked innocently. "Whatever for, Holmes?"

Holmes was puzzled. "Then you're not...but you said..."

"I said I forgave you, and I do," I said firmly, "but I'm not going back with you."

"Why?" he cried.

I rose from my seat. "I think that the more appropriate question is, 'Why not?' How do I know that you aren't going to do it again? I don't doubt the sin-cerity of your apology, but how do I know that you won't need to give me another apology, and another? You cut me deeply that night, Holmes; why wouldn't you do it again?" I shook my head firmly, cutting off his protest. "No, Holmes. Until you overcome your problem, I can't go back with you."

His face was bleak. "What can I do then?"

I gestured through the copse. "Take a walk with me."

He looked at me askance, but acquiesced.

We walked together through the trees in silence, skirting the edge of the pasture beyond. We emerged from the shelter of the branches onto a pictur-esque scene. An ancient oak, probably the forebear of the other trees in the area, ruled the scene atop a low hill. As far as the eye could see extended an ocean of land, green pasture giving way to purple moorland under the declin-ing September sun. I gestured to the scenery. "What do you remember about this place, Holmes?"

"I fail to follow you," he replied.

"Come on; there must be some obscure memory jogged loose by this sight. Tell me about it."

Holmes uneasily complied, casting about for a scrap of remembrance, his eyes lighting as he glanced at the stately oak tree. Beckoning for me to follow, he strode up the hill, seizing upon an old iron ring embedded in the trunk. "This," he declared proudly. "I used to tether my pony here."

"*You* had a pony?" I asked incredulously.

"I was a child once, Nona," he said defensively. "I had him when I was seven, shortly after we returned from the Continent."

"What was his name?" I asked.

"Pony."

"That's it?"

He grinned ruefully. "I was never one for names." He continued eagerly, needing no further prompting. "Occasionally I would ride out as far as the moors, spending the night in the wilderness, or at least what I thought was the wilderness. My mother always worried when I spent the night alone, but my father said…" He broke off, the delighted smile disappearing like smoke. "He said it builds character," he finished in a whisper.

This was it. I sat on the ground and pulled him down next to me. "This is what I meant, Holmes. This is what I tried to tell you back at Baker Street. I didn't do a very good job then, so I'm trying again now. You need to let this go."

"How?" he said bleakly, staring out at the horizon, his eyes brimming with sorrow.

I bit my lip in thought. "I…I'm not sure I know. Give it a little thought, at least." Rising from my seat, I could see that he made to follow, but I pressed him back down with a hand on his shoulder. "Stay here for a bit," I commanded softly, praying that I was doing the right thing. "Give it some thought, think about what's really important. Just remember…" I allowed my hand to stray upwards, burying itself in his thick black hair. "I care about you, Sherlock Holmes. *You*."

Leaving him under the tree, I turned and made my way through the trees and back to the edge of the clearing, sitting on the stone I had previously vacated and settling down for a wait. One hour passed, then two; the sun dipped lower and I continued to fidget. What on earth could be keeping him? The ache of worry in my stomach began to grow, and just as I was about to go search for him, I spotted his tall form heading this way through the trees. Instead of going to meet him, I remained seated, waiting for him to make his way over. I rose to meet him as he stood before me, his face pale but composed, his eyes slightly red. "How do you feel?" I asked shakily.

He parted his lips to release a single word. "Clean."

The gratitude in his voice brought tears to my eyes. As we stood together, a harsh and sudden gust of wind assaulted us, howling through the trees, and my foggy memory dug up an image of Holmes on that fateful, rainy night.

Holmes grimaced, as if reading my mind. "It won't be the same as before."

There was no need to ask what he meant. "I know," I admitted. "So this time we'll make it better." I turned back to the field, glancing back over my shoulder. "Ready to go home?"

A genuine smile was born on both our lips as we silently walked back towards the Manor, leaving the past behind us.

❧   ❧   ❧

Needless to say, I returned to Baker Street that very day. Virgil was disconsolate, but I promised to visit every month and he promised to have his scales perfected by the time I came back. Watson and Mrs. Hudson were overjoyed to see us that evening, although Watson seemed strangely withdrawn. The next morning when I awoke in my own room, I changed into a housedress and mobcap from my reclaimed wardrobe and fairly skipped into the kitchen. I was never so glad to see a pile of dirty dishes in all my life.

One more event bears mentioning. Only three days after my return to Baker Street, I was polishing silver in the kitchen when the door sounded with a knock. "I got it!" I called to no one in particular, relishing my presence here once again. Moving swiftly to the door, I admitted a lovely young lady with blond hair, dressed tastefully but inexpensively, who nervously bit her lip as she fished a calling card from her reticule. I took and read it, only the sheer force of my will keeping my eyebrows down. The plainly printed card read simply, 'Miss Mary Morstan.' With an unusually large smile, I assured her that Mr. Holmes would be delighted to see her and fairly dashed up the stairs to announce her. Without knocking I entered the sitting room, catching the tail end of a heated discussion over, of all things, Watson's pocket watch. I announced Miss Morstan aloud and received permission to admit her. Escorting her up the stairs, I entered first to monitor Watson's reaction.

Dr. John Watson looked at her.

Miss Mary Morstan looked at him.

And the rest, as they say, is history.

CHAPTER 15

In Which I Am Always a Bridesmaid and Almost a Bride

You may be disappointed to learn that I did not participate in the Morstan-Small case. My reasoning behind this was lack of interest. Thanks to a little volume called "The Sign of Four," I already knew exactly what was going to happen, and I did not wish to get in the way. Therefore, I was not surprised in the least when, as we were gathered in the sitting room at the conclusion of the case, Watson announced that Miss Morstan had accepted him as a husband-in-prospect.

Overjoyed, I threw my arms around him in an exuberant hug. "Bravo, Watson! Mucho congrats! I confidently predict many years of wedded bliss!"

Watson smiled his thanks and turned to Holmes for approval. The detective stood by the fireplace grate, pipe in hand, eyes boring through his friend. "Are you sure?" he asked finally. For some odd reason Watson shot a glance in my direction before turning back to Holmes and nodding solemnly.

At that, Holmes' face was wreathed in smiles as he stepped forwards and shook Watson's hand in delight. "In that case, my dear fellow, accept my heartfelt congratulations! I am sure that you and Miss Morstan will be very happy together."

What? That didn't sound right! "Holmes," I said curiously, "are you feeling all right?"

He looked up in surprise. "Perfectly. Why?"

"You aren't supposed to say that!" I protested, the pair of them giving me a look that spoke of Bedlam. In the interest of my sanity, I explained, "Holmes, one of your biggest trademarks is your disdain for the softer passions! That's one of the things that made you famous! What would your fans think if they heard you saying something like that?"

He raised a brow playfully. "Really? Well, we can't have that. Not to worry, Nona," he said with confidence. "Since that is the case, I am sure that if and when this account is ever published, my biographer can put some appropriately cold-blooded words in my mouth."

And, as I am sure most of you know, that is precisely what happened.

❧   ❧   ❧

Watson and Mary (as I was soon entreated to call her) spent the next few weeks almost exclusively in each other's company. Holmes and I were hardly put out by this; we were actually rather glad for it, as it gave us the space we needed to rebuild. Still, on occasion Watson would assist on some trivial case, leaving me in Mary's company.

Mary Morstan was the typical Victorian lady, sweet, proper, generous and demure. At first I had thought that my more contemporary views would offend her, but on the contrary, she had a well-developed and open mind beneath her hat. She was more delighted than shocked to hear of my time traveling when Watson told her. I was a bit miffed that he had spilled my secret, but he protested that he would keep nothing from his wife, and I was forced to concede the point.

Mary and I would often have tea together or traverse the length of Regent's Park, talking about the future. Through our conversations I came to realize that Watson, of course, had better sense than to fall for a piece of blond Victorian fluff. Mary was a woman of layers and depth, and we quickly grew to be fast friends.

Still, I was rather taken aback when she asked me to be her maid of honor. "Mary," I protested, "shouldn't that honor go to someone a little closer to you?"

She laughed merrily. "Oh, my dear Nona, I fear you don't understand. My only family was my father, may he rest in peace, and my only other close acquaintance is Mrs. Forrester, my employer, whom I fear is a bit too old for bridesmaiding. Anyway, you may think this silly, but I feel as if we've been friends forever! Isn't that odd? However, if you do not wish to, I shall understand."

"No, Mary!" I exclaimed. "It's not that! I just wanted to make sure. I'd be happy to be your bridesmaid!" I hastily changed topics. "Have you and Watson decided on a date yet?"

She colored prettily at the mention of Watson, the epitome of the blushing bride. "John and I were considering October tenth," she said.

"So soon?" I queried.

"I don't see why not," she replied a bit testily. "I have no relatives to please with an extended engagement, and John's relations in Edinburgh have long since abandoned contact with him. Besides, I should prefer the beauty of October for my wedding day than dreary November."

I could think of no better argument and earnestly told her so, soothing her sensitive feathers.

The day of the tenth dawned clear and cold. Poor Watson was a nervous wreck, clumsy with anxiety. I swear the poor fellow spilled his coffee and dropped his fork twice, and that at breakfast alone! My frequent exhortations that "everything will be fine" had little effect on him, and even my authority on the future as resident time-traveler did not reassure him. I suppose that his unease was justified; marriage was a great deal more final in Victorian times. Holmes was silent throughout the morning, eyes unusually dark throughout the day as we enjoyed Watson's last day as a Baker Street resident.

The wedding ceremony was scheduled for four o'clock, so as the hour approached, we retreated to our separate quarters to prepare. I changed into my nicest town frock, pinned my hair into a simple bun and decided to splurge on such a special occasion, hanging my diamond pendant around my neck. A brief application of cosmetics rendered me presentable in public and I went to fetch the groom and best man, whistling "Get Me to the Church on Time" as I fairly skipped up the stairs. I was so happy for Watson; the wonderful man deserved all this and more. The "more" would be the wedding present I had for the pair, a meager offering, but mine own. Coming upon the door to Watson's room, I paused as I heard my name mentioned through the cracked portal.

"...what you told me about Nona, after all. Are you sure that you are doing this for the right reasons?" That was Holmes' voice, quite serious.

"For the final time, Holmes, I am sure." Watson, sounding a bit exasperated. "After all, it is not so sudden a reversal. I do love Mary and I am glad for this."

"But after what you said, Watson! You may be making a grievous error!"

"And if I was, what could I do about it?" Silence from Holmes. "No answer, my friend?" A sigh. "I will be the first to admit that my love for Nona was once of a romantic tone, but that has…changed, some time ago."

Holmes, questioning. "You no longer love her?"

"No, of course I do, but not in the same way. I love her just as strongly; it is simply that I believe my love has transmuted into a more familial affection, leaving ample room for Mary. Does that make sense to you now?"

"Love never makes much sense, Watson, especially for this particular cur-mudgeon-in-training, but I believe that I…how does she say it? 'Get your drift.'"

In like vein I drifted away from the door back into the sitting room, collaps-ing onto the divan to ponder my stupidity. Watson had been in love with me? Oh, how could I have been so dense? I had never seen any sign of Watson's affection for me! Could he be that good of an actor, or had I simply not wanted to see? Had I been so wrapped up in Holmes that I ignored Watson?

As I reviewed my actions over the past year, I realized that I would not have changed them. Watson and Mary were meant to be together, that was obvious even to the simplest acquaintance. If I had recognized Watson's feelings, acted upon them, fallen in love with him, then where would Mary be? No, all things considered, it was for the best. I was interrupted in my thoughts as Holmes and Watson emerged, both exceedingly spiffy in their black suits and top hats. Determined to forget what I had just heard, I pasted on my most dazzling smile and complimented the men, allowing Holmes to help me with my coat. Checking one pocket for the ring I was to present during the ceremony and discreetly checking another for my gift, I took Holmes' arm and we went to the waiting cab.

The ceremony was a civil one, done with reverence and decorum, with Holmes and I as the necessary two witnesses. Mary was lovely in a simple, albeit white, dress, two of the Agra pearls sparkling as earrings in her ears. The service was short but heartfelt. At the speaking of the vows, I felt a pressing need for my pocket-handkerchief and averted my eyes to delay the inevitable.

Holmes caught and held my gaze, his eyes glowing with intensity such as I had rarely seen before. Was he casting his thoughts toward the future, a future with me? Could his piercing gray gaze penetrate cloudy images yet-to-come, where he and I swore ourselves to one another with eternal love as the fruit of our vows?

I was so caught up in the possibility that I almost missed my cue, hastily handing the plain gold band to Mary. She slipped it onto Watson's finger with infinite tenderness, breathing, "With this ring, I thee wed." The dams of my eyes trembled in their foundations. Watson accepted a daintier ring from Holmes and repeated the process with Mary, his whispered words giving no one any further doubt to his devotion. Was it my imagination, or did Holmes' eyes mirror that devotion as he glanced at me?

I would never know for the Justice of the Peace proclaimed John Watson and Mary Morstan man and wife, the groom kissed the bride, and I was left scrambling for my handkerchief.

After the ceremony the four of us went to dinner at Simpson's on the Strand, even Holmes caught up in the exultant rush. We were positively effervescent in our reminiscences as Watson accepted well wishes from several of his fans that stopped at the table. Holmes scowled his way through autographs for the aforementioned well-wishers, and after his third glass of champagne, he lost enough inhibition to manage a clumsy and halting toast to the Watsons.

Holmes cleared his throat hesitantly and stood with his glass in hand. "Um, yes," he began, casting about for something eloquent. "A toast to Watson and...Mrs. Watson. May they have, ah, years of happiness, and...may they never require my services again! I mean professionally, of course, since I normally deal with tragedies, and I surely would not wish that upon you both, but still, Watson, you are always welcome to collaborate with me on my cases, if you aren't too busy, and, ah...oh, drat it all...um, congratulations." He collapsed into his seat again, ears burning furiously as his eyes scorched a hole through his plate. We hid our smiles as we dutifully sipped our champagne, and Watson tactfully changed the subject.

Some hours later over dessert, I brought up the subject of wedding gifts. Watson and Mary protested, of course, but I waved it away and procured the envelope I had secreted in my pocket. Too curious for further argument, Mary opened the envelope and withdrew in shock forty pounds in various notes. "Forty," she breathed. "This is too much, Nona!"

"Nonsense!" I proclaimed, waving her objections away, "a mere trifle." Actually it was most of my savings, but I wasn't about to let them know. "It is a bit unsentimental, I know, but I think that this is more practical." The pair of them exclaimed their gratitude and I basked in their friendship.

"On the subject of gifts," Holmes echoed, a hand diving into his own jacket pocket and retrieving a similar envelope. "It is rather small," he continued, "but it was the best I could come up with on short notice." My eyebrows rose in a smile. Great minds think alike, I supposed.

Watson opened the envelope and withdrew what seemed to be a set of documents. The good doctor hastily perused them, his jaw literally dropping in shock. "A house," he breathed at last, turning widened eyes to Holmes. "A house in Kensington." Mary gasped aloud and her hand flew to her face as we three regarded Holmes, who was slowly turning pink under the scrutiny. "Holmes," Watson choked out, "I don't know what to say."

Neither did I. Holmes had bought them a house! Where did he find the money for that? The blackmail scandal? I knew that the august personage had been grateful, but I had no idea of just how grateful until now. Well, I surmised that it was either that or Holmes had gotten a loan from his brothers. Either way, it was a stunning gift.

Holmes ran a finger under his collar and tried to smile. "Think nothing of it, old boy. Only a fraction of that is a gift. Consider the rest merely accumulated back pay for years of employment in the Baker Street Agency for Detection."

Watson blinked hastily to clear away moisture, and Mary was tearing openly. Watson cleared his throat. "Holmes, I-I can't thank you enough."

For a brief moment a flash of public emotion glinted in the detective's eyes. "You already have," he said simply before reapplying himself to dessert and inquiring after the Watsons' plans for a honeymoon in France.

Finally wearied with good cheer, we stumbled our way out onto the darkened pavement and called a cab for the newlyweds. Wishing them good fortune on their impending honeymoon, we saw them off, both of us waving as the cab drove away. Only after it had disappeared did I allow myself to relax, drained of merriment after an emotionally trying day.

Holmes, equally drained, rolled his shoulders irritably. "Nona, promise me that you will never let me do that again."

I glanced up, shocked. "What, the gift?" I queried.

He shook his head. "The toast."

I suppressed a giggle at the memory. Glancing up, I found Holmes looking down on me silently. I considered referring back to his gift, curious as to exactly how he bought them a *house*, but I knew that he would find that uncomfortable. Instead I simply said, "Well, Holmes."

His eyes cleared at my lack of comment. "Well, Nona."

"Let's go home."

"A capital idea."

So, we went home.

❦   ❦   ❦

The lamplighters plied their trade as we dismounted our cab at Baker Street. Holmes paid the driver as I unlocked the front door, stepping inside. I was about to go to my room when I remembered a book I wanted to read before bed, currently residing on Holmes' bookshelf. With an irritated sniff, I trudged up the stairs and into the sitting room, swiftly locating the coveted volume. Turning to go downstairs, I paused as Holmes entered the room and shut the door behind him, shedding coat and hat onto the coat-rack. I clutched the book to my chest and tried to control my breathing. With Watson now married, I realized, Holmes and I were alone, very alone.

Speaking around the constriction in my chest, I muttered, "Goodnight, Holmes," and tried to brush past him towards the door.

"Nona." His low, taut voice froze me in my tracks just before I reached the door. He cleared his throat behind me. "Now that Watson has left these quarters, Nona, perhaps you would care to take up residence in his room. It should provide a larger modicum of comfort for you."

"That's very kind of you," I replied uneasily, "but I think that we should save it for Watson. Heaven knows that married life is no cakewalk; Watson may soon need to hide out here after some marital spat." That wasn't strictly the truth, but what could I tell him? *I want to keep my own room since my new one would only be a few steps from yours? That I'm afraid of what I would do, lying with just a wall between us, night after night? That I'm afraid that my unheeding feet might carry me into your arms and your bed one night and we might do something that we would both regret?*

"Well, then, we shall put him in the maid's quarters," Holmes said with an irreverent smirk.

My reply left my mouth before I could consider it. "At least he won't be thrown out to freeze."

I could have slapped myself as I saw Holmes recoil in pain. "Oh, God, Holmes!" I cried, aghast at my own density. "I'm sorry! I don't know what came over me! Oh, forgive me, Holmes, that was stupid and cruel-"

"And justified."

"And—no, no, not at all! Not at all! I already forgave you; I truly did, but…I fear that the effects are somewhat lingering." Holmes steadfastly avoided my gaze, standing stiffly near the mantle, suddenly finding something interesting in the fire. I placed my book on an end table, drew closer to him and tried to draw his eyes to mine. "And you, Holmes? Have you forgiven me for the awful things I said to you?"

He turned to me in shock. "Forgive you? Perish the thought! I realize now that I deserved those imprecations, each and every one. Selfish, stupid…"

It was still an open wound for him as well. I reached out and took his hand to silence him, feeling his slender fingers shaking in my grip. "Only time can heal this kind of thing, time, effort and forgiveness. Still, maybe it will make you feel better to know that…that I was overjoyed to come back with you. Secretly, so secretly that I didn't even know, I wanted you to find me."

His shoulders heaved as he clasped my hand, his face pale in the gaslight. "I tried to cast you away," he exhaled. "I tried to cast you from my mind, to rip you from my life and harden my heart against you, but it was no use." His hands left mine and went to rest on my waist. "Despite my efforts, Nona, I am but flesh and blood, heir to all of the tortures thereof." His voice dropped to a whisper. "I am not made of stone."

My vision was swimming and my throat burned. "I am glad for it…"

I love him; I love him so and I want him…

My hands slid up his arms to his trembling shoulders. "…for we would be very uncomfortable…"

I want every last part of him…

My voice dropped as well. "…if you were."

I want…

The door to the sitting room suddenly creaked open and Mrs. Hudson appeared!

"Mr. Holmes, will you be needing anything before-?" Holmes and I flew apart, blushing madly, but not before the redoubtable Scotswoman took in the situation and, regrettably, came to the correct conclusion. Her brows darkened and her Scotch lilt became more pronounced in her severity.

"Nona," she said heavily, dropping my pet name. I hung my head. "I think it be time for bed."

It would seem that we were not as alone as I thought. "But I-"

"*Bed.*"

The jig was up then. Shuffling my feet, I reluctantly turned back to Holmes. "Goodnight," I said again, a trifle wistfully.

He lowered his head to my ear and breathed, "'Sleep govern thine eyes, peace in thy breast," before walking proudly straight-backed to his own, empty bed.

I smiled as I mentally finished the couplet from, quite appropriately, "Romeo and Juliet." *'Oh, that I would sleep in peace so sweet to rest.'*

I turned and left the sitting room, hopping down the stairs with Mrs. Hudson at my back. At the door to my room I turned to face her. "What was *that* all about?" I cried.

"I'm wantin' an answer to that myself!" she retorted, hands on hips.

I kept my voice hurt and angry. "What's the big deal? I thought you wanted Holmes and me to be together!"

She shook her already-graying head. "I can't argue with that, lassie. If you and Mr. Holmes were to wed, my bird, I would skip to the chapel! But I don't want you to wed for the wrong reasons!"

I cocked my head skeptically. "S'plain," I commanded.

"If I hadn't come in when I did, Nona-bird, you wouldn't be in your bed come the morn. You'd be in *his!*"

I gasped in shock. "Mrs. Hudson!" As the product of a more decadent age, it didn't shock me so much that she *said* it, but that *she* said it. Martha Hudson was the most proper woman I knew; for her to say such things, right in the open, was practically scandalous!

She cut me off in her businesslike brogue. "Now, now, Nona-bird, I wasn't born with the Mrs. before my name. I know what it's like between a man and woman in love, and Henry and I, God rest his soul, came far too close once as well. Nona, dearie, do you not know the scandal t'would cause if you and Mr. Holmes were…" She hesitated, bowing to Victorian sensibilities before continuing. "It'd be monstrous! He'd be branded a ne'er-do-well, and no client would darken his doorstep again! You'd be called tramp behind your back! And," she added, "to say nothin' of my reputation as keeper of a respectable house!"

I thought about that for a minute. She was right; the consequences of our actions would run far deeper than anything I was used to before. Not only would my reputation suffer, but Holmes' as well, along with that of our friends. I sighed with regret. "You're right, of course, Mrs. H. Thank you." I grinned with sudden levity. "Heaven forbid should I tarnish your reputation!"

She smiled in relief. "Thank the Lord for that. I'm glad you understand, dear. Away with you now, birdie, and pleasant dreams." With that she walked down the hall and into her room. I opened my door and stood in the doorway, gazing up at the general location of Holmes' room. Maybe, just maybe…

"*BED!*" roared an unseen, vengeful Scot.

I dashed into my room and slammed the door, only to hear a similar slamming from the direction of the sitting room.

✤   ✤   ✤

I shall never know if Holmes came to the conclusion on his own or if Mrs. Hudson got to him first, but the next morning at breakfast he was courteous and polite, the perfect gentleman. By unspoken agreement that night was never spoken of between us again.

However, we talked about everything else. Oh, Lord, we talked! We used our newfound solitude to discover everything about the other and to open ourselves as well, building the trust necessary for a relationship. Hardly a pertinent topic escaped our thorough decimation. Holmes took many minor cases and he drew me into them, sometimes physically, sometimes intellectually, never excluding me from any facet of his life. I in turn introduced him to some of my more enjoyable activities, letting him know my preferences.

That is not to say that our lives were peaches and cream. As is bound to happen when two stubborn people are drawn together, we did have the occasional scuffle. However, none of these compared to the magnitude of our previous altercation. Most were resolved within a day or two. The worst of the arguments came about when Holmes expressed his disapproval over my sitting up for him when he was out late on a case, protesting that my health would fail. I threw the health argument back in his face, saying that I sat up because I was worried about him without Watson to guard his back. After three days of pouting in opposite corners, we compromised: I promised to go to bed earlier and he agreed to take a revolver on his "recon" missions. Of course, I neglected to mention that I would lie awake in bed, listening for the stealthy opening and closing of the front door before I went to sleep.

We grew into a routine, each completely comfortable with the other, our love growing daily. Little did we know that it would soon be torn asunder.

✤   ✤   ✤

Late at night on the sixteenth of October, Holmes and I were returning from a night on the town. I had finally dragged him to the Savoy to see Gilbert and Sullivan's comic opera, "The Pirates of Penzance."

The comic opera, which in my time are better known as 'musicals,' was one that I remembered from Broadway, and I thoroughly enjoyed myself. Holmes, however, complained that such base entertainments were beneath his intellect.

"Come on, Holmes," I protested as the hansom rattled down the dark streets. "That's a classic! People will be watching that in New York for a century and more!"

He snorted. "A lasting tribute to the American sense of humor."

"When are you going to stop picking on Americans?" I teased.

"When they give us our colonies back," he retorted.

I stuck my nose in the air. "Nobody likes a smartass," I quipped in imitation of his own Oxbridgian tones.

"Then everyone must hate you," he said with a smile.

I rolled my eyes as the cab ground to a halt in front of the flat. "Pay the cabbie, smartass," I threw over my shoulder as I hopped from the cab. He did so, and as I climbed the front steps with key in hand, I could hear him humming a melody from an hour past under his breath, base entertainments indeed.

Neither of us was tired, so we settled ourselves in the sitting room, nestled in armchairs before the roaring fire. Holmes was smoking his pipe and idly daydreaming, and I had changed into a housedress and was performing the bi-weekly chore of mending, plying needle and thread as I repaired one of his shirts that was damaged in a knife fight with a suspect. He hadn't wanted to tell me exactly how he ripped the shirt, but I had refused to mend it until he did.

We sat in a comfortable silence until the mantle clock chiming twelve brought a thought to my mind. "Holmes?"

"Hmm?"

"It's the seventeenth."

He glanced up at the clock. "So it is."

"Holmes, in a few days it will have been exactly one year since I came to London, to this time."

That got his attention. He glanced at the clock again and fixed me with an incredulous stare. "Only a year?" he asked in wonder. "It has felt as if you had always been here..." He smiled at me oddly before his ears reddened and he changed the subject. "Have you heard from Watson lately?"

I nodded. "Mm-hmm, I was over in Kensington just the other day. They're all moved in, and the house looks beautiful. Watson is still looking for a small practice to buy into, though."

"I can see that marriage has not yet driven him back to our arms," he quipped.

"Holmes," I said warningly, "marriage is not some chain that shackles you against your will. It's the greatest state of happiness you can achieve. Sure, you argue and scuffle; my own parents rarely saw eye to eye in their marriage, but my father told me that he wouldn't have it otherwise." I smiled at him. "Just wait until you're married." *To me.* "Then you'll see."

Holmes looked a trifle uncomfortable and puffed his pipe furiously, seizing a random book off of the side table. I couldn't see the title, but it looked unfamiliar. However, after only a few pages, Holmes snapped the book shut and rose with it, clearing his pipe. "I'm going to Watson's," he said tersely. "Don't wait up for me."

"What?" I asked incredulously. "Watson's? But, Holmes, he and Mary will surely be asleep by—" Even as I spoke, he shrugged on his coat and hat, snatched the unfamiliar book and was out the door. "-now," I finished to the closed door. I shook my head in wonderment. Never in a million, billion years would I understand Sherlock Holmes.

~*Excerpt from the private journal of Dr. Watson*~

The strenuous pounding on the front door jolted me from a sound sleep. Fumbling for a box of vestas, I lit a bedside candle, its light revealing the sleepy blue eyes of my dear wife raising her head from the pillow beside me. "What is it, John?" she asked wearily as the door sounded again.

With ill humor I rolled out of the bed and cast about for my dressing gown. "Go back to sleep, my dear, it's only the door."

"The door? At this hour?" said she, casting about for the bedroom clock, its hands yielding half-past midnight. "Don't tell me that Cullingworth has peddled off another of his hypochondriacs onto you!"

"It seems more than likely, dearest," I replied, fastening the tie of my dressing gown in favor of actually dressing, hoping that my obvious state of undress would discourage any less serious maladies. "Go back to sleep, now, I'll return soon."

"You do that," she smiled, turning over and rearranging the blankets over her slim form.

I descended the stairs of my new home, uncharitably cursing whoever it was to roust me from the warmth of my wife's company at such an hour. Therefore, imagine my surprise when I pulled the door open to admit none other than Sherlock Holmes! "Holmes!" I cried in disbelief. "Whatever are you-?"

He silenced me by raising a book for me to take. I recognized it as a volume of romantic poetry I had left behind at Baker Street, but surely the cause of his nocturnal visit was not to return a book! His next words, however, confirmed my doubt and rewarded me for at least a year of selfless patience.

"It makes sense, Watson. The damned thing makes *sense*."

~**~

I sat up in the sitting room, against my custom, waiting for Holmes to return. My mind was alight with curiosity. What on earth could have sent Holmes to Watson in such a hurry? Was he sick or something? If so, why had he taken that book with him? It was exceedingly odd, even for him, and it would not let me sleep.

After an interminable amount of time, though, I heard the front door crack open with more force than necessary and more quietly shut, followed by footsteps ascending the staircase. Holmes! I hastily returned my eyes to my sewing, rehearsing what I was going to say.

Without turning, I heard the door to the sitting room open, but failed to hear it close. "Before you say anything, Holmes," I called out without looking around, "I'm not waiting up for you. I simply wasn't tired." I peeked at the mantle clock; it read half-past midnight. "That was fast," I mused aloud. "Watson was asleep, wasn't he? I told you he would be." I waited for a sarcastic rejoinder, but Holmes remained silent, coming to stand directly behind me.

Puzzled at his lack of reply, I turned with a question on my lips, only to have it die as the blood froze in my veins. The towering figure before me was not Holmes. This individual was the rightful owner of a jail cell, a bad memory, a terrible lurking of my worst nightmares. For a merciful second, I imagined that I was dreaming, but the sound of his hated, mock-pleasant voice shattered my hopes completely.

"Why, if it isn't Miss Nona Brown!"

Darby Edwards.

CHAPTER 16

In Which I Follow my Instincts and Holmes Gets a Rematch

I gave myself no time to question the impossibility of Darby's presence in my home. Leaping from the armchair, I kicked the heavy thing onto him, knocking him backwards. With him thus occupied, I bolted for the door, screaming like a banshee to rouse Mrs. Hudson, the neighbors or some fortunately nearby constable. Darby snarled something coarse and leapt after me, but suddenly the doorframe filled with a hulking, unfamiliar man, his tiny black eyes glittering with a kind of brutish intelligence. The stranger almost casually backhanded me, knocking me against the wall with the force of it. I staggered against the wallpaper, fingernails scoring the pattern as I flailed for purchase. My head was muddled and my face felt aflame; I only dimly registered Darby's hissing, "No force, you idiot! She is to be left unharmed!"

Apparently the silent henchman had learned his lesson, for when he grabbed my elbows to subdue me, his grip was iron-firm but not painful. I cleared my head with a shake and turned to Darby, hardly knowing where to begin. "Where did you...How are you...Where is Mrs. Hudson?"

Darby smiled affably, his thin lips showing clearly now with his lack of goatee. His beard was absent, his hair cropped closely in what I assumed was a prison cut, and his skin was pale from confinement. However, his clothing was of a finer quality that anything he had worn as the impoverished esquire. He had broken out of prison and had a great deal of money. The question that remained was how?

"The housekeeper, my dear?" he crooned, removing a small bottle and a handkerchief from his pocket and drenching the cloth in the clear liquid from the vial. "Nothing permanent has befallen her, I assure you In fact, I shall do the same to you." Knowing what was coming, I averted my head and held my breath, struggling futilely as he pressed the soaking handkerchief over my nose and mouth. "A spirited woman," he mused thoughtfully, more to himself than to his lackey or me. "I begin to see why he would take such precautions for you."

I was growing desperate. Despite my best efforts, the fumes from the chloroform were drifting up my nose, and I was growing increasingly lightheaded. My lungs burned from lack of oxygen and tears of frustration stung my eyelids as I bucked and kicked, trying to find some weakness in my oppressor. Just as I momentarily freed an arm, I involuntarily breathed in through the cloth. Before I could realize what I had done, I thought that Darby had lost patience with me and cast me out of the bow window because I was falling...falling...

~*Excerpt from the private journal of Dr. Watson*~

Holmes' fingers drummed a staccato beat on the cab seat as we rattled down the cobblestones to Baker Street, the simple motion speaking volumes of unease in my usually reserved friend. Holmes had come to me in the absurd hopes of my revealing a sort of magic word that would enable him to reveal the depth of his love to Nona. I, however, hastened to explain that all there remained for Holmes to do was to tell Nona how he felt, without any flowery phrases that were so foreign to his very nature. To prove it I hastened to dress, explaining the situation to my then wakeful and highly amused wife, and fairly shoved the stammering Holmes into a cab and back to Baker Street, professing to accompany him for "medical support." In actuality I meant to exercise my meager eavesdropping skills at the penultimate moment of truth. I would not have missed this for all of the tea in India!

After what must have been an eternity to Holmes, we pulled up to the familiar address, greeted with a warm yellow light pouring through the bay windows of my former quarters. Nona was still awake. Holmes noted this as well, his eyes tightening in anxiety. We clambered out of the hansom, and Holmes had turned to pay the cabman when I noticed the front door slightly ajar.

I gestured briefly to Holmes, pointing out the aberration. His brows lifted in surprise, then furrowed in grim thought. "I remember locking the door,

Watson," said he. "I locked the door behind me…" Breaking off, he strode to the portal and bent to run a gloved hand along the doorjamb. With a hiss he straightened and stared, not at me but through me. "The door has been forced," he announced before pushing the door fully open and disappearing into the darkened interior.

Suddenly fearful, I tossed half a crown to the cabbie and instructed him to wait before dashing after Holmes and cursing my revolver, resting uselessly in my desk at home. The foyer was in almost total darkness, the only light cast from the door at the top of the landing, also ajar. I stumbled in the dark as I climbed the familiar steps and pushed open the door leading to 221B. My mind took a few seconds to process the entirety of the sitting room, but now I can recall it as if it were yesterday. The heavy armchair by the fire lay on its back, as if someone had knocked or pushed it over. The fire itself was still burning, as were the gas lamps. A few articles from Holmes' desk lay littered on the floor. And Holmes himself stood by the desk, a sheet of paper clenched in a white-knuckle grip, eyes closed and breathing slowly. Nona was nowhere to be seen. "Holmes, where is she?" I asked with growing apprehension. "Where is Nona?"

At the sound of her name, Holmes came to life again. He threw the paper onto his desk, seized his magnifying lens from among the assorted clutter and began traversing the room with utmost care. Lost, I picked up the paper that Holmes had discarded. The terse message, written in a slanted, masculine script, ran thusly:

> *My Dear Mr. Sherlock Holmes,*
>
> *I have the girl. If you wish to have her returned, unharmed, then be at Canary Wharf, Dock Seven, at precisely six o'clock on the evening of the seventeenth. Bring no one but yourself and nothing but the clothes you wear. If my instructions are not followed to the letter, the girl will die. Until then!*
>
> *Fondest Regards,*
> *Darby Edwards, Esq.*

Despite the terror that seized me at the reading, I believe it was the flippant closing of the terrible missive that set my blood to boiling. Darby Edwards! I had never met the man face-to-face, but after the travesty at Oakstaff Manor, his very name filled my heart with loathing. The monster was free somehow, and had kidnapped Nona! "Holmes!" I cried, the letter still in my hand. He was meticulously inspecting a wall, intensely concentrating on his task but otherwise seemingly unconcerned. I was shocked at his cold-bloodedness. "Holmes!" I repeated. "What the devil are we going to do?? We have to do something; we can't simply leave Nona in the clutches of that fiend! Holmes, are you even listening to me; you're acting as though you-"

He brusquely interrupted me, never taking his eyes from the wall. "Do shut up, Watson, and see if Mrs. Hudson is well."

This from a man on the brink of proposing marriage to a woman, who might well be dead, or worse! I bristled at his icy demeanor and was on the verge of snapping at him when I finally saw and understood. Holmes had been cut deeply and was burying his wounds behind a wall of aloofness. Obviously his concern for Nona was still raw, and he required time and space to surmount his emotions. Furthermore, he did have a point; we knew of Nona's fate, but what of Mrs. Hudson?

With a muttered excuse, I retreated down the stairs and across the hall to Mrs. Hudson's quarters. Knocking loudly and calling for her, I received no reply and, overcoming propriety for the moment, hesitantly opened the door, discovering a limp, shadowy form on the bed. Fearing the worst, I gave her a cursory examination, breathing a sigh of relief when I found her unharmed. I made no attempt to rouse her, though, for I had caught the telltale odor of chloroform; Heaven only knew when she would awake. Returning to the foyer, I just caught Holmes running down the stairs. He nodded perfunctorily at my report and fairly dragged me out of the door in his haste. "Quickly, Watson," he shouted. "We haven't a moment to lose!"

"But where are we going?" I asked foggily.

My query was answered in Holmes' bark to the cabbie. "To the nearest telegraph office and thence to Scotland Yard, my good man! A life is at stake!" Sufficiently roused, the cabman shifted in the folds of his overcoat and lashed at the horse, whipping the beast into a canter.

"What did you find?" I queried once I was settled in my seat.

Holmes tented his fingertips and pressed them to his lips before speaking. "Besides the obviously overturned armchair and the scattered knickknacks, I observed several scratches in the wallpaper, as if someone had attempted to gain purchase on the wall after...after being struck." He swallowed hastily and continued. "The armchair, however, did not coincide with the striking. I deduce that Nona, having spotted her attacker, overturned the chair as a distraction and fled for the door, only to be struck down as she reached the door, possibly by Edwards himself or an accomplice." He smiled grimly. "Most likely an accomplice; I cannot see Edwards alone vanquishing Nona."

The very thought of her trying to escape at all served as a reminder of her spirited and unconventional nature and only increased my worry tenfold.

Holmes continued, "Edwards must have struck almost immediately after I left. I can think of two explanations: he has the devil's own luck, or he had been watching the house. Needless to say, I strongly suspect the latter."

"But how has he escaped from gaol in the first place?" I expostulated.

"I will not theorize in advance of the evidence," he snapped, obviously frustrated at the lack of information.

We pulled up to the telegraph office and Holmes leapt from the cab, pounding strenuously on the closed door until it yielded a sleepy attendant. The flash of gold in Holmes' hand earned him admission, and he emerged no more than a minute later, resettling himself in the cab seat. However, he refused to tell me what he had written or to whom he had sent it, lapsing instead into a furious silence. We did not speak further until we reached the arch and drive of Scotland Yard. Holmes headed for the main doors, burning brightly with new Edison bulbs, as I remained behind to pay the cabman.

He accepted my offering and tipped his frayed silk hat with solicitude. "'Ope everythin' turns out, guv," he said before gathering the reins and clicking to his horse, off in search of more fares. I hurried to follow Holmes, catching him just as he was asking the suited constable at the front desk which inspector was on duty that night.

"That'll be George Lestrade," yawned the tired man. "But good luck digging him out; the Commish has him swamped in piled-up paperwork going back to…" His narrative trailed off as his audience receded down the hallway, Holmes scanning doorplates until he found Lestrade's cramped office, opening the door without knocking.

The little inspector was hunched over his cluttered desk, pen in hand, and blinked in surprise at the sight of Holmes in the doorway. "Mr. Holmes, good heavens!" he cried. "What brings you here at this hour?"

"A matter of the gravest importance, Inspector," Holmes replied tersely. "I need your immediate attention on this matter and as many men as can be spared."

Lestrade's eyebrows nearly disappeared into his hairline as he gestured to the stacks of documents engulfing him. "What? Are you blind, man? The Commissioner needs me to get all of this filed and sorted within a day! I haven't the time or energy to spare."

Holmes' fists and voice tightened. "Miss Nona Brown has been kidnapped, Lestrade, by one Darby Edward, a man I had assumed was in custody awaiting trial."

The inspector's eyes widened in shock. "Edwards? That's the blighter who got out of the clink?" He shook his head. "Well, I'm sorry to hear that, Mr. Holmes, but I'm afraid that I can't help you this time. If you just keep going down this hall," he gestured to the door with his pen, "you'll come to Missing Persons, see, and you'll find-"

He was abruptly cut off as Holmes brought both of his open palms down onto Lestrade's desk, the sound causing both he and I to jump. "I fear that you do not understand, Lestrade," he hissed, eyes boring a hole into the little inspector. "She is not 'missing.' My *fiancée* has been *kidnapped* by a man I had trusted was in the official care of the police. If we do not apprehend Edwards and rescue Miss Brown by six in the evening, she is going to *die* I'm sure that the negative publicity from the death of a woman thanks to the negligence of the police, coupled with a lawsuit for misconduct, would *hardly* endear you to your commissioner now, would it?"

Lestrade had grown distinctly pale during the course of this speech and jumped a bit at the word 'lawsuit.' He cleared his throat hastily. "Your fiancée, Mr. Holmes?" he stammered. "Well, that's a shoe on the other foot, of course! Of course we shall assist you; I'll just send a runner to rouse Gregson from his house, and you can fill us in on the details." He ushered us into the hallway. "If you'll have a seat, gentlemen," he said, gesturing to a hard wooden bench against a wall before turning on heel and marching down the hall as quickly as was dignified, no doubt anxious to put as much space as possible between him and the detective. Holmes, however, took no further notice of him, sinking onto the bench and fumbling in his pockets for his spare pipe.

I sat next to him but noticed that Lestrade had paused in the corridor and was speaking earnestly to a uniformed constable. The other man jumped in surprise and glanced in our direction, Lestrade nodding in confirmation. With a scowl of ill humor, the constable dug into his trouser pocket and handed a pair of coins to a very smug Lestrade before the inspector carried on. I smiled despite myself, having deduced the cause of this transaction. "Fiancée, Holmes?" I asked quietly.

He paused suddenly, fingers poised in charging his pipe with tobacco. After a moment's thought he cracked a sardonic smile. "I do believe it has a bit more pulling power than 'housekeeper,' my dear Watson."

And has made Inspector Lestrade a bit richer, I thought. As Holmes silently coaxed his pipe to life, I could not help but marvel at the strange course the night had taken and could not help but wonder if Nona was well.

~**~

My world was a gray mist, swirling and coalescing before me. Slowly, ever so slowly, I became aware of shapes through the fog. Sensation returned; my head pounded and my throat burned. My arms were bound before me with thin, coarse rope, as were my ankles. The floor beneath my limp body was hard, dusty wood. The fog then lifted and I was able to take in my surroundings. I was in an enormous chamber, filled with dilapidated crates and dusty sheets of canvas. A pungent smell of fish pervaded the air, and strong midday sunlight poured through the myriad gaps in the wooden walls and ceiling. A warehouse. My mind was swimming with questions. How had Darby orchestrated this caper? How had he come into such funds? And, perhaps most importantly, how the hell had he gotten out of jail in the first place?

Not far from where I was lying, Darby and the unknown man were hunched over a makeshift table and chairs fashioned from crates, while two piles of coins and a rather untidy stack of cards adorned the tabletop. Darby snuffed the stub of an expensive Turkish cigarette, flourished his hand of cards and collected the pot as his compatriot threw his own hand down in disgust.

Turning to light a fresh cigarette, Darby spied me and grinned. "Well, Briar Rose is awake, it seems. How do you feel, my dear?"

I open my mouth to say something rude, but only a harsh croak emerged.

Darby replaced his unlit cigarette and, picking up a chipped porcelain mug from the table, he walked over and helped me to sit up. "Here, drink this," he said, handing me the cup.

My hands were bound before me so I could hold the cup, but it was an awkward maneuver. I sniffed at the contents, expecting the bitter-almond scent of cyanide or the pungent reek of cheap alcohol, but was pleasantly surprised to find the liquid to be ordinary water. Without bothering to question his sudden kindness, I greedily gulped it down, spilling some down the front of my housedress in my haste.

Darby tried to reassure me as I drank. "Don't worry now, Miss Brown, you need not fear me. I am under the strictest possible orders that you remain unharmed." I had to give him that; my face smarted a bit still, but I had gotten worse falling off of my bike and considering what he could have done…"Of course, you can hardly be expected to understand this, and I am not at liberty to explain it, but I give you my word as a gentleman that you will not be harmed."

I stared at him in disbelief over the rim of my empty mug before I finally understood. He still thought I was a halfwit! My trump card was still good! If I could just play it to my advantage…Opening my eyes wide, I cooed in stage fear, "Why, Darby? Why did you tie me up?"

Darby sighed, a weary parent with a confused child. "I need to keep you here until tonight. Once Holmes comes, I shall release you."

"Why didn't you just ask Mr. Holmes to come? Oh, Darby, these ropes hurt!" With a bit of effort I forced tears into my eyes and allowed my lower lip to tremble.

With a kindhearted sigh Darby removed a jackknife from his pocket and began slicing at my bonds. At least I was mobile again with the added bonus of knowing that Darby kept a knife close at all times. As the ropes pooled around me, I flexed my wrists and averted my eyes. "Thank you, Darby," I murmured, trying to sound sincere.

He was fooled. "Not at all, my dear. Remember, you can't sneak away or I'll have to tie you up again." I nodded profusely and he helped me to stand. Turning to the bored lackey, he barked, "Murphy, go report to the teach. He wanted to know when she woke up." With another grunt Murphy shifted himself and trudged out of sight around some boxes, giving me an approximation of where the exit was. My stomach tense with fear, I allowed the smiling murderer to guide me to Murphy's vacated seat. "Do you know how to play cards, Miss Brown?"

"A bit," I allowed. Nona the Manhattan college student could have cleaned Darby out at cards, especially at blackjack, but Nona the London lady was appropriately clueless. Darby dealt me a hand of five-card stud, and I hesitantly began to play, already enmeshed in the most dangerous game of my life.

I played poker with a murderer for about an hour, careful to lose every hand. As I meekly reviewed my recent loss, an unseen door scraped open and shut, followed by the sound of two pairs of footsteps approaching. Murphy rounded the crates accompanied by an old man, tall yet slightly stooped, wrinkled hands grasping a silver-headed cane as he drew nearer. How had this venerable oldster gotten mixed in with Darby? An aging uncle of some sort?

Perhaps I could sway him to…My schemes trickled away as I realized whom I was facing. The reasons behind Darby's escape and his sudden funds were now clear.

The man's hair was white and receding, revealing the dome of his forehead. His blue eyes were piercing, as sharp as the line of his thin lips. But perhaps the most telling evidence was the slight, constant movement of his head, back and forth, as if he were negating the whole world. This was the brilliant mathematician, the genius of the shadows, the Napoleon of Crime, the apotheosis of all that was base, wicked or evil.

Professor James Moriarty.

My terror was no longer feigned.

The sinister man stared me down, his hard, flat eyes and the curious motion of his head proving his fabled resemblance to some cold-blooded and venomous reptile. "Wait outside, gentlemen," he said smoothly, never taking his loathsome eyes from me.

Darby started forward. "But what do you-"

"Leave." The professor's voice did not rise or change, but Darby recoiled as if shot. With nary a backward glance, he and the lumpish Murphy retreated around the piles of crates. I heard the door open and shut, leaving me alone with the snake.

I considered bolting past him, judging him physically unable to stop me, but Darby and Murphy were directly outside the only door, and I knew of no other exit. At a loss, I fell back on my strategy of playing dumb. "Who are you, sir?" I asked as demurely as I could, trying to imitate Mary Watson's dulcet tones.

Moriarty's hooded eyes remained expressionless as his thin, humorless mouth quirked into a smile. "I believe that you may drop the pretence, Miss Brown; we both know of your level of intelligence. I have been observing you for quite some time. I am Professor Moriarty; perhaps you have heard of me." It was a statement, not a question.

"In what context?" I asked, not realizing what I had said until the words were out of my mouth.

One of his silver eyebrows arched slightly in amusement. "Ah, my fame precedes me, I see. Master Sherlock has no doubt informed you of my varied, shall we say, extra-curricular activities. Do you know, Miss Brown, that Master Sherlock had the most difficult time with mathematics?"

I clasped my hands at the small of my back to hide their trembling. "I-I find that a learning impediment often has its faults with the instructor rather than the pupil." Not the wisest choice of words, but my pride demanded it. My heart was a block of ice in my chest, but I would be damned before I gave this devil an inch.

Moriarty's hands tightened on his cane and I flinched, sure that he would lash out at me. Instead, he smiled coldly. "You needn't be so paranoid, my dear; I am a man of my word. Mr. Edwards assured Master Sherlock that you would be unharmed, and unharmed you shall remain."

"How quaint," I crooned with saccharine sweetness, "a villain with morals." I drove my voice flat again. "Go to hell, you twisted son of a bitch."

Finally betraying emotion, Moriarty's eyes widened at my unladylike profanity, but the spasm was soon gone. Seemingly satisfied with his appraisal of me, he turned to summon Darby and Murphy.

I, however, was not about to let him go that easily. "What do you want with me?" I cried, launching myself from my seat.

Moriarty turned, amused. "You? I want nothing with you, girl; you are the means to an end. Tonight Master Sherlock will arrive, and Mr. Edwards shall make an exchange: your life for his."

My heart twisted at the thought of Holmes in this monster's grasp. "And if he doesn't come?" I asked unsteadily, fearing the answer but preferring it to any alternative for Holmes.

"He will come." Moriarty summoned the two stooges back into the warehouse for final instructions. "Bring the girl to the Canary Wharf, Dock Seven, promptly at five-thirty. My operatives will be in position by then. Once Mr. Holmes appears, make sure that all men have their pistols trained on him. Keep a gun on the girl at all times." He turned to go, but suddenly paused. "Oh yes, and Mr. Edwards…" He fixed me with a stare that gave me a sudden urge for the bathroom. "When Holmes is in hand, kill the girl." For all of his seeming kindness, Darby did not hesitate to nod.

"But you said I'd be released unharmed!" I cried desperately.

"And so you shall!" returned the professor. "But who can say, Miss Brown, that after you are released unharmed, Mr. Edwards does not shoot you?" With that rhetorical question, he bowed slightly and disappeared, returning to the safety of good society.

Utterly numb, I sank back onto the crate, no longer trusting my knees. From that moment on, I realized, I was a dead woman. My every moment, my every thought, my every breath was no longer my own. With the severity of the situation, I became consumed with only one thought: I must warn Holmes, save the man I loved from this monster and see that my death was not in vain.

❦   ❦   ❦

The hours dripped by like molasses as I sat on the ground and racked my brain, trying to come up with a satisfactory plan, but every scenario I formed contained some fatal flaw. I cursed the waning sunlight as it filtered through the cracks, bringing the fated hour nearer.

Suddenly Darby was before me, a revolver in his hand. "Come along, Miss Brown," he said pleasantly, as if he were taking me to lunch instead of my death. "It's time to go."

I rose without complaint and followed him through the warehouse, putting up a docile appearance. Darby had his back to me; once we were out of the warehouse, I would turn and run like hell. I could see the dying sun through the open door over his shoulder, and my muscles tensed for flight. We crossed the threshold, but as soon as we were clear, the muzzle of a gun was pressed into my back. I froze in fear and forced myself to look over my shoulder. Murphy grinned at me, finger tight on the trigger, eyes gleaming with an awful telepathy. He had known what I was about to do, and I knew that if I had run, he would have taken unprecedented pleasure in gunning me down.

Sandwiched between the villains, both of them armed, I was forced to let them lead me into a waiting carriage. Once inside, the pair did not restrain or blindfold me but obviously gripped their revolvers in case I had entertained any ideas of leaping from the moving carriage. The curtains were tightly drawn, preventing me from signaling for help as we rattled down silent streets. I could only sit helplessly, stomach knotted, shivering in my thin housedress, knowing that each revolution of the cab wheels brought me closer to my doom.

After what seemed too short a time, the cab ground to a halt and we got out, the cab driver steadfastly taking no notice of us as I was dragged across the large yard. We were in a dockyard, the rapidly declining sun outlining the shapes of small steam barges while huge buildings, obviously boathouses, loomed around us. The fog had crept up, lining the air with a faint mist. The temperature was dropping as night drew nearer, and my shivers became more pronounced as I squelched through icy mud, feeling it through the soles of my shoes. Darby, however, ignored my shivers. He had shed his genteel skin, the steel in his eyes no longer faint. He harshly pulled me across the yard and behind a stack of crates and canvas, where a group of four men crouched and spoke in nearly unintelligible mutterings.

They stood in silence as Darby approached. "Any sign of Holmes?" he snapped.

"No sign, sir," replied one of the thugs. "Was a couple o' dockmen 'bout 'arf an hour past, but they didn't see us. Prob'ly too drunk to 'member us if they 'ad."

Darby snorted in reproach and cast me aside, tripping me so I fell to my hands and knees in the mud. "Have a seat, Miss Brown," he sneered, his cruel personality finally brought to the forefront. "I am sure that the wait will not be long."

My hands clenched painfully in the mud as my hair fell around my face, hiding my snarl. I wanted to grab a handful of earth and hurl it all over his fine clothes. I wanted to kick and punch and scream obscenities in every language I knew until the air turned blue before me! Only the thought of Holmes, the knowledge of his danger, stilled my anger. I had to stay alive, if only long enough to warn him. Also important, though secondary, was the simple fact that I did not want to die. I wanted to tell Holmes how I felt, to feel his arms around me, to share his life in every conceivable way. Tears of helplessness and rage slipped down my cheeks as I fell back against a crate, arms wrapped around myself, trying to hold in the warmth.

The minutes dragged by as the blood-red sun scorched the earth in cruel fury, refusing to surrender without a fight. After what seemed an eternity, I heard the sweetest and most heart-wrenching sound of my life.

"Edwards! Where are you?!"

Holmes' voice.

Darby grabbed my hair and pulled, yanking me to my feet and further abusing my aching head. Wrapping an arm around my waist, he placed the muzzle of his gun to the corner of my jaw and walked me into the open yard, the five thugs following. My heart plummeted at the sight of Holmes, unarmed, standing only about thirty feet away. Even at that distance I could see the stricken look on his face as his eyes met mine. "Nona!" he cried in hope and fear.

I made to answer, but Darby prodded my head with his gun. "Now, now, Mr. Holmes, let's take care of business, shall we? You are alone, are you not?"

Holmes' hands clenched in fury. "Yes," he grated.

Alone? No! I had to do something! My mind racing furiously, I seized upon the first course of action presented to me. Giving a feminine sigh, I slipped into a seeming faint, causing Darby to shift his grip on me. My reasoning behind this action was twofold: firstly, it gave Darby an unwieldy load of dead weight to deal with, and secondly, it left me unnoticed to exercise my pickpocket skills, honed from practice with the Irregulars.

"Let's get this over with then!" Darby barked, shifting my weight in his grasp.

That's right, Darby, I silently coaxed, fingers creeping towards his coat pocket in search of the jackknife. *Keep talking...* With a swift flourish, my fingers dove silently in and out of his pocket, procuring absolutely nothing! His knife was in the other pocket, the one I couldn't reach! I gritted my teeth to keep from screaming in frustration and spoiling my ruse. Keeping my arms limp and out of Darby's line of sight, I clenched and relaxed my fists over and over, hoping Holmes would see and realize that I was still conscious.

"It somehow doesn't surprise me, Edwards," said Holmes with a sneer. What was he doing? "That you would stoop to kidnapping a woman merely to force a confrontation. What *is* the matter, not man enough to come and face me honorably?"

"Shut up," Darby called, the tip of the revolver wavering against my jaw. I fervently wished for the same; couldn't Holmes see that he was provoking the man?

"You were always cowardly, Edwards," Holmes continued, unheeding, "always running to hide behind your father. You hid behind him at the fencing tournament, and now you're hiding behind a woman!"

"Shut *up*!" The gun was quivering more violently and my stomach lurched. The thugs grouped around us were shifting uneasily, unsure of the circumstances.

"Why? Afraid to hear the truth, you spineless, weak, pathetic-"

"*Shut up! I'll KILL you!*" Darby howled, his grip on me tightening painfully as his insecurities were truly revealed. Terror gripped me as I realized that despite Moriarty's warnings, he would do exactly that.

I couldn't see Holmes' face, but the rage in his voice spoke volumes. "Then *kill me,* you weakling, and *be DONE with it!*" The gun whipped away from my head and...

I had once read that humans share the same basic brain stem with lizards, and this fuels our instincts and reflexes. I now wholeheartedly agree, for from the moment I felt the gun leave my head as Darby swung it around, my inner lizard was already moving. Without a single conscious thought, I hauled myself up with a hand on his shoulder, grasped his wrist with both hands, pointed the barrel of the gun at the cloudy sky and sank my teeth into his wrist!

Darby gave an unearthly scream and reflexively pulled the trigger before dropping his gun, discharging a bullet into the burnished sky. The recoil threatened to knock me loose, but I sank my teeth deeper, the copper taste of blood coating my mouth. He latched onto his favorite target, my long hair, and pulled viciously, bringing tears to my eyes, but I simply ground tighter, my every sense overwhelmed by the feral instinct to protect the one I loved.

A split second later, more gunshots and a hoarse cry sounded through the air, and some dimly rational part of me shrieked for Holmes. "Sniper!" I heard Murphy bellow. "Run for it, lads!" The thugs scattered in search of cover, their employer forgotten as they tried to save themselves. With a final blow to my head, Darby succeeded in loosening me from his wrist, and I slipped to my knees, coughing and spitting, as Darby seized his gun and fled towards the empty barges, in the opposite direction of the thugs.

Before I could contemplate events further, a pair of thin strong arms tightly enveloped me. "By God, Nona, are you all right?" Holmes pulled back to search my face anxiously. He seemed none the worse for wear. "Did he hurt you? What happened? Nona, say something!"

A joy that I had never known before engulfed me, and I launched myself into his embrace, letting my actions speak for me. Holmes returned the gesture, clinging to me as if he feared he would awake from a dream. *Holmes is here,* I told myself as I breathed the smell of tobacco and exhaustion. *Holmes is here, and I'm safe, and Darby is...*With that thought, I pulled away from Holmes with a jerk and flung an arm in the felon's direction. "Holmes! He's getting away!"

For a split second of indecision, Holmes hovered between staying with me and catching Darby, but with a coarse oath usually reserved for his baser disguises, he took to his heels in pursuit of the fiend, Watson right behind him. Wait, Watson? Where did he come from? Further down the dock, my unbelieving eyes took in several boatmen holding revolvers to Murphy and the captive thugs, led by a rather scruffy Lestrade. Lestrade...then the other men were undercover constables. They had come to rescue me! Secure in their capture, I pushed myself up and stumbled into an uneasy run after Holmes and Watson. Rather than sapping my strength, the exercise warmed my body and cleared my head. The paralyzing fear was gone, replaced with a burning need for vengeance. I was driven by a different instinct, one that demanded punishment for Darby's crimes. Another gunshot rang out and I followed the sound to a small barge seeing Holmes and Watson climbing aboard as it began to drift away from the dock! Putting my newfound energy to good use, I broke into a run and jumped the still-short distance between the boat and me, landing in an ungraceful heap at their feet.

"Nona!" Holmes cried in astonishment. "What on earth are you doing?"

"And here I thought you were a genius," I croaked, shakily rising to my feet and wiping my mouth, fighting the urge to spit as the adrenaline of my run wore off.

Holmes, to my surprise, began to actually shake with some strong emotion as he forced his words out. "You are in no condition to…You shouldn't be…This is too…Get off this boat, right now!"

"I'm afraid that it's a bit late for that, Holmes," called Watson, staring over the rail. As we watched, the distance between the boat and the dock steadily widened. If I got off the boat, I would be swimming.

I turned back to the detective. "Holmes, I want to get Darby just as much as you do. Seeing as how I was the one who was kidnapped, manhandled and nearly frozen to death, I think that I deserve to be a part of this, don't you agree? Besides," I interrupted before he could open his mouth fully, "I don't fancy a swim in the Thames at this time of year, so I guess you're stuck with me." I smiled ruefully.

Holmes once again hovered in indecision, but finally he gently took my hand and pulled me to him. "Stay close," he commanded, a revolver in one hand and my hand in the other, as we moved down the berthing stairs into the belly of the barge. I needed no further warning, walking as closely as I could to Holmes without tripping him.

The setting sun slanted through the portholes of the barge as the three of us tensely examined the captain's quarters, one of the storage chambers and the bunkroom before coming to an expansive galley. Long, heavy tables covered the floor space as one door led to the kitchen and another staircase led up to the deck. Almost immediately after we entered, shots echoed across the room. I barely had time to glance at an overturned table at the far end before both Holmes and Watson shoved me to the floor, upsetting a table for their own cover and crouching behind it. When the shots died down, Holmes and Watson rose up and fired, quickly dropping to reload with the loose bullets in their coat pockets. It was so much like an old spaghetti western that I felt a giggle of hysteria building in my throat. Harshly I pushed it away, promising my subconscious a bit of much-needed quiet time when this was all over.

The lethal give-and-take continued, Holmes and Watson rapidly firing and trying to duck the return fire as lead sang over our heads. As Darby, obviously carrying spare ammunition of his own, launched another attack, Holmes crouched down next to me, and I tried hard not to give in to the fear and hysteria. Suddenly he reached out and tightly grasped my hand in his, drawing my frightened gaze to his intent gray one. If I was surprised at this unexpected gesture, his next words completely blew me away.

"If we live through this, Nona Brown, will you marry me?"

I barely heard Watson gasp in surprise. I was so stunned the Darby could have shot me then and there, and I would not have flinched. The culmination of my hopes and my wishes; the final scene of so many of my dreams, was all here in a few simple words. All I could see was Holmes, his beseeching eyes begging me for an answer. Holmes loved me, as deeply as I loved him. He wanted to marry me, to have me as his wife until death do we part. Hell, I was so happy I was even willing to forgive the unromantic setting! Swallowing uneasily, I took a deep breath and gave the only possible answer.

"Okay."

He broke into a delighted grin, as if I had agreed to a day at the park rather than holy matrimony. "Good," was all he said, abruptly turning and firing two rounds at Darby before the revolver's chambers clicked hollowly. He furiously dug into his pocket but came away empty handed. "Damn!" he cried. "My bullets are gone! Watson, what of you?" The doctor could only shake his head mutely, his own supply of munitions depleted as well. Holmes risked a glance over the tabletop and quickly rose, gesturing with his useless firearm. "Look, there he goes!" he cried, pulling me to my feet before dashing away.

"Holmes!" I cried. "What about Darby's-" My warning was cut off as the trapped felon gave a shout of challenge and flung his own gun at Holmes' head, thankfully missing its target. Darby was obviously out of bullets as well. Now out of weapons, he turned and fled up the stairs leading to the deck, Holmes hot on his heels. As Watson and I gave chase, I could not help but notice a low hissing sound. I surmised that one of the bullets had pierced the stove, and I pitied the poor sailors who would return to this wreck when we were done with it.

We emerged onto the deck, now fully dark, the glowing gaslights of the distant shore giving the only illumination. Scrap metal from repairs littered the wooden deck. Along the way I could see Darby in his shirtsleeves, jacket discarded on the plank floor, bloodstained handkerchief clumsily tied around his wrist, standing shakily with a long, thin bar of scrap iron braced in his hand. "Stay back!" he screeched, his normally suave voice harsh with fury and terror.

Holmes had also shed his coat and stooped to grasp another piece of metal similar to Darby's. "Your father can't save you now, Darby," he taunted, stepping back and raising his makeshift sword into what I assumed was the *en garde* position.

Darby smiled and mimicked Holmes. "I've beaten you once, Sherlock," he rasped. "I can do it again."

I gasped in realization as the two men began to move, parrying and thrusting with lightning speed. This was a repeat of the infamous fencing match; the one on which Holmes told me Darby had cheated when they were fifteen. Watson and I watched in breathless silence, unsure of anything that we could do, as the childhood rivals swung to kill, no judge present save Death. I ached to do something, to grab a bar of my own and club Darby senseless, but instinct told me that this was Holmes' fight, his own personal demon to exorcise, and I was powerless.

Caught up as I was in the mortal battle, I failed to notice the heat rising at my back. Eventually I rubbed the back of my neck and it came away hot, so I turned in curiosity, stopping in fear. Watson imitated me; the only sound escaping him was a feeble, "My God."

The barge ran on steam power, fueled by a coal furnace. One of the stray bullets from our shootout had pierced the floor and ruptured the boiler. The hissing I had heard was not the stove, but the collapsing of the boiler, evidenced by the swirling, fiery maelstrom that had once been the galley.

The barge was in flames.

A hollow explosion erupted across the water, and the barge pitched violently, damaged timbers creaking as it rocked under the force of the blow. We were all thrown to the ground, Darby's makeshift foil careening out of his grip. Satisfied that Darby was unarmed, Holmes scrambled to his feet and turned to us. "Are you both all right?" he called anxiously.

"We're fine," I called back, "but the barge is—Holmes, *look out!*" As I watched, Darby sprang to his feet and dove a hand into his pocket, brandishing the forgotten jackknife as he lunged at Holmes' unarmed back.

By grace alone Holmes heard my warning in time. He pivoted and ducked, causing Darby to miss his thrust, and instinctively locking his arms around the criminal's waist, he heaved him up and threw him completely over the boat rail!

There was a barely audible thump as Darby hit the side of the barge and a much louder splash as he hit the water. We three dashed to the edge of the rail, peering into the dark water, waiting for some sign of the felon. A minute passed, then two, and Darby did not emerge. I could not help but breathe a sigh of relief at this ugly end for an evil man.

Just as I was about to speak, the boat rocked violently again as another explosion echoed through the ship and it began to quite noticeably tilt. I mentally changed what I was going to say. "Well, boys," I began blithely, "it's a lovely ship, but I don't think we should go down with it."

They nodded in all seriousness. "Ladies first," said Watson. These men found the oddest times to be chivalrous.

Nodding myself, I allowed them to help me over the railing until I clung to the wrong side of the rail. I was petrified, being no fan of great heights or deep water, but Holmes squeezed my hand reassuringly and I was able to steel myself. Taking a deep breath, I released myself into space and a moment later plunged into the water.

Cold! The icy river assaulted me on all sides, filling my nose and ears and eyes, numbing my hands and feet, deadening my limbs. I flailed through the thick, oily water, legs pumping as I strove for the surface. After an eternity, I broke to the surface, gasping for air and instinctively swimming away from the tilted barge as it slowly broke apart into useless flotsam. Seizing upon a floating plank, once a piece of the boat, I clung to it exhaustedly and scanned the water for Holmes.

My heart clenched as I found no sight of him, but soared again as he suddenly appeared from below the water with Watson not far behind. I waved and shouted hoarsely, causing them to swim over, Watson a tad slower due to his past injuries. Too shocked for words, we treaded water as we clung to the plank, watching the fiery spectacle as the barge slowly descended into the river.

"Halloa!" A foreign voice suddenly called out across the water. We craned our heads behind us to see Lestrade in a commandeered rowboat, a pair of constables with him pulling the oars for all they were worth. "Hold on, we'll get you out of there!"

If I weren't already spoken for, I could have kissed the man.

Lestrade was as good as his word. He hauled us all aboard, wrapped our shivering forms with thick blankets and kept us conscious with the promise of hot coffee. We disembarked from the rowboat into a state of chaos. Police wagons and ambulances moved in and out about as constables and doctors careened around in an official frenzy, mainly keeping back the suddenly pressing hordes of enterprising reporters, confused dockmen and other assorted rubberneckers.

I was pried away from Holmes by a nameless doctor who poked and prodded me, pronounced me alive, plied me with steaming black coffee from a steel thermos and sent me to sit in the corner. I eagerly did so, clutching my blanket cape-like with one hand and my mug of coffee in the other. Holmes and Watson were seated in similar fashion on a pair of crates at the far end of the crime scene, both unconsciously rising as I made my disheveled grand entry. Waving them down, I seated myself next to Holmes and drew comfort from his nearness. "How did you do it, Holmes?" I asked, cautiously sipping the coffee. It was black and burned, but it was hot, so I welcomed it.

For once Holmes did not have to question the meaning of the word "it." "It was very simple, my dear," he said easily. "Once I discovered your absence from Baker Street, I sent a wire to Mycroft and enlisted the aid of Lestrade and his men. A dozen undercover constables prowled Canary Wharf for a full day, waiting for Mycroft to supply me with a professional military assassin." He paused to sip his coffee. "The general plan was to have the sniper, hidden in one of the boathouses, kill or injure Edwards. With the leader gone, the constables could subdue the confused hirelings."

"But you almost got yourself killed!" I protested. "You antagonized Edwards!"

He coughed uneasily. "In order for the sniper to get a clear shot, the revolver had to be directed away from the hostage," he replied, as if he were reading from a textbook.

"It was necessary, Nona," Watson interjected. "If Holmes' had not done so, you might have been killed."

"And was that supposed to console me if you died?" I asked Holmes. He turned to me in mute appeal, pleading for understanding. I sighed in acquiescence. "Just…don't do it again."

He reverted his gaze to his coffee mug and after a few moments changed the subject. "I simply can't understand how Darby escaped from gaol in the first place. He is hardly the daring schemer."

"I can answer that in one word," I replied. As the men looked to me in startled expectation, I said simply, "Moriarty."

For a moment they ceased to breathe. Holmes was well aware of his former mentor's true nature, and despite misleading statements in his writings, so was Watson. Holmes' hand crept tenderly into mine. "Did he hurt you?" he murmured, the words laden with any number of meanings.

I shook my head. "No, just gave me the standard villain speech: 'I'll get Holmes, just you wait.'" I tweaked an imaginary mustache and threw in a

Snidely Whiplash evil laugh for good measure, failing to mention the dread the man had evoked in me. "He was none too pleased with me."

"Why is that?" asked Watson.

I smiled into my coffee. "I called him a son of a bitch."

Shocked, the men roared with laughter, and I quickly joined in as we released our pent-up emotions, the fear and anxiety of the day's trials evaporating with the sound of our laughter. When the fit subsided, Holmes wiped moisture from his eyes and shook his head. "Oh," he breathed, "what I would have given to see his expression!"

"You would have been disappointed," I replied unnecessarily. "All he did was raise an eyebrow." Silence descended once more, but this time it was uncomfortable. I had to say something to bridge the gap and test the waters of our new relationship. "Well, Holmes," I began.

He smiled at our usual repartee. "Well, Nona," he returned.

I took a breath and plunged in: "I believe that this is the part where the brave hero takes his fiancée into his arms."

His face was utterly blank for a beat and I cringed inside. Did he regret his hasty question, posed under fire? "As you know, Nona," he began finally, "I am a most unconventional man." I felt my face and my hopes begin to fall. "But," he hastily amended. "I suppose that just this once, I will bow to conformity." Saying that, he placed his coffee mug aside and opened his arms to me.

I needed no further encouragement. Placing my own cup aside, I abandoned propriety as I fairly flew to his lap, twining my arms around his neck as his own locked securely around me. The smell of his tobacco was overpowered by the reek of river water, but as I listened to the beat of his heart and the sound of his contented breathing, I just couldn't bring myself to care.

We were lost in each other's arms for an unknown amount of time, but the next thing I heard was Watson's insistent voice: "Come along, you two, Lestrade has called us a cab."

I reluctantly rose, sliding off Holmes' lap. A cab, a vessel to transport us home with its promise of hot baths and warm beds. Holmes and Watson shook the disguised inspector's hand as he uneasily clutched his cloth cap, and I smiled gratefully at him as he helped me inside the cab. Holmes seated himself next to me and took my hand, bringing a smile to both our faces. The cab ride seemed to have fewer bumps and jolts as usual, but that may be due to the fact that I felt as though he were floating.

Watson's house was our first stop, the windows glowing cheerily as Mary Watson and the household help waited up for him. He clambered out of the cab and turned back to me. "Come along, Nona; you shall be staying with me for a while."

"What?" I asked incredulously.

Watson frowned impatiently. "You and Holmes are engaged now, Nona. Did you really expect to sleep under the same roof?"

My anger flared suddenly. Damn these Victorians and their prudishness! I was about to open my mouth to retort when Holmes forestalled me. "It's for the best, Nona."

His calm tone effectively squelched my anger, and I realized that I was far too tired to argue. Besides, I rationalized, I could always argue in the morning. With an unladylike grunt, I disembarked and allowed Watson to guide me down the walk toward the house, every cell in my body crying out for sleep.

"Wait!" Holmes' voice arrested me as he climbed out of the cab and jogged over to me with an impish grin. "I do believe, Nona," he said, "that this is the part where the brave hero kisses his fiancée goodnight."

I could not count all of the times I had dreamed of hearing words to that effect. Now at long last, after a year of gain and loss, aggravation and betrayal, forgiveness and love, my dreams were a reality. I was so happy I couldn't think of a single witty retort as I blissfully stepped into his embrace. He held me for a moment, tenderly brushing away a damp lock of hair before grasping my chin and slowly lowering his face to mine.

A deep chuckle broke the spell. "Holmes," I breathlessly murmured, "Watson is watching."

He paused for a moment, and then grinned again. "Let him watch," was all he said before pressing his lips to mine.

There is a God.

Holmes' kiss was feather-light at first, but slowly deepened in intensity. My eyes slipped closed as I focused my every sense on his touch. I could feel exquisitely the play of his lips on mine, his hands as they combed through my hair, down my shoulders, around my waist, pulling me closer. I could feel my own hands moving across the length of his shoulders, up the back of his neck, through his dark, damp hair as I pulled him to me. It was perfect. It was heaven. It was pure and simple love.

He broke the kiss and we came up gasping for air, clinging to each other as the tremors of passion rocked us still. Sherlock's gray eyes were almost black as he drank in the sight of me. "I may not say this often, my dear Miss Brown," he gasped out, "but I love you."

I smiled despite myself. "Keep this up," I retorted, "and you won't have to say it." What possible response could there be but to kiss again?

The clearing of Watson's throat jerked us out of our second round. I was beginning to see spots from lack of oxygen. I loved those spots. "I believe that it is time to go inside," he said, trying to be stern.

I nodded absently and broke from Holmes, but as our eyes met again, we were suddenly back in each other's arms, a pair of travelers lost in the desert, who found an oasis in each other. This time Watson was a bit more forceful in his insistence. He took my arm and gently pulled us apart, walking me to the house. "I shall return here first thing in the morning," Holmes called to me, trying to walk backwards.

"I'm counting the hours," I replied, allowing Watson to drag me towards the door. "Sleep well."

"I will. Pleasant dreams."

"Don't worry; they will be. Goodnight!" We were babbling, and we knew it, just one of the pleasant side effects of love.

Somehow Holmes got into the cab backwards, never taking his gaze from me, and the hansom rattled off down the cobblestone street. Only after the cab had disappeared did I allow myself to enter the Watson home. However, due to the stress of the evening, the shock of Holmes' declaration, and the lack of oxygen, I only have the vaguest memory of Mary Watson fairly leaping into her soaked husband's arms before I did the most embarrassing thing that an emancipated woman of the twenty-first century can do.

I fainted.

Two days later, October twentieth, I was still on Cloud Nine with an excellent forecast of moving up to Ten. Watson and Mary were very accommodating hosts, allowing to come and go at leisure. They seemed to be resigned to my being an invisible houseguest, spending nearly every waking hour at Baker Street, stumbling back to Kensington close to midnight. It had taken Holmes a bit of getting used to, this new facet of our relationship, but after a few reminders he had stopped asking for permission to kiss me. Since Las Vegas was definitely out of the question, I wanted to run to the nearest Justice of the Peace and elope that first day, but Holmes quietly vetoed the idea, not wanting to leave family and friends out of the equation. I acquiesced, but not before teasing him about his latent sentimentality and vowing never to think that I had completely figured him out.

One evening the four of us enjoyed a late dinner at Simpson's and were leisurely strolling down the near-deserted Strand in the light of the gas lamps, looking for a brougham cab to take us back to our respective domiciles. Holmes kept my hand on his arm, walking on the curbside as solicitous as ever, but there was a certain restfulness on his face not usually there. I was inordinately pleased to have been the cause of such a welcome change and allowed myself to tune out the conversation between Holmes, Watson and Mary, content to let my thoughts drift.

A tap on the hand from my fiancé brought me back to myself as I regarded him with a silent question on my face, never breaking our pace. In answer, he turned the pocket watch in his hand towards me, the gaslight catching the face and revealing the time. "Happy anniversary," he bent and whispered for my ears alone. Blushing to my hairline with happiness, I glanced over my shoulder to see Watson and his wife exchanging knowing glances. I shot them both a "mind-your-own-business" glare before squeezing Holmes' arm where my hand rested.

The walk progressed onward with still no available cab in sight when suddenly Holmes stopped in his tracks, pulling me to a standstill, staring intently at a closed jewelry store a few yards down the street. "What's the matter?" I asked. I broke off suddenly as a flash of light inside the otherwise darkened store revealed what Holmes had deduced. It appeared that someone, likely with a covered lantern, had broken into the store and was busy relieving the owner of the contents.

"Wait here," Holmes said quietly before nodding to Watson and taking off towards the store, the doctor close at his heels as they disappeared through the broken and opened door. Poor Mary was white as a sheet and, I admit, I was also a little nervous as we stood together in a puddle of lamplight, straining our ears for any sound. The silence of the night was unbroken until we dimly heard the ring of shattering glass within the store. *Holmes!* Ignoring Mary, I took off for the store, running the best I could in a corset and dress, my only thoughts consumed by my fiancé.

Thus preoccupied, I was seized with joy when a tall figure came stumbling out of the store. "Holmes!" I shouted before seized in an unfamiliar grip by the figure, the cold steel of a gun barrel placed to my temple. My stomach plunged with recognition; it wasn't Holmes, it was the burglar! "Oh, God, not again…"

"Shut up!" the man cried hoarsely. I could see both Holmes and Watson now, Holmes with his hands raised in a conciliatory gesture, Watson with his pistol leveled at the man. Turning my head slightly, I caught a glimpse of the man's face as he walked us backwards, the light revealing the sickly pallor and hollow eyes of the opium addict. It was a common story even in the past, the junkie needing a fix, but it meant that this desperate fellow was probably not thinking rationally. "Put that gun down!" the man shrieked, sounding more afraid than me.

After a pointed glance from Holmes, Watson reluctantly placed the revolver on the ground, and the detective turned his attention to my captor. "We are not trying to harm you, sir," he said calmly. "We are unarmed. Please, put the gun down. I'm sure that you do not want to hurt the lady."

"Shut up!" the man rasped, grinding the gun harder against my head, backing up until we were nearly flat against a brick wall. "I'll kill her; don't think I won't!"

Oh, God, now what? As I racked my brain for a possible escape, a metal bucket came crashing down in the alley across the street, followed by the yowl of a cat. The addict nearly leapt out of his skin and pointed the barrel into the alleyway, leaving me free to act. I kicked the man's shin as hard as I could and tried to make a run for it, but his hand swept back and knocked me clear. Stumbling to the side, I fell to the ground disoriented, shaking my head to try and clear it before getting to my feet again. No one was in sight, and there were…I was…*oh, God, no!*

~*Excerpt from the private journal of Dr. Watson*~

The horror of this past night is nearly too much for the human mind to comprehend. Holmes is finally asleep, thanks to a generous dose of morphine from my own supply, but I have no such luxury. Even the consolation of my dear wife is no balm for me at this hour.

When we pursued the would-be burglar out of the store and onto the street, neither Holmes nor I realized that Nona was so close to the door. In but a moment the sick man had seized Nona tightly, pressing his ancient pistol to her head and backing further down the walk. I could hear Nona saying, "Not again," and my mind cast back involuntarily to the deadly situation only days earlier as I prayed that this instance would have a similar conclusion.

I loathed lowering my weapon, but even without Holmes' insistence, I could see that there was no other way. Placing my revolver on the ground, I could also see that Holmes' entreaties were useless against the man's drug-induced paranoia, evidenced further by his extreme reaction to the clatter in the alleyway. Nona reacted to the distraction with her characteristic quick-wittedness, but as the man pushed her away, she...I can hardly bear to write it...she fell straight through the brick wall!

The burglar was so terrified by such witchery that he fell prostrate on the ground in a faint, but none of us gave any thought to him. With a cry I had never heard from man or beast, Holmes flung himself at the wall, but it remained firm and unyielding. He continued to beat against it, futilely cursing and sobbing much as Nona herself had when she first arrived here. I thought my heart would surely give way from the strain of sympathy and loss. Mary came unsteadily to my side and I feared that she might swoon as well, but she merely wrapped her arms about me and clung as the detective's pleas echoed in the empty streets.

A passing Good Samaritan took in the situation and summoned a constable, who took the senseless burglar into custody. Upon our return to my house in Kensington, Holmes was delirious from pain, I gave him a liberal dose of morphine and settled him into bed in our guest room, his awful tears finally silenced in sleep. Now, as dawn creeps in through the windows, I sit at my desk and stare at the words I have written, scarcely believing them myself. I do not know how Holmes will deal with such a loss or how things shall ever return to some shadow of normalcy, but I shall support him as best I can.

And I pray that Nona, whenever she is, is well.

Epilogue

The door swung open and shut. The man in blue looked up from the papers on his desk.

"Grady? What are you doing back here, old man? I thought your patrol wasn't over until five in the morning."

"It's not. I had to bring someone in; hey, got any coffee left?"

"There should be some. Help yourself."

Footsteps, the sound of liquid pouring, a sigh.

"God, Mick, look at it come down. Cats and dogs got nothing on this."

"No shit. Something terrible must have happened."

"Come again?"

"My sainted Irish grandmum always said that a heavy rain meant a tragedy. 'The heavens are weeping,' said she."

"Knock it off, Mick, that's depressing."

"You want depressing? Come check out this paperwork, five yet unsolved murder cases in this precinct, for this quarter alone. Why can't life be like it is on *Law & Order*?"

"The guys on *Law & Order* don't always get the bad guy, buddy."

"Oh, yeah."

Silence.

"So what gives, Grady? How come you're here at the station instead of out in the wet?"

"Like I said, I had to bring someone in."

"Drug dealer? Pimp?"

"No, nothing like that, not even a crime. This lady went bonkers 'bout three blocks from NYU. I saw her when I drove past, pounding a brick wall, kicking and screaming, the whole nine yards. She wouldn't respond to Ortega or me, so we got her into the car and drove her here. She quieted down on the drive, long enough to talk for a while."

"What happened?"

"Her fiancé recently died. Seems that it just sunk in for her and she kinda lost it."

"Ouch."

"But that's not even the interesting part! Seems that this little lady had been on the Missing Persons list for a whole year!"

"No kidding? What happened?"

"According to her, she had a quarter-life crisis, dropped out of college and ran off to London to become an artist. She meets a detective, they fall in love, they get engaged, then the guy goes and croaks."

"How did he die?"

"I didn't ask. Anyway, after the funeral she hops the first flight home, no luggage even, and heads for the college in a daze. About three blocks away she breaks down."

"Wow, that's some story. Hey Grady, what's the matter?"

A sigh. "I dunno. It's like there's something she ain't telling, a lot of some-things. I mean, she's just a little girl, early twenties; I got daughters older than her. But she acts like she's twice her age, even wears some kind of old-fashioned dress. She doesn't strike me as the type to go AWOL on a moment's notice. Plus her whole story is shaky, like she just made it up."

"You gonna call her out on it?"

"Nah, no point. Not like she's a crook or anything. Besides, something hap-pened to her that made her flip out. I think the part with the fiancé, that was true. She's got this look in her eyes like…ya know, like the world ended or something. I tell ya, I dunno."

"What happens now?"

"She called her parents. They live uptown, so they're coming down to get her now. I set her up with coffee in one of the interrogation rooms; she should be fine."

"Man, Grady, losing her fiancé. That's rough. I mean, Sarah and me have only been married for five years. If she'd died before we got hitched, I don't know what I would've done."

"She's got her parents, Mick, and the rest of her family. She'll be fine."

"Well, all's well that ends well, I guess."

"Yeah."

Silence, the sound of rain.

"So, you catch the Mets last night?"

Look for the next Nona Brown novel,

Mayhem in Manhattan

Coming soon in 2007!

Chapter One
Home Sweet Home

"Steve, I need you to come in tomorrow. The Atwell account needs some last-minute touches."

"Tomorrow? No way, Bill! Tomorrow's Saturday! I'm headed up to the Catskills for the weekend, time and fish wait for no man."

"Well, I need someone!"

"Get Nona on it."

"Nona's worked the past four weekends, Steve."

"So? Nona has no life."

I hunched over my desk in my tiny office, painfully aware of the conversation that was taking place outside my cracked door.

"All right, I'll get her on it, but only if you bring me back some of that catch, deal?"

"Deal, man."

Bill Paisley poked his bony horse's face around my door. "Hey, Nona, I need you to-"

"No."

His brows lifted. "'Scuse me?"

"No, Bill." I fixed him with my iciest glare. "Regardless of what Steve says, I *do* have a life, and I have big plans for tomorrow. And since, like you said, I've worked for the past four weeks, you can find yourself another patsy. I finished my share of the Atwell account last week." Without waiting for a response, I returned my attention to the account sheets on my desk, hearing rather than seeing the door shut. The murmur of voices picked up again, this time indistinct. I had a pretty good idea of their topic of discussion, though. Nona 'The Ice Queen' Brown, resident workaholic. 'The Blessed Virgin.' 'Miss Frigid

Bitch.' Take your pick. I took off my reading glasses and pressed my hands to my tired eyes, telling myself that I didn't care. Now, if only that were true. I was fed up with their cavalier attitude towards me, and of course, waiting for a call from the doctor didn't improve matters.

I smiled grimly as I reviewed my 'big plans for tomorrow,' currently consisting of lounging in my sweats with a pint of Ben and Jerry's and the latest Preston and Child novel. "Steve's right," I moaned aloud. "I have no life. Especially," I added as I glanced at the wall clock, "since it's six-thirty and work ended an hour ago." With a sigh, I slid off my three-inch pumps, exchanged them for the pair of sneakers in my desk drawer, slipped on the more comfortable shoes and packed up my briefcase. In went accounting files, sketches for ads, all of the necessary accoutrements for an assistant manager for Kramer and Smith Advertisers, Inc. At twenty-six, I was a bit young for the job, but my "devotion to the company" had quickly elevated me. If only they knew the cause of my single-minded drive.

Clasping the leather valise closed, I pushed myself up and headed out the door, striding purposefully past the disgruntled Paisley, caught up in my thoughts. I needed to get home and feed Bug, do the dishes, fold the laundry, maybe work on that canvas before Maggie and Tony show up for dinner, did I remember to pick up that fancy salsa Maggie likes-?

Without warning, I slammed into a tall figure just before the elevators, nearly dropping my briefcase.

"Whoa, slow down there, little miss! I knew I had animal magnetism, but really!"

Oh, God. Ivan 'the Terrible' Kramer, my floor supervisor, stared down at me with his thousand-dollar smile. The name was not a coincidence; Ivan Kramer was the nephew of Stephen Kramer, CEO and joint owner of the company, and that was probably the only reason that he was still employed. Kramer was a chauvinist of the worst kind; he had slept with every woman on the floor, with only one exception. That unlucky woman was Kramer's only obstacle between him and a personal record, and consequently, he focused all of his odious attention on her.

Starting to see why I wanted to avoid him?

"Mr. Kramer, I'm sorry," I said as calmly as I could, craning my neck upwards and wishing for the extra three inches my heels granted me. "I'll try to pay more attention next time, and I'll bring in the Atwell papers on Monday. Good evening, sir." With that, I tried to slide past him.

No such luck. He slid with me and was once more in front of me. "Now, wait a minute, sugar." That's right: *sugar*. If I didn't know better, I'd say he was joking. "You never did give me a straight answer about tomorrow night."

He was talking about his most recent 'night-on-the-town' suggestion, made a couple of days ago. "I'm sorry, Mr. Kramer, but I can't-"

"What's it gonna take, darlin'?" he asked, moving closer. "What's it gonna take to get you to go out with me? It would be *lots* of fun, I guarantee." He grinned with slimy innuendo.

Stepping backwards, racking my poor, tired mind for some excuse, *any* excuse, I blurted out, "Mr. Kramer, do you play the violin?"

He stopped in surprise, processing the question. "No."

I shook my head firmly and I sneaked around and pushed the elevator call button. "Then I'm sorry, sir, but I won't date a man unless he plays the violin." Salvation arrived with an electronic ding as an empty elevator pulled up. I hastily climbed in and pressed the close button.

"Then I'll take lessons!" protested Kramer as the metal doors slid shut. "If that's all you need, then-" He was cut off as the doors fully closed and I burst out laughing and the metal box slid downwards. Violins! Where the hell did *that* come from?? It wasn't like I knew anyone who played the...

He reached for the Stradivarius, just within reach of the armchair where he had folded his long frame. Tucking the instrument under his pointed chin, closing his gray eyes in concentration, he drew the violin bow back and forth across he strings, coaxing forth an unconscious melody. His dark brows drew together as he played and pondered, searching the farthest recesses of that brilliant mind, seeking the one piece of data that would tie all together and bring the case to a close. After minutes of thought, he ceased his music making and lowered the priceless violin, turning to me in triumph. His eyes were alight with revelation. "Eureka," he said with a smile. "I've done it, Nona. I've done it."

An unknown tear trickled down my cheek and I hastily brushed it away as the doors opened with a ring. My stride had gone from purposeful to dejected as I crossed the lobby, nodded a distracted farewell to Jerry the doorman and stepped out onto the chilly October streets of the city. Scores of people flooded past, yellow taxis crowded the street, steel and cement skyscrapers loomed over my head like towers of Babel in stereo. The smell of sweat and exhaust and endless frustration permeated the stale air.

The city so nice, they named it twice: New York, New York.

Home, sweet home.

❦   ❦   ❦

Two subways and a four-block walk brought me to my humble abode, an ancient, decaying brownstone, broken into apartments. I let myself in with my key and tiptoed past Mme. Delacour's door. The cranky old landlady inhabited the first floor of the building, and her three tenants had quickly learned to give her a wide berth. Reaching the staircase, I bypassed the second floor, home to Tony Sinclair. Tony was only a few years older than me, transplanted from Iowa to pursue his dream of being a gourmet chef He was halfway there, employed as one of five assistant chefs in one of Park Avenue's finer establishments. I continued past the third floor, where Margaret Malloy resided. Maggie was thirty-six, or at least she said she was, and worked as an interior decorator. The eldest of our happy trio, she had taken Tony and me under her sophisticated wing. Finally, reaching the top floor, I unlocked my own familiar door and stepped inside.

A familiar meowing sounded from the vicinity of the living (*sitting*) room. I started at the involuntary flash of memory. Shaking my head, I hung up my coat and kicked my shoes into an untidy heap. "Can't hug you now, Bug, you'll get hair all over my suit," I called out lightly, trying to throw off my melancholy reminiscing. Dropping my valise carelessly by the door, I crossed the tidy living room and headed for the bedroom, stripping my business suit and skirt and donning a pair of shapeless sweats, worn with years of comfortable memories. Running fingers through my now-stylish, shoulder-length hair, I returned to the *living* room and scooped up the tiny ball of fluff that resided on my couch.

"Hey, Booger Bug," I cooed affectionately, stroking his tiny ears. "Do anything useful today?" The tabby kitten purred in response, burrowing his nose into my arm. Booger Bug and I had an interesting history: he had been a birthday gift for Maggie from her then-boyfriend. However, upon being introduced to her apartment, his first act was to gleefully attack her designer taffeta curtains.

Caught red-handed, Maggie had scooped the felon up, cried, "You little booger-bug!" and remanded the young criminal to my custody. Interestingly enough, the newly-christened Booger Bug had taken a shine to his jailer and had gratefully inhabited his prison for the past several months.

I carried Bug into the kitchen and set him on the stained linoleum, whereupon he promptly recommenced his demands for food. Smiling indulgently, I retrieved a can of tuna from the fridge and loaded his bowl, with Bug jumping in before I even finished. My convict satisfied, I replaced the can, did the few dishes and went down my short hallway into my studio, the spare room where I kept my current works-in-progress. I contemplated working on my latest oil, a rendition of the Lyceum Theatre, but as I gazed at the half-colored canvas, I turned and walked away, putting a pot of coffee on instead. Maggie and Tony were coming up for Chinese food later on, and I didn't want to start the evening sobbing into my mochaccino. To distract myself, I went to the phone and played back the messages on my answering machine.

BEEP.

"Nona, dear, it's Grandma. Listen, I'm sure you're at work, dearest, but you'll never guess who I ran into at Celia Garrison's today! Her grandson Harry, you remember him? Just back from Princeton, already climbing the ladder in his father's practice! Isn't that thrilling? Anyway, the first thing he did was ask about you! I know that you only remember a gangly boy who teased you all those summers ago, but I always knew that he had a feather in his cap for you! If only you could see him, darling, such a fine young man! Makes me wish I was four decades younger.

"So, of course I gave him your number, and he said that he would love to get reacquainted with you, so be sure and expect a call from him soon. I hope you don't think me forward, dear, but you really need to get out more. Ever since the London fiasco, you've been so withdrawn. You spend all of your time with that odd duck Maggie, and that cook fellow. How will you ever get anywhere if you don't get out in society? Well, I'm off to the Daughters of the Revolution luncheon, so be sure and tell me all about it when Harry calls! All my love, dear! Ta!"

BEEP. You have no more messages.

Disgusted, I threw myself onto the couch, fuming. *Dammit, why did Grandma have to go play matchmaker? With Harry Garrison, of all people! Still, she has a point. It was three years ago, girl. You're over this. You're over HIM. You need to move on.* It was a nice thought, but then I turned my gaze to the living room wall, with its' framed posters of the Empire State Building (*Big Ben*), Central Park (*Regent's Park*), and the Brooklyn Bridge (*Tower Bridge*) spanning the East River (*the Thames, the Thames, oh, God, why isn't it the Thames?*), I couldn't contain it any longer. Sitting back on the sofa, I drew a slender chain off of my neck, gazed at the simple gold band that hung there, and let my tears fall.

Oh, Sherlock.

❦   ❦   ❦

After some time, I'm not sure how much, I heard my front door open and close. "Nona!" called a female voice. "You decent?"

Jumping a bit, I shoved the chain under my shirt and scrubbed my face as I croaked out, "Come on in, guys." Despite my efforts, I was caught.

Maggie Malloy took one look at me, shoved a brown paper bag into Tony's arms, strode over to the couch and sat beside me, running an electric-blue fingernail down my cheek. "You were thinking about him again," was all she said, and I nodded miserably. She shook her head, sending her curls flying, their Irish red fire at least halfway due to a box of cranberry *L'Oreal*. "We've been through this, Nona," she sighed, letting her finger drift down to pluck fussily at the chain around my neck. "This isn't healthy."

"She's got a point, girl," said Tony, his dark, honest face frowning with seriousness as he set the bag on the coffee table. "I'm sorry, but he *is* dead. Even if you accept the Baring-Gould, he's been dead some fifty years."

"You could have gotten yourself mugged or killed, you know, throwing yourself into alleyways like you told us about," Maggie added, maternally brushing my chocolate-colored hair behind my ear. "You have to let him go."

"Will you guys get off my case?" I snapped irritably.

Tony spread his hands defensively. "Hey, you're the one who told us about it all."

"*After* you got me so smashed on sour apple martinis that I couldn't walk straight!"

Maggie rolled her green eyes heavenward. "And how were we supposed to know that you're a talkative drunk?" Maggie and Tony weren't the only ones to hear my outrageous story, but they were the only ones who actually believed it.

I crossed my legs and sighed, a heavy weight in the middle of my stomach. Maggie, a full six inches taller than me, drew me easily down to her shoulder and I went willingly, glad for the comfort from my "adopted" sister. Tony took the phone from its cradle and disappeared into the kitchen, passing a satiated Booger Bug. Ever eager to cuddle, Bug leaped onto my lap and I stroked him as I told Maggie about my grandmother's matchmaking.

"She may have the right idea, Nona," Maggie commented when I was through. "Even if this Harry isn't the one," I snorted aloud, but she ignored me," you'll be out of the house and out doing things! You're a Young Urban

Professional in the greatest city in the world! Go out, get drunk and get *laid*, for crying out loud!"

"Maybe, no thanks, and no, in that order," I replied, feeling a little more myself. I sat up and tried a smile. "I miss him, Maggie. I always will, and no amount of dating will change that. I just have to accept it. Thanks for helping, though." She still looked unsatisfied, so I changed the topic. "What's in the bag?"

She shifted and grabbed the bag, pulling forth a sewing kit and a small sheet of cloth. "I was wondering if you could do some of your scrollwork stitching on this, so the designer knows what I'm talking about when I see him Sunday."

"Sure," I agreed, happy for the diversion. "I can work while we talk, just let me order...hey, where's the phone?"

Tony emerged from the kitchen, bearing the errant phone and three bottles of Corona. "I made the order," he said simply.

"What?" Maggie wrinkled her nose in distaste. "Tony, I thought we agreed that you wouldn't order chinks anymore!"

"Well, you were busy," he protested. He passed me a beer. "Feeling better?" he asked, and I nodded in reply.

"You always order too much!" Maggie protested.

"Better too much than not enough," Tony quoted blithely.

"Will you two stop bickering and put some music on?" I asked, crossing my eyes as I threaded the needle from the sewing kit.

"Oh! Dibs on Sinatra!" Maggie leapt up and sprang to the CD player, slipping Frank Sinatra's Greatest Hits into the player. She took a seat on the floor and cracked her Corona as the rest of us did likewise.

After half an hour of conversation, I was halfway done with the scrollwork and Tony got up for more Corona, returning with three more bottles. "These are the last ones, Nona."

I clicked my tongue in irritation. "Do you guys have any?" I asked.

"Miller Lite," replied Tony.

"Guinness," chimed Maggie.

"Gross and grosser," I said, putting aside the cloth. "I'll run down to Karansky's and get some more."

"I'll go with," said Tony, getting up. "It's getting dark."

I went to the door and grabbed my purse, coat and sneakers as Tony found his own accoutrements. "Maggie, can you stay put in case the delivery boy shows up?"

She lifted her fresh bottle in salute. "Ten-four, Zebra-3."

Tony opened the door for me and we headed down the stairs and out of the building, bundled up against the March chill, headed for Pete Karansky's convenience store two blocks away.

Tony glanced at me as we trudged. "You okay?" he asked.

"Yeah," I returned.

"Wanna talk about it?"

"Not really."

"Okay." Tony, wise man, knew when to push an issue and when to leave it alone. He meant well, I knew, they both did, but I also knew that I would live my life alone. There was no alternative.

Little did I know that, when I returned to my apartment, my opinion would be, quite seriously, altered.

Chapter Two
The Narrative of Dr. Watson

As I reflect upon the extraordinary events of 1890 and the years that followed, if not directly on the calendar, at least in the span of our lives, I am struck by their singular, almost impossible proceedings. Thanks to the intervention of the Fates and the companionship of my two remarkable friends, Mr. Sherlock Holmes and Miss Nona Brown, I was set upon a greater adventure than anyone, even the esteemed H.G. Wells, could conjure upon the pages of fiction.

Of course, I am surely committing the cardinal sin of authorship and beginning my tale in the middle, as Holmes has often and rightly accused me of, so I shall strive to put the facts of this remarkable case into a clear and orderly manner. Whether or not my strange tale is to be believed remains at the discretion of the reader.

♦   ♦   ♦

It was a cold and damp evening in October of 1890, with the yellow fog boiling out of the Thames to steam its way through the streets of London, as Sherlock Holmes and I crouched in the shadows near the Canary Wharf, waiting for our quarry to emerge from a dilapidated dockhouse. I was greatly uneasy for my friend's welfare, for I was sure that this area and this particular date, the twentieth of October, would recall memories of the kidnapping and subsequent rescue of Miss Nona Brown, the only woman to win the Great Detective's heart.

Nona had been, as difficult as it may be to fathom, a time traveler, sent accidentally to our era from her own more than a century in the future. She was intelligent, charming and as unconventional as Holmes himself. His acceptance of her love, and his own returning of the emotion, was as much a surprise to him as it was to those who knew him, but after an eventful year and the strangest courtship I have ever witnessed, the pair became affianced and began to plan for their future together. However, it was the future that undid them; on the very eve of Nona's first full year in London, not but a few days after their engagement, Nona Brown fell through a solid wall before our very eyes, vanishing from the face of the earth. Confronted with this impossibility, Holmes and I bleakly deduced that Nona had been called back to the future by the same forces that had brought her hence.

If Canary Wharf was the bearer of bittersweet memories, no trace of it showed on the harsh lines of Holmes' implacable face. In fact, very little emotion had registered on his features for quite some time. To those who did not know him well, Holmes was virtually unchanged over the three years since her disappearance; perhaps a bit more cynical, a bit more detached from humanity. To those who knew him, however, the change in him was immense.

Nona had succeeded in coaxing forth life from Holmes, causing him to betray the emotions that marked him as human: happiness, warmth, even exuberance. Since her departure from this plane, Holmes had completely reverted to the shell he had once inhabited, becoming cold and distant, living only for his work, more machine than man. He was unfeeling towards his clients, more scornful than ever of his official counterparts at Scotland Yard, and almost remote even towards myself.

Yet, his valiant efforts would be momentarily undone. When alone and unbothered in Baker Street, he would unconsciously turn a well-worn pocket watch in his nervous grasp, or take up his violin and play a tune that would not be officially composed for another hundred years. The bonds of true love were not easily severed, as I well knew since the death of my own beloved Mary, not four months before. Thus, I had returned to Baker Street, to Holmes and the life I had left behind, and was able to drown my own sorrows in work.

I was startled from my thoughts by a sharp gesture from Holmes. "Watson!" he hissed softly. "There he goes!"

Just through the fog, I could see an indistinct, man-sized shape, moving with the lurching gait that characterized our suspect. Motioning me to follow, Holmes pulled his traveling cap lower and started forward, silently creeping after the villain. I followed in turn, one hand securely in the pocket of my overcoat, grasping my revolver. We followed the man for some distance out of the wharf, back into residential and business streets, when my boot accidentally scraped on a patch of gravel. The small sound carried through our silence. Our quarry's head snapped toward us before he broke into a surprisingly swift run.

"After him!" Holmes cried, the need for stealth gone. We stumbled through the fog, the thick air clogging our lungs as we gave chase. Thanks to the head start he had gained in our caution while following him, the scoundrel soon vanished completely from our sight, rounding a corner some distance ahead of us. Holmes stopped for half a second, evaluating our options. "We can cut him off," he declared, seizing my arm and pulling me into an alley between two shops. "This way, Watson! Hurry!"

We dashed into the blackness of the alley, our footsteps echoing off of the walls until I could see a splash of light ahead. Holmes and I broke into the lamplight, frantically casting about for the villain we pursued. However, a completely different sight met our astonished eyes. The cobbles in the street were gone, replaced by some type of smooth black sheetrock. A verdant park lay directly across the street, with a large expanse of water faintly seen behind it. The gas lamps were incredibly tall and bright, and the thick fog was suddenly absent. The scene was so foreign that I cast a glance behind me, towards where we had come, but my gaze met only the solid face of a wall. Most incredibly of all, as my eyes traveled up the face of the building, I found it towering to such an unthinkable height, as could never be realized by any architect. Stunned, I did not realize myself stepping backwards until I had stumbled off of the curb and into the street. A harsh, mechanical roar filled my ears, disorienting me further.

"Watson, look out!" Holmes seized my arm and hauled me onto the walk just as a transport of some fearful kind, the source of the noise, came hurtling past at an unearthly speed. One glance at Holmes informed me that he was as terrified as I. Simultaneously gripped by the need for cover, we hastily crossed the foreign street and dashed into the park, under the shelter of the shadowy trees, not ceasing until we reached the water's edge, both of us heaving with fear and adrenaline.

"By God, Holmes," I gasped out. "Where are we? What is this devilish place?"

"I-I do not know," said he. "My mind is racing with any number of possibilities. This could be some conniving scheme of Moriarty's, to disorient us."

As I caught my breath, I caught sight of something familiar in the distance, in the middle of the harbor. "Holmes…"

"We may have been exposed to some hallucinogen in the air…"

"Holmes!"

"Causing some kind of simultaneous delirium..."

"*Holmes!*"

He snapped toward me, nerves strained to breaking. "What *is* it, Watson?" In answer, I grasped his shoulders and spun him round, so that he could see the object of my conclusions, illuminated by artificial light. At the sight, the detective's voice grew very small. "The Statue of Liberty?"

"I believe so," I rejoined in equal awe, "but Holmes, it's green! I thought the Statue was constructed of copper!"

Holmes' face took on a sudden light, a quality I had not seen in three long years. "Copper will corrode into a greenish hue," said he, "when exposed to the elements...for a long period of *time.*"

The realization shook me to my very core. "You don't mean-"

"I do," he interrupted eagerly. "I do mean, my dear Watson." We turned our gaze to the city, the towering buildings clearly visible over the trees. "We are in the twenty-first century."

❦ ❦ ❦

I had wanted to sit on the grass for a moment and collect my bearings, but Holmes afforded me no such opportunity, tearing down the walkway and leaving me to flounder in his wake. "Now that we know where and *when* we are," said Holmes, setting a brisk pace down the street, the unnatural electric lights illuminating our path, "it now only remains to find her."

As I tried to keep up with Holmes, still reeling from the shock, I found that I did not to question of whom he spoke. "But Holmes!" I gasped, dividing my attention between my companion and my unthinkable surroundings. "If memory serves, this city now contains eight million people! How are we to find one soul amongst eight million? Furthermore, how do you know that Nona is even here?"

"She is here," was his curt reply.

"But how can you be sure?"

Upon receiving no answer, I realized that he was not sure. For the first time in years, perhaps in decades, Holmes had placed his trust in faith rather than reason, with nothing to guide him but hope. I hoped as well, for my sake as well as his, that his faith was not misplaced.

"Ah!" Holmes cried in revelation. "Here we are!" We had stumbled upon a curious glass booth, lit by the ever-present electricity, a sign atop it proclaiming "Telephone" The machine within resembled no telephone I had ever seen, but the slot at the forefront was easy enough to recognize.

"Holmes," I began, "how are we to use this? Unless my eyes deceive me, it takes coins to activate it, and I doubt that any currency on our persons would help."

"We don't want the telephone," he snapped. "We want the telephone directory!" He grasped a book of an obscene size, chained to the telephone machine, and opened it, revealing lists upon lists of addresses and calling numbers. "It seems that Nona's tales have not deserted either one of us, my dear Watson. This should narrow our field of inquiry quite admirably!" Without further ado, he searched out the 'B' section, his long fingers nervously tracing the pages. "Brown," he muttered under his breath as I attempted to read over his shoulder. "Nathaniel Brown, Nicole Brown, Norman, no, too far, ah…" He hissed in frustration. "Nothing! No entries for a Nona Brown!"

"Perhaps she has listed only her initials," I expostulated, knowing the dangers of any large city for a single young woman.

Hastily paging backwards, Holmes gave a cry of triumph. "Brilliant, Watson! N. Brown! There are two entries."

"Shall we pursue them both?" I queried.

"No need." He pointed to a note under the second entry, which read, 'Gaslight Gallery, Fine Victorian-Style Art, No Portraits, Please. Contact Ms. N. Brown.' "I do not believe in coincidence, Watson," said Holmes, a joy tingeing his voice. Tearing the page from the book, he read the address aloud. "1236, E. 4th Street, Apt. 4. Now all that remains is to get from here to there. Didn't Nona say that there are a multiplicity of cabs in this era?"

"Indeed," I assented, "and all are a uniform yellow color."

"Like that one headed toward us?" I followed Holmes' pointing hand and espied a bright yellow vehicle, moving at a much slower pace than the one we encountered earlier. Holmes experimentally raised a hand in the air and the vehicle pulled over and rolled to a stop before us, allowing us to read the words *United Taxi Co.* on it's side. "Well," Holmes quipped breathlessly, as staggered as I at the sight of this advanced machine. "Nice to see that some things never change."

After a moment of fumbling, Holmes was able to manipulate the handle and open the door, sliding into the low seat. I followed and shut the door behind me. Our driver, a thin Negro with a profusion of braids in his hair, leaned over his seat and cast us a wide grin, overflowing with uneven teeth. "Where can Ah take you fiiiine gennelmen?" he asked, in an accent I would later learn was Jamaican.

Holmes recited the address again and the cabbie pushed a lever by the steering wheel, causing the contraption to move forward at a smooth, even pace. Both Holmes and I were rapt with awe as the cityscape flew past our eyes at a pace we had only experienced on trains. Shops, restaurants, all wondrously foreign, careened past the tiny window. Our host and driver, thankfully, did not attempt to engage us in conversation, casting strange glances into a mirror that allowed him to see us without turning his head backwards. I pitied him his first impression of us, reflecting back to my confused thoughts when I first made Nona's acquaintance.

The thought of Nona troubled me more than I cared to admit. The absence had been three years for Holmes and I; had it been as long for her? Longer, perhaps? Did she remember us? Had she forgotten us, dismissed us as some traumatic hallucination? Had she gone on with her life, been courted and married? Did she have children of her own? Would she have a place in her life for us, and a place in her heart for Holmes? I dared not voice these misgivings aloud, for I could read the same turmoil in my friend's formerly jubilant face.

After some travel, we pulled to a halt on a quieter, tree-lined street. The cabbie turned to face us again. "That'll be twenty-two fifty," said he.

Now Holmes and I were in a true quandary: how to pay the man. Digging in his pockets, Holmes seized a sovereign, a kingly sum for a cabbie in our era, and thrust it at the man, fumbling at the door.

Just as Holmes unlatched the door, the man cried, "What da H-ll is dis? Dis ain't money! You can't give me dis sh-t!"

"Now, see here," began Holmes uncertainly, "That is all we have, and you can't expect us to-" He was cut off as the cabbie resumed his diatribe, making some questionable remarks about Holmes' parentage.

When he threatened to 'call da cops,' I intervened with the only thing that sprung to my mind. "It's gold."

My announcement quieted the cabbie, who now regarded the sovereign in his hand with reverence. "Gold?" he echoed.

"Solid gold," I assured him, remembering Nona's bygone comment that gold had drastically increased in value over a century's worth of inflation. Holmes took advantage of the lull to launch himself from the seat, with myself hot on his heels. Once we were out into the open air, with the door shut behind

us, the cabbie leaned out of his window, uncertainty and guilt plain on his features. He knew as well as we that we were being short-changed. "Ey, dat's
good'a you gennelmen," he said. "Yo, if you eva need a favor, you call me," he
slapped a dark hand against the sign on the cab's side, "an you ask for Ratty. I
owe you gennelmen, and Ratty, he makes good on what he owe, dig?" We
assured him of such and he drove away, his conscience appeased.

1236 E. 4th Street was a crumbling construct of dingy brown stone, worn
with years of abuse. Nearly trembling, Holmes climbed the stone steps and
tried the door. It was locked, of course, so he instead turned his attention to
the row of names beside it. I almost laughed aloud as Holmes removed his
deerstalker hat and ran a hand through his hair before depressing the button
next to the name Brown.

Neither of us was sure of what would occur, so we were equally surprised
when a woman's voice emerged from the plate by the door. "You'd better be the
delivery boy."

Whoever this voice was, it was not Nona. Looking a bit foolish, Holmes
cleared his throat. "Hello," he called loudly into the plate. "I'm here to see Miss
Nona Brown."

"No need to shout," came the woman's voice. "If you're from the office, go
away and come back on Monday. Give her a break!"

Holmes shot me a silent look of exultation. *She is here!* "Is she there? Please,
let me speak to Nona!" he cried.

"And who shall I say is yelling?" the voice retorted.

He replied easily, "My name is Sherlock Holmes."

There was absolute silence on the other end as Holmes and I held our
breath, anxiously awaiting to hear from the object of our impromptu journey.
Instead, we heard a heavy thumping sound from within the building, like
someone running down flights of stairs. A moment later, the front door flew
open and a tall, redheaded woman reared back and slapped Holmes across the
face!

"You b-st-rd!" she spat at him as he reeled from the blow. "How dare you! I
don't know who the h-ll you think you are, or how you found out, but this is
one sick joke! You are d-mn lucky that Nona's gone right now, 'cause if she
heard that, I'd *really* be pissed!"

"Madam!" Holmes barked, the image of the affronted gentleman. "You
assume too much! I insist on speaking to Nona!"

"Get the h-ll of my property!" roared the redhead, prodding him roughly
with a blue-lacquered fingernail. "I'll call the cops!"

Holmes' nerves were reaching the breaking point. I could see him clenching his fists in anger. "Call them, then!" he retorted through clenched teeth. "I shall not leave until I see Nona! Now move out of my way, or I will not be-"

The sound of shattering glass brought our attention round. For a moment, I did not recognize the too-thin young woman who stood not a dozen meters away, accompanied by a tall Negro man. She was staring in unmitigated shock, wrapped in a voluminous coat, her brown hair clipped short. A brown paper bag lay at her feet, a dark, spreading stain attesting to the sound of broken glass. However, my mind soon saw through the change the years had wrought and I saw Miss Nona Brown, my dear friend, and I knew that Holmes saw her as well.

978-0-595-35686-7
0-595-35686-9

Printed in the United States
32721LVS00003B/54

9 780595 356867